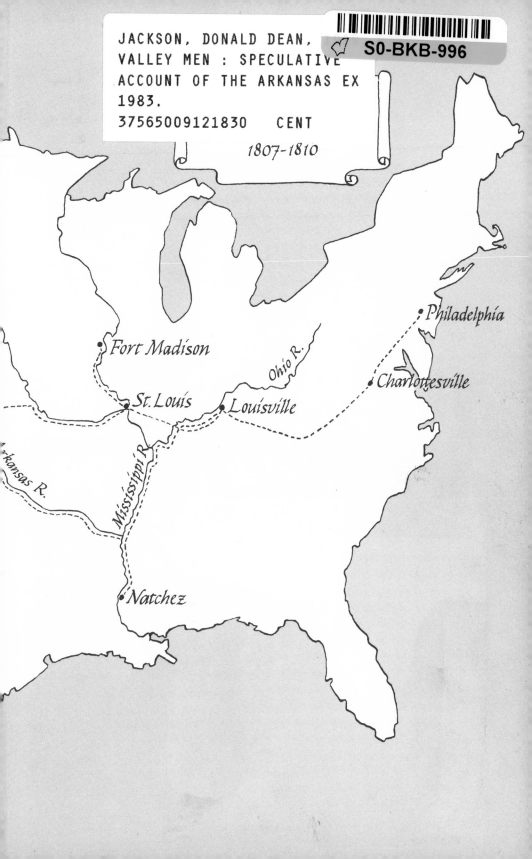

1807-1810

Philadelphia

Fort Madison

Ohio R.

Charlottesville

St. Louis

Louisville

Arkansas R.

Mississippi R.

Natchez

VALLEY MEN

Historical Works by Donald Jackson

Black Hawk: An Autobiography
(editor)

*The Journals of Zebulon Montgomery Pike:
With Letters and Related Documents*
(editor)

Custer's Gold: The U.S. Cavalry Expedition of 1874

The Expeditions of John Charles Frémont
(editor, with Mary Lee Spence)

George Washington and the War of Independence

The Diaries of George Washington
(editor, with Dorothy Twohig)

*Letters of the Lewis and Clark Expedition:
With Related Documents, 1783–1874*
(editor)

*Thomas Jefferson and the Stony Mountains:
Exploring the West from Monticello*

VALLEY MEN

*A Speculative Account
of the Arkansas Expedition
of 1807*

Donald Jackson

Ticknor & Fields
NEW HAVEN AND NEW YORK
1983

Library of Congress Cataloging in Publication Data

Jackson, Donald Dean, 1919–
   Valley men.

   1. Arkansas River — Discovery and exploration — Fiction.
2. Southwestern States — History — Fiction.   3. West (U.S.)
— History — To 1848 — Fiction.   I. Title.
PS3560.A2135V3   1983   813'.54   83-4995
ISBN 0-89919-198-3

Printed in the United States of America

D   10 9 8 7 6 5 4 3 2 1

Endpaper map by John O. C. McCrillis

In Memory of Meriwether Lewis

Turn safe to rest, no dreams, no waking;
    And here, man, here's the wreath I've made.
'Tis not a gift that's worth the taking,
    But wear it and it will not fade.
          — A. E. Housman, *A Shropshire Lad*

CONTENTS

We was all valley people in them days. Never heard of no mountain men. I come out of the Shando Valley and down the Ohio, and on up the Missisip to the lower Missouri. Valleys is the way we traveled.

                                   — Fur trader in St. Louis

I do hereby certify that Raphael Bailey has pursued under my direction, these two years, the study of Physick, Surgery, and Midwifery. From his natural Abilities and his Attention to the Prosecution of his Studies, I am fully convinced that he is qualified to practice in these branches of his Profession. Should he now attend the medical college in Philadelphia, as he proposes, his Competence will be greatly enhanced.

                                   — Dr. Prentiss Puckett
                                    Charlottesville, Va.
                                    1 Sept. 1805

Preface

I AM GRATEFUL to Thomas Jefferson for presenting me an already organized and working expedition to serve as a basis for this fictional narrative. My hope at first was to invent a plausible western expedition, set in the early nineteenth century, the account of which would evoke the drama and dangers, and emphasize the profound importance of such undertakings. Such an account would have to fit the history of the times, involve travel to logical places, and reveal discoveries in keeping with the state of geographic knowledge about the West. Then I remembered that a proposed expedition up the Arkansas River had been conceived, planned, and actually set in motion by Jefferson and his associates in the spring of 1807. Before it could move beyond Natchez it was canceled. I decided to take it over, with the cast of characters already chosen, and send it up the river as if it had never been called off. It would be mine to manipulate, but its very existence would bear a stamp of Jeffersonian approval. The notion of making this aborted plan of Jefferson's the core of my narrative became irresistible.

For a few weeks in the summer of 1806, Jefferson had every reason to think that no American effort to explore the new Louisiana Purchase was going to succeed. Lewis and Clark had not been heard from for more than a year. Zebulon Pike was somewhere in the West, with instructions to look for the headwaters of the Red River in territory claimed by the Spanish, and there were third-hand reports that he had been cut off. Jefferson had received word that the expedition up the Red River, led by Thomas Freeman, had been intercepted and turned back by the

Spanish. Considering these difficulties, the president would have had good reason to reconsider the next exploration on his agenda, a voyage up the Arkansas River planned for the spring of 1807.

He finally heard from Meriwether Lewis in late October 1806, with the report of his successful return. No one in government then knew that the Spanish had made at least three attempts to intercept that expedition. Nor could anyone predict that Pike would be arrested on a branch of the Rio Grande during the coming winter, taken under guard to Chihuahua for questioning, and escorted back to the American border by Spanish soldiers. Only after receiving Freeman's report, explaining that his two boats and a contingent of twenty-one officers and men had got no farther upriver than what is now Texarkana, Texas, did Jefferson have clear proof the Spanish were trying vigorously to discourage American inroads.

Despite the omens, Jefferson was determined to go ahead with his master plan of exploration. He assigned the surveyor general the job of exploring the upper Mississippi and expected Congress to authorize the examination of western rivers. "I should propose," he said, "to send one party up the [North] Platte, thence along the highlands to the source of the [South Platte], and down that to its mouth. Another party up the Arkansa to its source, thence along the highlands to the source of the Red River, & down that to its mouth. These surveys will enable us to prepare a map of Louisiana which in its contour and main waters will be perfectly correct." He does not mention Lewis and Clark, or Pike, in these plans because the Lewis and Clark expedition is already in progress and Pike's travels are not, to him, genuine journeys of exploration, but rather military reconnoiterings.

To oversee the Arkansas venture, the president chose a man who was already closer to the scene than he and one who had the resources and talents appropriate to the task. William Dunbar (who does not appear in my narrative) was a Scottish planter and amateur scientist who lived near Natchez, in Mississippi Territory. He not only arranged Freeman's trip up the Red in 1806, and the Arkansas expedition of 1807, but made a personal inspection of the Ouachita as far as the Hot Springs. The strenuous portage required on the latter voyage persuaded him that going up one river and down another was a logistical mistake. So the Red and Arkansas project was separated into two.

The Red River expedition, led by Freeman and assisted by scientist Peter Custis, left Natchez in the spring of 1806, traveled about six hundred miles upstream, and was stopped by a detachment of dragoons that greatly outnumbered the men of the expedition. Had Freeman succeeded in his mission of finding the headwaters of the Red and exploring the mountains beyond, he would have simplified the great boundary dispute with Spain, contributed to Jefferson's understanding of the Purchase, and enabled the U.S. government to proceed with the projected map of the entire Louisiana Territory. Instead, Freeman returned to Natchez, reported his failure to Jefferson, and went forward with plans for the Arkansas enterprise set up for the following spring.

Incredibly, because of the age-old problem of delays in the mail, William Dunbar and the participants in the proposed expedition were still hard at work on it, and looking forward to its success, six weeks after it had been canceled. On March 30, 1807, Secretary of War Henry Dearborn wrote Dunbar that Congress, "by some mistake or inattention," had made no appropriation for the expedition. He said that Jefferson had directed him to inform the principals that it was necessary to suspend all plans for the current season.

The explanation given by Dearborn may be the correct one: Congress just forgot to provide the money. But considering Jefferson's long interest in exploration and his daily contacts with congressmen — considering the fact that Congress already had authorized the expedition in principle and needed only to vote the funds; considering that among the congressmen on the Hill were several who were fanatic in their determination to move the United States rapidly westward — the theory of an inattentive Congress is less than completely tenable. Senator Samuel Latham Mitchill, for example, who once urged Jefferson to claim all the land lying across the central part of the continent as far as the Pacific, was not likely to let Congress forget the Arkansas expedition.

Among other possible reasons for the cancellation, a few seem to have merit:

Jefferson was tired of public life. At about the time in early 1807 when he should have been pushing the appropriation for the Arkansas venture, he wrote his old friend John Dickinson: "I am tired of an office where I can do no more good than many others who would be glad to be employed in it." He may have sensed that 1807 was to be a burdensome year: the year of the Aaron Burr trial in Richmond, in which Jefferson was to become emotionally involved; the year of the embargo against England, which was to put him under fire from his Federalist critics — all this, and his term in office still had more than two years to run.

When the Arkansas expedition was called off, Zebulon Pike still had not been heard from, and it was widely assumed that the Spanish had taken him. Coming so soon after the debacle on the Red River the previous summer, the concern that Jefferson felt for Pike could itself have caused him to put off the Arkansas adventure and the risk of further encounters with the Spanish.

For whatever reason, Jefferson abandoned the Arkansas plan and left it for me to complete. Beyond certain limits that he had already set, I was free to do with it what I wished. This freedom carried the risk that I might lose my head. When a friend who knew of my intentions asked me where the Arkansas River ran, I replied imperiously, "Any place I want it to."

As Jefferson had not yet chosen a scientist to accompany Freeman and the two officers, it became necessary for me to invent one. He proved to be Dr. Raphael Bailey. The story is peopled by several other fictional characters, some important enough to have names and personalities. Like Rafe, all the Baileys are invented. So is Callie, and so is Mlle Marie-Louise Gratiot. Siegfried Burger, also known as Burgoo, is not real, either. The rest of the characters, for the most part, actually existed. I take responsibility for their behavior and have tried to put no real-life figures into situations or places where they might not have been during 1807–1811.

Because these people led real lives that extended beyond the confines of the narrative, I set them forth below in summary.

Philadelphia

All members of the medical faculty at the University of Pennsylvania are well known in medical history. Charles Willson Peale, the artist and museum curator, was a lively member of the nation's artistic and scientific circles.

Until recent years when I published some notes on Mahlon Dickerson, his close friendship with Meriwether Lewis had been known only through a single letter he had received from Lewis. Dickerson was adjutant general of Pennsylvania, governor of New Jersey and senator from that state, and from 1834 to 1838 was secretary of the navy. Apparently he met Lewis in Washington in April 1802 when he was Jefferson's dinner guest. Lewis then visited Dickerson the following month on a trip that seems to have had no connection with his duties as secretary to Jefferson. He socialized often in company with Dickerson then, and saw him again in 1803 and 1807 when he went to Philadelphia on business.

In his diary, now at the New Jersey Historical Society, Dickerson comes across as effete, well educated, with European tastes and the politics of a Jeffersonian. He was a dilettante scientist — member of the American Philosophical Society — and his friends and dinner companions during the period 1803–1807 included the governor of Pennsylvania, the Spanish minister to the United States, and most of the scholars and literati in the city.

Dickerson's diary entry for October 22, 1809, reads: "A very cold winter's day — read the horrible account of Capt. Meriwether Lewis's death on the night of 10th Oct. I think he was the most sincere friend I ever had."

The Expedition

Thomas Freeman served on the expedition as an employee of the surveyor general of the United States and remained in that service for the rest of his life. By 1810 he had opened an office in the little town of Washington, near Natchez in Mississippi Territory, where he was assigned to begin a survey of public lands below Tennessee. When Alabama Territory was formed in 1817, the necessary surveys became a part of his assignment. A coincidence links him with the tragic death of Lewis. When Lewis's body was found in Tennessee, and it was apparent that he carried important maps and papers generated by his own expedition, Freeman happened to be in the vicinity and available to carry those documents to Jefferson and the secretary of war. He died in 1821 during an inspection trip to Huntsville, Alabama, and was eulogized by the Washington, Mississippi, *Republican* for "the urbanity of his manner, the amiability of his disposition, and the honorable uprightness of his deportment."

James Biddle Wilkinson, son of General James Wilkinson, became a captain in 1808 and spent the rest of his short life never far from his father's solicitous eye. By 1809 he was stationed at Fort Stoddert, on the Mobile River about fifty miles above Mobile, Alabama. When Judge Harry Toulmin, former secretary of the state of Kentucky and president of Transylvania University, moved near Fort Stoddert with a family of daughters, the captain soon married Hannah Toulmin and produced a son. Never a sturdy man, Wilkinson fell into poor health. In 1810 he was directed to explore an area between Mobile and eastern Tennessee. In respectfully declining the assignment in a letter to his colonel, he wrote: "I am much mortified & chagrined, that the remains of a lingering nervous disease will prevent my undertaking it." He was still at Fort Stoddert — and serving as its commander — in 1813 when the War of 1812 brought action to the area. By this time his father had gone north to conduct operations in Canada, and Captain Wilkinson opted out of the army. He obtained an appointment as postmaster at Mobile and resigned his army commission. Shortly afterward, in September 1813, he died at Dauphin Island, Alabama.

Thomas Adams Smith's army career was not much longer than Wilkinson's, but was much more illustrious. He and his brother Reuben had been commissioned on the same day in 1803, and — except for some thoughts of resignation in 1806 — Thomas seemed committed to the army. By May 1810 he was a captain commanding Fort Hawkins in Georgia, and by November 1811 he was a lieutenant colonel in Regiment of Rifles, stationed at Frederick Town, Maryland. He served well in the War of 1812, especially at Plattsburg and Sackets Harbor, and was breveted a brigadier general for meritorious conduct. In 1817 he was stationed in St. Louis as commander of the Sixth Military Department and was active in organizing a proposed expedition to the Yellowstone. During this period a fort was established at Belle Pointe, on the Arkansas, and named Fort Smith in his honor. He might have gained further distinction in leading the Yellowstone expedition (which later was terminated before reaching its destination), but he resigned to become the receiver in the U.S. land office at Franklin, Missouri. He died in Saline County, Missouri, in 1844.

Two men who do not appear physically in the narrative are never far offstage: General James Wilkinson and Captain Zebulon Pike. The general had long been a principal figure in Spanish attempts to subvert western settlers into seceding from the United States. His involvement may have been even deeper than his son suspected, for not only was he receiving a "pension" of four thousand dollars a year from Spain, he also had taken an oath of allegiance to His Most Catholic Majesty, the king. Today he is generally believed to have motivated Aaron Burr in the famous conspiracy to separate the West from the United States (perhaps), and to lead a filibustering expedition into Mexico (more likely). He survived several judicial inquiries into his activities and was commanding general of the army during most of the War of 1812. He was relieved of command and court-martialed on various charges concerning his conduct of the war, but was acquitted. Honorably discharged in 1815, he died in Mexico ten years later.

In a way, Pike shared Rafe Bailey's dread of becoming "a second Lewis and Clark." He was overshadowed by those two superior explorers in every way and expressed his resentment in his letters. He tried in vain to get extra compensation for himself and his men. At one time he billed the government for extra pay as a surveyor during his expedition. Although his ambition for greater recognition as an explorer never was realized, he rose rapidly as a military officer, thanks to his close relationship with General Wilkinson. By the end of 1809 he was a lieutenant colonel and had become a full colonel by the middle of 1812. In March 1813 he was elevated to the rank of brigadier general and adjutant general of the army. After the battle of York in Canada, in April 1813, he was killed by the explosion of a powder magazine.

Nothing is more frustrating than trying to recover the names of enlisted personnel from old army records. The surviving muster rolls in the National Archives are few, and a researcher is lucky indeed to find one covering detachments assigned to early western explorations. I was fortunate to find a muster roll of Smith's detachment from the Regiment of Artillerists. I have used some of these names for men on the Freeman and Bailey expedition, but have invented Private Henry Macomb and Corporal Jonas Gardner, and three deserters.

At the Arkansas Post, Dr. Abraham Stewart and factor John

B. Treat left no trail of genealogical data that I have been able to follow. Stewart did in fact command the fort in the absence of a line officer; then he disappears from my view. Treat was active as a factor and Indian agent, and a collection of his papers would be a welcome find.

In the episode with the Spanish, three men are historical figures: Governor Joaquín del Real Alencaster, Lieutenant José Raphael Sotelo, and Bartholomew Fernandez. Alencaster, during his governorship of New Mexico (1805–1808), not only apprehended Pike but made several attempts to interdict Lewis and Clark. The two Spanish army officers were in charge of the detachment that discovered Pike on the wrong side of the Rio Grande.

St. Louis

The two significant figures in the St. Louis episode are, naturally, Meriwether Lewis and William Clark. Lewis's star was waning by 1808. What some of his friends, including Jefferson, had always seen as a streak of occasional melancholia was now becoming a problem. Lewis had contained it well during the expedition and had come home a hero, not only to the public but to the men who served with him. I can cite no instance in which the soldiers and civilians who traveled with him to the Pacific ever disparaged his valor, leadership, or amiability.

Americans have always found it difficult to honor their heroes appropriately. A splendid desk job is usually the reward of choice. Soldier Ulysses S. Grant became a president of little distinction after his notable service in the Civil War. Explorer John Charles Frémont was put up for president against James Buchanan and, luckily for him and his country, did not win. He would have been a wretched political leader. In Lewis's case, Jefferson rewarded him by giving him the governorship of upper Louisiana Territory.

It may be that Lewis did not relish the appointment from the start. He became governor in March 1807 but dawdled along the way, attending dinners in his honor, visiting old friends, and arranging for publication of the book of travels he now proposed to write. When he finally reached St. Louis a year later, he began a lackluster governorship over what must have seemed an ungovernable populace of longtime French inhabitants and new American speculators, opportunists, and political hacks. He began to speculate in lands; he quarreled with his colleagues; he bemoaned to Mahlon Dickerson his inability to find a wife; and he fretted ineffectually over the stack of morocco-bound journals that he and Clark had produced during their expedition. With Jefferson out of office in 1809, Lewis lacked a friend and protector in Washington. His unauthorized use of funds in returning an important Mandan chief to his village far up the Missouri was disallowed by an unfriendly Department of State — and the debt fell personally upon Lewis.

These calamities, perceived and real, must surely have contributed to Lewis's steadily growing addiction to alcohol. The fact that he drank to excess is now documented to the satisfaction of all but his most doggedly loyal admirers. In my first edition of the Lewis and Clark letters (1962), I wrote that Lewis almost surely died by his own hand at Grinder's Tavern along the Natchez Trace in Tennessee. I was not the first to make this assertion, but acceptance of the conclusion has been slow in coming. That the weight of scholarly opinion is shifting more rapidly toward an assumption of suicide, rather than murder by a highwayman, is seen in an article by a psychohistorian who espouses the belief that Lewis was suicide-prone from childhood.

As I planned this narrative, I did not realize how painful it would become to deal with Lewis's last, dark years. Those who read western American history may find evidence on library shelves of the earnest attempts I have made, during the last quarter century, to promote a better understanding of Lewis and his traveling companions.

In the popularity contest that followed the expedition, William Clark was a dark horse. The expedition as arranged and masterminded by Jefferson was Lewis's from the beginning — Captain Lewis's tour. The captain was authorized to appoint a partner and very nearly got Lieutenant Moses Hooke. Second choice was Clark, who happily accepted when Hooke declined.

Clark's post-expedition appointment to a generalship in the militia, and to the superintendency of Indian affairs in the new territory, marked the start of a notable career in public service. Besides serving the Indians well until his death in 1838, he was governor of Missouri Territory from 1813 until the state was formed in 1821. Julia died in 1820 after bearing five children. Two sons were born to Clark and his second wife, Harriet Kennerly Radford, whom he married in 1821.

His compassion for the Indians in his care never flagged. In 1826 he wrote Jefferson: "It would afford me pleasure to be enabled to meliorate the condition of those unfortunate people placed under my charge, knowing as I do their wretchedness, and their rapid decline. It is to be lamented that this deplorable situation of the Indians do not receive more of the humain feelings of this Nation."

When Lewis died, his publisher complained to Jefferson that not a line of the proposed book of travels had ever reached Philadelphia. Through Clark's effort, and with Jefferson's persistent encouragement, Nicholas Biddle was persuaded to write a narrative account of the expedition. Published in 1814, it satisfied public clamor but not Jefferson's desire to see a more detailed scientific work. Nearly a century was to pass before the journals themselves, with scholarly annotation, were published in 1904–1905.

Fort Madison

People come and go at a busy military installation. All those in my chapters about Fort Madison are real except Rafe Bailey. I have compressed some events and shortened chronology here and there, for the sake of a story, but the account follows the history of the fort quite closely. The installation survived until sometime in the fall of 1813, when it had to be abandoned by its commander, Lieutenant Thomas Hamilton. Indian harassment was increasing, the contractor had stopped shipping food and supplies, and the factory that the garrison was meant to protect had been burned for more than a year. The men slipped out to their boats one night after setting the buildings afire, and hastened to St. Louis.

In June 1965 I helped to excavate the site of the fort, discovered in the parking lot of the Sheaffer Pen Company, Fort Madison, Iowa. The state archaeologist and the state historian supervised the excavation of some foundation stones, the burned timbers of one blockhouse, and traces of the palisade fence that had surrounded the compound. The building stones and artifacts were preserved for possible use in a reconstruction, but the actual site was to be reburied.

I present here a few notes on the later lives of the Fort Madison cast:

Hannah Stark bore a daughter, Rosanna, in September 1810 at the fort — the child becoming the first white baby born in my native state of Iowa. Hannah's next pregnancy did not go well and she was sent down to Bellefontaine for her confinement. The Starks had friends there, Lieutenant and Mrs. John Cleve Symmes, who promised to care for Hannah while her husband remained at Fort Madison. In September 1812 she gave birth to a son, whom she named Horatio. Childbed fever followed. She was tended by Mrs. Symmes (who was also suckling the child), and was treated by the best physician in St. Louis — Dr. Bernard Farrar — but she could not be saved. As John Symmes wrote to Stark: "All reasonable exertions were contrived, but she dropped off in the cover of the night."

Horatio Stark left the fort late in 1812 and was one of the many career officers discharged with the reduction of the army in 1815. By then he had become a lieutenant colonel, and upon discharge he tried his hand at writing a new drill manual which he had begun at Fort Madison. The manuscript has not been found. In 1817 he was in Woodville, Mississippi Territory, raising corn and cotton in partnership with his brother. After Hannah's death he had married Mrs. Penniman, who had cared for the baby boy in St. Louis.

Alpha Kingsley was discharged in 1815 and settled in Nashville, Tennessee, becoming the friend of Andrew and Rachel Jackson. In 1821 he took over the management of Jackson's favorite haunt — the Nashville Inn. Another friend, Sam Houston, called him "a very amiable man, and a good member of the Church." He died in 1846.

Thomas Hamilton was retained, brevetted a major in 1816, and stayed in the army until 1824. He died in St. Louis in 1833. His wife Catherine survived him for more than forty years, proud to be the aunt of a promising artist, James McNeill Whistler.

Nathaniel Pryor and his partner, George Hunt, were attacked

by Winnebagoes at their lead mines early in 1812, barely escaping to St. Louis. Pryor spent long years campaigning to collect from the government for his losses of lead and other goods. During his later years he married an Osage woman and traded with the Osages. Students of the Lewis and Clark expedition have always suspected that he kept a journal which will someday be discovered.

John Johnson was assigned to a new factory at Fort Crawford, near present-day Prairie du Chien, Wisconsin. After becoming wealthy through lead mining in the region, he moved to St. Louis in 1822. Upon the death of his Sauk wife Tapassio, he married again, served for a time as mayor of St. Louis, and died in 1854. His three half-blood daughters "married well."

Dr. Robert Simpson rebelled at Horatio Stark's cruelties and tried in vain to bring charges against him. He married Brecia Smith and took her to the fort — where she and their child nearly died of malaria. Discouraged and frustrated, Dr. Simpson resigned in 1812, started a medical practice in St. Louis, and became an early champion of women's rights. He was one of the first antislavery advocates in the area. For a time he was sheriff, then city comptroller, and cashier of the Boatman's Savings Institution. When he reached his eighty-eighth birthday in 1872, he was hailed as the oldest living American resident of St. Louis. He died the following year.

During the period covered by this narrative, the Arkansas River was variously called the Arkansa, Arcansa, or Arkansaw. I have called it the Arkansa, as Jefferson frequently did.

Donald Jackson
Colorado Springs, Colorado

VALLEY MEN

1

The Arkansa Expedition of 1807

THE DRUMMER always beat the staccato taps that came before reveille when he could see a thousand yards in the dawning light. Twenty minutes later he would sound reveille itself. This morning the orderly drummer for the day's guard detail drew himself heavily from his tent and scuffed across the sand to a point at the river's edge. Aboard the smaller of two keelboats, young Dr. Rafe Bailey was already awake. He heard the drummer fussing with his sticks, clearing his throat as if he were going to make the signal vocally. Then the first taut beats rang out like unexpected musket shots to awaken the men of the Arkansa River expedition.

Rafe had slept aft on the deck, near the tiller, on a pallet of dirty ticking filled with dry grass. The night air had dampened the ticking and stiffened his blanket. Lying on his back, he could see a trace of willow foliage as the tree line began to show against the lightening sky. As he organized his thoughts for the routines of the day, he started to compile a mental list of men who probably would appear for sick call after breakfast. Later, when he stood up to pull on his trousers and looked out across the double row of tents facing the river, the events of last night came suddenly to him and he realized that today would not be routine. Although the cooks were poking up the cold fires and the camp was stirring, there was a difference; the tents were not being struck.

The doctor tucked in his clammy shirttail and tightened his belt. *I wish this day were over. Double damn.* He was capable of fiercer oaths, but this one had stuck with him since boyhood and, now that he was twenty-three, it still served. He sat on the gunwale and felt for the queue of yellow hair that hung past the nape of his neck. It needed some work but that could wait. Rafe's face was broad and open, his nose flat-tipped and without distinction. His cheeks and forehead were slightly rubbled from childhood smallpox. "At least he's going to be tall like his father," he had overheard his mother saying long ago. Now he was even taller, maybe six feet two.

"Morning to ye, doctor." Thomas Freeman, who had slept on a bench inside the cabin of the boat, came on deck carrying a shaving brush and a tin cup containing a shard of yellow soap. Propping a tiny, mottled mirror on the low roof of the cabin, he began to shave with a bone-handled razor.

Like Rafe, Freeman was a civilian assigned by the president to this venture into the unknown West. The voyage would be known some day as the Freeman and Bailey expedition, but to the soldiers who had come along to protect them it was merely "the tour." The role of the army was to see that these two men, one a doctor and naturalist fresh from medical school, the other a mature and experienced civil engineer, came safely home with information about the new Louisiana Purchase. Freeman was a ruddy Irishman of stocky build, so nearly bald that he no longer bothered with a queue but let his sandy hair run ragged. The left side of his scalp, just above the hairline, bore a healed gash made by a Kickapoo tomahawk.

"We aren't breaking camp," Rafe said.

"Not after what happened last night." Freeman dabbed a patch of thin lather onto his cheek. "I think we'll be having a court-martial today."

Rafe went in and got his own razor, and the two stood side by side while shaving. Last night, before turning in, he had walked in the dark to the timber's edge and discovered Private Henry Macomb asleep at his post. He had gone back to the boat and told Freeman, naively, "I just saw one of the sentinels snoozing behind a log." In an explosive reaction that surprised Rafe, Freeman had jumped to his feet, cried "Hell!" and scrambled ashore. A flurry of subdued activity had followed; there were raised voices and some cursing from the officers' tent. The rest of the night had been an uneasy one for all. *Double damn.*

"I wish I had pissed over the stern," Rafe said.

"The wind was against you," Freeman said. "And now, son, I want to emphasize one thing. I'm the chap who turned that rascal in. I'm the one who found him asleep, called out the corporal of the guard, and it doesn't matter that you told me about it first. You're new, the men like you, and you're their doctor. I've got a suspicion that if you'd been more familiar with army ways you'd have tiptoed away from that sentinel and said nothing. Wrong thing to do! He endangered us all. The fuss he caused should tell you it's a serious matter. Less serious than if we were farther up the river, but plenty bad. If I know Lieutenant Wilkinson, he will render justice very quick to set an example. And I'll testify, not you."

Army life had begun to seem more complicated. Rafe wondered if he should have thought longer before applying for an appointment as surgeon's mate. The application had not gone through yet, but it was surely too late to head it off. He supposed he would know more about how to behave as an officer as he watched the two who were leading the detachment. Second-in-command was Lieutenant Thomas Adams Smith with twenty men from the Regiment of Artillerists. His superior was Lieutenant James Biddle Wilkinson with twenty from the Second Infantry. It had puzzled Rafe to learn that the assignment of command had fallen to the son of General James Wilkinson, who commanded the entire U.S. Army, until he was reminded that young Wilkinson had come down the lower half of the river a few weeks ago, on another assignment, and knew what to expect.

"What'll they do to Macomb?"

"Court-martial him, find him guilty, and flog him."

"My God! Is that the only way to punish him? And so soon."

"You paddle a dog's ass as soon as you can after he nips you on the leg."

"But why flogging? Why not something else?"

"There isn't anything else, doctor. You can't put him in irons and lock him in the hold, because we need him to push a pole or handle an oar. If we come under attack by Indians we need his firepower. Can't afford to take him off the duty roster for more than a day or so."

Rafe handed Freeman a vial of dilute camphorated spirits, which they had been using for shaving lotion since the expedition had left Natchez. The vial was almost empty and they were only ten days out — just barely into the Arkansa and headed west. *This stuff isn't going to last until we reach the mountains.* He would break out another vial.

The older man slapped his cheeks smartly as the lotion burned, then Rafe reached for the vial. "What's a flogging like?"

Freeman fanned his face with a great, gnarled hand. "Let's just say that you ought to be running over in your mind how to treat a badly lacerated torso."

Across the bow, Rafe could see a much larger keelboat, which lay moored along the sandbar. It was the *Columbia,* which its two officers sarcastically called the flagship of the flotilla. The smaller boat which Rafe and Freeman occupied, and which was headquarters for their surveying and collecting, was called the *Lewis and Clark.* The name made Rafe wince — and the wincing made him briefly ashamed. He was still confused about the hostility he felt toward Meriwether Lewis and William Clark, who now were heroes after their recent expedition across the continent to the Pacific. He had disliked hearing his father, on their Virginia farm, boast to a neighbor that his son was going to be "a second Lewis and Clark." He hated to think back on his last few weeks in Philadelphia, when — in addition to the strain of finishing his exams and getting his diploma — he had encountered Meriwether Lewis under puzzling circumstances.

Mrs. Crawley's boarding house on Second Street is at one corner of a rectangle that encloses Rafe's world in Philadelphia. From his garret room he can go straight west to the hospital which he visits daily, turn north to the new medical school on Chestnut, then easterly to Surgeons Hall on Fifth Street. When he occasionally wanders outside his quadrangular route it is to stroll along the docks, sometimes walking across the frozen Delaware from the Race Street wharf to Cooper's Ferry and back, mingling with thousands of citizens sleighing and celebrating winter on the ice. Sometimes he goes to the schooners along the piers to buy sweet Malaga wine and other imported delights.

Philadelphia is a wondrous city to a rural lad from the Piedmont slopes of Virginia, but an untidy one. Rafe is accustomed to the dung of animals in a rural setting but somehow disturbed by the piles of horse manure along Market Street where the stables are. At home he loves the sight of fat sows rooting in the oak-maple forests, but here he hates to see them snuffling through the offal in the streets. On the farm, human excrement is kept discreetly out of sight; here, even as a medical student becoming inured to malodorous unpleasantness, he is galled at the sight of human waste in the gutters.

In this last year of his medical education, Rafe has bought tickets to five courses: Benjamin Rush on physick, Caspar Wistar on anatomy, William Shippen on surgery, James Woodhouse on chemistry, and Benjamin Smith Barton on natural history. He also is working several hours a week at Charles Willson Peale's famed museum in the State House. That labor brings him a little spending money, an occasional meal at the Peale table, and useful experience in preparing specimens of birds and animals for study or display. It was here in the museum that he first learned about the Lewis and Clark expedition, when Peale received a shipment of wondrous Indian artifacts and plant and animal specimens, shipped down the Missouri by the two captains.

All this will end when he receives his degree. To join the other members of the Arkansa expedition, now forming at New Orleans, he will have to take his exams early, hasten to Albemarle County to bid his parents farewell, and make his way to Louisville for a water passage down the Ohio and Mississippi. To have been selected to serve as naturalist of the expedition, by Jefferson himself, is an honor that he prizes.

Then comes that incredible day. The whole scientific community has been awaiting the arrival of Captain Lewis, who is coming to renew old friendships and arrange for the publication of his journals. One of the men most anxious for Lewis's return is Mahlon Dickerson, who has introduced himself to Rafe and taken him to taverns now and then. Dickerson is a kind of dandy, thin-faced and spare, wearing the latest in fine clothing. Rafe recalls seeing him once in yellow pantaloons, taut and slim, with Hessian boots of the softest leather, a coat of dark blue cut very high in the back, a white satin waistcoat, and a powder-blue beaver hat.

It is important to Rafe that he meet with Lewis, so he waits in the city longer than he should. After he has bought supplies and medical instruments, and said good-bye to his professors and classmates, he decides he can wait no longer. He must be off to Virginia, but first he will make one last call on Dickerson — who would certainly have any news of Lewis's arrival.

He goes to Dickerson's quarters in the heart of town and finds a note on the door: *Ne troublez pas, s.v.p.* It is like Dickerson to suppose that anyone worth visiting him will know French. Rafe wanders over to Surgeons Hall and spends a few minutes watching a lithotomy being performed on a man in anguish from bladder stones. He feels the old urge to take notes but has no writing material with him.

On the chance that Dickerson's note was only meant to discourage early callers, he waits until midafternoon before returning to the door. The note is there. Resentment rises in him, directed not at Dickerson but himself. Intrepid explorer, new M.D., too timid to knock on a door that bears a warning. So he knocks, not gingerly but with four or five resounding knuckle raps, like a real doctor making an urgent house call.

Sounds of movement come from inside — and possibly the hum of suppressed voices. After a full minute the door opens a few inches and Rafe hears a sigh from Dickerson.

"Whatever is it, Dr. Bailey?"

"I'm leaving for home tomorrow."

Dickerson steps into the hallway in a rumpled dressing gown, his eyes pink and his hair untidy. His cheeks wear a beard of perhaps two days' growth. He holds an empty glass.

"Pardon my appearance," he says, rubbing his bristly chin. "I really have not been myself for the past few days. I am *bien chagrine.*" That is his euphemism for a hangover. "Too bad you are going to miss my birthday party at Fouquet's."

"Sorry to miss that occasion, but I have waited for Captain Lewis as long as I dare. Will you make it clear that I tried hard to see him? I am riding out in the morning, going first to Charlottesville and then to the West."

Dickerson hesitates, staring into the depths of his glass. "I'll certainly tell the captain. And I wish you the very best. You're going to be the second Lewis and Clark!"

They shake hands and Dickerson turns to go inside, opening the door just far enough to slip through. A wisp of stale air strikes

Rafe's nostrils, heavy with tobacco haze and alcoholic vapors. The room is dark, the shutters drawn; a lamp burns on the table.

For an instant the figure of a man is visible, seated at the table with a glass before him. Had he been facing the door, Rafe might not have recognized him, but now his head appears in profile in the yellow glow. Rafe has never seen this man before but he certainly has seen the profile, in a crayon drawing hanging on display in Mr. Peale's museum.

It is Meriwether Lewis.

Breakfast on the day of the flogging was venison steak, biscuits, and bitter coffee, followed by the sound of the whisky drum. The men seemed even more eager than usual to draw their half-gill of Monongahela whisky. When the detachment paraded for roll call, Lieutenant Smith — as officer of the day — assigned several fatigue parties, including a hunting team and one to dig a latrine trench because of the extended stay, and others to air bedding, scrub decks, and inspect arms. Men with specialties were detailed to mend rifles, tailor worn clothing, or do a little carpentry. The sentinels were told off, a corporal of the guard named, and the password and countersign announced. Smith had chosen those two words with a glint in his eye. The password was "sleep" and the countersign "danger."

Rafe felt shabbily dressed as he viewed the assembled soldiers and their officers. His frontier garb ran to browns and blacks, dun broadcloth and leather. *I'm out of uniform, as they say.* The soldiers wore bright blue coats with scarlet lapels and cuffs, white shirts, white pantaloons, dark linen gaiters, and black shoes. Their caps were black cylinders seven inches high, with the brims hand-rolled, and bore the insignia of their outfits. In the heat of this June morning, all hands soon would be doffing their coats and caps, and their shirts would go limp and gray with sweat as they slapped mosquitoes and got to work. The officers wore the great chapeaux bras adorned with black cockades and colored plumes. Each wore an epaulet of dangling wire ringlets on the left shoulder to denote rank. Stowed with their gear on the *Columbia* were their swords in gleaming scabbards, worn only when they served as officer of the day.

Before dismissing the formation, Smith read an entry from the orderly book: "A garrison court-martial will assemble at one o'clock in front of the officers' tent, for the trial of such prisoners as may be brought before it. Lieutenant James B. Wilkinson, commanding this detachment, will serve as president. Lieutenant Thomas A. Smith and Sergeant John Steele to be members."

Among the men in ranks no eyes shifted, but from his position outside the formation Rafe could look directly into the face of Henry Macomb. He was sturdy enough to take the lash, but no tower of strength. Medium build, fair hair, and light skin now reddened by the sun, with eyebrows bleached white. His uniform was noticeably neater than some, the white linen unsmudged, the leggins brightened with pipe clay, and the shoes blacker than circumstances would require. He had never reported himself sick.

As Rafe knew, at least half the men in the group — those in Wilkinson's detachment — felt a kinship with Private Macomb. All twenty were from Pennsylvania. While it was true that the army swept up men of all conditions and stations, most of them even lacking the bond of literacy, the system had one salutary effect. When a newly promoted young captain was sent out on recruiting duty, his mission was to form a company of his own. He might go into a small frontier town and sign up three or four men, often related, and the prospect was good that his entire harvest of new soldiers would hail from the same part of a single state. Because neither of the two officers were captains, the detachments were not actually theirs. They were borrowed from captains back in the states. There was a mild rivalry among them because Smith's twenty were all from Virginia and the South, but daily mixing and a hard life shared had made them almost a unit by now. If Private Macomb dreaded what was to be done to his body this day, the rest dreaded it also, for they would be forced to watch the ordeal of a countryman from Lancaster.

When the troops were dismissed and Rafe had returned to the boat, Sergeant Charles Russell, orderly sergeant of the day, brought him the sick report. It was a printed form, and in the column headed "Name of Patient" the sergeant had scrawled, "Noboddy sick To-day."

"I guess they're forgetting their own ills," Rafe said.

"Looks that way, sir."

"What sort of soldier is Macomb? How will he hold up if he's punished?"

"He's a Pennsylvanian, sir. You'll see how them kind takes it. I'm from Germantown."

"I've been there."

The sergeant hesitated, then left. Rafe sat at the cabin table alone (Freeman was away conferring with the officers about his role as witness) and made a brief list of medicines he might need for Macomb. "Laudanum for pain. Ointment. Poultice makings. Adhesive plaster. Suturing equip." He would not use precious linen unless the man got very badly cut and would require a big roller bandage. Inspecting his laudanum supply, he decided he was running low. He sifted an ounce of powdered opium into a pint decanter of brandy, shook it well, and set it aside. It should have aged for a week, but no matter. He laid out a jar of basilicon ointment made of wax, olive oil, and Venice turpentine, and saw that he had strips of cloth, gum arabic, and resin with which to make plasters. For a poultice he had a canister of fine bread crumbs that he would dissolve in water, the nearest he could come to the standard bread-and-milk concoction.

While wondering how he might divert himself during this stressful day (he did not feel like gathering plants or hunting new birds), Rafe heard an exuberant whinny. From the front port of the cabin he saw Mancha, his spotted pony, and Blue, the old Bailey-family mule, being led across the sand by a soldier. Rafe had brought the animals from home, and now two farm boys from Kentucky were detailed to ride them along the riverside until, when the expedition had to abandon the boats in shallow water, they would be essential.

Mancha and Blue required the usual nose-rubbing, ear-scratching, back-stroking, and rump-patting. "Easy, Blue," Rafe crooned. While the horse and mule stomped in the wet sand and plied their tails against the tiny black midges that swarmed about them, Rafe inspected their legs for cuts and bruises. The soldier offered his own appraisal.

"The gelding he's fine but that-ere mule, he's threw his shoe somewheres."

Rafe already had noted the holes in Blue's left-front hoof where the nails had pulled through.

"Are you a farrier?" he asked.

"A what, sir?"

"Can you shoe a mule?"

"No, but I seen old Burgoo working a forge down there in Natchez before we left."

A grim German, named Siegfried Burger and called Burgoo, was the expedition's interpreter and guide. Freeman had hired him after failing to find a Frenchman who would have better fit the traditional image. Burgoo was fat, short-legged, with unkempt white hair and a yellowing beard. Eventually he would be wearing buckskins, but now he wore the garb of an eastern farmer: Osnaburg trousers, a dirty shirt and mended jacket, heavy boots, and a black roram hat. A stringy red kerchief hung around his neck. He agreed to do the shoeing for two dollars, plus an extra dollar for making the shoe. Rafe borrowed an anvil, tools, and charcoal from the army stores, and together the two built a fire in the sand and brought it to white heat with a set of leather bellows.

Burgoo complained as he pounded away at a length of red-hot strap iron. From constant pipe-smoking, the inner edge of his lower lip was slightly extruded, a bit too moist and red, and on his nose and cheeks was the pattern of rosaceous veins that a lifetime of heavy drinking had stenciled there.

"Mules, zey don't need shoes," he said.

"I'll feel better if he's shod," Rafe insisted.

"Chust pump a lot more, den, vy don't you?"

Blue stood calm, his lower leg folded into the half-lap of the crouching farrier. Once he took his foot back to stomp at flies, and the underside of his hoof had to be scraped clean of damp sand.

"*Dummkopf!*" Burgoo said in a gentle way. He already had given Blue a couple of furtive pats and mumbled to him in German. When the shoeing was finished, the mule walked away cautiously, as if his leg had been put in a cast.

Rafe paid the bill. "I heard you playing music on some kind of flute last night after supper. I've never heard an instrument like that, and I enjoyed it very much."

Burgoo nodded. "*Blockflöte.* Fery goot music it makes. Zuch a mellow zound." As the old man watched Blue departing, he added, "I play for you venefer you vant."

After the noon meal and shortly before the court-martial, Tom Smith came to the boat and joined Rafe in the cabin. They were on a first-name basis now, having discovered they were fellow Virginians, Smith hailing from Essex County, and both were Jeffersonian Republicans. He was Rafe's ideal young officer: tall and slender, tanned the year around, quick to praise or defend his men but keeping an appropriate social distance from them. His eyebrows tended to grow together at the bridge of his nose, and he always bore a small cut or abrasion where he had parted the brows with a razor.

"I dread this flogging crap," the lieutenant said. "But I guess it's necessary."

"Maybe," Rafe said. "I get the impression that Macomb will get the lash regardless of his reason for falling asleep."

"Not inevitably. The court could recommend leniency. The problem is that he did fall asleep. The duty of a sentinel is to stay the hell awake."

"I like the civil system."

"We can't come much closer to it than we have. Don't forget that a garrison court may save more punishment than it hands out. It keeps a savage officer — and I've known a few — from administering pure torture on his own. The commander of an army unit is like a ship's captain, a sort of god. Some need to be kept in check."

"But flogging, for Christ's sake!"

"I hope you won't think I'm unfeeling, but for some soldiers it's the only solution. We get some pretty hard men in the service — although Macomb surely isn't one of them. And don't forget that we're all in prison here. We can't desert without facing great hardship; we're walled in. So locking this fellow up is no punishment. We have to hurt him, unfortunately."

"Officers don't get flogged. Do they get away with much?"

"Hell, no. They get court-martialed right and left, and on some trivial charges. We military people are a quarrelsome lot. Litigious, one of my lawyer friends calls us. We bring charges against our tent-mates for silly infractions, and when we do that a whole complicated system of justice goes into effect. A general court-martial, really a pageant, with a judge advocate and an orderly drummer, sometimes a fifer if there's one in the area. Written records, oral testimony, all that. Once I rode two hundred miles to serve on such a court. I was ordered to, of course."

"What's the punishment for an officer?"

"He gets cashiered. Ask any officer who's lost his commission, and thus his standing in the community, if he'd rather be cashiered or given the lash."

And there's always tar and feathers. "I've been mixing some fresh laudanum for Macomb," Rafe said. There's a little brandy left in the bottle. Want some?"

"Save it for me. I owe it to Macomb to hear his testimony with a clear head. I hope that doesn't sound idiotic." The boat teetered slightly as Smith stepped on the gunwale and jumped ashore.

As the afternoon dragged on, Rafe glanced occasionally at the figures squatting on buckets, kettles, and driftwood in front of the officers' tent. When it seemed that the trial must surely be about to end, Sergeant Russell came to the *Lewis and Clark* and, saluting unnecessarily, asked for a word with Rafe.

"Sir, I'm going to be doing the flogging — assuming that he gets a guilty verdict. I don't see it no other way."

"You're probably right, sergeant."

"And I just wanted to be sure that you — that you are going to take good care of Macomb."

"And why shouldn't I?" Rafe snapped, the strain of the day apparent in his voice.

"Wait, I never meant that! It's just that I have to look to my men. I wasn't suggesting nothing." The sergeant turned to leave, and Rafe stopped him.

"Hold on. If you want to do something for Macomb, see that he gets his medicine on time."

"Is he sick? Sick enough not to be punished?"

"Afraid not. But I've been treating him for a little cough and I want you to be sure he gets something for it. What time will the punishment be given?"

"At retreat, sir. Just about sundown."

"All right. Exactly an hour before that time I want you to have him drink this." Rafe took an empty four-ounce vial from his medicine chest and poured it full of laudanum, hoping he was judging the prisoner's body weight correctly and not overdosing him. The brandy would give him a nice glow and the opium would take the edge off the pain. *I might try some myself before this is over.*

"I'll see that he takes it, sir. I wish to Holy Jesus that I didn't have to fling that cat-o'-nines at him."

"Go get that cat and let's look at it. I've never seen one."

The sergeant dashed off across the camp and returned with a contraption of leather thongs held together by a woven leather handle. It was made like a hydra-headed bullwhip. An ugly implement, each of the nine thongs was about two feet long.

"What are these wire tips at the end of the thongs?"

"That's what makes it a wired cat. Them little wires can really eat into a man."

"Do they have to be there?"

"Well, sir, sometimes the verdict is for so many lashes with a wired cat."

"Cut those blasted things off. Nobody in this command would order such cruel treatment." *I'd better be right.*

Together they hacked the wire tips off the thongs with their hunting knives and hurled them into the river. "I'll be on my way, sir," the sergeant said, going ashore with the bottle in his hand.

The court-martial adjourned, the fatigue parties came in, and the cooks served an early supper while the sun still was high. No joking or jostling in the messes.

Evening parade was held near the *Columbia* on a patch of sand now well stirred and pocked by the passage of many feet. Rafe noticed that neither Sergeant Russell nor his prisoner was present in the formation. Apparently they were in the cabin of the keelboat, awaiting the reading of the court's findings. Lieutenant Smith read solemnly from the orderly book:

"Proceedings of a garrison court-martial held on the Arkansa River expedition pursuant to an order of 12 June. The court being duly sworn in the presence of the prisoner, proceeded to the trial of Private Henry Macomb, of the Second Regiment of Infantry, for violation of the forty-sixth article of the Rules and Articles of War, namely, that any sentinel who shall be found sleeping at his post, or shall leave it before he shall be regularly relieved, shall suffer death or such other punishment as shall be inflicted by the sentence of a court-martial. The court did, upon hearing the testimony of the prisoner and a sworn witness, find Private Macomb guilty of sleeping at his post on the night of the eleventh instant, and did sentence him to receive twenty-five lashes on his bare back.

"The commanding officer of this detachment has reviewed the circumstances and the testimony, and does hereby approve the findings of the court. He reminds every man in this command of the seriousness of the charge, and believes the sentence to be a lenient one. He hopes that the punishment of the prisoner will serve as a warning to all members of the command. Sentence is to be carried out at evening parade on the 12th Instant. Signed, Lieutenant James Biddle Wilkinson, Commanding."

The drummer began the "Rogue's March," and Sergeant Russell appeared at the gangway with Private Macomb. The private was stripped to the waist, the whiteness of his hairless chest and shoulders contrasting with the ruddy hue of his neck and face. As he walked down the gangway, Rafe noted his studied walk and decided that the laudanum had begun to take hold. Macomb seemed aware of what was happening but did not seem afraid. He was mainly concerned with not stumbling.

The two men marched to a spot in front of the formation where a willow pole had been fixed upright in the sand. While the drummer's doleful cadence, traditional at floggings, rolled out across the river, Macomb was tied to the pole. Gratefully, Rafe saw that the sergeant was tying the boy's wrists at about chest level, rather than stretching his arms high and thus tautening the skin of his torso. The leather would do less damage this way.

"Thwack!" sang the lash as the first blow raked Macomb across the back and shoulders. Each of the thongs cut or abraded him in a different way, and upon his face there came a look of surprise and anguish.

Rafe steeled himself as he used to in Surgeons Hall when an amputation or trepanning was in progress. *I should have used more laudanum.*

"Thwack! Thwack! Thwack!" The sergeant laid them on rapidly, anxious to be done. He stepped back to get a better grip on the whipstock with a sweaty hand. Macomb took the willow post in his arms and clutched it. He may have been sobbing.

"Thwack! Thwack!" On and on it went. Rafe felt he must watch. The boy was his patient now.

At the nineteenth or twentieth stroke — Rafe had tried to count them — the prisoner sank to his knees, his back now crisscrossed with bleeding incisions. The sergeant stopped and looked inquiringly at Lieutenant Wilkinson, who was standing just outside the range of the flailing leather. Even the drummer paused.

Wilkinson raised his hand. "That's twenty-five," he said. "Get this man cut down." The soldiers in the formation relaxed noticeably, though still at attention, and those who had been silently counting the strokes must have noted that an act of mercy had occurred during an act of official brutality.

"At ease!" Lieutenant Smith barked. He held up the rest of the retreat ceremony while the sergeant untied Macomb and knelt to keep him from falling forward. Rafe hurried to help steady him. "Don't get sand in those wounds. Let's see if he can walk."

They lifted him gently by the arms and felt his legs stiffen and take hold. "It's all over, Macomb," the sergeant said. "The doctor's going to take good care of you now."

They walked Macomb slowly toward the *Lewis and Clark,* where he would be spending the night in Rafe's care. As they shuffled to the boat, the drummer beat retreat, some muffled orders were shouted, and the men of the Arkansa expedition drifted off toward their tents as twilight faded.

Macomb had two visitors during the evening. He was oblivious to both. Heavily sedated by another draught of laudanum, and lying on his stomach alongside the cabin of the boat, he slept restlessly but deeply. Only a few of the wounds had required closing with plasters and none had needed suturing. Everything looked clean to Rafe, none of the incisions was jagged, and he felt that normal adhesion and healing would occur — leaving only scars that young Macomb might someday show his children with perverse and bitter pride.

The first visitor was Wilkinson. He came aboard quietly as if entering a sickroom. From inside the cabin, Freeman — who was doing some drafting and journal-keeping by candlelight — handed a bottle of whisky out to Rafe and Wilkinson and was not heard from again.

The lieutenant knelt beside the sleeping soldier. "I know this boy's older brother. He keeps a fine tavern in Lancaster and he's going to give me a real caning next time I see him." Wilkinson patted Macomb's sweating head and sat down on the gunwale while Rafe poured two drinks.

His nickname was Bid, a shortening of Biddle, and he was three or four years older than Rafe — thin-faced and quiet, as if trying to seem the very opposite of his posturing and flamboyant father, the general. He had been sent to school in Philadelphia and was preparing to enter college when he suddenly decided (or was persuaded) to accept a cadetship in the army. He soon became his father's aide-de-camp, living at various headquarters with as much pomp and luxury as conditions could provide. His father had sent him west from St. Louis last year with Zebulon Pike, instructing that when they reached the Arkansa he was to return home. His descent of the river from the Great Bend, with five reluctant soldiers, had been a nightmare. He had lain ill in the boat for days while the men, some with desertion on their minds, had dragged and poled the craft through the icy shallows. This was his meager qualification to lead an expedition back up the Arkansa.

Rafe could see no sign of military temperament in Wilkinson. Already it was plain that Tom Smith was quietly shouldering many of the cares of command. Smith, who sang loudly around campfires, a queue of glistening black hair slapping his collar. Wilkinson was of a different breed.

"You must call me Bid. All my friends call me that."

"Right. Does it bother you that we've lost a day of travel?"

"Certainly. But we got some things done that we couldn't have done if we'd been under way." He noted a scattering of plant specimens that Rafe had been drying in the sun. "Some of your natural history stuff, I see. I wish you would take me collecting with you sometime."

"Easily done, since I've got a horse and a mule. I notice that you like to sketch. I'm terrible at it. You might draw a plant or two for me."

"Make it birds. I'm in love with birds."

They talked of their schools and of Wilkinson's ambition to read law. They spoke of army life and politics, and when Rafe mentioned his parents, Wilkinson explained that his mother had died in New Orleans only a few weeks before the expedition had left there. He spoke admiringly of Lieutenant Smith.

"Tom's a real officer. I'm just a fellow trying to get up the ladder and using the army to do it, with an occasional lift from my daddy. Sometimes I think the general sent Tom along just to keep me out of trouble. I hope he does."

"I would like to meet the general someday," Rafe said.

"Wait as long as you can and don't let him take you under his wing. He'll smother you."

Bid Wilkinson stared into his empty cup, from which he had drained more whisky than he was accustomed to having.

"I shouldn't have said that," he continued. Rafe poured another splash into his cup. "Right now my father is in Richmond testifying against Aaron Burr. He claims that Burr had some plan to invade Spanish territory, and so on. But if I know dad, he had a hand in it right up to the elbow. I guess we won't know until we get home, but I'll bet a good American dollar that he comes out of this as clean as a whistle. Burr's reputation will be ruined even if he isn't convicted, but the old general will come strutting out of the courthouse, with that bantam-rooster walk of his, and maybe go have a bowl of rum with the chief justice. He's such a damned schemer."

"You don't need to tell me all this," Rafe said, but the lieutenant continued.

"There's something worse. I've got an idea that Spain is slipping my father some *reales* for services rendered. Or for information. If that's so, he's the one who ought to be on trial. For God's sake, the man is commanding general of the army and may be in the pay of a foreign power!"

Silence. Then Wilkinson put down his cup and rose unsteadily.

"Are you all right?" Rafe asked.

"Williamsburg," he said.

"What's that mean?"

"Williamsburg. The old capital of Virginia. When I can say it without getting my tongue in the way, it means I'm still all right. It's been my test since I first learned to drink. I do think I'm a little flusticated, though."

He walked down the short gangway and disappeared in the

darkness, whistling as if to show that he was in full control of his faculties.

Rafe called after him. "Williamsburg to you, too." He was pleased that Wilkinson had opened up to him, and was for the present unaware that his whole conception of the expedition would change. There were two men of power and influence, far away, who directed the exploration as surely as if they had been aboard the boats — President Jefferson and General Wilkinson.

A second visitor appeared almost as soon as the lieutenant had gone. It was Burgoo, whose heavy step Rafe heard as he was covering Macomb with another blanket.

"Guten Abend," Burgoo said. "How iss der young von dere?"

"Sleeping and doing nicely."

"I play for him, *nein?"* Burgoo took his block flute from under his arm and sat down on a wooden chest.

"That would be very nice. He may not hear you, but I will."

"He vill hear. In his zleep he vill hear."

While the river rolled quietly past, with only the light from Freeman's candle casting an occasional glimmer on the water, Burgoo played haunting country tunes from his homeland. Macomb slept on.

It was late in the night when Rafe finished his journal entry. He had decided to call his daily notes *Remarks & Occurrences,* following the example of George Washington, who had kept a diary all his adult life. Rafe made a few comments from an earlier trip onshore, recording his wonder at the sight of an enormous cypress tree: "Marvelous, with trunk straight as an arrow, rising bare of limbs to 80 ft. or more. It has a rather flat top formed by horizontal branches, & the foliage is almost proof against the sun. At the foot of the trunk there are many roots, radiating & forming stout knees (as they are called) which support the tree. These giants grow densely in land so unstable that I sink to my thighs in mud and water. In places the soil produces tall, thick grass."

He was sitting on the sail locker in the stern, listening to the sentries at the four corners of camp calling out "all's well" to one another in the night. He imagined that after Macomb's experience they were trying to sound particularly alert and wakeful. He thought of something that Bid Wilkinson had said: "This expedition is going to make you and Freeman another Lewis and Clark."

Wonderful.

2

To the Last Army Outpost

THE FLOGGING of Private Macomb mortified Rafe. He had
seen bodily punishment in and around Charlottesville when a slave
was beaten, and he considered such treatment obscene. To see it
administered by men he respected introduced a new factor into
his notion of how human affairs should go. In the days that followed he gradually absorbed this hard fact of military life. It
helped to see Macomb playing ball with his fellow soldiers before
retreat each evening, including the sergeant who had swung the
lash.

The keelboats were now two weeks out of Natchez, proceeding
west on the lower Arkansa. When the expedition had been on
the Mississippi the wind had blown fair for a part of each day,
and at times the vessels had been under sail. Now, with an un-
favorable headwind and little room to tack in the narrower channel of the Arkansa, both were being alternately poled and rowed.

The *Columbia* was a sixty-foot boat, twelve feet wide amidships. Loaded, she drew about eighteen inches of water. A box-
like cabin ran nearly the length of the vessel, with a catwalk on
either side where the soldiers worked the poles. A single mast just
forward of the center line stood high above the flat-roofed cabin.
The square sail was now lowered and furled; atop the slender
pine mast flew the United States flag of seventeen stars. At the
stern, on a shorter staff, hung the blue and white regimental standard of the Second Infantry.

Unlike a seagoing boat with a fixed keel, the *Columbia* was

built with a flat bottom for shallow waters. Hanging in the water
behind the stern, like the lashing tail of a sea monster, was a
detached keel of planking set at the end of a long, curving oar.
When the helmsman moved the oar in its pivoting lock, the boat
answered leisurely but surely.

By comparison, the *Lewis and Clark* was tiny. Had it not come
with a squat little cabin, two catwalks, a mast, and a swinging
keel, it might have qualified as a large canoe or — as the French
settlers would have called it — a pirogue. Like its larger sister, it
was freshly painted in the army's standard color, Spanish brown.

In its lower reaches the Arkansa was a typical southern river,
edged with brackish bayous in which the cypress trees hung full
with moss and the black water of the quiet places was topped
with algae and ensnared by vines. In midstream, however, the
river was turbid from rains, and the current was so swift that the
boats could make little way. The bowsmen kept them close ashore,
where the going was easier.

The river played with sand and soil, scooping a bend on one
side, building a point on the other, shaping itself into patterns
that never were quite the same from season to season. Each time
the boats neared a point extending into the stream on the inside
of a bend, where the current was swift, they were compelled to
cross the river to the quieter convex side.

Most of the advice that Lieutenant Wilkinson gave the newer
men began with the words "watch out." Watch out for planters,
which were sunken trees fixed to the river bottom by their roots,
thrusting their branches solidly upward to gouge out the bottom
of a boat. Watch out for sawyers, which were loose and bobbing
trunks that rose and fell as they yielded to the current. Watch out
for wooden islands of driftwood, which were more dangerous
than real islands because the river had not yet tapered their sides
with sand. And take care that you never put ashore near a point,
which can crumble and crush your vessel, but rather in the cove
below the point, where the willows will cushion the shock as you
come aground.

Such lore came fast to men whose mode of travel was the tricky
western river. Although the soldiers-now-boatmen of the expedition were drawn from the ranks of the army in New Orleans,
they already were attuned to the scuffle of feet on the catwalks

as the polers worked, and their eyes were alert to the perils of the stream.

Last night the boats had been moored at a sandbar, upon which everyone had slept without pitching their tents, had cooked their meals and stretched stiff muscles by racing and wrestling. Some of the men had fished for catfish — unsightly fish with flattened heads and whiskerlike barbels, having no scales. One experienced New Orleans fisherman used pungent animal liver for bait.

"It's got to be really rotten for channel cat," he claimed. "If y'all cain't stand to smell it, then it's jist right to be catfish bait."

This morning Rafe had held sick call ashore in the shade of a large willow, until the drumroll had signaled time for departure. Now he sat in the bow of the *Lewis and Clark*, tending a sick man who lay on the deck in front of the cabin. Rafe had rigged a mosquito netting over the restless soldier and given him an extra mattress. Private Wyatt Ranson drank often from a canister of river water and groaned quietly when the pain flashed anew through his midsection.

"How is it now?" Rafe asked.

"Not too bad, sir," Ranson said. Gangly and curly-haired, he had signed on in a hasty moment while watching a recruiting officer and squad of musicians in Richmond. The lilt of the fife and the irresistibility of all those red lapels had sent him to the sergeant, hungering to sign the recruiting roll. He was not soldier material, Rafe knew. *Should be at William and Mary.* He had been quickly assigned by Wilkinson as his waiter — a kind of body servant and private secretary combined.

Ranson was fascinated by Rafe's profession — not the medical aspects, but the study of natural history. The idea that a doctor would come so far to press plants between sheets of paper was what he wanted to talk about.

"We had this flower garden at home," he said, grabbing at a mosquito that had slipped through the netting. "My father explained to me about Latin names. A clever system. Invented by a Swede, wasn't it?"

"Carl Linnaeus," Rafe said. "We just use his last name."

"I wish you would run through that part again about how the plants get their names."

Rafe explained that the person who first described a new plant or animal in print, according to certain rules, was privileged to assign the name. Each species had two names, the first for genus and the second for species. "Sometimes the discoverer of a new plant or animal will honor a friend by naming it for him. The genus of plants called *Claytonia* was named to honor the great naturalist John Clayton."

Ranson smiled and nodded, then his face went gray and he drew his right leg up in a spasm of pain. It was time, Rafe thought, for another dose of laudanum.

His patient had reported to sick call two days ago with a pain in the umbilical region. He had complained of nausea, vomiting, and costive bowels. Yesterday the pain had shifted to the right-lower quadrant of his belly, and he described it as sometimes dull, sometimes severe. There was a mild fever and the pain was worse when he coughed or sneezed. Once, when the boat ran aground with a heavy jolt on an underwater bar, Ranson had cried out.

The only other case of intestinal inflammation as severe as this one had killed Rafe's sister's husband. He could bleed this soldier and be generous with the opium, and little else. Thus far he had taken eight ounces of blood from Ranson's arm and given him laudanum in modest doses. He was holding off on the cathartics without quite knowing why. Perhaps later he would resort to Dr. Rush's purgative pills as an extreme measure.

Sick call for the rest of the men was almost a relief. He realized, filling out the morning report, that his men were a healthy lot and their minor ills were what his teachers had called self-limiting. ("Count yourselves lucky, my young friends, that most of your patients will recover by themselves," Dr. Wistar had said in his first lecture.)

Some of the men had chronic malarial fever and ague, to which they had grown accustomed. They took their doses of cinchona-bark tea, endured the fever, and when it came time to shake with the chills they did it resignedly. Rafe hoped that his case load of cinchona-takers would diminish when the expedition had cleared the miasmic airs of the lower river and reached the dry climate of the plains. Until then he was thankful for the bark, perhaps the one medication in his baggage that would control a specific agent. Well, no, there was also mercury for venereal complaints.

When Ranson drifted off into fitful sleep, Rafe watched the crew at work. Four men on each side of the cabin, along the catwalks, drove their spiked poles into the sandy river bottom and worked in unison, pushing the boat into the current. Ahead, the *Columbia* required eight men on a side. At the front of each boat the bowman watched for tiny ripples that might indicate underwater obstructions. At the stern the helmsman held the end of the oaken keel oar in both hands, keeping it steady until commanded to change direction.

In the cabin, Freeman was preparing his chart of the river. He had built a table upon which to work, and his drafting instruments were laid out beside him as he bent over his compass or peered through the window to estimate the distance to the next bend. As he scratched away with his pen he hummed old Irish airs, and every half hour or so he stepped out on deck to chat with Rafe.

"How does the laddy seem?" He stepped carefully around the dozing patient.

"I'm getting concerned."

Wearing a cheap gray jacket and linsey-woolsey trousers, and a pair of indestructible jackboots that once had been black, Freeman was not a commanding figure. He seldom wore a hat, and Rafe wondered why. Maybe to avoid chafing his tomahawk scar. He had come from Ireland to work as a surveyor back in the eighties and served for a while as inspector of the port of Plymouth, Massachusetts. When the new District of Columbia and the federal city were laid out, he worked on that project. He began a project under Andrew Ellicott in the 1790s, marking the southern boundary between the United States and the Spanish colonies of East and West Florida, but had quarreled with Ellicott and resigned. His next assignment had been to lay out and supervise the building of Fort Adams, below Natchez, and by the summer of 1802 he was surveying up along the Wabash for Governor Harrison. By this time he was a respected professional in the office of the surveyor general, and when Jefferson had needed a surveyor for the Red River expedition of 1806, Freeman had been assigned. When the Spanish had intercepted the party, Freeman had negotiated until it became clear that he must turn back, and after that fiasco Jefferson had held him in reserve for this voyage on the Arkansa.

"If you're just going to be sitting around, I'll give you the compass and let you keep the headings," he told Rafe.

"That's risky. My father gave up trying to show me how to measure a field. I never understood the metes and bounds."

"Fields are nothing compared to rivers. I don't mind working a meander line by time and distance, but I sure don't care for the quadrant. I warned the president that I was a surveyor, not an astronomer."

Jefferson. The man in charge. Rafe's visit with him a few short weeks ago had been exciting and inspiring.

With his diploma in his saddlebag, he has ridden out of Philadelphia toward home, coming down across the Brandywine and the Susquehanna, on to Baltimore and Georgetown, then into his beloved Virginia. He has made the ride in six days, in the prime of an April springtime, and has decided to stop at Monticello before going on home.

At the president's house a black servant takes charge of his horse and directs him to the front entrance. In the hall where he is asked to wait he sees more of the marvels collected by Lewis and Clark — a bow and quiver of arrows, a rich and soft antelope robe, a box of mineral specimens, earthen pots with incised designs, the antlers of a deer with a different conformation than those of the white-tailed deer around home. On the wall, an enormous buffalo hide covered with pictographs drawn in bright colors. His fingers are brushing the incredibly thick leather, and he is about to sniff it, when Jefferson speaks from behind him.

"The Mandan tribe sent it back with Captain Lewis. I've been trying to decipher the story."

Rafe turns, and his first thought is of how Jefferson has changed since he last saw him. He is wearing a brown homespun coat, corduroy knee breeches, a faded red waistcoat, hose that seem not quite secure at the knees, and scuffed leather slippers without heels or buckles. He is holding a soil-caked trowel which he hands to a servant. Rafe last saw Jefferson crossing the courthouse square in Charlottesville, maybe five years ago, in riding garb. At that time he seemed tall, virile, even dashing. His hair was sandy red then but now is gray, drawn back to a queue. He stoops noticeably, his jowls are full, and there is a suggestion of a double chin.

"I'm Raphael Bailey, sir. Anthony Bailey's son."

"*Doctor* Bailey, isn't it?" They shake hands. "I know and admire your father. Tell me what you think of my Mandan pictograph."

Rafe studies the great primitive panorama, with its stick men and stick horses drawn up as two opposing war parties. He has never thought of Indians as picture-makers.

"I've been thinking what it would be like to see the Battle of Monmouth done by the same hand," he says.

Jefferson smiles. "No doubt you would see the great and fierce Chief George Washington on his famous steed Blueskin, charging up and down the ranks, exhorting his warriors to rally and charge. He would wear a glorious headdress and his angry face would be very red."

They tour the gardens behind the mansion and Rafe is introduced to Martha Randolph, the president's married daughter, who has come from her adjoining estate to wait upon her father during his brief time away from the capital. She wears a bright calico morning dress and muslin cap, and presents her teen-aged daughter Ellen, whose gypsy hat of straw is jauntily tipped and held fast by a blue chin ribbon.

The president shows Rafe his new flower beds on the east and west lawns, where he is planting tuberoses, anemones, tulips, lobelias, and pinks. He points out a flowering pea from the prairies and a yellow lily from the Columbia River, brought home by Lewis and Clark. The rich brick and white trim of the noble Palladian house, the fine old trees surrounding it, and the view of the Blue Ridge to the west are wholly stunning to Rafe.

"We'll go to my study now," Jefferson says. There Rafe runs his eyes along more rows of books than he has ever seen before: classics in Latin and Greek; works of moral philosophy and European history; and wonderful, tempting volumes of geography and natural history that make him feel totally uninstructed. Lying open, with a reading glass upon it to mark the place, is Alexander Mackenzie's *Voyages from Montreal*. In Philadelphia it is being said that Mackenzie's work had spurred Jefferson into sending an expedition to the Pacific.

"Dr. Bailey, I don't want to keep you from the arms of your parents, but I should like to hear a bit about your life. Your education, perhaps."

"My mother taught me at home when my father was General Washington's farm overseer at Mount Vernon. And when my family left that place, upon the general's death, they bought a farm along Doyle's River in western Albemarle. I boarded at Mr. Robertson's school for two years."

"A fine old Scot. Did he introduce you to Tacitus?"

"He tried, sir. But I had a hard time with it."

"Indeed you must have. I still never read him without a translation at hand. Please go on."

Rafe continues, taking the story through his attendance at Washington Academy in Lexington. "My father naturally wanted me to go to a school so recently named for the general, and I studied there for two years." He tells of being ready to enroll in the medical department at Philadelphia when he learns that to earn an M.D. he first must spend two years with a preceptor. "I chose Dr. Puckett, here in town, and read medicine with him, riding home most nights to be with father, mother, and my sister Frances. Then, when I was twenty-one, I went to Philadelphia and have spent the past two years there."

"Let's get to your exciting tour up the Arkansa," Jefferson urges. "You are highly thought of at the medical school and I have no doubt that you are the person we need to complement the work of Mr. Freeman. As you know, Captain Zebulon Pike is out in that area now. There is some reason to think the Spanish have molested him, but I doubt it. Old General Salcedo down in Chihuahua made a great fuss about my sending out Lewis and Clark, but it was pure bluster. If you and your fellows are prudent and alert you will have nothing to fear.

"You are to be the surgeon, of course, but I hope that the distribution of some of Dr. Rush's famous and nearly incendiary pills will be the extent of your medical duties. I want you to do as Captain Lewis did and collect all that is new to you. What you cannot collect you must describe minutely in your journals. Don't expect to start finding new things immediately you enter the Arkansa. Lewis and Clark were out for three months before they found their first new bird, the black-billed magpie.

"When you put a written description in your journal, and perhaps a sketch of a new species, be sure to tell exactly where it came from. Don't merely write 'Banks of the Arkansa' or 'Stony Mountains,' but explain the soil, the growing conditions, and the adjacent vegetation. Some of your observations will not deal with new species, but will be helpful in our understanding the range of those already known — and variations induced by different environments.

"I suspect that many of your findings will overlap those of Lewis and Clark. I've been reading their journals and inspecting their collections. It may be that a tree which thrives at an elevation of five thousand feet in the Northwest may thrive as well, at the same altitude, in the Southwest. The same may be true for animals and birds.

"Your collecting will consist mainly of plants because they are easy to dry and transport. Bird skins are somewhat bulkier and more difficult to prepare. But the animals — especially the larger ones — are the worst. You will wish many times for a wagon. A grizzly bear's hide might weigh a hundred pounds. Spare me any more of those, please. And don't burden yourself with rocks of any size unless they are precious ore. Just a small chip will suffice. Concentrate on coal, lead, or other minerals of some economic value. I am impatient with geologists who scratch up the earth's surface in quest of useless knowledge about the age of the universe."

"What about ethnological data on the Indians?" Rafe asks.

"Get all you can. Mr. Freeman knows Indians well, but I suspect he will chafe at collecting data. No doubt you will see, besides the Osages, a weak and friendly tribe called the Quapaws on the lower Arkansa. And later, some Pawnees, perhaps. The ones to watch out for, the Ietans or Comanches, you may come upon as you near the mountains. I am going to give you some printed vocabulary lists that I have drawn up. It would add much to a collection I have been making all my life if you would try to get the equivalent words in various Indian tongues."

Holding the bundle of printed forms tied with a brown string, Rafe thinks the time has come to bring up his interest in receiving an army appointment. "Mr. President, I have the notion that I'd like to become a surgeon's mate. Dr. Barton was the one who first suggested it, and the idea has rather possessed me as if it were my own."

"Of course. It's an honorable calling. I have no doubt, though, that you could easily receive a commission as a lieutenant in the line instead."

"Perhaps later, but right now I want to practice medicine, and this seems to be the way I can serve as a doctor and an officer at the same time."

"You'll only be a warrant officer, not a commissioned one, and your superiors may not always think of you as a genuine equal. But if that's what you want, I shall write the secretary of war at once. Your appointment will have to be approved by the Senate and I fear the papers won't reach you before the expedition departs. I'll have them sent to New Orleans and they'll be waiting for your return."

Then the president hesitates and says, "There's one thing that I must ask you about. Your party affiliation. Because we Republicans inherited an army that was mainly Federalist, I have had the double necessity of reducing the size of the military and getting more Republicans into the officer corps. It might surprise you to learn that when I hired Captain Lewis as my secretary I wanted him mainly to help me evaluate the officers he had come to know so well, from the standpoint of both capability and party leanings. Sending him out to explore was a later inspiration." He smiles and pauses.

"I'm a good Republican like my father, sir."

"The secretary of war will be delighted. Of all my cabinet members, Henry Dearborn seems the most party-minded. I think you may consider your appointment achieved — assuming that the Senate approves.

They talk for another quarter-hour. "If you encounter the Spanish," Jefferson says, "Mr. Freeman and the officer in charge of your armed escort will do the negotiating. The agreement drawn up by General Wilkinson last fall, neutralizing a strip of land between the Sabine and the Arroyo Hondo, has cooled tempers for the time. And that area is much farther south than you will be. The boundary of Louisiana Territory is still to be agreed upon, but that is a job for diplomats. We now have a claim on the country even beyond Louisiana, on the western slope of the Stony Mountains, through the legal principle of jus gentium, meaning that when a nation takes possession of a river's mouth, the ownership is considered to include all the waters draining into that river. Captain Gray sailed into the Columbia in 1792 and established our claim there. Lewis and Clark strengthened that claim. But I concur with Lewis that we shall have a much stronger case when we have put a trading post at the mouth of the Columbia. In this we are competing with the British. The Spanish question is a stickier one, and I shall await the results of your tour with anxiety. It is foolish of us and the Spanish to speak of boundaries until we have accurate maps of the drainage systems."

"Won't our expedition be duplicating Pike's?"

"No, Captain Pike is an untrained observer, sent by General Wilkinson on a number of errands into the West. What he learns will be helpful, but his is not a definitive tour."

Jefferson rises and so does Rafe. "Do you know Spanish?" the president asks.

"Only some French, sir."

"Spanish is easy. I learned it while sailing to Europe years ago. I'll give you a little grammar and dictionary if you don't fear it will add too much to your baggage."

"I'd like to have it."

The president walks with him to the front entrance and along the brick walk, where his horse is standing in the care of a stable hand. She has been brushed and fed, and looks rested. Her ears swivel forward when Rafe appears.

"Write your parents every chance you get," the president urges. "It is a terrible thing that people wait until they have much to say, when just a line would be so welcome."

Rafe laughs and mounts the mare, and when he looks back for the last time he sees that Jefferson, now standing in his doorway, has already recovered his garden trowel and is ready to dig.

In midafternoon, Bid Wilkinson realized that if he did not stop for the day he would be arriving near dark at the Arkansa Post. So he signaled from the *Columbia* that he was making for a protected cove and would camp there. The Arkansa Post was both a small French village and a minor United States Army post, the only such garrison the expedition would see in ascending the river. The lieutenant preferred to arrive in the morning, rather than disturb the garrison and perhaps alarm the sentinels by appearing after dark.

Once ashore, the men assigned to the various messes began to pitch small tents while the cook for each mess got out his kettles to hang over a fire. There were five messes; the officers plus Rafe and Freeman made up a smaller sixth. Ordinarily, Wilkinson used his waiter Wyatt Ranson as cook, but tonight it was Smith's waiter, Joseph Ironmonger, who brought food to the officer group from one of the other messes. (The officers ate some of the food from a different mess each day, to be reasonably sure the men were properly fed.) Everyone in camp knew that a locker aboard the big keelboat contained raisins, lemons, candy, and nutmeats with which the officers supplemented their ration. For the men, the only treat was the half-gill of whisky they received twice a day.

"How much is half a gill supposed to be?" a soldier asked, peering into his cup.

"That's easy," another said. "Suppose a bat was to fly into that cup of yourn, and puke till his little stomach was plumb empty. You'd have half a gill." Actually it was two ounces. Wilkinson insisted that each man drink his ration at once instead of hoarding it for a drunken spree.

While the men sat on white, barkless logs washed up on the sandbar, and hoped the smoke from the fires would keep the mosquitoes quiescent, the four men of the officers' mess took their wooden trenchers of salt pork and white beans aboard the *Columbia* and sat in the bow. Rafe had taken his patient ashore and put him in a private tent, after failing to persuade him to taste a little broth.

Freeman spoke first after everyone had eaten for a while in silence. "Tell me, Mr. Wilkinson, who issued us this monster of a barge? She rides high in the stern, doesn't answer the tiller well, and sloshes about in the water like a log raft. I can hardly bear to watch the poor old girl from back there in our little boat."

"Blame my father the general for that," Wilkinson said. "He had her on his hands, tied up at the presidio, and checked her out to me. I had no choice." He tilted his trencher to get the last of the salty gravy.

"You'd think a general's son could talk back to him," Tom Smith said.

"Tried that just once," Wilkinson said, and did not elaborate. "How's my sick man?" he asked, turning to Rafe.

"I'm worried about him."

"I'll look in on him after parade. And tomorrow you'll have another doctor to consult, up at the post."

"The damned boat almost broached today when we tried the sail," Smith said. What he did not add was that, at the moment of danger, Wilkinson had been sitting in the stern with a sketching pad on his knee, unaware of the situation.

"I think you might as well stow the sail when it gets good and dry," Freeman said.

"We'll do that," Wilkinson said, assigning the job to Tom Smith with a glance.

In the first cool of the evening, when the willows along the bank were throwing a jagged line of shadow across the sandbar and out upon the water, the drummer beat the call for parade. For the first time since leaving Natchez, the men paraded under arms. Their clipped and varied voices sounded roll call. The colors were paraded while the drummer beat retreat. The soldiers stood in formation and Smith read from the orderly book:

"Tomorrow after breakfast we shall be passing the village called Arkansa Post and proceeding to the garrison of the same name. While we are at the fort no man is to consort with any French inhabitants of the town. Only Sergeant Steele is authorized to buy food from them at prices to be set by this command. At the fort there will be no fighting with soldiers stationed there, and absolutely no drunkenness. Those who see this pause as a last opportunity to desert from the service of their country are reminded of Article Twenty of the Rules and Articles of War."

Sentries were assigned their watches, one on each boat and four posted about the camp. At 9:00 P.M. the drummer beat tattoo, the signal for all men to be near their tents and ready for bed. Half an hour later he beat taps. Fires were doused, candles snuffed out, and there was little human sound except the periodic calling of the sentinels.

Rafe returned to Private Ranson. There was barely room inside the tent for both, especially as Ranson thrashed and turned constantly. By midnight he seemed to have entered a new phase of his ordeal. Because it hurt so much to move, he lay very still. His breathing was shallow, his pulse fast and thready, and his abdomen was distended. When Rafe put an ear to his belly he could hear no bowel sounds. The doctor and his patient lay quietly together. Tomorrow, Rafe decided, he would have to take more blood.

In the morning Ranson seemed slightly better. He called for something to drink, took some wine and a sip or two of venison broth. Encouraged, Rafe blistered his abdomen with cantharides and drew another ten ounces from his arm with the spring-loaded venesection knife that he carried in his pocket. Ranson seemed ready to talk for a while.

"What day is it, sir?"

"No idea. But I'll try to find out."

"Have you been out gathering plants?"

"Not yet. Got to get you back on your feet first."

"I was thinking," the soldier said, "about this business of finding plants and naming them. That's what I want to do. I want to go out collecting and watch how you do it. Maybe I'll find a new plant of my own."

"We can talk about that later," Rafe said. "Pretty soon we'll be raising the Arkansa Post and I can move you inside the barracks to get you away from these goddamned mosquitoes. And the rocking of the boat."

Ranson did not respond, having drifted off again. His legs were pulled tightly against his abdomen and Rafe straightened them with difficulty. *I'd give a lot to talk with Dr. Rush right about now.*

The village now coming into view around the bend had grown up beside an old French fort established more than a century earlier and later occupied by the Spanish. After the Louisiana Purchase it had become an American military post. Retaining its French character, it was headquarters for traders and a place for Indian delegations to stop by from up the river. The village itself stood apart from the fort. Its four-hundred inhabitants, mainly French, included thirty or forty slaves. Its buildings were in the New Orleans style, with open galleries all around, many doors, no glass in the windows. The village gave the impression of being always on the move, the flimsy houses edging back from the shoreline as the river changed course every spring.

As the boats passed, those villagers who had heard the signal shots came down to the landing: the men in overalls of homespun and moccasins of deerskin, blanket capes over the shoulders; the women in plain dresses; and both sexes wearing red madras bandannas as head coverings. The blacks, all waving, were garbed like their masters, although Rafe saw one with a white jacket and trousers, a stiff collar, checkered apron worn high on his bulging waist, and large gold rings hanging from his ears. The servant, perhaps, of an affluent trader.

Freeman and Rafe stood in the bow as the tiny flotilla approached the fort. "That's the meanest-looking army post I ever saw," Freeman declared.

A dozen soldiers had come to the landing and were laughing and shouting, waiting to help tie up the boats. "Look at those sloppy uniforms," Freeman said. "See that tall chap holding a coil of line? Hell, he's dressed worse than me."

The fort — decrepit buildings surrounded by a palisade or stockade of logs fourteen feet high — had been in a poor state of repair when the Spanish had transferred it and was nearly a shambles now. The front side of the stockade was only a few paces from the boat landing. Another year of high water might bring the river to the gate. Inside the stockade were the officers' quarters and a barracks building for the men, both with clay chimneys, and a storehouse which also contained the kitchen and powder magazine. All were made of sawed boards and roofed with cypress shingles. At three of the stockade corners, uncovered bastions contained raised platforms for cannon, but only one six-pounder was visible. The United States flag hung from a tall staff on the parade ground in the center of the stockade area.

Outside the fort, and sitting well back from the river, was the only sign of new construction. A building made in two sections, with an open gallery between and a cellar underneath one wing, stood still-unroofed — its freshly cut siding boards gleaming in the sun.

"That new structure must be the factory," Freeman said. "That's for the factor or government trader who deals with the Indians. And there's the shed beside it where the tribes stay when they bring their furs down to trade."

A sallow, stocky man in full-dress uniform stepped through the stockade gate and hurried to the landing. Rafe recognized the dress as that of a surgeon's mate, a blue coat trimmed in white lace, a black plume on the tricorn cap. He wore a short sword, or dirk, and his pantaloons were rumpled as if they had been packed away. When the bow end of the *Columbia* nosed in and bumped the rotting dock, Dr. Abraham Stewart smiled happily. When Wilkinson jumped ashore, the doctor cried: "Bid Wilkinson! By God, you must be my replacement. What a happy day!"

They exchanged salutes. "I'm not here as your replacement, Abe. Are you still in command?"

"Christ, yes. Can you believe it? Where's that contractor's boat? Did you see anything of it?"

"Not a sign. Is it overdue?"

"We haven't seen the rascal since September. My men are short of salt, blankets, clothing, whisky, anything you can name. When we heard the shots from your bow gun we thought you were the contractor. Then we saw the flag and I concluded that you were someone coming to take command. I need to talk to you, Bid. Glad to see you are in better health than last time."

By the time the boats were secure, Rafe and Freeman had joined the officers on the rickety landing. Everyone was introduced.

Rafe lost no time. "Dr. Stewart, I've got a pretty sick man with me."

Stewart detailed two soldiers to carry Ranson to the barracks, where a small partition at one end defined the sick ward. Then he led the way to the dayroom in the officers' quarters.

They were joined by John B. Treat, the factor, who brought a bottle of spirits of wine that he kept for certain chiefs. As if no one knew the story of Bid Wilkinson's recent descent of the river, Treat took the matter up at once. "By thunder, when I saw that dugout floating downstream, whirling in the current, I thought she was empty. Then this ragged figure stood up, all wobbly, and started to wave an old rag."

"I had some better brandy in my hospital stuff," Dr. Stewart said, not caring to hear the rest of a well-known tale, "but I'm afraid that little by little the men have nipped it all away."

Stewart had trained in Massachusetts and taken a surgeoncy in the army a dozen years ago. When he was posted to the Arkansa nine months earlier he had expected a short tour and an early relief. The government had not sent a full company to protect the factory, but only a detail of sixteen men commanded by a lieutenant. One day the lieutenant had taken off for Fort Adams, claiming official business and leaving Stewart in command. He never came back. While the doctor was learning to handle soldiers, and to fill out morning reports, sick reports, returns of equipment, muster rolls, and the company book, he had sent pleading letters to Washington asking to be relieved. Matters grew worse when James Morrison of Lexington, having a contract to supply several of the posts in the Mississippi Valley, failed to deliver. Even worse, the district paymaster had not been around for half a year. Luckily the Quapaw, Choctaw, and Osage Indians who came to the factory were peaceable enough. As for the French settlers in the town, they kept apart. Stewart heard singing and fiddling when they held dancing assemblies, but no one had ever invited him to attend.

Wilkinson agreed to leave a few articles of clothing and some blankets that had been designated as Indian gifts, but he could do no more. In the evening, at a parade over which he presided, he posted extra sentinels to the *Columbia* to guard the stores and the liquor supply.

In the twilight, after Rafe had fussed over his patient and Wilkinson had tried by candlelight to make sense of Stewart's record-keeping, Freeman and Rafe went to the factor's quarters and talked long past taps about the Indians upriver, the condition of the stream, and what might lie out on the high plains. Treat showed them copies of long letters he had written to Jefferson about the Indians in the region. His assignment as factor was to trade white men's goods — guns and traps, kettles and trinkets — for Indian furs. He had not been very successful because the French in the village had an established trade. The house of Morgan and Bright, based in New Orleans, was especially well entrenched. He said that when he got his factory built he would spend all his time proselytizing the Indians.

"You aren't going to get much higher than the Three Forks with the bigger boat," he told Freeman. "You should have been on the river by January at the latest to catch the spring rise."

Freeman explained their plan of sending both boats home when they ran out of water, and trying to get horses from one of the tribes to push on to the mountains.

"In that case you might coax the smaller boat a good bit higher upriver and try the Pawnees for horses. Wilkinson knows the

Pawnees along the Republican River, as he was there with Pike. And, incidentally, who put that young fellow in command of your party? His father?"

"I should think so," Freeman said, but did not comment.

Wilkinson and Smith joined them at that moment and, while the men of the garrison slept, all five drank the bitter concentrated wine and talked of home.

Next morning, Rafe was eager to go on his first collecting trip in many days. Ranson was in and out of delirium, much weaker, but Rafe felt confident in leaving him under Dr. Stewart's care.

"Have you tried a purgative? Any jalap or calomel?" Stewart asked.

Rafe said he had not.

"You've bled him?"

"Twice. About eighteen ounces. And when he was vomiting I tried ten drops of spirits of turpentine every four hours. Didn't seem to help."

"Any clyster injections?"

"A couple. He hates those enemas worse than anything."

"You go on along and I'll do what I can for him. Haven't had an interesting case here in a long time."

Because he was not expecting to engage in any fancy horsemanship, Rafe opted to ride Blue. His light musket was charged with No. 12 shot for birds, and he carried a tin box with a strap handle for plants. His field notebook was safely wrapped in oiled linen and stowed in a saddlebag. Dr. Stewart had told him of a lake two miles south of the fort, said to mark the beginning of a huge prairie covered with grass and shrubs.

There was one false start. He was nearing the lake and letting Blue find solid ground while he admired the countryside. He had steered the mule to a flat green glade that seemed to provide a way to higher ground, when the wary animal hesitated. Rafe dismounted, found a moss-covered stick, and heaved it into the middle of the area. It disappeared with a plunk, then rose bobbing to the surface of the black water. As the ripples subsided, the carpet of green algae closed and repaired itself. *We won't go that way, Blue.*

He glimpsed his first live ivory-billed woodpecker, big as a crow, garish and bold, moving from one tree to another with a single sweep of its wings. He had seen a mounted specimen at Peale's, but its stuffed and dusty body had lacked the gloss of this one, and the singular white markings on the wings, neck, and bill had turned to gray. This living bird was as gaudy as a colonel in full dress. His bright yellow eyes kept Rafe in view from high behind a sycamore trunk. Not expecting to find so large a bird, Rafe had charged his musket with shot too fine to bring it down. He was rather glad.

The plants he saw were not new to him. He had either seen them before or read of them in William Bartram's *Travels,* but he practiced ticking off the names in his mind. At the edge of the prairie he saw bur oak, willow oak, and black tupelo. There were blue violets and a kind of alyssum. He saw a button snakeroot resembling the one that Virginia mountain people used as a diuretic.

Dismounting again and leading Blue through the lush herbage, he stopped now and then to make an entry in his notebook. He bent to dig a wild onion from the sod, root and all, and savored the aroma. It was another reminder of home, for Old Sally often cooked a mess in the spring and called it "ramp." This plant was plainly an *Allium,* but not quite like the ones he knew. It might be his first discovery. He dug out a better specimen and put it into his box, then rode off — chewing one of the stems so vigorously that his eyes watered.

He nooned on a small rise where there was shade and a breeze, and grass to divert Blue. Nibbling on biscuits and cold venison, he lay on his back and longed for the red clay and blue-ridged vistas of home.

It is Easter Sunday and Mrs. Eleanor Custis Bailey is planning a happy, festive meal for her son who is soon going out West. The walnut dining table is covered with two damask cloths. Her best silver and china are spread on the sideboard. As she hurries about the house she already is dressed in her second-best gray and white outfit and wears a white cap with a cluster of violets pinned over the right ear. Her fair hair is graying now, and the ringlets she has carefully arranged at her forehead are damp with perspiration.

In the kitchen behind the house, where the steam from the

cooking pots, the smoky odors from the spit and roasting pan, and the tang of baking pastries co-mingle, she checks the work of the two women who are bent to their tasks. One is Old Black Sally, the other Frances Bailey Armistead, the widowed daughter who has come home to live. Tall and yellow-haired like her mother, but unsmiling and with a perpetual look of dismay that so much could have happened to her so early, she still wears the mourning dress that her husband Jack would have hated. The respected townsman died of bilious fever.

"What about the turkey? Is it getting tender?" Rafe has shot a wild one on the mountain during one of his rides.

"Not quite, Miz Eleanor," Sally mumbles as she lifts the roaster lid to give the bird a stab in the breast with a fork.

"Mother, dear, if you don't watch out I'm going to send you upstairs to rest," Frances warns.

"I can rest all evening. What time do you think Dr. Bailey would like to eat?"

"Dr. Bailey? Do you mean homely little Raphael Bailey, with red mud all over his feet, the runny-nosed one who used to race through this kitchen half naked? Do you mean *that* Dr. Bailey?"

In a sense the meal tells the story of Rafe's family. They have been exposed to the gloriously rich life of the aristocratic and powerful families of Virginia and now are farmers in the Piedmont. The glamour of the tidewater plantations, the Old Virginia below the waterfall line where the rivers slowed and life was abundant, is a life they have walked away from. But it calls to them.

At the head of the table, Anthony sits in a blue coat that was in high fashion twenty years ago. Now the collar is too low in the back and the linen is not quite right. His waistcoat had been brightly striped once, and now the stripes are hard to see. The military mien of the soldier has gone. Anthony's family and neighbors often tease him with the claim that, since he gained thirty pounds, he resembles the portraits of the late Benjamin Franklin. For this reason he refuses to wear spectacles and combs some of his sparse hair forward to look less Franklinesque. Already the April sun has tanned the lower part of his face, while his forehead, shaded by his hat brim when he rides the fields, is winter pale. He is a man respected not only in western Albemarle but in the legislative halls of Richmond. Last year he stood for election to the House of Delegates and narrowly lost.

Anthony says grace. Once he asked Rafe to perform this ceremony and was surprised to learn from the polite refusal that his son's religion did not include personal supplications to God. Rafe considers himself a Deist when asked, because Jefferson is one, but has put off for now the chore of understanding Deism.

While the father carves the turkey and roast of pork, Peter and Sally hover and serve, until finally there has been a general distribution of beefsteak pie, sausage and fried apples, beaten biscuits, and spoon bread. The vegetables are hominy, sweet potatoes, squash, black-eyed peas, and greens from the turnips that have survived the winter on the sunny side of the barn.

After dinner, while Anthony and Rafe are sitting in chairs on the veranda, Frances calls to Rafe from an upstairs window.

"Could you come up here? Mother isn't feeling quite right." And in the examination that follows, Rafe decides that Eleanor Bailey is seriously afflicted with a heart condition. She relates the classic symptoms of angina pectoris.

Later, Rafe lies to his father. "She can go on this way for years. She might even get over the pains. I don't think you should worry, or that she should, either. I'm going to make up some doses of foxglove. I'll crush the leaves and put them in little packets, and if she ever gets really bad and doesn't respond to bed rest, I want you to give her decoctions of the foxglove four times a day. Also, plan to move her into town where she can be nearer Dr. Puckett. When he sees her, be sure to tell him that she is on the medication."

He writes some instructions for his mother's care, stacks his medical books on the library table, and goes into the kitchen to put a new candle in the lanthorn. He slips on an old coat and, carrying the light, goes to the barn. It is a fragrant night, lit with stars and a full moon just rising, and he can see the Blue Ridge slightly darker than the sky in the north.

The horses, standing asleep, stir and snuffle as they become aware of him. The white tail and speckled rump of Mancha stand out in the flickering light. The little horse is restless; the straw beneath its hind hooves has been chopped into mingled earth and chaff. The mare named Maude, which he rode home from school, dozes blearily in the adjoining stall.

The lie he told his father: was it a doctor's lie or a son's lie? Or worse, the lie of an ambitious young man who wants to be on his way to adventure with a clean slate and the blessings of a strong and healthy family? Dr. Shippen had said something once in class: don't try to treat your parents or your children. Emotion will cloud your reason.

How can he leave this old barn, this farm, and these people that he loves, to ride toward strangeness and danger; how can he bear the burden of Jefferson's confident expectations? How can he leave a mother who is ill?

He goes to Mancha, walks alongside him, and strokes his nose. The horse lifts his head as if to increase the weight of the friendly hand and crowds toward Rafe in a gesture of affection. Rafe presses his chin against Mancha's warm back. *Good-bye, mother. Frances. Father. Good-bye old barn.* He weeps for them and for a childhood blown away by the beckoning winds from the west.

Late in the day, Rafe approached the Arkansa Post from the rear. A sentry sighted him as soon as he was in the clearing, and waved. They knew his mule. He rode around to the front gate and a soldier offered to take Blue to the stable. Lieutenant Smith hailed him from across the parade ground. "Go see Dr. Stewart right away."

"Where?"

"Maybe in the sick ward."

Hurrying into the barracks, he made his way along the corridor to Private Ranson's dark corner. The bunk was empty. "Oh, dear God," he whispered, and ran back across the parade to the dayroom.

Dr. Stewart sat at the table, a copy of Cullen's *Practice of Physick* open before him. He looked up and shook his head.

"Lost your patient, Rafe. I've put the body in the storeroom until morning."

"What happened?"

"The usual termination of severe intestinal inflammation. Intense splinting of the abdominal muscles. Abdominal distention, chills, then fever. I gave him ten grains each of jalap and calomel, but nothing helped. He died about half an hour later in a paroxysm of vomiting."

"Maybe if I'd given him the purge yesterday —" Rafe began.

"Who can say? I think we did what we could. Is this the first patient you've lost?"

"That depends. If my mother —" and Rafe could not finish the sentence.

So that a regular fatigue party could open a grave soon after assembly, the burial ceremony was held early in the morning. The flag was pulled to the top of the staff, then brought halfway down. A detail of six men, three of Smith's and three of Wilkinson's, was selected to fire the salute. Six others carried the cypress casket, hammered together overnight by the Creole carpenter and his black helper who were building the factory. The ceremony was brief, held far enough behind the stockade that the daily business of the garrison would not later disturb the grave. Wilkinson, unhappy to have lost a man and squeamish, anyway, about death, asked Rafe to read a chapter from the Bible. When Rafe's voice broke, Dr. Stewart took the book. "I am the resurrection and the life," he repeated, and went on from there. Five of the rifles discharged properly but one with a bad flint hung fire. "Goddamn it," said the soldier whose weapon had not worked. "Excuse me, sir. Sorry, sir," he said to no one in particular.

One of the casket-bearers opened his jacket and brought out a spray of marigolds he had picked from along the barracks wall. As he laid them on the mound of dark clay, he impelled Rafe to hurry back to officers' quarters and get his own tribute for the grave. He returned with a handful of green: a plant so wilted that he had to arrange it carefully on the grave, blossom head at the top, then the stem, and the bulbous root. When he stepped back, only Lieutenant Smith remained at the graveside.

"There were more marigolds you could have had."

"This will do."

"What is it? Some rare kind of plant?"

"It's a kind of wild onion. I'm going to call it *Allium ransoni.*"

That night he made an entry in his *Remarks & Occurrences,* and could not bring himself to write about Wyatt Ranson. Instead, he summarized a letter that had come for him while he had been riding:

An express came in from Natchez with dispatches for the officers & a letter for me. It was not from my parents, as I had hoped, but from Meriwether Lewis. He virtually demanded that I not publish any of my natural history findings until he has come out with his announced journals. I am partly puzzled, partly furious at the stand he has taken, for priority of publication is an important part of any scientist's satisfaction for his labors. Captain Lewis has ample time to get his findings in order whilst I am away, & his demand that I hold back is intolerable. I think of his drawn face in that smoky room of Dickerson's, & wonder just what is going on. I think Lewis was drunk & it looked as if he had been so for some time. I feel as if I were carrying a sorry secret, unknown to the President &, of course, to my countrymen who are making a hero of him. He has been my hero, too, & I hope this all blows over by the time I get home.

3

The Quapaw Village

WHEN THE BOATS left Arkansa Post, so early that mists
still sat low on the river, the men were feeling good about their
final stop on the way into the wilds. Black terns glided overhead,
pelicans fished intently along the shore, and the whole glowing
scene — turbid water and sun-washed trees — was gray green in
the June sun. Wilkinson had sent a rider with an urgent dispatch
to his father, advising of the situation at the fort. Freeman had
gone through his inventory and left behind all the supplies he
dared give up. As the flotilla pulled away from the landing, Dr.
Stewart stood at the gate of the palisade and waved until a bend
in the river put the expedition out of sight.

Aboard the *Columbia*, Sergeant Steele had decided to take advantage of the breeze that by midmorning had freshened from
the northeast. "Make sail!" Rafe and Freeman heard the command with their usual amusement, knowing the sergeant's memory of seafaring days had taken hold again (he had been in the
rum and molasses trade between New England and the West Indies). Making sail today consisted of running up the single patch
of square canvas and hoping it would ease slightly the work of
the poling soldiers.

"Stand course!" the sergeant shouted. The steersman at the keel
oar, a sturdy artillerist from Tennessee, paid little attention. His
aim was to keep the boat out of midchannel on the one hand and
away from the marshy shallows on the other.

By noon they were approaching the first of three Quapaw villages, all on the south side of the river and within two-dozen miles of the post. The Quapaws claimed a large tract of land on their side, while newly migrated bands of Chickasaws, Choctaws, and Cherokees, all refugees from the leading edge of the white frontier, were establishing themselves across the river. The Quapaws were a small tribe of sedentary people, living more from agriculture than the hunt, friendly toward the Americans and — luckily for them — in no danger of attack from upstream by the warlike Osages, with whom they shared a common Siouan language base.

Because the lower village was the home of the principal chief, the *capitaine* in French parlance, Freeman had decided to put ashore there. As the boats approached the place where many Quapaw pirogues were tied up at the bank, one of the larger ones was seen putting out into the stream. So the signal went up to drop anchor offshore and wait. The *Lewis and Clark* was eased against the stern of the larger boat and made fast. Freeman jumped across to join Wilkinson on the *Columbia*'s deck, while Rafe remained behind, delightedly studying the first Indian village he had ever seen.

The grandmothers sat plaiting mats outside the lodges while the old men gambled and smoked in the sun. The younger women swarmed across the fields behind the lodges, gashing the soil with their hoes and hilling up mounds of earth around the new corn and bean plants. Children, playing with seed rattles and willow squirt guns, scampered brown and naked along the shore. Young warriors were fishing along the bank or — behind the village and the fields — racing their horses and playing ball. Some were drinking whisky. They would drink until their ribald good nature turned from rowdiness to lewdness, then to wild frenzy. By nightfall, many would lie insensible in the village streets.

Incredible. Rafe started to make notes.

The approaching pirogue contained a man and a girl, seated in the middle of the craft between two oarsmen located fore and aft. It came to, amidships on the port side of the *Columbia,* and the man stood up to be helped aboard. He was a chief of stately bearing, about sixty, dressed in deerskin leggins, breechclout, and with a bright blanket about his shoulders. His head and ears were painted with vermillion. His head was shaved and his eyebrows plucked, leaving only a plaited scalp lock decorated with feathers and silver baubles. After a handshake all round, he sat down cross-legged on the foredeck, along with Freeman, Burgoo, and the two officers.

Standing in the bow of the *Lewis and Clark*, Rafe felt left out until his eyes fell again upon the girl who sat waiting in the pirogue. She was perhaps eighteen and trying hard to ignore the soldiers who were grinning, waving, but not daring to call to her. She wore a dress of immaculate buckskin, girdled with a beaded belt, and leggins and moccasins of the same material. Her black hair hung far down her back, unbraided, and she idly lifted it at the nape to let a bit of cooling air touch her skin. Next she rolled it into a loose bun, patting her neck with the other hand to cool and dry it. She felt about her person to see if she could find a bone pin with which to secure the hair. Finding none, she let the splendid cascade fall back again and shook her head vigorously to resettle it.

Rafe permitted himself a quiet groan. *Double damn, she's beautiful.*

Freeman returned to the boat for an item he had forgotten and went inside the cabin. When he emerged he whispered, "She's something, isn't she? Her father was French. She's the chief's granddaughter."

By now the girl had noticed Rafe, perhaps because he was not in uniform and thus not someone to be automatically distrusted. Her smile caused him to step across to the stern of the *Columbia* and walk forward until he was directly above the bobbing pirogue. He knelt on the deck and put himself nearly at her eye level.

"*Bonjour,*" he said. "*Je ne parle pas bien français.*"

She nodded. Rafe pointed to his chest and said, "*Je m'appelle* Rafe." She nodded again and her dark eyes flashed. Just as he was wondering if she understood, she laid her hand on her breast, below the throat, and said, "*Caille-de-prairie.*" Then she giggled.

"That's your name? *Que veut dire cela?*"

She smiled but said nothing. He worked on the name. *Caille* meant quail. Quail of the prairie. He rather liked it. Then she said haltingly in something like English, "Mead-do-lark."

A bright, happy bird with a beautiful song. He tried to imitate the unique call of the meadowlark, and made her laugh. "Mead-do-lark!" she cried.

We've got a real start here, Rafe told himself. Now what shall I say? *"Je suis médecin,"* he told her.

She put a slim hand over her mouth to show how impressed she was, and rubbed a finger across her forehead when she saw the old traces of Rafe's boyhood attack of smallpox. She pointed to his forehead and said *"variole,"* the French word for pox.

"Oui," Rafe said. *"Il y a de nombreuses années."*

She seemed excited, pointing first to Rafe and then to her bare upper arm, and drawing a tiny, invisible circle on the flesh. *"Je ne voudrais pas petite variole,"* she said, shaking her head gravely.

He understood at once: vaccination. He had brought cowpox vaccine, the new preventative for smallpox — and had given no thought to it since packing it away in his gear. He had not supposed he would ever vaccinate an Indian without heavy persuasion, and now this ravishing maid named Meadowlark was asking for the treatment. *My practice is expanding.* He extended his hand to help the girl out of the pirogue, then led her along the catwalk of the *Columbia* and across to the deck of his own boat, closely followed by the two Quapaw men.

When Rafe motioned for her to enter the cabin, she hesitated, then cast an imperious glance at her kinsmen (stay outside, her eyes said) and stooped to enter the crowded little room ahead of Rafe. She sat on the bench usually occupied by Freeman when he was mapmaking, and began to inspect a half-completed chart of the lower reaches of the river.

"Poste aux Arcs," she said, pointing to Freeman's rough plan of the Arkansa Post. *"Il y a ville des Quapaw. Voila!"* Possibly, Rafe thought, she has been away to school in New Orleans.

He found his packet of vaccination quills in a roll of paper at the bottom of his medical chest. In his childhood, the fight against smallpox had centered around inoculation — exposing oneself to the disease and living in isolation or with others similarly inoculated in the hope that immunity would follow a mild case of the pox. But recently Dr. Benjamin Waterhouse had borrowed from abroad the technique of causing the patient to contract cowpox, a usually uncomplicated disease which had the wondrous quality of creating immunity to the often-fatal smallpox.

From Dr. Waterhouse himself, Rafe had received about fifty doses of what he called "cowpox matter." He took from the packet a tube made from a goose quill, sealed with wax, and opened it by scraping away the wax with his thumbnail. Shaking it over the table, he extracted a needle dangling at the end of a short length of white linen thread. The unseen magic lay in the thread, which had been passed with the needle through a lesion on a person with an active case of cowpox.

The girl knew what was expected of her. She extended her arm.

Rafe was sorry that his modest command of French did not include that useful phrase, "This may hurt a little," but he suspected that she knew, anyway. He pinched up a ridge of skin on her brown arm (he did not notice at the time how good that felt) and worked the needle into it, guiding it to penetrate only far enough that the thread could be pulled through. As he drew the thread, and a drop of blood appeared, the girl smiled.

"*Voila!*" Rafe said.

She rubbed the blood away with her palm and let her short buckskin sleeve fall over the tiny wound. "*Merci.*"

He toyed with the notion of explaining some precautions to her; a warning of possible complications. But that, too, would need to be done in French that he did not have. No doubt her tribe knew European diseases, including smallpox, or she would not be asking for the vaccine. If she developed a rash or fever, the old women of her lodge would have a dozen remedies in their materia medica, gathered from the fields and bayous. He decided to say nothing.

There was no excess of gratitude in her manner. She had asked a favor and thanked him for it. As if she knew that her beauty alone was remuneration for small debts of this kind, she looked into his eyes for a moment. And with a half-smile she said, "I learn *anglais,*" and was gone. He heard the gentle sound of her moccasined feet along the catwalk, followed by the heavy steps of her escorts as they returned to the pirogue.

As he stood watching her reestablish herself in the pirogue, three old men in another one came rowing out to beg, crying "*pitoyable!*" He could see the serrated, age-old skin of their throats, with soot and oil worn into the creases. Men with their pride gone, too old to keep their heads plucked; too old to bother with ornaments in their pierced ears — the stretched lobes hung shriveled and gaping.

But the girl. Oh, the girl.

The expedition camped that night on a bar below the second Quapaw village, which Freeman and Wilkinson had decided not to visit. The evening was unusually free of mosquitoes, and Freeman called a meeting of the "leadership," as he termed it, after retreat. As darkness fell they dragged two willow logs close to a subsiding campfire.

Burgoo sat beside Rafe. "You haf goot eye for sqvaw," he said, slapping his knee in approbation.

The remark got past Rafe at the time, but later he disliked the old man's use of so crude a word as "squaw." He knew it was the common word for any adult female Indian, but it seemed ugly, pejorative, demeaning.

Apparently Freeman was just now realizing how late he was in sharing with the others the gist of Jefferson's instructions to the expedition. He began to read a six-page letter, which started: "The government being desirous of informing itself of the extent of the country lately ceded to them under the name of Louisiana, and to have the same with its principal mass geographically delineated, you are appointed to explore the interesting portion of it which lies on the Arkansa River, from the confluence with the Mississippi to the remotest source of the main stream, and the high lands connecting the same."

"Is that just the first sentence?" Tom Smith asked. "How many pages in that thing?"

Freeman began to summarize, describing his duties as surveyor in "taking note of all remarkable places" and touching on the duties that Rafe already had been told of in his conversation with Jefferson.

Rafe nodded. "And you all thought I was just here to give purgatives and treat piles."

"Never mind," Freeman said. "There's plenty for everyone to do. For example, here Jefferson says to 'court a relationship with the natives as extensively as you can.' "

Wilkinson laughed. "I saw Rafe courting a relationship with the chief's granddaughter only today."

"She implored me to give her medical attention."

"Without her grandfather's permission," Freeman said. "Lucky those two guardians she had didn't bruise you up a little with their tomahawks."

"I never thought of that. But I think she'd have pushed them over the side."

Freeman summarized the rest of the instructions, which dwelt heavily on the need to establish trade with the tribes and to advise them that trading houses would be established. "It's a big assignment. I'm glad that Bid here has been down the lower part of the river, at least, and can tell us what to expect."

"Remember," Wilkinson said, "that it was in the winter and I saw most of the country while lying flat in the bottom of a canoe, sick and hungry."

Next morning, while the men were breaking camp and the officers were conferring with a wandering Choctaw who was rafting downstream to sell a load of deerskins, Rafe made a collecting tour. He was back in an hour, happily bearing the leaves, twigs, and embryonic fruit of what he felt was a new species of nut tree. By digging carefully in the moldy forest floor beneath the tree, he had recovered three or four whole nuts from last year's crop. After turning Blue's reins over to the private who usually rode him, Rafe went to his quarters on the *Lewis and Clark* to study his finds.

He had also brought in a passenger pigeon, a handsome bird with buff breast and soft blue wings, knocked down from a tree where a large flock had gathered. The bird was of little scientific interest to him, for the species was well known at home; he had seen clouds of pigeons darkening the sun on his ride through Kentucky. But the carcass was not damaged, and he decided to practice his skinning technique.

Holding the carcass on his knee, he made a deft scalpel incision down the middle of the breast and began to work the skin loose. When he had finished, he had extracted the entire body, except head and legs, from the skin — which he treated amply with white arsenic on a swab. His final step was to fill the skin with cotton to give it some semblance of pigeonhood, then to drop it head-first into a paper funnel that he sealed and labeled. He would be repeating this procedure many times as the expedition moved toward the mountains.

The night's camp was a few miles above the uppermost Quapaw village, at a horseshoe bend that provided a good bar and plenty of downed wood. Both boats were nudged far enough onto the sand to be secure. As it was an early stop, Rafe and Freeman took advantage of the remaining daylight to work. On the deck, Rafe reshuffled his growing plant collection, pressing the specimens between fresh papers, spreading the damp sheets out for reuse when dry. Freeman, inside at the table, sketched out the day's travel on his map, double-checked the readings of the sun's equal altitudes that he had made at midmorning and midafternoon, and determined the approximate latitude. For now, he must estimate the longitude by dead reckoning, waiting for a long day in camp to work out a closer figure by means of lunar distances.

"Sometimes I think the most important stuff we carry is paper," Freeman said. "Every time I spoil a sheet I feel as if I'd dropped a keg of powder into the channel."

By age and education, Rafe should have been drawn more closely to the officers than to this woodsman of another generation. But the confined quarters they shared, and the respect each had developed for the work of the other, became the basis for a growing friendship and many hours of good talk.

"From what I saw of the Quapaws, they're good people," Rafe said.

"Very decent, except when the young men get hold of whisky, and quite friendly toward us Americans. The tribe is in for trouble, with the Cherokees and Choctaws crowding in on them. The chief — the one who came aboard at the first village — was upset because he had given up his Spanish medal when the territory changed hands and hadn't ever got his American one. They consider those big silver medals their badge of authority. Personally, I wouldn't want one of the damned things banging me on the chest all the time. But I gave him one."

"His granddaughter," Rafe ventured. "What about her?"

"Pretty little thing who lost her mother at birth. No telling where her father has gone by now. The French always mix well with the Indians and intermarry with them much of the time. I guess that's why they do so well in the fur trade. It appears you took quite a shine to the girl."

Rafe braced his knee against a bundle of pressed plants, leaned with his whole weight against it, and drew the binding strap tight.

"I did, sort of. Almost jumped ship and volunteered to become a Quapaw."

"I've had a couple of Indian families myself," Freeman said, and Rafe sensed that the subject was not open for pursuit.

"Let me show you a little botanical find," he said, and he laid out the leaves and nuts he had gathered. The long, compound leaves with their array of leaflets were limp, and he patted them onto the bare table until they had returned almost to their original shape.

"Found some pecans, I see," Freeman said. "Those sure taste good on a winter night. Some folks call them Illinois nuts."

I'll be double damned and dipped in brine. He quickly thought of a way out. "I picked them up to see if I've established the western edge of their range," he said. Then he quietly went on deck and eased the specimens over the side.

He sat on the gunwale to enjoy the night. The camp was silent after taps and the fires were burned down to a few spots of pink coals strung along the sandbar.

Callie. That would be a fine name for the Indian girl. A sloppy adaptation of Caille but with a pretty sound. Callie. He was not sure how to interpret her last words to him. "I learn *anglais.*" Was it a promise? Did she mean she was studying English, or did she seem to say that she would now do so? Was it a girlish boast or an affirmation that she wanted to do it for him? *No matter. She's gone now.*

That night in his bed he permitted himself an elaborate fantasy. He pretended that Callie had asked if she could accompany the expedition, and her grandfather had consented. She would be useful, she claimed, because (at least in the fantasy) she could speak Osage, Pawnee, and Comanche. Clearly, she wished to be with him. So he reminded Freeman that Lewis and Clark had taken an Indian girl named Sacagawea across the mountains to the Pacific with them.

He was high in the Stony Mountains and the camp was quiet. Vistas no American had seen had been spread out before them for days. All the camp was asleep, but in his own tent someone stirred beside him. She awoke briefly, reached out to touch him, and together they shared the warmth of their bodies under a buffalo robe. He drew his hand along the length of her leg and thigh, across her abdomen, and up to the unbearably firm-soft round-ness of her breast. Their bodies fit together like two bright silver spoons as they slept the night away.

At daybreak she awakened him with a caress and a movement of her hand that aroused him quickly and brought them together in the sweet desperation of lovers first making love.

The fantasy ended and Rafe, perspiring lightly, saved for his memory what he could of the fading sensations. It could never have happened, he knew. The whole dream went sour as he be-came aware of why he did not, in fact, want Callie to come with the expedition. He did not want her to be a second Sacagawea any more than he wished to be known as the second Lewis or Clark. But the notion was born in him that he would see her again and that she would love him.

"I learn *anglais*." He put himself to sleep with the remem-brance of her promise.

4

With the Osages at Three Forks

〰〰〰〰〰〰〰〰〰〰〰〰

IT WAS mid-June now, and the expedition was toiling toward the next pause and a council with the Osages. At times the gray brow of an island in the stream far ahead, frosted over with white mist, reminded Rafe of scenes at home. The flat sandbars were feathered with willows, and the sand tapered off thinly into shoal water. The water did not lap the shore in waves, but simply rinsed the thin crust of shoreline with small, nudging motions. Gray claws of long-fallen trees lined the river's edge — convenient perches for herons and other water birds.

Rafe filled many pages in his journal, *Remarks & Occurrences*, as the boats proceeded toward the Three Forks of the Arkansa.

13 June. We are now bound for a place nearly 350 miles from here, & expect to average about 10 miles per day. Saw redbud trees today, their bloom gone. They grow aplenty at home on Fox Run Farm, especially in the high meadow. A fruit that I have not seen before & which may be unreported is a kind of *Vitis* which Bid Wilkinson calls the June grape, now ripening. Birds & animals in this region all known to science. Animals include black bear, raccoon, river otter, puma or lion, gray & red squirrels, beaver, & of course the deer. Anxious to see our first buffalo.

Callie. Cally. Meadowlark.

When I first joined the expedition I was mainly concerned with my medical chores & my observations on natural history. Now I begin to take a livelier interest in our route, destination, the demeanor of the tribes we shall encounter, &c.

Query: What became of Captain Pike? He has been unreported since Wilkinson left him at the Great Bend of the Arkansa last fall, Pike going on westward & Wilkinson coming down the Arkansa. We shall be on the watch for signs of him as we gain the highlands.

Query: Just where does this river begin & where does it lie in relation to the Red and other rivers? That is the most important thing we are assigned to discover.

Query: Will we meet the Spanish? Wilkinson thinks not; does not fear a parley with them. They can only turn us back, he says.

The Freeman & Bailey expedition. The Bailey & Freeman expedition.

16 June. Yesterday we passed the worst sandbar thus far, the channel very narrow & intricate. The men so tired that we camped at once after rounding the point beyond Plum Bayou. Today we passed what Burgoo and Wilkinson say is the first of several pine bluffs within 20 miles. This one a low ridge, pine-covered, & in walking along the river below it I saw cottonwood, sycamore, maple & black ash. Beyond the river are groves, glades, & uplands that seem to await cultivation. My father would never believe the richness of the soil.

19 June. Much time spent today getting around a large loop in the river. Chagrined to find it only 40 ft. across at the neck. Perhaps the next big flood will cut through the neck & turn the loop into a bayou.

20 June. At a place called the Little Rock we saw the first sign of rock in the banks of the river. Camping here, we saw clusters of holly, the first I have found, & a species of *Prunus,* short of stature & growing in thickets, which Burgoo calls the Chickasaw plum. I continue collecting everything that seems new. My plants will dry faster when we get into the drier air. I must continually shuffle them about, change the papers, doing some damage to the plants each time.

21 June. At the mouth of the Mamelle. Cliffs along the river are broken into shelves & brightened with fern & red cedar. On our left are round-topped hills, one — which from a distance appears conical & volcanic — is called the Mamelle. All the men cheered by the progress indicated by change of scene. The rocks, cedars, & pines present a view much different from the alluvial floodplain through which we have been passing since the Miss. Rain fell all morning, followed by a heavy fog during which our boats got separated. The helmsmen kept in touch by blowing on tin sounding-horns. Everyone wet, steamy, but my buckskin shirt & trousers shed the water well.

23 June. At the mouth of Cadron Creek, a name whose origin Burgoo does not know. There is a cove of rocks here providing a comfortable harbor. Tonight the wind has risen from the northwest & the river is rising. Velocity of current 4 or 5 miles an hour. New plants found today include an *Eriogonum* that tastes like rhubarb. Prickly *Opuntia* cactus first seen.

26 June. A low ridge called Dardenelle Mt. has been in sight all day. Beyond it we see Magazin Mt., the highest "peak" observed so far. Current very strong below the mountain. When I climbed a height after supper I could see three chains of low mts. in the southwest, & behind us the Mamelle still in view.

3 July. Passed Mulberry Creek. The river in this area resembles the Ohio, with gravelly rapids & many islands. Willow along the banks which may be new; I collect a few specimens, but begin to think that *Salix* is a very complex genus.

4 July. Independence Day. We have made such good time that we declared a day of rest & celebration. Tom Smith issued 5 rounds of blank ammunition to each man. Much random firing after the official salute at daylight. An extra gill of whisky to the men at noon. The soldiers paraded in uniform in midafternoon and no fatigue parties were assigned today.

5 July. An agreeable stretch of river terminating in a high bluff called Belle Pointe. It is located at the confluence of the Poteau & Arkansa, affording a fine view up and down the Arkansa. We spent a night here & I rode Mancha for a short way up the Poteau. (Not all our names for rivers, &c., come from Burgoo. Mr. Freeman is carrying a sketch map given him by Mr. Treat. Says we shall run out of names at the Great Bend & will start assigning our own names.) I found today a new species of *Monarda,* or mint, with the usual pleasant taste (our mess discovered it makes a passable julep). Also several plants that may be new, including a lilac-colored daisy, a new figwort, a *Tradescantia* with large flowers, some phlox, a verbena, & a kind of wild hyacinth. A curious tree already known to Mr. Jefferson through Lewis & Clark is seen here, the bois d'arc, or orangewood. Its wood very tough & its color may provide a good dye.

8 July. The country has begun to open up since passing Belle Pointe. Sometimes I feel a pang of homesickness for the Blue Ridge. I feel we are soon to be seeing changes in flora & fauna.

10 July. At the Falls of the Arkansa, a cascade of 2 or 3 ft., probably much more in low water, with a chute at one side over which we drew the boats with ropes. We did not have to lighten the large boat although this was considered. Later, Lt. Wilkinson says he was very ill when he came down this stretch but thinks the cascade was about 7 ft. high.

11 July. Our first buffalo or bison today! Shot by the soldier riding Mancha. It is a fat cow & several men were sent to butcher it & bring in the best parts. Burgoo says we will not see many of these animals until we are beyond the Osage hunting grounds. I found the meat of the hump, as it is called, very tasty. Burgoo is doing something detestable with the intestines, producing without much preparatory cleaning an eellike sausage which he calls "boudins."

A good omen today was the finding of a new bird that is almost worth the whole journey to me. Much like a cuckoo but lives on or near the ground, runs very fast, & presents an almost comical appearance. Its tail quite long, & although I skinned & preserved this specimen I rather doubt that I can get it home with tail unbent. I might propose calling it *Coccyzus ludovicianus,* or Louisiana Cuckoo.

For some reason my thoughts tonight have been on Meriwether Lewis. I often wonder if my glimpse of him in Dickerson's quarters was not chimerical, imaginary. Even if he were there, which would be a most mysterious kind of behavior, I cannot fault him for the spectacular expedition that he & Capt. Clark have executed & which I appreciate more & more as we attempt a similar adventure.

Memo: see if a flute like Mr. Burgoo's is available in New Orleans. Get printed music.

They tied up at a point of rocks where the Verdigris River came into the Arkansa from the north. About a mile downstream the Grand also flowed in from the north, forming a convergence of streams that had been called Three Forks for as long as Indians or Europeans could remember. Freeman advised that they not make a substantial camp until they knew where the Osages would put theirs, and until the mood of the Indians became evident. He and Burgoo supposed they would come in from the west, having been hunting buffalo on the prairies, but it was impossible to say which side of the river they would descend.

"Are we halfway to the mountains?" a soldier asked.

"Halfway? Not till we get to the Great Bend, a long way up."

"Damnation!"

It seemed to Rafe that they were in a transitional zone between the lush and hilly terrain behind them and the arid plains ahead. Trees had been thinning out — the evergreens gone entirely — but a few ample groves of oak and hickory remained. He collected a dozen new plants on his walks. As for birds, he had a gull with white spots on its primary wing feathers and with a different call than that of the laughing gulls at home. He had seen a flycatcher with a long, deeply forked tail, so long that when he first saw an adult in flight he thought it was carrying a streamer of dried grass to its nest. One of the men had brought in a creature that nearly defied description: a small, armored mammal with large ears and an opossumlike tail. A private who had been to Texas said he had seen one there.

Rafe wondered if the Indians would arrive in close ranks like a Roman phalanx, or come clamoring along in great disorder like the riders in a Virginia fox hunt. When they appeared, it was their quietness that surprised him. A couple of riders appeared in late afternoon of the second day, across the river in the neck of land between the Verdigris and the Grand. They raised their arms in greeting and galloped away. Four or five more riders came in, and soon the entire rolling plain between the two rivers was being converted to an Indian village.

The warriors rode about aimlessly on their best horses, tiny bells on the scarlet bridles jingling faintly in the breeze. Each rider wore leggins, breechclout, and a blanket, with a round leather shield slung on his back. Some carried smoothbore muskets — they seemed to have no rifles — and each had a scalping knife and tomahawk. Some wore eagle feathers attached to their scalp locks and even dangled a few from the tails of their horses. They seemed eager for the women to get on with the making of camp.

"Why do some of the horses have pink tails?" Rafe asked.

"That's red dust from the plains to the west," someone explained.

The women traveled in single file, members of each lodge staying together. On their packhorses were great bundles loosely wrapped in skins, each forming a depression that held infants, young puppies, and the bric-a-brac of households everywhere. Small naked boys, five or six years old, rode bareback on the yearling colts, controlling them with rope halters. Except for the children, no one shouted, no one sang. There would be time for that when the lodges were in place.

When the women were assembled, they took the reins from the men and tethered all the horses at the edge of the clearing. The men sat down and lit their pipes while the women spread sunshades of buckskin or blankets for them. A few women from each lodge went to the river to cut saplings for their shelters, which would be less carefully made than their permanent homes upstream on the Verdigris. Two rows of saplings were stuck in the ground and lashed together to form a series of arches. Buffalo skins were thrown down to make a floor, and others were tossed upon the arches and fastened to make a roof. The lodges — about thirty of them — all faced east and received light and air from both ends.

When they had trenched around each lodge to drain away rainfall, dug firepits, cut stakes to support the cooking pots, and brought in wood and water for the evening, the women slacked their pace and began to enjoy the shade in the lengthening shadows of random trees. Most of the men had gone to sleep.

"They're friendly this time," Bid Wilkinson said as the members of the officers' mess sat by the water, near the boats, and ate their evening meal.

"They act as if they don't know we're here," Rafe said, but at that moment a brown little boy ran into the water and threw a stone in their direction. Then he laughed, waved, and splashed back to shore.

"They know," Freeman said. "Dozing Indians aren't hostile, and that's a good sign. Keep your eye on the biggest lodge, the one in the center of camp. That's Chief Clermont's place. Tomorrow there'll be a big marquee out in front of that lodge, to shade us while we hold the council. That will be his invitation for us to cross over."

"How did they know we were coming?"

"Well, if Pierre Chouteau from St. Louis did what he was told by the War Department, he's been out here on a special trip to tell Clermont we were on the way. Chouteau not only trades with these people, but he's now their agent. He's probably asked them to cooperate with us."

"Will they?"

"They usually see things his way. The Chouteau brothers are a powerful French family, with fur-trading interests all along the Mississippi and lower Missouri. We are lucky to have them on our side."

Wilkinson said: "Something else to remember. These fellows that you see here are dissidents. Until a few years ago they lived up north with the main Osage nation. Then some tribal disputes and trading rivalries brought them down into this region. Chouteau had something to do with it, I think. Clermont is a shrewd man. Full of vanity. He needs a lot of wooing from the government, especially since the Spanish influence has been strong in the tribe."

"So," Freeman said, "when the Spanish turned us back on our Red River trip last summer, it seemed best to make sure the Osages would let us come up the Arkansa."

"You mean we are counciling with them just to butter them up?" Rafe asked.

"Damn right," Freeman declared. "Nothing wrong with that. Every contact they have with Americans, if it's friendly, is in our best interest and helps to draw them away from the Spanish and French. They've got to learn to fear and respect us, and get to depending on us for trade. It's time they realized that the old days of Spanish and French control are gone. We want them not to prohibit American traders from coming up this river."

"And not to scalp us," Tom Smith added.

"Amen," Freeman muttered.

Clermont's Indian name was *Gra-Mo'n,* which meant Arrow-Going-Home. The French had gallicized the name and later the Americans would call him Claymore. Since the death last fall of *Ko-Zhi-Ci-Gthe,* or Makes-Tracks-Going-Home, whom the Americans called Great Track, Chief Clermont had been the undisputed leader of the Arkansa band. His gens, or clan, was that of the bear, from which came all the great chiefs of the Osage, and some said he was eligible to become the principal chief of all the bands, including the great northern division. Now, having assented to Chouteau's splitting of the tribe to get sole trading rights to the southern branch, Clermont was considered a renegade. The northern chiefs derided him to the Americans. He was unmoved.

This morning he stood on the riverbank, with several influential men of the tribe and two young women who brushed flies from his face with eagle-wing fans, and watched the Americans crossing the river in a pirogue. He stood very tall, perhaps a few inches above six feet. His deerskin leggins had been whitened with gypsum, and a glistening buffalo robe hung from one shoulder. Beneath his necklace of bear claws, his chest showed a pattern of intricately worked tattoo marks. Adorning his scalp lock was a roach of deer's-tail hair and the beard of a turkey gobbler. His face was painted black and red, and he carried as a symbol of rank a staff decorated with swanskin. He made no sign of greeting as the officials of the Arkansa expedition approached and landed.

The delegation included Freeman, Burgoo, and the two officers. Rafe had come along to watch, and four enlisted men were rowing the pirogue. Back at the keelboats on the opposite shore, the rest of the detachment pretended to be going about their duties casually — but their rifles were charged.

Freeman seemed relieved as he viewed the scene. "No problems today."

"Just endless talk," Smith predicted, "with lots of smoke from cheap government tobacco."

And plenty of mosquitoes. Still, Rafe did not expect to be bored. When the principal men of the tribe were seated under the marquee, and the American delegation had joined them in smoking a pipe of peace and friendship, each Osage man muttered a brief prayer to the smoking pipe as he took it, and the council began. Freeman's fair knowledge of the language enabled him to carry the introductory exchanges without Burgoo's help.

"The Great Father in Washington sends me and my nephews with greetings. As he is also *your* Great Father, he wishes us to bring you gifts and to remind you that your people are now members of the seventeen council fires of the United States of America."

"That is not a new message," Clermont said. "The Heavy Eyebrows have been telling me for two years that I must lead my people away from the Spaniards." The Heavy Eyebrows was his term for Americans. "I am thinking about it."

"Your Great Father also wishes you to be at peace with the other Indian nations. He stresses this particularly."

"That is well, but the Great Father should tell that to the Pawnees, and to the Comanches far to the west, who raid us all the time."

"He knows it. He has authorized me to tell that to the Pawnees and the Comanches. He wishes you to smoke the pipe with them."

"We will think about it. When will you send us more traders?"

"That is another important thing," Freeman said. "We know that the trading house at Arkansa Post is not much used by the Osages. We shall build another one somewhere."

"Chouteau does well by us, but he only brings us the goods he wants us to have, and pays us what he wants for our skins and furs."

Within five minutes, Freeman and Clermont had covered the most important aspects of U.S. policy toward the Indians: acceptance of U.S. sovereignty, peace among the tribes, and increased trade. One other aspect remained.

"Your Great Father promises that he will protect all his Indian children from their enemies. You will be safe to bring your goods to our trading houses and to move to and from your hunting grounds. The American soldiers will protect you."

To Rafe, not involved, that seemed a hollow promise. He slipped out of the council at the first opportunity and strolled about the camp. The men were tall and handsome, as Jefferson had declared, but the women seemed homely. Not like Callie. They were short and stout, their hair long and not well tended. Some had tattoo lines on their necks, chests, backs, and arms. Only one woman, a young chief's wife, attracted him. She wore a calico shirt, buckskin skirt, and red leggins, and her hair was neatly tied in the back. She rode at the edge of camp astride a gray horse, proudly carrying her husband's lance and shield.

Better than most.

When he returned to the council and sat down beside Smith, all policy matters had been covered and Clermont had been told of their plans to get horses from the Pawnees at the Great Bend.

Burgoo was translating for Clermont now: "You cannot take the boats to the Great Bend because the water is too low. The small boat can go on for several days, but the big one will come aground in the shallows."

Freeman spoke to Burgoo. "Ask him when we'll get to the Bend, and also when will we see the mountains."

The translation: "He says we will come to the Great Bend in the Yellow-Flower Moon, by which he means August, and to the mountains at the end of the Deer-Hiding Moon, which is September."

Wilkinson whispered to Freeman, who nodded; a quick decision had been made.

"Burgoo, tell him we want to barter for horses. We'll get them from him instead of from the Pawnees."

Clermont would not talk horse trading, for a cloud had come in from the west and cloudy days were not propitious for counciling or bargaining. He dismissed the council until the next day. Freeman gave him a bottle of cheap peach brandy and poured a splash of whisky into the cups of the lesser chiefs. He gave each one a twist of tobacco, told them there would be more gifts tomorrow, and waved them back to their lodges.

Next morning, a fatigue party under Sergeant Russell started bringing trade goods up from the hold of the *Columbia* and stowing them on deck. Bales and crates were hauled out and opened, revealing a rich hoard of necessities and trifles designed to catch the Indian eye.

Clermont and three other chiefs came across in a pirogue and climbed on deck. He said the beaver traps had weak springs and he had no blacksmith to repair them. The muskets, he said, were the cheap kind with a small bore, made just for the Indian trade.

"Blow up in face," he said in English, illustrating with a quick thrust of his fist toward his eyes.

A shrewd old bastard.

"Tell him he will have a blacksmith when the new trading house is built," Freeman said to Burgoo.

Finally, when Clermont had seen the quantity of goods available in exchange for horses, and inspected a few crates in consultation with his fellow Osages, he shook his head in the universal gesture of disapproval.

"I want boucher," he said to Burgoo.

A moment of silence as the Americans looked at one another in puzzlement. Tom Smith understood what the chief meant.

"His English has been tainted by the Spanish. He wants a *voucher*. He wants money instead of goods."

"Oh, God," Freeman said.

Burgoo conveyed Clermont's elaboration. There were goods aplenty to be had from St. Louis, sent by Chouteau. The Osages could get anything Freeman was showing. What they could not get was money to spend as they wanted — as the white man did.

Clermont wanted a slip of paper that would convert into American dollars.

But there was more. Clermont engaged Burgoo in an exchange which the German did not comprehend at once. There was head-shaking by Burgoo and tough talk from the chief. Once Clermont laughed and looked directly at Rafe, and the mystery grew. When Burgoo turned to Freeman with a summary of the conversation, there was disbelief and amusement in his eyes.

"He vants der doctor's horse."

Everyone was silent, staring at the deck to avoid Rafe's eyes. *That son of a bitch wants Mancha?*

Around the campfire later, Freeman discussed the day's events while a canteen of whisky passed from hand to hand. Although he seemed to consider the matter of Mancha secondary, he understood fully — Rafe hoped — that the beautiful animal had come directly as a gift from the president.

It is the Easter Sunday a couple of days before Rafe is to leave home. After dinner he has gone into the parlor and is repairing and tuning Franny's harpsichord — a prized French import which he loves to hear but scarcely can play. For years he has repaired the snapped strings, kept the quills and felts in order, and tuned the instrument with a special wrench. Franny always claims she could tune it as well, but it has had a specially brilliant tone after he has tempered the thirds and fifths and tested all the octaves. He hopes he can do it well this time, as a brotherly farewell gift to Franny. When he has finished, he plays a simple Couperin gigue, one of the few selections he knows.

While Rafe plays and Anthony and Franny listen, they all sense that Peter is waiting patiently in the doorway. The old black head is sodden with sweat from the kitchen heat, and his palsied hand shows crumbs from his interrupted meal.

"Colored man come ridin' up here, leadin' a horse behind his-self, already got 'cross Fox Run," Peter says.

The Bailey men go to the front door and step into the late afternoon sun. The rider comes in from the east, shading his eyes with one arm. He rides a bay mount — a common riding horse — but the animal he leads is far from common. It is black with white spots and patches, roman-nosed, short-coupled as if it lacks a vertebra or two, and is no more than fourteen hands high. Its eye is bright, its tossing mane glossy white — the kind of horse that seems to know how handsome it is and to revel in admiration.

"That's an Indian pony or something," Anthony says. "Haven't seen one since the Cherokees stopped coming this way."

The horseman stops and nods. "I'm Isaac, sah, come from Mist' Jeff'son. Brought thisyah paper." He pulls a folded note from his pocket and hands it to Anthony.

"It's addressed to Dr. R. Bailey, Esq.," Anthony says, and passes it on. Rafe breaks the seal of red wax and opens the message:

Dr. Bailey:

I send by Isaac a fine wild horse from Texas, shipped to me by friends of the late adventurer Philip Nolan, who traded in these animals. As chief executive I do not accept such gifts, and am pleased to think that this gelding might be of service both to you and our country. He is a bit shy when approached from behind on the off side, but has learnt much.

Captain Lewis tells me he saw many horses with these peculiar markings among the Indians of the pierced noses in the Northwest. I have no doubt this animal is descended from the famous steeds of Araby.

I should think that your expedition, even though it begins on water, will require a few horses for hunters to use in ranging the shores. And such a creature as this will also aid you much in your collecting. My little granddaughter, with some prompting, has been calling the horse Mancha because of his interesting spotted and speckled markings.

Let me say again how delighted I am that you have accepted this important assignment. Please extend my good wishes to your esteemed father and mother, and to your sister, to whom I add my heartfelt condolences for her bereavement of some months past. Wishing you every success, I am, my dear Doctor,

Yr. Obt. Servt.
Th. Jefferson

Rafe and Anthony stare at the horse while Isaac tries not to watch them. They reexamine the letter. Sally and Peter come out to look, then Frances appears, too.

"My Lord, what an animal! And what a gift!" Anthony cries, stepping over to rub the gelding's white roman nose.

"Yessa, Mist' Bailey," Isaac agrees.

Rafe pulls his hand across the short, broad back and admires the curious coloration of the hide. "Mancha," he says. "I'll have to check my Spanish book."

Anthony instructs Isaac to take both horses to the barn and care for them, then return to the kitchen and call upon Sally for food. "You'd better stay the night, too. It would be dark long before you could reach home."

It is the same afternoon on which his mother first reveals her illness to him. So the arrival of Mancha and the somber aspects of his mother's condition are bound together forever in Rafe's memory.

His colleagues seemed impressed by his account, and he sensed there was general opposition to the idea of letting the precious animal go with the trade.

"We'll talk about that later," Freeman said. "The important thing is this damned voucher that he wants. There's no way the War Department would authorize payment retroactively. I'd be stuck with the bill personally. We've got to convince Clermont that these goods are worth having in exchange for horses."

"It's all high-grade stuff," Bid Wilkinson said. "I watched it being packed in New Orleans. The old chief is bluffing when he says he can get the same quality and variety in St. Louis from his private trader. I'd like to have some of this merchandise myself."

Rafe ventured an idea. "Setting Mancha's fate aside, but only for a moment, I have a suggestion. Let's move the *Columbia* across the river and set up a bazaar here on deck. Invite the people aboard to look at the goods more closely. I got the impression that Clermont's mind was made up and that he really doesn't know what is here. Let's show it to everybody."

"Von't vork," Burgoo ventured. "Dey take everysing."

"Maybe," Tom Smith said, "but they'd have to come down the gangway and we could watch them. We might lose a little of our stock, but it is worth a try."

Freeman agreed to the plan. He also vowed to Rafe that Mancha would not be traded. "I have an idea about that," he said. "Something that we could settle for."

When the Osages roused themselves in the morning, the *Columbia* was moored along the riverbank below their camp. At first the Indians paid no heed, for the morning wail was in process. The Osages traditionally sent up a lamenting prayer to their Grandfather Sun at dawn — crying real tears and filling the river valley with the shrill, echoing sounds of seeming grief. Then they pulled themselves together in an instant and went about the business of the day.

Across the river, Rafe had spent the night on the deck of the *Lewis and Clark,* with Mancha tied alongside, secured to an oarlock by his halter rope. It was apparent that Clermont had somehow found out the horse had belonged to Jefferson and wanted him for his promise of magic, strong medicine, and prestige. After breakfast, when Rafe saw the Osages filing onto the big keelboat across the river, he left Mancha in the care of a corporal and crossed over in a pirogue.

The Indians waiting in line to go up the gangway reminded Rafe of people at the piers along the Philadelphia river front when a rich vessel would come in from Plymouth or Canton. There was much pushing and shoving, men and women vying for position. Two unarmed sentries stood at the foot of the gangway, and Rafe noticed that several of Wilkinson's most reliable men were on the deck to watch the goods.

No longer were the tribes so inexperienced in trade that they would sell a year's catch of furs for a few beads. Yet it was plain that bright fabrics and ornaments were tempting. Both men and women looked hungrily at a crate of gilt-framed mirrors, so convenient for applying paint to the face. The men were admiring the boxes of mock garnets, brass finger rings, gorgets, plumes, and a wondrous variety of ear bells, cow bells, and sleigh bells that would lend beauty and excitement to their dances.

The drygoods were superior: heavy woollen blankets, bolts of red and blue stroud, white and green baize, embossed serge, red and yellow flannel, calico, twill coating, striped gartering, and swanskin. Even Clermont, who had strode on board to see the display, reached out to finger a bolt of yellow silk. But he quickly moved on to the hardware, seeming to like the brass tomahawks, the curb bridles, fishhooks, spurs, and fire steels.

Tom Smith joined Rafe to watch the scene. "We've figured out what we need in the way of horses."

"Does everyone get a horse?"

"Of course. Even infantrymen get to ride on this tour."

"How many horses do you intend to buy?"

"Well, if we send about nine men back we'll need thirty mounts for the enlisted personnel and five for us. Add five packhorses and that makes forty. These Osages can give up that many and never miss them. Clermont must own a hundred by himself."

"And my little Mancha?"

"I think that's being taken care of," Smith said. "Ask Freeman."

Rafe found Freeman in the cabin of the *Columbia,* where he had been conferring with Clermont. He was grinning. "We've made a fine trade for forty horses, all to be of sound wind, none with foal, and none smooth-mouthed or lame."

"And Mancha?"

"Your little horse stays with us as I promised. Counting him and your mule we have forty-two mounts."

Rafe impulsively shook Freeman's hand. "I'm relieved. I was going to make an ugly scene."

"We were lucky, but you lost something just the same. I persuaded Clermont that it would be an affront to all Heavy Eyebrows, and to the Great Father personally, if we bartered away such a gift that had been bestowed on one of us. Then I told him the Great Father might be inclined to let you give up your saddle. A beautiful saddle, made across the bright waters in England, which has borne the exalted body of the Great Father and fit smoothly beneath his exalted posterior. Clermont grabbed that idea and now he can't wait to get his own ass hoisted onto that saddle."

On a stifling July morning, the mounted expedition left the Three Forks and moved out along the north bank of the Arkansa. Some of the soldiers were experienced horsemen, but others — the boys from the seaboard cities — had never ridden before.

"Christ, it's a mile to the ground," cried a corporal from Baltimore.

"I ditten know you had to spraddle your legs so damned far," said an artillerist from Savannah. "My balls gone git smashed."

Rafe watched a swarm of tiny black insects hovering near Mancha's moist, flaring nostrils as he pranced and tossed his head in annoyance. At the end of a halter rope, close behind, complacent old Blue ignored his own swarm of frantic little flies and plodded along, bearing his pack with scarcely a waggle of the ears.

The new saddle would take some getting used to. It was of Osage design, made from forked branches held together by wooden crosspieces and covered with folded deerskin. The stirrups were nearly too small for the toes of Rafe's boots, and the leathers were uncomfortably short.

Wilkinson left the column and cantered back to spend a few minutes with Rafe. "Do you miss life aboard ship?"

"Beginning to. I'm getting chafed already."

"I was surprised that you gave up your other saddle so willingly. It must have been a valuable souvenir."

"It was," Rafe said. "But it wasn't from the president. My father traded a crate of hens to Brightberry Brown, up in Brown's Cove, for that saddle when I was a baby. It's a family heirloom."

Clermont, who had been riding at the head of the column with several warriors, waved good-bye as he dashed past the departing expedition. He was resplendent, regal, and proud as he bounced along on the Bailey-family saddle.

5

The Secret of the Big Cottonwoods

AT THE END of the first day's ride the men were sore and, as one said, "tireder than if I was polin' the blasted boat." The evening ball game was canceled; the whisky drum brought out an unusual crush of eager clients. Later there was concern over how to stake out the horses for a night's grazing.

To Rafe, the most troublesome new factor in the routine was not horses, but arms and ammunition. Until now the boats had borne the weight, and now the weapons had to be carried: rifles, lead, and powder. Except for the officers, who had sidearms, and Rafe with his birding gun, all hands were equipped with a heavy flintlock built at the arsenal in Harper's Ferry, Virginia — a long and cumbersome rifle not ideal for use on horseback. Besides the weapon itself, each soldier had to worry about his rounds of ammunition, his cartouche box (for paper cartridges), his powder pouch, and a few extra flints. He had to keep checking to be sure that the ramrod was fixed securely under the gun barrel and that prairie winds had not swept the powder from his priming pan.

Rafe was content with his lightweight musket. On the second day, as the mechanics of covering ground became less preoccupying, he began to record the gradual change in topography and wildlife. The new birds fascinated him. Most species were familiar, but many were showing minor differences. The noisy kingbirds were now of two kinds, including a western subspecies with a small bit of red on its crown. The meadowlark had a different song than those at home. A gray kite with white wing bars chased a chimney swift across the sky, while yellow-billed cuckoos foraged for caterpillars and a hairy woodpecker clung to a high cottonwood stub. Overhead, nearly out of sight, red-tailed hawks were circling. Rafe shot a new kind of cormorant with a curious double crest and a patch of bare, orange skin beneath its bill. It was as heavy as a goose, so he skinned it at the next rest period and discarded the carcass.

Burgoo came to Rafe early in the evening, obviously in pain. Lately, Rafe had done little in the way of medicine but bathe a few swollen eyes with sugar of lead and treat a few cases of poison ivy. Now he seemed to have a patient more likely to tax his medical skill.

"Bad pain," Burgoo said, hobbling up to Rafe's tent. *"Ich habe hier Schmerzen,"* he repeated, holding both hands to his groin. His face was more flushed than usual and he explained that he had been having difficulty in voiding urine.

A damned stone, maybe already in the ureter. A lithotomy was out of the question. The old man haughtily declined Rafe's request to let him feel for the stone by way of the rectum. Once Dr. Puckett had related an anecdote about flushing away a stone with copious doses of drinking water. It might work, although he had never seen Burgoo drink anything except whisky.

On the riverbank, screened from camp by a scattering of young trees, Rafe kept Burgoo on his knees while he scooped up water in a canteen and handed it to the moaning patient. After the third cupful, he gave the man a swig of laudanum, then more river water. Within two hours, resting on hands and knees and uttering dark Teutonic oaths, Burgoo got rid of the stone. Then he sank to the ground and began to perspire. *"Danke, Herr Doktor,"* he murmured as he drifted off into heavy sleep.

When they passed the mouth of a large tributary flowing in from the south, Wilkinson called it the Red Fork and said it ran through a great salt plain to the west. The Osages brought home salt in baskets. Freeman said he figured the rumors of this large, salty area had given Jefferson the idea of a "salt mountain," which had so amused his Federalist opponents. The river was murky with red particles and broken by wide bars and crumbling banks. Rafe found tracks of deer and elk, and the ever-present droppings of buffalo herds. He collected a new *Gaura,* or evening primrose, a purple sand grass, some salt grass, and new species of *Arundo* and *Donia.* He noted in his journal that he had seen no canebrakes since leaving the Three Forks.

One evening the men caught a fifty-pound paddlefish, blue gray and with no scales. Its spatulate bill, Rafe decided, was too delicate for ramming a boat, as one soldier speculated, and must be a sensory organ.

Continuing north, the expedition touched upon the tall prairie vegetation that covered vast stretches of the middle plains. Bluestem grasses rose ten feet tall, and to collect a complete plant Rafe had to cut it into a dozen lengths before drying it.

The Little Arkansa was a fine stream of cool water, meandering through a dense stand of trees and shrubs. Rafe saw honey locust and sycamore here, but the predominant trees were cottonwood, elm, and ash. Prairie-dog towns were everywhere; the men had learned to keep their horses clear of the burrows.

Tom Smith often rode beside Rafe. "I'm one Virginian who isn't a horseman. I've never even tried a fox hunt. Took a lady riding one afternoon and the horse I picked for her turned out to be a farter. Broke wind the whole afternoon. I could have died."

"Poor sphincter tone," Rafe speculated.

"Poor attitude, more than likely."

Freeman kept at his mapmaking. Rafe had come to admire the engineer's ability to sit up late at night, swatting mosquitoes while turning out beautiful river charts and drawings of the surrounding terrain.

"These are just preliminary," Freeman insisted. "Wait till you see what the engraver does with them." He held his most recent chart at arm's length, looked at it over steel-rimmed glasses, and seemed pleased. "I sweat so much over the last one that I had to throw it away."

By now the buffalo were as familiar to everyone as cows in a pasture. Rafe watched a hunter assigned by Wilkinson shoot half-a-dozen animals without frightening the rest of the herd. The stricken bulls stood their ground, as if unhurt, until they collapsed. The survivors finally fled in wondrously fast time, sticking their short, tufted tails in the air as they dashed along.

At the Great Bend of the Arkansa, where the river course turned to the southwest, the expedition made camp in the afternoon of August 1, 1807. Although the riverbed was perhaps four hundred feet wide between banks, the stream itself was merely twenty feet wide and about six inches deep. It was a dreary site, the blankness relieved only by a faltering line of cottonwoods along the north bank.

After evening mess, the four leaders sat in the shade and played keno. "I need something to collect," Rafe said. "It's been dull today."

"We'll find you a grizzly someday," Tom Smith promised.

"You can collect all you want for a few days," Wilkinson said. "Mr. Freeman and I are going to take Burgoo and a few men, and ride north to have a little parley with the Pawnees. It's in our instructions. Besides, I want to see if they have any word about what might have happened to Captain Pike."

With Smith in command of the camp, and Rafe secretly pleased to have a respite from long marches, the expedition settled in to await the return of the travelers. The gunsmith repaired flintlocks, the best tailor in the outfit patched up pantaloons torn by cacti and worn through by saddle friction. The cooks strained to devise a diet consisting of more than the usual venison or buffalo, coffee, and cornmeal cakes.

One of the hunters brought in the first pronghorn antelope, to be sketched by Rafe and eaten by the detachment. Within two days, the doctor's natural-history collections had been increased by the addition of a jackrabbit, horned toad, and a small prairie fox. All these new things, he supposed, had been collected by Lewis and Clark — but he took no chances.

He spent one day a few miles north of the river in an incredible area of wetlands, covered with cattails and bullrushes, and inhabited by thousands of birds: great blue herons, white pelicans, avocets, stilts, sandpipers, terns, and untold redwing and yellow-headed blackbirds. As he approached camp at sundown, loaded with bird carcasses, Sergeant Russell rode out to meet him.

"Some of the men's sick, sir."

"What's the trouble?"

"Looks like they took something. They won't say what."

At first Rafe assumed that someone had broken into his medical supplies. He found nothing amiss in his tent. Some soldiers were grouped around three men on the ground by the river, all apparently quite ill. Two were lying down and the third sat with his head in his hands.

Later, Rafe was to reflect upon his reaction to this emergency and realize in dismay that he was not yet living up to his own image of a physician. He had come quickly to a diagnosis and to the important question: How can I help them? But not before three other questions had passed through his mind. Is this my fault? Will I look bad if I can't figure out what's wrong? And (worst of all, as he looked back on it), are these good or bad soldiers? *So much for Hippocrates.*

It happened that they were bad, the three worst men in the command, always lagging, always bullying, forever plotting insubordination while not actually committing it. Private Delaney was a tanner from Delaware; Private Fowler a tinsmith from Maryland; and Private Agan, barely old enough to enlist, was a giant farm boy from the Piedmont area of North Carolina.

Rafe made the diagnosis almost by accident. While checking Fowler for pupil dilation, strength and rate of pulse, and respiration, he knelt close to the man's face and caught a familiar aroma. It was not the fetid and repellent odor of a sick man's breath, but something sweet and almost attractive. It reminded Rafe not so much of the dank wards at Pennsylvania Hospital, but of the sunny kitchen at Fox Run Farm. A cooking odor or, more precisely, a baking odor. It seemed to come straight from his mother's baking pans, and for a moment he was overwhelmed by images of home. He sniffed the man's breath again, then checked the other two. In a gesture of relief that was almost exultant, he stood up and announced his diagnosis to Tom Smith.

"These men have been taking nutmeg!"

Smith did not quite understand. "Is that harmful? We used to put it in pumpkin pie."

"In large amounts it can produce hallucinations and make you very sick."

"We've only got a small bit for the officers' mess. I don't think the men have any at all."

"Then someone has been carrying it just for this purpose," Rafe said. "Let's get them into my tent and see what I can do for them."

In the end he decided he could do nothing but let them sleep off the effects. Nutmeg was a prisoner's drug, used by men who could obtain no liquor or opium and who were willing to endure the awful side effects in exchange for a brief flight of euphoria. For most users, a tablespoonful of ground nutmeg in hot water would bring on visual and auditory fireworks, accompanied by headache, dizziness, nausea — the most monumental of hangovers.

Private Agan described the sensations to Rafe when he was feeling better. "You cain't imagine how turrible it is. Bitter-like. It don't even dissolve good, and you got to gulp it down like wet sand. Then it makes you want to puke. Ol' Fowler he did actually puke, but us other two we kept it down. Then Delaney he begun to giggle. Just sat there snickerin' and gigglin', and then I went to doin' the same. Couldn't hep ourselves and ditten know why we was gigglin'. My mouth went dry. My nose took to runnin' and I laid down on 'at riverbank where y'all found me, and damn if it ditten feel lak floatin' on a cloud. I seen thangs, doc. Purty thangs. Don't know as I could describe what I seen. Colors, all goin' in this big circle. There was music, too. That was the best. Fiddles, banjoes and all, jest playin' the dangest purty tunes I ever did hear. I shore wish my daddy coulda heard them fiddles."

Take him a bag of nutmeg and he will. Rafe patted Agan's shoulder. "Try to get some rest."

Late into the night, Rafe and Tom Smith sat on a length of rotten driftwood before a small fire, debating what to do with the miscreants.

"I'm not up to a triple flogging," Smith said. "I don't think the detachment is, either."

Rafe poured a finger of brandy into his canteen cup, and both men seemed to have the same thought. Smith drained his liquor in one gulp and idly tapped the empty cup on his knee. "You thinking what I am?"

"Sure. We're drinking brandy and the enlisted men get just enough army whisky to remind them what it tastes like. And we wonder why they turn to nutmeg."

"I suppose the ultimate irony would be to take away their whisky ration. I can't do that."

Smith closed the episode next day by making an entry in the orderly book: "The officer in charge takes due notice of the fact that Privates Delaney, Fowler & Agan have become ill by drinking an unauthorized substance and are guilty of misconduct, having reduced the firepower of this detachment during their illness. Under other circumstances this infraction would be dealt with by a garrison court-martial. In this case it is ordered that a decision on the matter be postponed until a later date, when conditions are more suitable for deliberation."

When Rafe asked how Wilkinson would react to the order, Smith's reply was confident. "Bid Wilkinson never reads back in the orderly book."

The delegation to the Pawnees returned with sobering news. The Pawnees themselves had been friendly, to a degree, the chiefs recalling Wilkinson's visit during the Pike expedition of last summer. They had accepted a few gifts, including medals and a flag, and had tried to sell Wilkinson and Freeman a few more horses. At the same time, they warned about dangers ahead, not especially from the Spanish but from the Comanches. Recently a Pawnee hunting party had been jumped by a larger party of Comanches and thoroughly defeated. Was it just a random raiding party, wandering far north of its usual territory in the lands the Spaniards called the Llano Estacado? Maybe, said the chiefs, but there were a few Comanche bands near the upper Arkansa, too.

"It makes me worry about Pike," Wilkinson said at supper. "He's bullheaded enough to head right into hostile territory."

Rafe wondered about that. *We're doing the same.*

Wilkinson continued, "We've got more than twice the men Pike had. It's a big country and there's no reason to think the Comanches will just automatically find us."

Freeman spoke. "You're forgetting something. I've got instructions in my pocket that says we are supposed to council with the Comanches, not avoid them."

A week in camp had spoiled the men and horses. When they marched off along the north bank of the river, the soldiers complained about the weight of their flintlocks, and the horses capered, reared, and shook their manes at the prospect of more plodding in the August sun. From now on the terrain would be new to everyone including Wilkinson, who had never been beyond the Great Bend.

Tom Smith, who ordinarily rode behind the column while Wilkinson, Freeman, and Burgoo took the lead, rode along beside the file of horsemen and issued instructions that were new and sobering.

"No excursions today. Nobody goes off chasing antelope. Keep the column in sight. If anybody is short of ammo, check with the orderly sergeant. Fill your canteen with water as soon as it's empty in case we get caught somewhere away from the river. Tonight, when we make camp, don't pitch your tents until I show you how we want them."

Pulling up beside Rafe, Smith chatted for a moment. "Got any nutmeg?"

"Just enough for myself."

"I learned something from Bid. He said Burgoo wasn't worth a damn with the Pawnees. Couldn't speak their language well enough to interpret. Sulked a lot, too."

"Let's sign him on as a musician and just let him play the block flute," Rafe suggested.

The days wore on, each taking the column into a more arid part of the plains. The buffalo grass sustained the horses but seemed shorter and drier than before. Rafe was seeing an *Artemisia,* tough and aromatic, which Freeman and Burgoo called sagebrush. Prairie-dog towns were often a mile square.

The only natural feature that broke the monotony of gently undulating prairie was a lone rocky promontory overlooking the river, such a novelty that Wilkinson called an early halt so that it could be explored, sketched, and admired. Rafe found ancient Indian petroglyphs gouged into one of the flat surfaces but no signs of recent Indian visits. A more exciting discovery was made by Wilkinson, who seemed to know what he was looking for. He spent an hour scrambling about the crevices and pacing on top of the rock, and near sundown the men in camp heard him shout.

"Found it, by God!" He motioned to Rafe and Smith, who were at the base. Wilkinson had discovered the inscription "ZMP 1806," which undoubtedly had been left by Pike.

"What's the 'M' stand for?" Rafe asked.

"Montgomery. He calls himself Montie now and then, so people won't confuse him with his father, Major Zebulon Pike. But he's Zeb to most of his friends."

Somehow the initials heartened the men. Another American had passed by, one they knew. Wilkinson spent the evening talking to little groups around the cooking fires, describing Pike's command.

"He had about thirteen men with him after I was separated to go home. And a couple of civilians — Dr. Robinson and an interpreter named Baronet Vasquez. We'll watch for other signs of them now."

"Why are we just duplicating what he was doing, sir?" a soldier asked.

"We aren't. His was a military tour and ours is scientific. He didn't even know how to use the quadrant until just before he left. And he draws the funniest maps you could imagine."

"Well, he got this far," someone ventured, and there was a silence suggesting uneasiness.

"So have we," Wilkinson said. "You'll all be home before snow flies."

Before leaving the big rock, Rafe made a cache of his earliest and driest collections, wrapping them into two large rawhide bundles, which he would retrieve on the homeward journey. Near the river he found a place — exactly south of the rock — where the soil was almost pure sand, easy to scoop into a hole. He covered the cache with heavy stones to foil coyotes, which now were so common that the men had been ordered not to waste ammunition by shooting them, especially now that gunfire might attract the attention of Indians.

Having lightened Blue's load by burying part of it, Rafe began at once to increase it with new finds. He collected a bird much like the whippoorwill but with a different song. In the grass along the river he found a western version of the indigo bunting, nesting in a tangle of low vines. Overhead, small falcons wheeled in the air, dwarfed in silhouette by a buteo hawk, the largest he had ever seen, its legs feathered all the way to the toes. Almost everything he was collecting he felt was new to science; he gathered in specimens greedily. When he shot several grouselike birds nearly as large as turkeys, and turned them over to the cooks, the men rejected the meat because of its strong taste and odor. *I guess they feed on sagebrush.*

Freeman calculated that another week would bring them within sight of the Stony Mountains — or Rocky Mountains — which were their goal. If he were going to measure the height of the peaks and ranges, he would need a baseline of predetermined elevation. By calculating the estimated fall of the river per mile, he had determined that the elevation of the land at their present location was about four thousand feet above sea level, higher than the Alleghenies and rapidly going higher. He had verified the figure by measuring the temperature of boiling water, finding it consistently and calculably lower than that at sea level.

On a simmering morning in August, when the column had been westering across the sandy barrens since dawn, the men in the lead came up over a rise and saw a wondrous sight: a low line of green lay along the horizon. Unmistakably a stand of trees.

"Could be a mirage," Wilkinson warned. Violating his own order about staying in formation, he raced his mount ahead a quarter mile or so. "Trees," he shouted as he returned to the column.

At noon they reached an unbelievable grove of giant cotton-woods, extending half-a-mile deep on either side of the river. To the men it meant shade, wood, and protection. To the hungry horses the sweet inner bark of the younger trees would provide relief from the crackling buffalo grass.

"What do you make of it?" Smith asked Rafe as they entered the first scattering of cottonwoods.

"The leaves are different than our species back east."

"Oh, thunderation! What do you think of it as a phenomenon of nature?"

In the quickening breeze, the leaves quaked and rustled like a flock of tiny, chattering birds. The gray trunks, some six feet in diameter, rose staunch and high, standing so close together that there was little underbrush.

"When you put it that way —" Rafe said. "It just goes on forever, doesn't it?"

After the noon meal the men lounged in the shade, listening to the tree sounds and watching the horses strip away the outer bark of the saplings. Rafe had found a patch of sod, in a sunny spot, just about large enough to cushion his body. He lay with his hands behind his head, chewing the bottom end of a grass stem, and pondered the fact that tomorrow would be his twenty-fourth birthday. *Up from brathood.* He would be in his family's thoughts. What had finally convinced him to come on this trip? Had it been Jefferson's imperious persuasiveness? The enthusiasm of Dr. Barton and Dr. Rush at school? The beckoning call of the West? Perhaps all of these, but for giving him the final shove he would have to credit Mr. Peale and that cluttered, cobwebby museum.

To artist and museum curator Charles Willson Peale, every day is Christmas and the universe a giant toy. He delights in the new, the curious, and what he likes to call the "marvelous." He can paint a portrait better than anyone else in America, then spend an hour celebrating the arrival at his museum of a calf with five legs. The museum reflects the boyishness and all-embracing interests of Peale and his family. The displays range from works of sublime art to gadgets of the sheerest trivia.

Rafe thinks the old man's family is as marvelous as his exhibits. Peale has sired seventeen children, of which perhaps a dozen are living (Rafe has never tallied them), each named for an artist that Peale has found listed in Pilkington's *Dictionary of Painters.* Rembrandt Peale, Titian Peale, Rubens Peale — and so the roster runs. Rafe's favorite is Raphaelle, a quixotic wit and masterful painter, now in his thirties, who drinks too much and whose hands are wracked by pain that he attributes to the arsenic he uses to prepare animal specimens for the display cabinets. Raphaelle concedes that Rafe outranks him because he is named for an archangel.

It is late afternoon when Rafe climbs the State House steps, and the oil lamps in the long exhibit hall are freshly lit. A few women and children are touring the room, examining the pipe organ not yet fully installed, or having their silhouettes cut for eight cents each by Moses Williams, a mulatto who is skillfully using a contrivance that Peale has devised to trace the outline of the human head. The physiognotrace.

Later Rafe would make his own tour of the Long Room, as he does almost daily, to see what new wonders are finished. First he goes into the small preserving room at the top of the stairs, where the reek of arsenic and corrosive sublimate, and the musky odor of bird skins and animal furs, are now familiar. Today no one is working. A brown pelican stands coldly on the work table, its glass eyes yet to be inserted, its massive throat pouch not yet touched up with pigmented oil. Rafe's working area is a corner table where he writes in large blank books the names of specimens under the various classes and orders of the Linnaean system. (Sometimes he takes a large tub down into the yard and, surrounded by cages of scampering monkeys and tanks of alligators from the Floridas, mixes arsenic water for the preserving room.) His problem today is that he has given the same catalog number to a hawthorn from the Illinois country and a new species of grass from the West Indies. Now he must check his records for the whole week.

He is rummaging through a stack of mounted plants, each attached to a folio sheet of heavy paper, when Peale himself comes in and puts a hand on his shoulder. "Rafe, my son! Dr. Barton says you have been given a fine opportunity. I am simply out of my mind with envy." The old man's eyes gleam. His pink, balding head glows in the lamplight.

"Thank you, sir. I was hoping you would come in. I haven't accepted the invitation yet."

Peale feigns shock. "What arrant nonsense! You are merely considering such an offer — from Mr. Jefferson himself? Shame!" He buries his face in his hands as Rafe grins nervously. But Peale's admonitions are always blunted by the smile that follows, and Rafe is soon at ease.

"You wouldn't want me to accept without consulting you, sir."

"Now you have disarmed me. Bless you."

Peale fills a pan with arsenic water from a cask and, wearing thick gloves, begins to wash down the pelican's plumage, working the solution well into the feathers. He talks on, saying all the right things, assuring Rafe that he is a promising botanist, a fair zoologist, and by all reports an excellent doctor; that the practice of physick or medicine can wait a year, but the chance to explore the wondrous West might never come again; that Meriwether Lewis will be proud to see another Albemarle man chosen for a western expedition.

"If I go I'll certainly want to talk with Captain Lewis first."

"You'll go. I have set my heart on it." Peale bends close to Rafe as if to reveal a profound secret. "Before you leave tonight, go have a look at our new exhibit in the far corner. Something there might interest you."

Rafe works only a bit longer and with diminished zeal. When he wanders out into the hall called the Long Room there are no patrons. Moses Williams is sweeping the floor before the first evening visitors arrive. Rafe walks slowly from exhibit to exhibit, stopping as always before the crayon portrait of Meriwether Lewis made by Saint-Mémin from a tracing. It is the fresh-looking face of a handsome man, hair tightly queued, lips firmly set, eyes seemingly on the horizon. By now the Lewis and Clark story is strong in Rafe's mind, and the notion that he has been chosen to emulate Lewis both attracts and repels him. A second Lewis and Clark.

Recalling Peale's reminder about a new exhibit, he strolls to the end of the hall to see what is new. He finds a freshly installed but empty display case in the corner, its green baize shelves ready to accept something awesome and mysterious from yet another far place: an empty case with a sheet of paper attached to the glass, bearing a handwritten notice by Peale:

This cabinet reserved for the discoveries of Dr. Raphael Bailey, of the Arkansa River expedition, sent off by the Honorable Thomas Jefferson in the spring of the year 1807. May God go with him.

The dear old man has tricked him and he knows that he is no longer uncertain about accepting the assignment. He turns to find Moses Williams behind him, broom in hand.

"We gone git you famous," Williams says. "Like Cap'n Lewis is."

Two soldiers ran up from the riverbank, their eyes wide and their faces as ashen as windburned faces can be, their babbled words suggesting they had come from a scene of great and terrible import.

"Bones! New ones!" cried the first.

"Skeletons. Four skeletons!" the other said. He was trembling and pointing to a gap through the trees where the riverbed was visible.

"All right," Smith said. "Get Lieutenant Wilkinson. Alert the corporal of the guard. Sergeant, have the drummer beat to arms. Nobody else go down there without an officer." And as an afterthought: "Get the horses in."

Wilkinson, Freeman, and Burgoo quickly gathered to hear the story from the two shaken men. "We was fishing. Right down there. John he seen it first, being ahead. These skeletons and a lot of other stuff scattered along the bank. At first we thought they was just old bones, like animal bones, but they ain't old, sir. The coyotes had worked them over pretty good, but they've still —"

"Still what?" Wilkinson demanded.

"Still got some meat on the bones, sir."

The group fell silent while Wilkinson decided what to do next. "The doctor and I will have a look. And Mr. Freeman. The rest of you stay alert. Remember, there's no sign of any immediate problem; just some bodies. We'll give you all the full story in a few minutes."

The three walked quietly to the scene, and Rafe knew what Wilkinson dreaded to find — evidence that his friend Pike had got only this far.

Later in the day, Rafe would write this entry in his journal: "The bodies were adult Caucasian males, stripped of all clothing and badly ravaged by animals. From the appearance of the skulls, the men were killed by blows to the head and, in some instances, evidently scalped. I found a metal spear point in the rib cage of one body. At first glance, there was little left by which to identify the group."

Wilkinson seemed heartened, after his first moments of revulsion, by the probability that the bodies were not of Pike or his men. "Too recent," he said. "These chaps were killed within the past few weeks."

"I'd say a couple of weeks," Freeman said. "These damnable coyotes and wolves are fast workers."

"Let's get these — these bodies buried," Wilkinson said. "But first I want you — Rafe — to make every observation you can that might help to tell us who they are. I'll detail a few men to comb the area for evidence. Burial service tonight before retreat. Let's go."

With the guard doubled and each man sleeping beside his rifle, the camp settled down for the night. Rafe and the other leaders sat by candlelight inside a tent and studied the artifacts before them: several yards of colored fabric, found deep in the grove where it might have been dropped by a departing Indian; a scrap of paper not yet deciphered, from the wet sand along the bank; and an oval planchet of silver, three inches long, stamped with a faint design.

Freeman was thinking aloud. "The cloth would be in demand in Santa Fe, which leads me to think these men were traders. This piece of paper has got to be a rough map of the route to Santa Fe. Look here in the lower right-hand corner — that's the mouth of the Platte. And in the upper left are the letters *SF*. The dotted line is the route and the branching lines are the rivers. I make out the Republican, the Smoky Hill, and right about here is where we are on the Arkansa."

Smith asked, "Who could have made such a map? There's no trade between us and the Spaniards yet."

"Some old Frenchman, probably, who thinks he knows the way even if he hasn't been there. I make out the name 'Cardinal' on the back of the paper. That could be one of the Cardinal brothers, either Polite or Jean Marie. They both trade along the Platte."

"What about the chunk of silver?" Rafe asked. "It looks military."

"It *is* military," Wilkinson said. "One of Smith's men brought it in a while ago and said he recognized it as a cap insignia of the artillerists, rolled from a silver dollar and crudely hand-stamped. Said he saw it being worn by a soldier in New Orleans who bragged that he and his captain were heading for Santa Fe as soon as they could get out of the army."

Smith had the answer. "Then the captain has got to be John McClallen. He was itching to get into the Santa Fe trade as soon as a safe route was opened. I guess he couldn't wait any longer."

"My father set him up for this," Wilkinson said. "I suspect they were partners, with father helping him to buy his goods. I know that when the whole command moved out to St. Louis, two years ago, McClallen was attached to our headquarters cadre and had more gear than anyone else. Word got out that it was trade goods. Later I heard my father say that McClallen was resigning to do a little trading on the Missouri. That could have been a feint, the real destination being Santa Fe."

The remaining question on everyone's mind was the nature of the raiders. Burgoo had found the remains of an Indian camp across the river. The party had left twenty-one buffalo skulls arranged in a circle and painted with black stripes, and also four peeled sticks driven into the ground, decorated with leather thongs. Burgoo thought the peeled sticks indicated four scalps taken, but the arrangement of buffalo skulls puzzled him. He seemed unable to decide whether the Indians had been Pawnees or Comanches.

Freeman thought he knew. "If they were Pawnees it would have been just a chance meeting by a raiding party coming back from Spanish territory. If they were Comanches, as I suspect, then the risk ahead is greater because they are operating north of what we think is their territory. More chance of meeting up with them."

The night passed restlessly for Rafe, although to be awakened by the silken chatter of the cottonwoods was a pleasure that almost masked yesterday's wretchedness. He prolonged the awakening as best he could, lying on a doubled buffalo robe with a couple of blankets over him. When a leaf fell on his cheek — a sign that summer was not interminable — he first brushed it away, then opened his eyes to pick it up. The teeth around the margin of the leaf were finer than those of an eastern cottonwood. Yesterday he had noticed that the buds were slightly more hairy.

Watching the top branches of the huddled trees respond to a gust of cool wind, he became conscious of a hard object wedged against his body. When he felt for his musket, and found it lying a foot or so away, he reached beneath the blankets to see what else might be there. The dark, gleaming wood, the slim cylinder that he had admired so often — it was Burgoo's block flute.

He sat up quickly. Burgoo had turned in early last night. The flute had not been there when he himself had fallen exhausted into bed. Idly he raised the instrument to his lips and made a soft, throaty sound.

Burgoo is gone. That has to be it.

He got up and buttoned his shirt. All hands had slept fully clothed, so he was basically ready for breakfast. He hurried to Wilkinson, who was just leaving his tent, and held up the flute.

"Burgoo left me this little present. I think he is gone."

Wilkinson seemed unsurprised. "No great loss. But let's see if he took anybody with him. And whether he got away with any horses or supplies.

His flute, for God's sake.

Instead of spreading an immediate alarm, Bid Wilkinson waited for morning roll call. When the men assembled, each in his regular place, there were gaps in the ranks. The orderly sergeant reported the results of the muster to Wilkinson.

"Three men not accounted for, sir."

"Who are they, sergeant?"

"Delaney, Fowler, and Agan, sir." Rafe glanced at Tom Smith, whose face was stony. The nutmeg-eaters had taken off with Burgoo.

6

The Shores of Purgatory

RAFE'S COLLECTION of *Remarks & Occurrences* was now so comfortably rich in descriptive passages, narration of events, and random musings that he began to think of the expedition primarily as grist for a book. Recalling the marvels in Duane's bookstore in Philadelphia, he could now picture his own published work shelved beside Mackenzie, Bartram, and perhaps Captain Cook's *Voyage to the Pacific*. He planned a gracious preface giving credit to Freeman and the officers for their steadfast support, without whom the book would have been impossible. Then would come about three hundred pages of daily journal entries, set in the new type by John Baskerville that was catching on with the better printers. Some botanical plates would follow, perhaps engraved from drawings that Mr. Peale would make for him. Unfolding from inside the back cover, and big enough to cover a library table, would be Freeman's map — carefully worked out with latitudes and longitudes shown in the margins, and with mountain ranges shaded to simulate three dimensions.

A devil in him suggested the possibility that Lewis's work would not yet be in print when his appeared. He even developed a statement to use in the preface, humble on the surface but with a tiny sting concealed: "To Captain Lewis, whose own travels are yet to be published, I extend the hand of a fellow researcher and my best wishes for the eventual appearance of his own findings." *A great sentence.*

The column had left the cottonwood grove and veered from

the river, skirting the timber by traveling across open prairie. A new set of marching orders, issued by Wilkinson after a campfire discussion of cavalry tactics, had shortened the column. The horsemen were ranked four abreast, officers in the lead and pack animals in the rear. Flanking the column were four riders, standing out from the troop to scout for any sign of Indians.

They had left the Three Forks with thirty-one men, two officers, and three civilians. Now the defection of Burgoo and the others — with half-a-dozen horses, some ammunition, and an unfortunately large quantity of beans, flour, and coffee — had put the command in a critical position. Wilkinson said he now wished he had beached the boats and not wasted the hands he had detached to return them to Natchez.

No attempt was being made to recover the deserters or to punish the sentinels whose carelessness had let them slip away. Survival was now the first goal, and that meant keeping the expedition intact, on the move, and in fighting spirit.

A long day's march put them beyond the cottonwoods and they moved again toward the river. Rafe was not permitted to range afield with Mancha or Blue, though sometimes he rode with one of the scouts or went with the hunters, always staying within sight of the main party. He found a small, spiked wheel which he decided was the rowel from a Spanish spur, and which provided some conversation in the evening.

"It's got about a year's rust on it," Freeman said. "What else have you been finding, Rafe?"

"Today I found a plover that nests on the bare ground, and a new wren that lives in rocky outcrops along the river. There's a finch or bunting that's all black except for white wing patches — the male, that is."

Tom Smith asked: "Isn't it time you found something big and ugly, with long hair and enormous fangs?"

And Wilkinson added: "Let's hope we don't encounter a fierce *Comanchia indianus* with fire coming out of his nostrils."

Freeman was studying the crude map that he had recovered from the effects of Captain McClallen. "There's just one more tributary on this map, and we'll be reaching it tomorrow. Runs in from the south and is labeled 'Purgatoire.' "

"I hope that doesn't mean what I think it does," Smith said.

"Most rivers get their names from obscure events or ordinary travelers," Freeman said. "I wouldn't worry about the Purgatory. I'm just glad it isn't called the Styx."

When the little branch came in sight the next day, a murmur of delight ran through the column. The area of rich bottomland at its mouth promised an oasis even better than the cottonwood grove. The stream came in from the southwest, running almost parallel with the Arkansa for some distance. The hunters were eager to look for deer in the glades, and Rafe noted an unusual number of black vultures riding the updrafts in wide circles overhead. An inviting place, but forbidding, too.

Parleying about a site for camp, Wilkinson and Freeman chose a spot north of the Arkansa and opposite the mouth of the Purgatory, an open ground. An island blocked the view of the confluence, but the rest of the terrain — forming a kind of basin — was all visible from the campsite.

Smith complained to Rafe. "It's a camp in the clear, all right, but if I were a band of Comanches on the move I'd be coming right down the Purgatory. We should have pushed on until we were out of sight of the fork."

"Why don't you say something to Bid?"

"Well, he's my superior and Freeman is an old Indian fighter. I'm just an artillerist without a cannon."

Before supper, Rafe had found a species of small, round gourd, orange in color, and had tasted the bitter chokecherries near the river. The yellow-flowered *Senecio* and the yucca were thick in the uplands.

In camp the men were stacking their impedimenta, including saddles, into a breastwork fronting the river. They reinforced the barricade with a few dead logs from the shore. The horses were allowed to graze for an hour or so, while a picket line was fixed so they could be tied and guarded during the night. The evening whisky drum was canceled and the men seemed to understand why.

"How do Comanches come at you?" Rafe asked Freeman during supper.

"Hell, don't ask me. I'm used to fighting Shawnees and Kickapoos in the hardwood forests. That's why I wanted us out here in the open. If I can see an Indian I can lick him. But if the bugger is behind a tree he's dangerous."

"Has Wilkinson ever fought Indians?"

"Not that he mentions. You got a rifle handy?"

"Just the musket I use for collecting."

"So you hope to kill an Indian without mussing his feathers. Is that it?"

"I'll get a rifle from the sergeant."

The night was long. Fires were doused early and the men sat in small groups for a while, speaking low and listening to the barking of coyotes. The horses on the picket lines snorted restlessly. Rafe checked through his chest of medicines and instruments, then propped his back against it to await sleep.

Too bad, he thought, that he knew so little about Indians in the flesh. Artifacts, yes. Literature about them, plenty. But he could recall nothing of the time that old Chief DuCoigne of the Kaskaskias had stopped at home and bounced him on a buckskin-clad knee. When delegates from the tribes had come to Philadelphia to visit Peale's displays, it was their trappings and ornaments that attracted him — not their faces. Yet they were people whose languages, according to the word lists he had made at the Three Forks and those which Freeman had brought from the Pawnees, were sophisticated. Conjugations and declensions. At Washington Academy, a professor had claimed there were no tribes anywhere in the world, from the islanders of Owyhee to the Hottentots of Africa, that did not have a fully developed language.

When a drumbeat sounded at dawn, Rafe thought at first that he was hearing the usual reveille. It was a different beat, though — a long roll that aroused the camp instantly. He sat up and saw men running in the half-light.

"What's going on?" he called to a soldier who was strapping on his cartouche belt as he hurried toward the barricade.

"Call to arms," the man cried without pausing to explain.

It has to be Comanches. Double Damn.

Freeman crept toward him, crouching low. "Get that medicine chest over behind the barricade." Crouching in imitation of Freeman, Rafe dragged the oaken box to a place behind a stack of logs and looked across the river where the attention of the command was focused.

About twenty mounted Indians were milling about at the edge of the island, where a firm sandbar had formed in front of a willow thicket. For the first time, Rafe heard the war whoops that every Indian fighter spoke of with quiet awe. The Comanches were reining their horses into a tight circle, and their cries grew louder and more frenzied.

"They've got no guns!" Rafe exclaimed.

"No, sir," said a soldier beside him, whose rifle was resting against a log and aimed toward the river. "But look at them bows and arras, and all them lances and shields. Shit, doc, they don't need guns!"

The Comanches were fearsome men, their copper bodies bare to the waist, their stout legs encased in hip-high deerskin leggins ornamented with silver and beads, their foreheads smeared with black pigment. Some were bareheaded, revealing braids of flying hair, but others wore headdresses made of the horns and scalps of buffalo. Their horses were an amazing mix of white, black, bay, sorrel, roan, and dun.

Vikings with Mongol faces. How long can they shout like that?

A soldier pointed with his rifle barrel. "That's Portwood layin' out there." Rafe saw a man on the ground by the riverbank, dead or unconscious.

"He was on guard duty," the distraught soldier said, "right where he's layin'. One of those big bucks came splashing across the river, hit him alongside the head with the butt of his lance, and started back. But another sentinel got the bastard in the back with a rifle ball."

The officers had positioned all hands behind the barricade. The horses were brought together in groups of half a dozen, their heads tied together to prevent their escape. In their excitement they fanned out like the spokes of a wheel.

Smith, moving from man to man to issue instructions and check their readiness, stopped to talk with Rafe. "Too small a band to take us on, ordinarily, but now they're angry. That warrior who ventured across the river wasn't trying to kill the sentinel but only touch him. Wanted to count coup on him. If he'd got away with it, the whole bunch would have let us alone. But now they've got to kill one of us. At least that's the way Freeman has got it figured."

"It's a little late to ask," Rafe said, "but I wonder how many really seasoned men we've got."

"Quite a few, luckily. You can tell by watching them when the shooting starts. The good soldier loads fast without jabbing you in the ribs with his ramrod. He doesn't spill powder all over the ground when he primes, and he doesn't drop cartridges in the grass when he takes them out of the box.

"When does the shooting start?"

"Right now," Smith said, and called out "Here they come!" to the men along the line.

Instead of riding as a group, and charging head-on, the Indians rode singly into the shallow river and guided their galloping horses on a course parallel to the barricade. Each rider slipped down along the side of his mount, to shield himself, and discharged several arrows under his horse's neck before circling back to the island. From three to four warriors were thus passing the barricade at once, and the men behind it were firing feverishly. Too feverishly, Rafe thought as he watched a ramrod go sailing out across the river from the rifle of a soldier who had forgotten to remove it before firing. Another man excitedly loaded his rifle three times without firing, then had to discard the weapon and pick up another.

Some of the horses were struck by arrows, but it was apparent that little injury was being inflicted on the men. The trajectory of the arrows was too flat, and the whirring shafts passed harmlessly overhead. The Comanches, realizing the futility of their attack, became less willing to ride the length of the barricade exposed to the gunfire of thirty rifles. One of their horses had fallen dead in midstream, but the rider, bent low behind his shield of buffalo hide, had withdrawn safely.

"Mother of God, I swear I hit that shield direct," a soldier muttered.

The moment came when there were no horsemen in the stream; Smith called out "hold fire." Several men rose to their feet and Wilkinson, observing something unusual occurring among the Indians, yelled "get down!"

One of the warriors had hurled his bow and quiver to the ground and, armed only with lance and shield, was riding directly toward the barricade.

"Fire," Wilkinson commanded, but most of the men had failed to reload after the last volley. A couple of shots failed to stop the desperate horseman, whose pony leaped directly atop the barricade, stumbled, and fell among the confused men.

"Somebody fire, damn it," Wilkinson yelled. Later he would curse himself for a decision he had made in Natchez to leave all bayonets behind.

A dozen men had thrown themselves upon the unhorsed Indian, pounding him with rifle butts and flailing away with hunting knives, until a corporal managed to reload and send a ball into the fallen man's chest.

"All right, all right. Get back," Smith called out. "He's dead."

The corpse was short-legged, stocky, not well made like the giant Osages. The men looked down at him in silence until one said, "I guess the horse was part of him. He don't look all there without it."

The spotted animal had galloped fifty yards, slowed to a trot, and now stood winded in a clump of cactus and sagebrush, its saddle pulled off-center and its bridle reins dangling.

Most of the men had reloaded and were down behind the barricade again. Rafe moved along the line to check for injuries. A few of the men had arrow wounds and one had been trampled by horses as he had struggled to tie them together before the skirmish.

Without waiting for an order, two soldiers had raced to the fallen sentinel — still alive — and dragged him back to safety, while the Comanches, their interest flagging, watched complacently and then began to vanish into the willows. Within a minute there was no sign of their recent presence except the trampled sand.

Wilkinson climbed atop the barricade and raised his arms. "Pay attention. Get any wounded men over here to Dr. Bailey. Move that Indian down to the river, where the ground is soft, and wait for a burial detail. There will be no mutilation of the body. Absolutely none. You can pick it clean for souvenirs and that's all."

The silver hair ornaments and greasy moccasins had already disappeared from the corpse. His lance and shield had been commandeered by Wilkinson. Some of the men were recovering the horse.

Rafe set up a small hospital in the officers' tent and evaluated the injuries. He thought the unconscious sentinel with the depressed skull wound would die, so he ignored him for the moment and turned to the men with arrow wounds. One arrow point was imbedded in Private James Quinn's shoulder and could be excised. An arrow had passed through the flesh of Private Jacob Weaver's thigh and was protruding; Rafe let the man's friends cut the shaft and remove it while he examined the leg of Christian Krips, an artificer with Smith's detachment who had been trampled by the horses. The tibia was fractured midway between ankle and knee, and a jagged end was visible in the narrow wound. Rafe decided to reduce the fracture first, then take care of all the arrow wounds.

"Any bad ones?" Wilkinson asked, sticking his head inside the tent. He had lost his cap, and his forehead — usually shaded — was white and plastered with sand.

"I've got a broken leg to set and splint, and some flesh wounds to handle, plus an unconscious man who may not survive."

"What help do you need?"

"Two men to help me with this leg."

"Right. And we want to move the hell away from here as soon as we can."

Two soldiers helped Rafe with the compound fracture while he kept up a running commentary, partly to keep the men calm and partly to remind himself of what had to be done.

"Both you fellows hold his leg down very firmly. I'm going to get his foot pointed in the right direction and try to persuade the bone to slip back where it belongs. That will relieve some of the pain. Here we go. Press down. Looks good, but don't get the idea that the bone is set. First we have to see to the wound. Not too bad. The edges will come together nicely. A couple of sutures and we'll be all set. What's the name of the poor devil over there? Henry Portwood? I'll do what I can for him later. Now then, both of you men get around here and grab this leg below the knee. I'm going to hold the foot with both hands, over the tarsus and behind the heel, and pull. Now, I'm turning the foot from side to side. See? I'm trying to work those bone ends together. Pull! That does it. Just let go gently and I'll get a splint and dressing in place. See how nice and easy the bone lies, even though it took all three of us to put it back? Isn't that the whisky drum I hear? You fellows can go now."

The pale helpers seemed glad. Rafe realized that the injured man had been screaming and that he had been shouting his instructions.

At least they were more scared than I was.

Private Portwood, crumpled on a pad of buffalo hides, stirred and moaned. His head bore a half-inch depression on the left side, extending — as Rafe later wrote in his journal — "from the frontal sinus obliquely toward the coronal angle of the parietal bone." A tiny line of pink serum oozed from the wound.

"Portwood," Rafe said, bending close to the ashen face.

"Sir," the man said, but he would say no more and lapsed back into senselessness.

Outside, the men were preparing to march again. Freeman and Smith kept looking into the tent to check on Rafe's progress. He washed Portwood's face, arms, and legs with a camphorated spirits and bled him. When the man returned to semiconsciousness again and called for water, Rafe gave him some with laudanum in it. Portwood took the liquid without choking, so Rafe followed it with calomel and jalap.

Smith stepped inside the tent. "Can he travel?"

"On a litter. In fact, we'll need two litters — one for this chap with the broken leg."

"Could have been worse."

"Not for this man with the bashed head."

Two of the gentlest horses were rigged to carry between them the litter of the soldier with the fracture. When that seemed to work to Rafe's satisfaction, a second litter was prepared and Portwood placed on it. Rafe rode one of the horses transporting him.

Under Freeman's direction, the body of the Comanche was buried near the river while the rest of the expedition waited, already mounted. The column moved out at noon.

Rafe concluded that Portwood had a massive subdural hematoma and that only a trephining operation to cut out a portion of the skull would remove the pressure. If he were to try that, the expedition would have to halt and wait until Portwood could travel again. Obviously, Wilkinson would resist stopping, with the Indians so close. And the delay would make it difficult for the expedition to return before bad weather.

In late afternoon they found a bit of high ground where, beneath a rocky outcrop, they could set up a defensible camp. Wilkinson called a halt and the troop dismounted with relief.

When they removed Portwood from the litter, he was dead.

At the sundown burial service, Freeman read a few verses from the Bible and the drummer beat a slow roll as the body was lowered into the ground. Freeman had covered all the traditional dust-to-dust clichés and had a go at exhorting the living to lead more exemplary lives. He had added in a brief prayer the assumption that God would concede that everything possible had been done for Portwood.

Rafe felt tears coming. *That was for my benefit.*

After supper, Rafe and Freeman sat on a limestone ledge overlooking the river and passed a cup of brandy back and forth as they talked. It had been days since they had had a private conversation, "as one civilian to another," Freeman put it.

Rafe asked: "The Indian who struck Portwood — what was he up to? What's counting coup mean?"

Freeman's lips lingered at the rim of the brandy cup, like those of a man who had been through a lot for one long day. "If you're an Indian, it's a great honor to lay hands on your enemy, to touch him with a weapon or even a stick. You don't have to kill him to get the credit."

"I understand — maybe. Another thing I'm curious about is that shield we took off the dead man. Buffalo hide. Do you think it can really turn a rifle ball?"

"I don't just think it, I know it. That thing is built up with layers of hide from some old bull, and it's got fur packed hard between the layers. Then they cure it before the fire and put all those magical decorations on it. I don't suppose it would turn a ball at point-blank range, but it can from twenty or thirty yards."

Rafe had the cup now. The liquor felt so good in his mouth that he hated to swallow it. "Are we rid of the Comanches now?"

"Wilkinson thinks so and I do, too. They know we're too strong for them, and by the time they can send for help we'll be well out of their territory. They're plains people and don't care much for uplands and mountains, from what I hear."

"So what's our goal now?"

"Keep on the Arkansa, find where it heads, make some observations for latitude and longitude, draw some sketches, and get the hell home." Freeman declined the cup and wiped his mouth with the back of his hand. "What's that you're always smearing on the bird and animal skins you keep? Some stuff in a jar."

"That's white arsenic. Very poisonous but a great preservative. Why do you ask?"

Freeman reached for the cup again. He paused for a long time. "Can I trust you? Of course I can. Stupid question."

Rafe nodded and Freeman unrolled a swatch of deerskin that seemed to contain a treasured object. Something fell to the ground and he snatched it up quickly, shaking off the sand. He started to hand it to Rafe, then changed his mind and spread it out on the deerskin.

The object was a patch of hair about for inches square, clotted with dark blood and still attached to the skin that had held it in life.

This old boy has scalped that Indian.

"I don't know why I did it. I've never been one of these hair-buyers. But when I took the burial party down to the river, and we had the grave dug, I sent the men back to mount up while I stayed behind to scoop the hole shut. That's when I did it."

Without standing up, Freeman hurled the scalp into the air. It caught the wind and sailed away from camp, toward the darkening western horizon, spinning and wobbling. It fell in a clump of sage, caught on a branch, and hung there — bobbling like a redwing blackbird singing his final song of the day.

"I'll get rid of it in the morning," Freeman said. Rafe offered him the canteen cup and he declined with a wave of his hand. "That stuff'll give you a belly ache."

In the early hours of morning, a dream began that promised at first to relieve Rafe from the burdens of the previous day. He was in Philadelphia on a glorious spring afternoon. His frontier clothes were gone and he was in his school garb, the brown frock coat with the shadbelly cut, the nankeen breeches, and a quilted green waistcoat. To verify his transformation, he looked down to see shining buckles on his calfskin slippers. His hose were new and clean, tightly secured at the knees.

A big event was scheduled and he could not remember what it

was. He strolled the streets, pondering, hoping someone would tell him what he was supposed to do. That was no hardship. He wandered from Broad Street down to the Delaware riverside. Children romped in the alleys and old men had thrown off their greatcoats to laze in the sun. A light shower had freshened the new greenery in the parks; robins and finches sang from the wakening trees. For a while his eyes followed a striking girl whose pale yellow hair was done in ringlets and whose walking dress and loose spencer were of apple green, her hat a bonnet of white with a straw brim. He quickened his step to see her face, and she hissed something at him. "The meeting, you fool. Get to the meeting!"

But what meeting? The girl was gone.

Apparently he had found his way to his familiar bench in the amphitheater of Surgeons Hall. The aged Dr. Shippen came through the door at the back of the room and strode down the creaking ramp. He wore a powdered wig, a sure sign in 1807 of a man holding close to the past. On a table in front of him lay a draped body. Oh, God, it was dissection time again. Rafe got up to leave and Dr. Shippen called to him. "You there. Bailey. *Habeat hydrargum submuriatis et oleum tiglii. Admoveatur emplastrum cantharidis capiti.* Tell me what that means, my good sir." But Rafe could not and he fled.

Fifth Street was thronged with people, and at last he realized where he was supposed to be going. Everyone was hurrying into Philosophical Hall on State House Square. The society was meeting! He started toward the hall but his slippers kept coming off. He hopped back into them, one at a time, again and again, and began to fear he would never reach the meeting. Suddenly he was not on Fifth Street at all, but back down at the docks, buying Belgian and Irish linens for his mother, Hebrides tweed for his father, and bolts of Canton silk for sister Franny. Now he was dragging an enormous bag made of hemp sacking, filled with his purchases, back toward Philosophical Hall. He jammed his feet into his slippers each time they fell off, and it seemed that he was slowly drawing closer to the door of the hall.

At last he was in the lecture room and seated; his purchases were gone and he was surrounded by old friends and acquaintances, all waiting for the proceedings to begin. Mahlon Dickerson, sitting next to him, complained, "You really should have waited for my birthday party before going west." On the other side, Dr. Benjamin Waterhouse — visiting from New York — whispered to him: "I have plenty of smallpox vaccine. I can let you have it cheap."

A beefy man in a bulging general's uniform — it must have been General Wilkinson — stood nervously at one side of the room, glancing often at the door. He was florid, sweaty, and obviously distraught. "Captain Pike should be here by now," Rafe heard him say. Rafe called to him. "I know your son James." The general frowned. "My son is a bootlicking little prick. He'll never make captain."

In the first row of chairs, Rafe's mother and father sat with their backs to him. He sprang to his feet and cried, "Mother! Your hair is so gray! Take your medicine, your medicine." She did not seem to hear.

A hush fell and Meriwether Lewis was on the speaker's platform, standing at an elaborately carved lectern draped with red, white, and blue bunting. He wore new buckskins festooned with ermine tippets, and on his head sat a great Indian headdress of eagle feathers. He raised a hand for silence.

"Wondrous things! I have brought unimaginable wonders from the Stony Mountains and the South Sea!"

Then Lewis laid his hand on the shoulder of a young Indian girl who stood beside him. "I want you to love my companion. Her name is Sacagawea. Legends will arise about her, and statues will appear in your city parks. She has served me well. You must love Sacagawea."

The girl looked up at Lewis with adoring eyes, and Rafe was struck with horror. "No, no! You are all mistaken!" he cried. But nobody listened, for they were applauding the girl whose face had become incredibly radiant, full of dark beauty.

"Callie! Callie! Callie!"

7

Climbing Bailey's Peak

ON THE MARCH next morning, Rafe rode at the head of the column with Freeman and the officers, pausing at times to inspect the yucca plants that appeared everywhere, their swordlike leaves rising in clusters from the short, patchy buffalo grass.

Wilkinson was giving Smith a lesson on the subject of misfires: "You can have a bad flint, or a weak feather-spring, but it's usually just a bad job of fixing the flint in the cock. I usually put the flat side down and make sure that the whole front edge strikes the hammer. That way, you're striking fire from a larger surface. Yesterday, every time there was a lull in the firing I checked the men's flints to see if they were screwed in well and hadn't got jarred loose."

"How did my artillerists do?" Smith asked. "Were their flints all askew?"

"They did well for cannoneers. You can be pleased with them."

When Rafe lagged behind the next time, he stayed longer than he had expected. He was dismounted, kneeling to inspect a tiny plant, and when he stood and glanced toward the column it had stopped. The horses stomped at flies and tossed their heads impatiently, but the men were motionless, their eyes on the horizon. No one spoke as Rafe galloped forward to join them, so he turned his gaze toward the hazy line where sky and land came together in the west.

"What is it?" he asked a soldier.

"Mountains."

At last, there they are.

Perhaps a part of the blue mass that lay so faintly on the rim of earth was clouds, but there was one unmistakable hulk — too bold for a cloud, darker blue than a cloud. A mountain for certain. The silence of the men bespoke a longing for that distant blue. Most of the riders had lived within sight of mountains all their lives. Their memories embraced the Smokies, the Poconos, the Cumberlands; there was a blue mass in the childhood recollections of every man. Now, after months of mountain hunger, they saw an end to the infinite flatness of the plains. Their silence became a low murmur.

"There they are, the beauties."

"Shade and clear, fast water."

"Pine trees again. No more cottonwoods."

"Cool air all the time."

The column resumed the march — the men tense and revived, the horses stoically unimpressed.

To the leaders the blue haze was not only a haven but also a destination — a place to start home from. Freeman said he expected the Arkansa to originate not too far beyond the first ridges. He would chart the river to its head, probably to be found in an area of converging smaller streams, and declare his mission achieved. Wilkinson and Smith were grudgingly ready to ease up on security, almost convinced there would be no more Comanches. There might be encounters on the homeward journey, but there was time to think of that later.

"Good collecting ahead," Wilkinson said, reining in beside Rafe.

"I may need another packhorse."

"We can arrange that."

"How long do you think we'll stay before starting home?" With September approaching, there was a chance that winter might overtake the expedition.

"We'll stay until Freeman has his maps and you've got your specimens, and I've got what I want." The lieutenant removed his cap and dabbed at the sweatband with his sleeve. "I want to find some evidence that Pike has been out here."

Rafe did not respond. *That's not in our orders.*

At roll call on the following morning, Smith addressed the command. "Several of you have expressed a wish to reach the mountains as soon as possible, and I can't say I blame you. So today we'll move as fast as we can and stay in the saddle a long time. But remember that some of your horses have arrow wounds, some have sore backs, and all are just plain tired. Besides, we've got one man with his leg still in splints. Let's not get foolish about those mountains. Sergeant, dismiss the men."

Forever lagging behind as he made new finds, Rafe felt a new and bracing thinness in the air. He gathered three plants that he thought were *Dalea, Euphorbia,* and *Eriogonum.* He found a stunted cedar clinging to a rocky projection by the river, the first he had seen for weeks. He shot a black-billed magpie and skinned it in the shade of a cottonwood.

The buffalo were scarce now. The last fresh meat was gone and the cooks were relying upon the dried kind until Wilkinson, scouting ahead of the column, shot a fine antelope with pronged horns. Later the lieutenant learned that by sitting motionless on a rock he could induce the naturally curious animals to come within range of his rifle.

At the noon halt, Freeman built a small fire of sagebrush stems and cottonwood twigs, boiled water in his canteen cup, and took the temperature. "Two hundred and four degrees. That puts us at about four thousand feet above sea level," he announced.

Higher than Old Rag at home. Higher right now than any mountain Rafe had ever seen, and they were still on the plains. The large peak now bore north, sixty-eight degrees west, and two other isolated promontories had appeared bearing south, forty degrees west. The current of the river had quickened — about six miles an hour, Freeman declared — and the water was getting deeper. It ran a serpentine course, shifting from side to side within the confines of its valley, and at the sharper bends there always was a cluster of cottonwoods. In places where the stream had changed its bed, the old channel was filled with stagnant backwater.

By midafternoon the mountains had clouded over and even the large peak had disappeared. Enthusiasm yielded to fatigue and the need to go easy on the horses, and Wilkinson put the men into camp an hour or so earlier than he had planned. They had come thirty miles. After supper, Rafe helped Freeman by holding the chronometer and taking notes as the engineer made observations of the moon and a few stars, hoping to get raw data that could later be turned into measurements of longitude.

"If we had a strong telescope, I could see the immersion and emersion of Jupiter's satellites and get some good figures. I'm using lunar distances instead, and that's harder and less accurate. I'll save the spherical trigonometry until we get home. Hate the stuff, anyway."

"How far to the base of those mountains?"

"Another two days."

Too long, too long.

They were seeing an occasional Spanish trail on the south side of the river, leading off toward Santa Fe. Because the Purgatory had been the last topographical feature with a name they knew, the leaders now showed great interest in assigning names to the streams and major landforms. During five days of travel west from the Purgatory, they passed two substantial streams coming in from the south, and Freeman gave the officers the assignment of naming them. Smith named the first one Claiborne Creek, after his old Virginia friend Bill Claiborne, who was now governor of Orleans Territory. Wilkinson chose Biddle Creek as the name for his, in honor of his late mother, Anne Biddle Wilkinson. Everyone kept an eye on the mountain range now coming into clearer view, each peak waiting to bear a name to honor the expedition and its loved ones at home.

"Next one's mine," Freeman said. "We're sure to find a good stream coming in from the north, flowing from the vicinity of that big mountain." He was so certain of this that Rafe began to think of the imaginary stream as a base camp from which to approach the mountains.

On the fifth day after the encounter with the Comanches, the hunters brought in three elk, the foothills turned from hazy blue to clear green, and they reached the creek. Spirits were high. The setting was much like that at the mouth of the Purgatory but with everything reversed. From the northwest came the clear stream, twenty yards wide, fringed with willows and joining the Arkansa almost in the shadow of the foothills.

Opposite the mouth of the creek, on the south bank of the Arkansa, a surprise awaited. They found a crude stockade of cottonwood logs, hardly more than a breastwork, five feet high on three sides and the fourth side opening toward the river. Not far below the stockade, at the very edge of the river, stood a simple corral of willow poles, now falling into ruin.

Wilkinson detailed three men to ride with him to the stockade, cautious lest they alarm someone encamped there. The place was vacant and they returned to the column. "There's been a latrine trench outside the structure, and there's an aspen tree with a lot of initials carved into the bark." Wilkinson stood in his stirrups, excited by his find. "We recognize the initials as possibly belonging to some of Pike's people."

This time the whole command rushed to the stockade, tying up hastily and gathering at the aspen tree which grew in a little ravine behind the stockade. A corporal who had been in St. Louis, and knew Pike's detachment, inspected the initials on the trunk as everyone crowded in.

"There's *A.V.* That could be Antoine Vasquez, the interpreter that everyone calls Baronie. And *T.D.* could be Tom Daugherty. He was a farmer from Pennsylvania. *J.B.* might be John Brown, who traded me this hunting knife before he left. And *A.R.* is maybe Alexander Roy, a Frenchman."

"That's strong evidence," Lieutenant Smith said, "but it could be coincidence."

"I'm going to settle it," Wilkinson said. "There apparently was one chap in the outfit who used his middle initial. Look here at this one. *J.R.J.*"

"Hell, that's Jeremiah R. Jackson!" the corporal exclaimed. "I couldn't forget the bastard who always beat me playing billiards."

"I think that settles it. We're standing on Pike's old campsite." Wilkinson was grinning.

To celebrate their happy find, and their arrival at the foot of the Stony Mountains, Wilkinson ordered the whisky drum to be beat an hour early. The orderly sergeant was authorized to pour a double ration. When a new latrine had been dug and the corral repaired, and details told off for the building of a few huts the next day, the men dined on fresh elk, corn bread, and coffee. They played ball on a dry section of the riverbed, while the officers chatted inside their tent. Rafe and Freeman walked a few hundred yards up the creek and studied the massive peak rising in the northwest, its bare summit thrust darkly into the twilight sky.

"We're going to stay here several days," Freeman said. "Why don't you take a couple of men and try to climb that thing? You could be back by tomorrow night. I'll spend the time taking readings and going up the Arkansa to look for its origin."

"How high would you say it is? The mountain."

"That's for you to find out. Take my thermometer along and boil some water. I should have brought a barometer, so we could tell for sure, but I didn't think I could get this far with it on horseback. While you're gone, I'll ride out where I can get a clear view and do a triangulation as an added check."

"If I climb the mountain do I get to name it?"

Freeman nodded, and Rafe saluted the peak with a raised arm. "Get ready, Mount Bailey, I'm on the way." He cupped his hands around his mouth and yelled, "coming up!"

Remarks & Occurrences

1 Sept. 1807. We left camp at dawn this morning, Lt. Smith accompanying me as well as Pvt. Macomb, the capable young soldier who was flogged for falling asleep. He has since become a reliable hand. The stream we are following (& which Mr. Freeman has named Corral Creek) takes off in a northwesterly direction & we hope it will lead us to the big mountain. Tom Smith already calls it "your mountain," referring to me.

We have spent this first day entirely on the open prairie, & begin to think our plan of getting back to the Arkansa by tomorrow night is too ambitious. Our three horses are packing a good lot of antelope & elk, some dried buffalo, as well as blankets, guns, a few medical supplies, & my collecting gear. The thermometer is troublesome, being designed more for hanging on a wall than for carrying into the wilds. I have it splinted & wrapped in a soft deerskin. My plant press rides behind my saddle in its usual place & I have today placed a few *Compositae* in it. Also got two bluebirds, one I suppose to be the western counterpart of our Virginia kind, & the other having no rust color on throat or breast.

2 Sept. Another day in the valley of Corral Creek has persuaded us that eastern travelers must adjust their perception of distance out here. We followed the stream (although Smith was at times tempted to cut across country & head straight for the mt.) through barren country, gravelly soil intermixed with jasper. On our right, along the perimeter of the valley, a ridge of pines. On the left the unbroken chain of mts., green to the tops except for Mt. Bailey & a flattopped summit south of it, both quite bare.

I shot a rattlesnake with a curious pattern of hexagonal blotches. It measured 72 in. and there is no time to skin out such a serpent.

At evening we are camped where the creek turns west & leads directly into a *cañón* at the base of the mt. I see that I have used two Spanish words (counting *corral*) in a single entry, appropriate for the country we are in. Surely we shall gain the summit tomorrow. With my pocket telescope I observe snow in crevices near the top. Twilight is extended here because the sun drops behind the *cordillera* of mountains (another Spanish word!) earlier than one would expect. Macomb wants to give the name Twilight Cañón to the deep ravine which we shall enter tomorrow. At home we would call it Twilight Hollow.

3 Sept. At sunrise we saw crags & spires of red sandstone between us & the mt., & lost no time breaking camp. By noon we had entered Macomb's ravine, narrow & rocky, interrupted at right angles by ridges of sandstone, & it became apparent that we must soon leave Macomb at a suitable place with the horses while Smith & I go ahead on foot. The spot we chose was a curious one, as we were surprised to come upon two hot springs much like those in Va. They were white basins or fountains of immaculate water, steaming slightly, the lime deposits having built up the sides of the basins until they overhung the stream beside them. We found the water agreeable to taste, reminiscent of that in Bath County, & I measured the temperature at 70° by Fahrenheit's scale, while the air temperature was 50°.

From the discovery of trinkets glinting in the bottom of the springs, & the trail leading past them and rising to the northwest, we conclude that this place has been frequented by Indians. Saw no recent tracks. Leaving Pvt. Macomb in a patch of grass overhung by pine branches & sheltered by an overcrop, Smith & I took what we could carry — no food except a little meat — & set out for the summit.

The bed of the *cañón* rose sharply. We stepped from stone to stone in the stream until we both had slipped several times, then took to the steep sides of the chasm where freezing & thawing had reduced the rock to chunks & gravelly inclines. When we had struggled for two or three hours under these conditions, we stopped to rest in a small grove & decided to go no further this day. Lt. Smith complains in jest that I am better off with my lightweight collecting gun than he is with his heavy rifle. He also has a pistol. Our blankets are thin & we expect to spend a chilly night with our heads toward the fire.

Wilkinson & Freeman will be alarmed when we do not return to camp tonight.

4 Sept. At daylight we left all but our guns, my notebook, & a mouthful of dried meat each, & set out again. The early-morning climb much like yesterday's until we came to another chasm coming in from the south, & in the triangle formed by the two intersecting chasms we found a level tract of pine & aspen which provided easier walking for a while. It was here that Smith concluded we should bear to the north, then go up a northeasterly face of the mt., circumventing a craterlike formation dead ahead, which looked impassable.

At last we began to lose the trees, which became sparser until finally we could look down & see a distinct line where forest left off & bare mountain began. We panted for breath in the thinner air. I got a headache for which I had brought no medication. We rested often, but the breeze had got so chill that it was more comfortable to climb. Smith was the first to find a patch of snow, lying in a shallow depression & dusted over with sand. He made a little snowman about a foot high. I saw some dwarfed trees which had become acclimated to the great height & incessant wind, so that they were naked of bark & limbs on the upper side. The vegetation above the limit of the forest is entirely new & undescribed. I collected what I could, especially prizing a miniature willow about six inches high which appears fully mature. I suppose the Alps of Europe produce similar diminutive plants.

They reached the summit at about four in the afternoon and were too miserable to feel exultation until they had rested. For a while they crouched behind one of the few rocks on the nearly level surface, and Rafe gathered some twigs into a sheltering crevice to build a fire. When he melted snow in a cup to take the temperature of boiling water, he and Smith were amazed to see that the boiling point was about twenty-eight degrees below that at sea level. If Freeman's formula was correct, that gave Mount Bailey a height of fourteen thousand feet.

Smith whistled in surprise. "A noble peak now named for a noble family. We ought to have some kind of ceremony." He then went off to look for a cairn or other sign that Pike had been there — and they concluded that he had not. The lieutenant made a rapid sketch of the land lying to the west, to aid Freeman in completing his map. They were surprised to see that the Arkansa, curving around from northwest to south, was greatly diminished in size along the base of the next range.

"Some of those peaks over there are just as high as this one if not higher," Smith observed. "More snow, too."

It was as grand a sight as Rafe had ever seen — a breathtaking, unimaginable view. To the west and north were the towering mountains. Behind them the flat, hazy prairies (*Did we come all that way?*) which now they must traverse again. He felt a longing to show this scene to his father. He stared, scanned, studied. Who would come here next? Well, not Jefferson, and for Jefferson's sake he must drink it into his pores. Take some home.

"If I'd brought Burgoo's flute and could play it, this place could inspire great music," Rafe said.

"That's it! We'll have some music." He jumped upon a flat-topped boulder of granite and stood looking at the western mountains, as if waiting for an inspiration while the wind whipped at his jacket. Then he sang:

> Come, O my guilty brethren, come,
> Groaning beneath your load of sin.
> His bleeding heart shall make you room,
> His wounded side shall take you in.
> He calls you all, invites you home,
> Come, O my guilty brethren, come.
> Outcast of men, to you I call,
> Harlots and publicans and thieves:
> He spreads His arms t'embrace you all.
> Sinners alone His grace receives.

They stood a while longer, watching the sun grow red as it lowered toward the peaks. Then they left the summit and began their descent.

"Funny that I should think of that old hymn," Smith said. "Hope you didn't mind."

"I thought it was a fine choice."

By dark they were back in the parklike area where a crevasse came in from the south, and had made camp. In the firelight Rafe sat surrounded by almost more natural-history specimens than they both could carry: twigs, flowers, roots, and several birds which Rafe was transporting in an improvised bag of vines. For his journal he compiled a catalogue of the day's finds with satisfaction and amazement, and thought that perhaps no other naturalist had ever accomplished so much for science, in terms of new species, in a single day.

Birds: Three finches, one with more brown on wings & breast than the purple finch of the East; another with unstreaked sides & belly; a third, above the forest line, with gray crown. A dark gray bird with short tail, which feeds underwater, walking on the stream bed. A kind of flycatcher and a grosbeak with black head in an open stand of trees. Hummingbird with broad tail. Tiny nuthatch which hangs on the underside of branches to feed. Dark green woodpecker with black rump and red face.

Animals: (Noted but not collected.) A beautiful black squirrel with large, tufted ears. A curiously flattened mammal, perhaps of the raccoon family, with very long front claws adapted for digging. A weasel with buffy underparts & long tail. And seen from a distance, several of the sheep described by Lewis & Clark, with massive curved horns on the males.

Plants: (My pride & joy.) Four undescribed pines, including some very old trees high up the mountainside, crippled by the wind. A brown-barked birch & a new maple; a scrub oak on the dry slopes of the foothills; and a spruce & fir, both new, found about midway up the mt. In the tundra region I collected alpine forms of the rush, lily, bistort, buttercup, clover, primrose, and could have spent days gathering more of these nondescripts had time permitted.

At dawn on the morning of the fifth, Rafe rekindled the fire and reviewed his notes while Smith made coffee. "How can I get my name into all this?" Smith asked. "Can't we call this mountain the Bailey-Smith discovery?"

"What if I name a plant after you. How does *Pinus smithii* strike you?"

"Do you have anything with big, red flowers?"

They began the last leg of their return in a jaunty mood. Humming loudly, Smith went on ahead while Rafe lingered to make sure his pack of collected material was secure for carrying, and to revel in the canopy of aspen leaves which seemed almost afire with color. Down on the plain the autumn hues had not yet appeared, and he could not resist pulling off a sprig of yellow and orange leaves to thrust into his hat as a reminder of what was to come.

He had nearly crossed the level area, just above the deep crevasse, when he was attracted by an unusually large patch of his new birches. He had missed them on the upward climb. Hardly more than shrubs growing densely in the shade of a pine cluster, their leaves were turning to russet.

The sound he heard next almost persuaded him for an instant that he was back in his beloved forest above Bluebird Meadow at Fox Run. It was a kind of snort, almost a snuffle, as if a fat sow were happily rummaging in the acorn mast, her pendulous belly swaying, her pink snout dusted with the compost of decayed leaves. This was the time of year when he and his father used to bring a few of the most promising hogs in from the forest, to be plied with corn and pumpkins. A wonderful sound, that snuffle and snort, which sent a pang of homesickness through him and held him motionless.

If the sound had mesmerized Rafe, what happened next sent him into sheer paralysis. There arose from the birch thicket the blunt, fearsome head, the interminably wide shoulders, the stout and shaggy forearms of a grizzly bear. The animal extended its hind legs to thrust its ponderous body even higher above the thicket-top. It snorted again — the sound no longer bespeaking contentment, but annoyance. The great body sank a few inches, as if the creature were dropping to all fours again. Had Rafe stayed transfixed, the bear might have ambled away. But in a movement as automatic as had been his momentary paralysis, he clutched his musket tighter and moved a finger cautiously into the trigger guard.

It was a trivial moment but it changed the bear's intention. With a bull-like roar, then a lunge, it came for Rafe. Teeth like sabers, mouth like a bucket of hot coals. Rafe fired his pitifully weak charge of bird shot, fell to the ground, and rolled. The bear reared when the pellets seared into its face and then, with a shake of the head, came again. No time to reload, no place to run, no way to resist the avalanche of muscle and fur. He lay motionless, face down, his arms thrown across his head as he felt the scorching breath upon his neck and the wide jaws groping for a place to hold and crunch.

"Smith! Oh, God! Smith!" His cry was muffled, but the lieutenant had heard the shot and was racing toward him. The sound the bear was making came also from Rafe's childhood days, being precisely like the eager, guttural murmuring of a hound worrying a fox to death.

Smith knelt to steady the rifle and fired a round. The bear looked up as if puzzled by the new shock that had jolted its rib cage. One eye was closed by the bird shot and blood ran from it. With an eye gone and the other nearly blinded, and this new ball of fire in its belly, the animal drew back and sat on its hindquarters.

Rafe lay still while Smith reloaded. Although years of practice

had given the lieutenant a soldier's deftness, the delay was ago-
nizing. He loaded as if doing it by the numbers from the manual
of arms. He half-cocked the lock, drew a paper cartridge from its
pouch at his belt line, tore into it with his teeth, shook a measure
of powder into the open pan, closed the pan, dumped the remaining powder into the barrel, crammed the paper-wrapped ball
after it, and drew his ramrod. He shoved the powder, paper, and
ball as far in as he could, yanked out the ramrod, cocked the
hammer fully, and raised the rifle to his shoulder. All that in less
than half a minute.

But he held his fire. The first ball had done no great injury to
the bear, but combined with the splatter of bird shot to the eyes
it was at least more than a distraction. Lying motionless, Rafe
offered no resistance. Perhaps in whatever mental process an animal uses at such times, this one told itself, "It isn't working and
isn't worth the trouble." With a red rivulet still creeping from the
closed eye, the bear swiveled on its haunches, dropped to all fours,
and shoved its insulted body into the clump of birches.

Smith held the rifle trained upon the receding buttocks until
the thicket closed around them. Quietly he reached Rafe, whose
neck and scalp were bleeding, and lifted him to his feet. Clinging
together and clutching their belongings between them, they hob-
bled and ran down a rocky incline until it seemed certain they
were out of danger. They had reached the creek where Rafe could
lie on a flat bed of gravel and be inspected. He was conscious
and not yet feeling pain.

"Stop the bleeding right away," he said.

"You've got a big gash on the side of your neck. The other
wounds are just through the skin."

"Press something tight against my neck."

"How about a patch of this?" Smith tore a swatch from his
blanket.

"Fine. Don't let me lose any more blood. Get me down to the
horses where I left my instruments. Have you got my specimens
and notebook?"

"Got 'em." The spray of aspen leaves was still in Rafe's hat,
and Smith pressed it into his hand. "Here's a specimen for you
to hang onto."

By the warm springs, Smith and Macomb bathed Rafe's wounds

in clear, sweet water and set about mending his head and neck. Rafe had directed them to check his scalp wounds to determine if any had penetrated his skull, and they had decided those wounds were not serious. As for the gash on the side of his neck, it was deep but not bone-deep. From their description he decided it could be sutured.

Macomb gratified Rafe by knowing what to do with a suturing needle and a length of catgut, and his skill as an untaught surgeon extended to making small talk.

"Sir, this is just the right place for a scar. Like a souvenir of our trip. You can keep it covered until you want to show it off. Then you can pull open your collar so folks can see what a grizzly bear did to you."

Eased by laudanum but still aware of every needle thrust, Rafe did his best to take a detached point of view.

"Don't draw the catgut too tight or we'll get swelling and inflammation. The idea is just to bring the wound gently closed. Don't put any ointment on it. The best healing agent for a wounded surface is the opposite surface of the same wound. Adhesion. Adhesion is the thing. When you get done, put some court plaster over the wound to take the pressure off the sutures.

"What if those stitches don't hold?" Smith asked. He was working some of the clotted blood out of Rafe's hair.

"No real harm done," Rafe said. "Then the wound will have to suppurate and subside, and it can be closed again. I'd have a thicker scar, of course."

In an hour Rafe was sitting up at the edge of the springs, neck throbbing, head still wet; patches of his hair had been cut away with Smith's hunting knife. He drank several cups of the slightly effervescent water.

Macomb's gentle touch and solicitous care were gratifying. No one needed to remark upon the reason — that he was responding to the care Rafe had given him on the worst day of his life, with bleeding stripes across his back.

When Rafe was ready to joke again, Smith was ready, too. "I've seen you collect sparrows with that toy gun and now I've watched you collect a bear. I'm glad you aimed for the eyes."

"Aimed? I think I was throwing my musket in his face and it

went off. Macomb says you got off a round, too. I don't remember hearing it."

"I thumped him in the ribs, but you got him where it was important."

The ride back to the Arkansa was slow and, for Rafe, excruciating. Even the common movements of his body, rolling and pitching slightly to accomodate Mancha's brisk walk, were constantly painful. The worst times, though, came when the horse elected to trot. After two of these episodes, Rafe surrendered the reins to Macomb, who led Mancha at an even pace down Corral Creek toward the expedition's camp.

The second day was easier. "I don't think Meriwether Lewis brought back a grizzly-bear scar," Rafe said suddenly, breaking a considerable silence.

"Don't be so sure," Smith replied. "He'll top you if he can. You'll be sitting around at an explorers' reunion, twenty or thirty years from now, and he'll turn his head and lift up his queue, and there will be *two* scars, both prettier than yours."

"And bigger," Macomb ventured.

"I see it differently," Rafe said. "Lewis will be so busy trying to get his journals into print before I do — even after all that time — that he will forget about his scars. Maybe I'd better just cut out for home tomorrow and start writing."

"Virginia in November. Not a bad place to be," Smith said. "Frosty mornings up in the Blue Ridge. Hazy days along the Shenandoah. Bluefish biting in the surf along the coast. Shocks of corn in the fields."

"We'll surely be heading home in a day or so," Rafe said. And when Smith did not acknowledge the prediction he repeated it. "Be going home soon. Right?"

"I've been speculating about that. Bid feels much attached to Pike, and now that he's got evidence of Pike's group being out this far, he may not be satisfied until he finds out more. When we found that camp, and the initials on the tree, our whole journey may have turned into a search for those men, or at least for some sign of where they went. I don't know. I'm not even sure of what I'd do if I were in command."

"But Freeman's in charge. He's the one to say when we start back."

"He's in charge but he isn't the general's son. We'll just have to wait and see."

Double damn. His neck throbbed and Mancha was trying to trot again.

8

Entrapped at Wilkinson's Cove

WHEN THE THREE mountain climbers returned to the Arkansa, they found a camp so well established that the soldiers were calling it a cantonment. Beside the river stood the officers' tent, near the entrance of the three-sided stockade. Farther back, against a willowed bank, were four lean-tos made of saplings and brush. The men had voted by acclamation to move the horse corral a few hundred feet to the east, downwind from the camp, to reduce flies and odor. The smoke of cooking fires drifted across the valley.

Freeman had not yet returned from his foray upstream. He had taken five good infantrymen, well provisioned, and no one was worried that they had been out for a week. Rafe and Smith spent a day or so loafing, but Wilkinson went out every morning with a detail of a dozen riders, returning with crudely sketched but highly detailed maps of the area. He claimed the drawings were to help Freeman with his general map. But it seemed more likely that his aim in making the trips was to look for signs of Pike. Thus far, the stockade and the initials on the aspen trunk were all that attested to Pike's recent presence.

"He may have gone south along the foot of the mountains," Smith reasoned. "He certainly didn't return down the Arkansa."

"Wasn't he under orders to look for the Red River?" Rafe asked.

"Yes, and Bid seems determined to find signs that he went down that way."

Macomb came around one morning and said, "Let's have a look at your neck, sir." He had dressed Rafe's wound daily since the encounter with the bear and, while the dressing was off, invited the men of his mess to take a quick look at the suturing he had done. Rafe tolerated what he felt would be a lifetime of stares at the claw mark of the beast.

"Not as red as it was," Macomb said. "Not as puffy, either."

"Good. I think the sutures ought to come out." Rafe tested the area with cautious finger pats and decided it was less sore than yesterday.

He sat on a log while Macomb, with the instrument case beside him, went about clipping and drawing the sutures. The scene might have been that of an officer having his hair dressed by his waiter.

"Hey! That one stung a little."

"Sorry, sir."

"Put some camphorated spirits on it and a clean plaster. Then bring me another bear."

"Right. Shall I make sure your toy gun is loaded?"

"No, I'm going to use a stick this time."

When Rafe and Smith talked, often strolling to a sandy point downriver, the subject always was Wilkinson and his obsession with trailing Pike.

"Our commander is filled with self-doubt," Smith said. "He's the general's son and has a free ride in the army if he wants it. His daddy coddles him, thinks he's weak. And he doesn't even like the service. Did you know that he read law for a year? Now he's out here in charge of an expedition, but not really in command because it's Freeman's show, and yours, and he only gets to yell 'Charge!' when the Indians show up. Now he has this notion that Pike's assignment might have turned out poorly; he won't ever forgive himself if he pulls out for home without knowing. He's a better soldier than his father thinks."

"Where do you suppose Pike is right now?"

"Back in New Orleans bucking that old chain of command, scrambling to advance, and milking whatever glory he can out of his expedition. Pike and I are born to be soldiers, so I understand that. I also know that he would not want us risking our lives a single moment on his behalf."

"Is Bid afraid of his father?"

"Damn right. It's all the worse because he's continually obligated to the old turd."

"Well, I'm willing to hang around here for a few more days if it will make Bid feel better."

"You're forgetting the time of year. Late September already. This outfit might not make it home without a rough time unless we start down the river within a few days."

They both knew that Freeman was the one to decide. Like everyone in camp they glanced up the river a hundred times a day, waiting. When Freeman finally came in with all hands well, he brought a tale that for the moment eclipsed Mount Bailey, the bear, and even the debate over when the expedition would start home. He told of an enormous rift in the earth through which the Arkansa ran, a chasm a quarter-mile deep, its sides plunging down to the whitecapped waters with breathtaking steepness. They had ventured into the lower end of the chasm until the horses could no longer find footing, then had returned to an incline easy enough to ascend. They had then ridden along the rim of the precipice, awed by the marvel, until once again the river was near ground level. Three days farther, the stream had begun to narrow and take on the characteristics of a mountain river, and Freeman had decided he was near enough to the headwaters that he could return and make a map.

"We saw your mountain from the back side," he told Rafe. "It's an imposing thing, but I've got to say that it doesn't compare to that row of peaks that lay off to my left as I went up the river. I'd sure love to see them in winter."

"Maybe you will. It looks as if we'll be here that long."

"Nonsense. We're going home as soon as I get my field notes in order."

"The men will be glad to hear that. They think that Wilkinson isn't anxious to start back."

"He isn't in charge."

Rafe realized that the command was dangerously split. Freeman carried the civil authority of the president; Bid Wilkinson had the power of the army. Not just the firepower — the weaponry for protecting all hands — but the ultimate authority of a young officer whose father was the commanding general. He did not need to flaunt that power; only to have it.

After taps, when the men were quietly disposed in their shelters, raised voices were heard in the officers' tent. Rafe and Tom Smith sat in the lean-to that had been designated the hospital, not far from where Freeman and Wilkinson were debating their future course.

"I heard Bid say something about discretionary orders. What are those?" Rafe asked.

"In army terms, it means the officer in command is to size up the situation and make his own decisions in the field."

"Do you think Bid has discretionary orders?"

"More than that, I supect that he has verbal orders. The old man calls him into headquarters, hands him a set of written orders for the record, then says he is free to look around for evidence of Pike when he gets out here. Within reason, of course."

"Freeman is a shrewd man. And plenty hard."

"Not hard enough to take an army detachment back down the river in opposition to the commanding officer's orders."

At breakfast, Freeman was unusually quiet until, with a nod, he signaled Rafe that he wanted to talk with him alone. They carried their coffee, venison, and corn bread to the hospital lean-to. In a parallel action, Wilkinson had taken Smith to the officers' tent. The men of the command, squatting or sitting about the breakfast fires, ate and waited.

"I've decided to let Wilkinson have his way for a while," Freeman said. "We'll head south for two days only, looking for signs of Pike. I have the man's word that we'll double back then and take off down the river. I could have outshouted him and put this outfit on the road to home at once, but not without consequences. I traded two days of travel time for the cooperation and morale that we need to get us all safely home, you with your collections and journals, me with my maps. When I get back to Washington I may have something to say to the president about it all."

To sweeten the announcement that the command was detouring, there was a double ration of whisky. The men cheered the whisky and cursed the delay.

Rafe idled the rest of the day away, giving up one last chance to collect upstream. Now that the return trip was so near, his thoughts flew half a continent away as he thought of school and home.

The faculty seems benign to him now, the professors no longer as formidable as they had been the first year, and he is able to evaluate them with more maturity. The renowned Dr. Benjamin Rush, with his oversimplified theory of disease (in which most ills are defined as a kind of fever). Dr. William Shippen, not nearly so polished a lecturer as Rafe had expected. Rush and Shippen are the old-timers; the others are in their forties. Dr. Philip Syng Physick, who is defensive about having a curious surname for a medical man, and who teaches surgery in a precise and distant manner, never using notes. Dr. James Woodhouse, whose chemistry lab on the ground floor of Surgeons Hall sends sulphurous fumes up through the floor of the amphitheater. Dr. Caspar Wistar, fluent when lecturing on anatomy but easily confused at the operating table. And Dr. Thomas Chalkley Jones, practicing and teaching midwifery and gynecology, who still cannot help blushing while demonstrating models of female pelvic anatomy. Rafe remembers squirming with embarrassment for him.

Of all the faculty, he feels closest to Benjamin Smith Barton, who has taught him natural history, taken him collecting near Philadelphia, and is an established scientist. A man more respected by his students than by his colleagues. Barton keeps two plaster busts in his office at the new medical building, of Linnaeus and Göethe. Someone has told him that he resembles Göethe, and he in fact does have what one of his peers called "Göethe's forceful mien." Some of the faculty say that his forcefulness surfaces mainly in displays of temper, and that he is dilatory, disorganized, and prone to make promises he cannot keep. His desk and office are a jumble of plant specimens, zoological parts in jars of alcohol or formaldehyde, and stacks of uncompleted manuscripts. Although he is superb as a botanist, he is less proficient as a doctor. About once a year the rumor goes around that he did not receive an M.D. while studying in Edinburgh and Göttingen, as he claims.

Barton has chosen Rafe from among the seniors to accompany

the tour at Jefferson's request. "I shall get a letter off to the president today, giving you high marks," he says. "And there's one thing I must not neglect to tell you. You can travel to earth's far corners, and bring home tons of specimens, but if you don't publish your findings you will have spent the time for naught. Unpublished research is worthless. Take the word of a man who is far behind with his writing."

Now Rafe is with his father in the little experimental plot behind the barn. Anthony is showing him the progress of the crops he is developing to improve Fox Run Farm. The early-maturing Indian corn from New York is for those times when spring rains keep the men out of the fields too long and shorten the growing season. Several patches of wheat from Europe and America are being tested for their resistance to the Hessian fly, lately seen in Albemarle. And here is a new kind of legume from the Eastern Shore, which Anthony and Rafe cannot decide whether to call a pea or bean. The ageing farmer bends slowly, because his hips are arthritic, and pulls a weed.

Callie coming aboard the keelboat. How do they walk so quietly, so surely? She does not flinch from the needle as the vaccine is drawn into her supple arm. A chief's granddaughter. And Burgoo, the scoundrel, calls her a squaw.

It seemed good the next morning to have the whole command together and on the march again. Rafe supposed he ought to spend at least some time considering butterflies, for soon the autumn frosts would take them. He watched a purple and black specimen, probably one of the hairstreaks, foraging among the leaves of the scrub oak. He remembered that he had brought no collecting bottle. Someone else could take care of the butterflies. *I can tell I'm ready for home.*

The terrain beyond the river, as they made for the mountains to the southwest, was the usual foothills shrubland — savannahs of upland grasses alternating with rocky patches of juniper, oak, and cedar. By midmorning he had found yet another kind of pine, short-needled and with a nutlike seed. Empty nests among the

branches seemed to have belonged to a new jay, short-tailed and
solid blue, now gathering in flocks among the clumps of pines.

Two isolated peaks stood out in the south, apart from the others. They looked easier to climb than Mount Bailey. *My mountain's better.*

The officers took no precautions against Indians anymore, letting the men straggle out in single file or ride in small groups if
they chose, so long as they presented the general appearance that
all were riding to the same place. Water was plentiful in small
streams that intersected the route. At noon, each man sat on the
ground with a chunk of bread in one hand and the reins of his
bridle in the other. Only Wilkinson kept busy, ranging out ahead
of the command, eyes on the ground or sweeping the horizon.
About midafternoon of the second day, he disappeared over a
rise for half an hour and came hurrying back with a piece of
news.

"We're going to come to a stream that flows down from that
low range, and I've found some tracks along the bank. Quite a
few horses."

"New tracks?" Smith asked.

"Can't tell. Can't tell if they're shod or unshod, either."

Freeman asked, "What do you want to do, lieutenant?"

"I want to go up that stream until sundown and see where
those tracks lead. We'll camp over by the mountains, plenty of
wood and grass, and we can get ready to start for home tomorrow."

When the word got out, the men resumed their old four-abreast
formation without being ordered. As they neared the stream, the
column halted while the officers, Freeman, and Rafe rode ahead
to look at the tracks. The only consensus they reached was that
there had been many horses, some weeks ago, and that they were
traveling downstream toward the east.

"Could it have been Pike?" Rafe asked.

Freeman shook his head. "More horses than he had. And the
tracks are more recent than those we found at the corral."

"Let's find out where they came from," Wilkinson said, and
gave the order that put the column in motion again.

They followed the little river as it bent around and led them
directly toward the mountains. A fringe of cottonwoods enabled

them to see its course in the distance. Within an hour or so it had begun to sink into a deepening crevasse in the earth that Rafe supposed the Spanish would call an *arroyo*. As the stream was now unfordable, the column stayed on the north side, to a point where the water seemed to slice through a hogback ridge of reddish sandstone.

The tracks were no longer discernible on the rocky banks. A man was sent ahead to look for a campsite; when he returned he was anxious to talk. "Goldamndest thing, sir. Kind of a cove or something up ahead. Level grassland, and this river breaks up into two or three streams that feed into it. Mountains all around, like there was only one way into the place."

"How big a cove is it?" Freeman asked.

The soldier was a North Carolina farm boy. "More'n a thousand acre, I'd say."

"How much is that?" someone asked. "We ain't all farmers."

"Couple of miles square," Rafe said.

"Of course, it ain't square," the returning scout explained. "More like a funny triangle."

The column worked its way over the hogback, along the *arroyo*, and by sundown had reached the flat valley that did indeed remind Rafe of a cove along the Blue Ridge. To the west were mountains which, with a couple of exceptions, were forested to the top. To the north and south, foothills. And to the east, the gap or notch through which they had come. It was a lush spot, timbered here and there, and Wilkinson chose a place for camp along the middle fork of the stream.

"You could put a cork in that gap and just live here forever," Freeman said. He was sketching the area while waiting for the venison to roast and the coffee to boil.

"Now you've got to name it," Smith reminded him.

"I've got it labeled already. This is Wilkinson's Cove."

"Do you think Pike was ever here?" Rafe asked.

"I don't think about that anymore. I just think about good beds with clean sheets, Madeira wine, and slabs of ham with sweet potatoes."

"Back home you'd think venison was a real treat."

"It would be, back home."

Next morning, for the second time since the start of the expedition, Rafe was awakened by a long drumroll calling the men to general quarters. He threw off his blanket and sprang up, the memory of the Comanche raid giving him extra incentive. His first thought was of his medical supplies; they were safe and whole at the base of a tree outside his hut.

Leaving the horses picketed, Wilkinson had called the men into formation, facing the gap in the eastern ridge through which they had filed the day before. Two ranks, the front rank kneeling, all rifles charged.

"What the tarnation's going on?" Freeman called to Rafe. He had sat up but kept his legs under a blanket.

"Something downstream. Can't tell what."

Freeman got up then. "I can make a good guess."

Carefully the two stalked out to inform themselves. A mile to the east, along the stream bank, stood a cluster of mounted men — motionless and dimly seen as the dawn brightened behind them.

"Did you guess right?" Rafe asked.

"Spanish troops. Not a new sight to me. *Qué diablo!*" Freeman muttered, as if practicing to think in another language.

Rafe watched two riders leave the group and come carefully toward camp. When they were within a hundred yards of the firing line, one man dismounted and handed the reins of his pinto horse to his partner. He came on foot toward the Americans, a hand held high in greeting.

"Hold fire. Nobody get excited," Smith called out.

As the Spaniard approached it was clear that he was an officer, brown-skinned and lean, walking awkwardly as horsemen often do just after dismounting. His spurs tinkled on his coarse, black boots.

"*Buenos días, señores. Quiénes son ustedes?*"

He had addressed nobody in particular and neither Wilkinson nor Smith appeared to know what he had said. Freeman turned to Wilkinson. "He wants to know who we are. Shall I speak with him?"

"Please do."

Freeman and the Spaniard shook hands. By this time the soldiers were at parade rest and the tension had eased. The two men spoke for a minute or two, then Freeman introduced the stranger.

"This is Don José Sotelo, a lieutenant in the army of New Spain. He says he is somewhat embarrassed by our presence here."

"Why is that?" Wilkinson asked. "We're in American territory."

"He is confused about that. Says his superiors would consider it Spanish territory."

"Well, Jesus, this is no time to debate the Louisiana Purchase. Ask him to bring in his men and we'll talk."

"I've done that. But he also says something very interesting. He arrested Pike last winter and took him to Santa Fe. I think he wants to do the same with us."

"Oh, horse shit!" Smith said under his breath. Rafe was stunned and so was Wilkinson, who shook his head slowly but said nothing. Lieutenant Sotelo saluted — at no one in particular — and mounted up to return to his company. Wilkinson ordered his own men to stand down but to keep their rifles unstacked. He disappeared into his tent, still shaking his head.

In about an hour a party of horsemen was seen galloping toward camp. What puzzled Rafe was the fact that about half the Spanish detail remained behind.

"Now what!" Freeman had been resting against a log, and sat up abruptly.

Fifty men of the Spanish party rode to a grassy spot along the creek, not far from the expedition's camp, and prepared to bivouac. Almost the same number had stayed behind and were now making their own camp at the gap in the cove.

"They've got us hemmed in," Smith said. "Can't say that I blame them. A smart move."

Corked in the bottle. Rafe could think of nothing more productive to do than get his journal and read his recent entries. As darkness came, the Spanish camp became noisy with the sound of guitars and fiddles. The cooking pots steaming with meat and chilies sent strange aromas into American nostrils. ("What kind of crap is that they're eating, for God's sake?") Some of the foreigners were regular cavalry, wearing long leather jackets and broad-brimmed hats, and armed with shields and lances as well as rifles. The others were militiamen, dressed in a variety of tatterdemalion clothing and armed with old muskets. A few had made their own lances by lashing iron hooks to willow poles.

Although it was well understood that the Americans were hostages, there was no friction. Men from the two camps began to mingle as the evening wore on, apparently confident that their leaders would talk matters out.

Rafe became acquainted with the only other officer besides Sotelo. He was young and dark, with teeth that shone white in the firelight. He had a quick laugh and spoke some English. When he learned that Rafe was a doctor he introduced himself.

"I am Bartholomew Fernandez, *soldado de cuera.* Cavalry. It is my good fortune to meet a *médico.* I want much to talk with you, for in my province of Chihuahua I, too, wanted to study medicine. Perhaps I shall do it later. I should like to sit on that log and share my *aguardiente.*"

"Certainly. I'm pleased to hear you speak English, as my Spanish is terrible. *Mi espagñol no es muy bueno.*"

Fernandez laughed. "That is better than you think. Perhaps I teach you more."

His liquor was the strong and bitter *pulque,* suggesting liquid cactus, and Rafe soon brought out his own supply of Monongahela whisky. Fernandez choked on the first drink but took another one soon. "This will make me *borracho.* Drunk."

"We were planning to start home tomorrow," Rafe said, letting his disappointment show in his voice.

"Please pardon if Sotelo decides that is not to be."

"Why would he do that?"

"He has orders to detain you."

"You mean you knew we were coming?"

"Not me, my friend. But I think Sotelo did. He will explain to your officers."

During the evening Rafe learned what he could from young Fernandez, while the *pulque* and whisky gradually disappeared. Zebulon Pike had been intercepted on the other side of the Rio del Norte, to the southwest, and escorted to Santa Fe for questioning. There the governor had decided to send him down to Chihuahua, where the commanding general of the Interior Provinces had questioned him further, reprimanding him for penetrating Spanish dominions, and sent him under guard to the American border on the Red River. By appearing south of the Rio del Norte, which Jefferson called the Rio Grande, Pike had clearly entered Spanish lands. But Fernandez, who seemed to know about the Louisiana Purchase, had a very fuzzy notion of how far north New Spain extended.

"Our president thinks the Red River is the boundary," Rafe said.

"We do not think that. It is not for me to decide, of course. But I think my *gobernador* in Santa Fe would say you are sitting on a Spanish log at this moment — with your feet on Spanish soil." Fernandez patted the log possessively, grinning, teasing.

"*Qué diablo!*" Rafe exclaimed, and that amused Fernandez. He put his arm around Rafe's shoulder and they drained the *pulque* bottle.

Wilkinson had not left his tent all evening. Freeman had been entertaining Lieutenant Sotelo alone, with Smith (who spoke no Spanish) sitting helplessly beside them. Wilkinson obviously was awake — the canvas wall of his tent was aglow from the light of a wavering candle — but there were no moving shadows.

"Your commander is a quiet man," Sotelo said to Freeman.

"I'm going in there and coax him out in a minute."

There was no need. Wilkinson crawled out of the tent, stood up unsteadily, and grasped the tent pole momentarily for support. Like everyone else, he had been drinking. He walked carefully toward Sotelo and Freeman at the fireside, and stood above them with hands clasped behind him.

Rafe sensed what was coming and grimaced.

"My father," Wilkinson began haltingly, "my father is the clothier general of the United States Army. I mean he *was* the clothier general. Now he is the commanding general. Top of the line. Brig–Brig–Brigadier General James Wilkinson."

Awkward pause. "I know of your father, señor," Sotelo said.

"First a volunteer in the Pennsylvania Rifles," Wilkinson continued. "Captain in the continental infantry. Went right up from there. Served with Greene, Arnold, Gates, and with George Washington himself, by God."

Freeman made a small hand signal as if to quiet him. "I'm sure that Señor Sotelo is getting tired."

"My father has been very close to the Spanish government. You might be surprised to know how close. He has worked with some of your highest officials."

Here it comes. Rafe tried not to listen.

"My father the general receives an honorarium from time to time, I believe, as a token of gratitude from His Most Catholic Majesty, King Carlos. He —"

Freeman got to his feet and took Wilkinson's arm. "Bid, I think you've got yourself a mite tiddly." He seldom called the lieutenant *Bid.* Now he hustled him toward his tent, mumbling to him as they moved away. All that Rafe could hear of the exchange was Wilkinson's, "I'm all right, damn you."

Sensing that his new American friends were experiencing a moment of dismay, Fernandez spoke cheerfully. "The log. Let us forget who is the rightful owner of this rotten old log. There is room for both of us. But wait! I must get up because I have something in my saddlebag that might be interesting to you. Two copies of your famous newspaper, the *Intelligencer Nacional.*"

He went to the Spanish camp and came back with the papers, creased from many foldings. "I learn some English from these," he said, and put them into Rafe's eager hands.

"You have no idea how precious these are," Rafe said. "We've had no news of home since we left the lower Arkansa in the spring."

"Keep them, *amigo.*" He waved good night as he walked away. "*Hasta mañana.*"

Finding an unoccupied fire, Rafe kicked it to life and started to read. He scanned the pages hungrily, learning that Aaron Burr had been acquitted (which must have upset Jefferson), and that there was an embargo on British goods. The U.S. frigate *Chesapeake* had been fired upon by the British frigate *Leopard,* off the Norfolk Roads.

He turned to the small talk of American life on the inside pages where — scattered among the advertisements for runaway slaves, and mill sites for sale — there were the ordinary chronicles of the land he missed so grievously. A name caught his eye and he tilted the page so that the firelight shone more brightly on it:

DIED. In Charlottesville, Virginia, on 1st July, Eleanor Custis Bailey, wife of the well-known agriculturist Anthony Bailey and collateral descendant of the Custises of Williamsburg and Mount Vernon. Of a heart attack.

He took the news surprisingly well, as if his mother's death were too remote in time and distance to affect him. July, the services in the family plot at the upper corner of Bluebird Meadow, a few friends from around the county and all those Browns from Brown's Cove. Now it was September and the grave would be grassed over, Franny's weeping muted, his father's terrible grief beginning to wane. *I couldn't have saved her.* He had left the medication for her and prepared the family for the worst. No doctor could have done more for Eleanor Bailey.

But I could have been there. Rafe the son, not Rafe the doctor.

He went quietly to bed, sure that when the whisky had burned out of his brain he could face her death and think about it. Until then he would sleep long and heavily, he promised himself.

But in the night he awoke and cried.

9

Santa Fe Autumn

~~~~~~~~~~~~~~~~~~~~~~~~~~~~~~~~~~~~~~

OCTOBER 1, with a light rain falling, and here and there a bright clump of snow, moving airily through the slanting raindrops and winking out before reaching the ground. Half the Spanish detachment was moving, Indian file, along the river — which they called the San Carlos — and into the *cañón* leading east out of Wilkinson's Cove. In an hour the horsemen would be able to climb out to level ground, turn south, and begin to skirt the gray mountains on the way to Santa Fe.

At the head of the column, along with Lieutenants Sotelo and Fernandez, rode the semihostages from the expedition: Freeman, Wilkinson, Wilkinson's waiter Jonas Gardner, and Rafe. Back in the cove, watched over by a *sargento* and the rest of the Spanish, Tom Smith was under orders to command the detachment, begin drying meat, and be ready to start down the Arkansa as soon as Freeman's group returned.

The journey to see the governor was only a formality, Sotelo had said. *"Lo siento,* but I have my instructions."

Rafe and Fernandez rode together after they had cleared the *cañón*, Rafe riding Mancha and leading Blue with extra gear for himself and the others. There was no animosity. Up ahead, Freeman talked with Sotelo in better Spanish than Rafe supposed he could ever manage. Wilkinson joined in, with English, and often there was laughter.

"An opportunity," Rafe said to Fernandez. "I can collect in a new area, and Mr. Freeman can try to figure out where all these rivers have their origin. The Red River especially."

"Ah, the Red! Señor Freeman may not learn much about that from my governor. It is our river, of course."

Maybe, but Rafe was not going to worry about it. He studied the garb and equipage of the cavalrymen and saw a sense of artistry in all they carried. The blades of their lances were handsomely forged; their buckskin cartridge belts bore embroidered designs; their bullhide shields were gaudily painted. Instead of boots they wore heavy leg coverings and simple moccasins. Their leather jackets, cumbersome when they walked, must have been designed to deflect arrows. And their flattopped hats were almost tough enough to qualify as helmets. They were a frightening troop until, suddenly at random, one of their number began to sing.

When the rain stopped and the clouds melted away from the mountains, Fernandez pointed out a promontory lying due west. "That is Cuerno Verde, the Greenhorn Mountain, named for the great Comanche chief whose forces were routed by Governor de Anza many years ago. My uncle rode with the cavalry and was killed by the chief himself." Fernandez crossed himself and whispered a Latin phrase.

"I climbed a mountain," Rafe said. "A big one northwest of here. The biggest. What is it called?"

"I think Sierra de Almagre. We Spanish seldom travel that far north."

"It has an American name now. Mount Bailey."

Fernandez nodded, conferring the mountain on Rafe as if by international agreement.

The Spanish horses, with rumps and withers steaming now that the sun was out, formed a *remuda* of many sorts. There were steely Arabians, tails arched and feet dancing, in bay, chestnut, white, and nutmeg roan. Little barbs like Mancha, pied with large spots. A few Indian horses, some cream-colored with black manes and tails. Several militiamen rode worn-out nags, hammerheaded and ill-groomed, eyes on the ground as they trudged homeward. A train of pack mules followed, bearing saddles made of straw-stuffed bags. *"Mulo!"* their drivers cried, as if ever fearful of being left behind.

When Rafe collected plants, Fernandez helped and so did some of the men, bringing in armloads of the shrubby, yellow-flowered *chamisa* that was everywhere, and explaining how the spiny arms of the *cholla* cactus were good for fence-making. Every plant had curative powers or household uses. The creosote bush, *hediondilla,* to sprinkle in the shoes and prevent rheumatism. The willow, *jarita,* whose leaves could be chewed to strengthen the gums. Dried leaves of the horsemint, *oregano,* to soothe the stomach and flavor the stews. And the edible seeds of the *piñon pine,* the name the men gave to one of Rafe's discoveries, the cones now opening so that a few soldiers ranged far up the hillsides to gather the nuts for roasting.

It would take seven days, Fernandez said, to reach Santa Fe. They crossed the scant sources of the Huerfano flowing down from the mountains, and went around the tip of the range to head west up a pass which marked a change in watersheds. The next range, snow-topped, was the one Rafe supposed he had seen from the summit of Mount Bailey. "Sangre de Cristo," Fernandez said. "They say from the color of Christ's blood when the late sun strikes the rocks."

"Es muy montañoso," Rafe said, drawing recklessly upon his meager Spanish.

They descended Sangre de Cristo Creek and entered the valley of San Luis, always bearing south, crossing Trinchera and Culebra creeks and other tributaries of the Rio del Norte. Now the chain of snowy mountains was on their left as they followed the old trail from the Arkansa to Taos. During a rest period, when Rafe and Fernandez sat together at the base of a vertical pane of soft, smooth rock, the Spaniard scratched an inscription above their heads with the tip of his hunting knife:

Paso por aquí R. Bailey y B. Fernandez

Passed by here. It reminded Rafe of Pike's initials on the rock in the plains, and of all the beech trees in the forests of home that bore his childish messages to the world. If his fellow townsmen ever put up a monument to him in the courthouse square, he supposed that *Paso por aquí* would be a good thing to say on it. Even on a gravestone.

The idea of the gravestone set him thinking of his mother. He fell so silent that Fernandez walked away and left him alone, to grieve and remember.

It is the Sunday before he is to leave her — the day he first realizes how ill she is. She has always seemed strong, like all the Eastern Shore Custises who came from that strangely different part of the commonwealth across Chesapeake Bay. He knows so well the story of how she met his father in 1784 when, traveling to Mount Vernon with her uncle to deal in sheep, she sat across from the young farmer at the dinner table. They married the next year and lived in the house on one of the Mount Vernon properties until General Washington died in 1799. They found the Doyle's River place the next year, attracted by the fact that slavery was on the wane in the western part of Albemarle County. Her urgent request to her father was that her dowry should include only two blacks, Peter and Sally, the house servants. Now she lies ill in the house while Peter, Sally, and the family await some word from Rafe about her condition.

Into the night Rafe sits in the little room off the parlor that Anthony calls the library, and goes over all the notes he has ever taken about diseases of the heart. He combs through his books and an old article in *Medical Transactions* that discusses angina pectoris. He even turns in some desperation to Tennant's *Every Man His Own Doctor,* outdated and simplistic, but the only medical book the family owns.

Rafe knows of no treatment for angina, does not even know the mechanism that causes the pain — although one scholar has written of spasms in the arteries. A fragment in his notebook, open to the lectures of Dr. Rush, catches his eye. "Dr. Rush says may be inherited tendency."

He finds the family Bible lying open on a table and turns to the back pages where the births and deaths of his mother's people have been entered for more than two centuries. He notes the entries for his mother's five brothers and sisters. He had known none of these Custises himself but had heard them discussed at home. All died in their early fifties. There is nothing unusual in that. But he notes the supposed causes of the deaths, jotted down in his mother's hand:

> Solomon Custis, b. 1743, d. 1794. Died of the dropsy.
> Mary Custis Bates, b. 1746, d. 1799. Died in her sleep.
> Adam Custis, b. 1753, d. 1803. Of a seizure.
> Sarah Virginia Custis Wells, b. 1754, d. 1777. In childbirth.
> Elizabeth Custis, b. 1755, d. 1805. Of failing heart.

Each of these deaths except that of Sarah Virginia could have been caused by a disease of the circulatory system. And even

Sarah, had she not died young of childbed fever, might have met the same fate in later years. Rafe's mother has just turned fifty and her dangerous years — if heredity means anything — are just at hand.

The chill abruptness of that discovery in the family Bible would haunt him forever, now that his mother was gone. *My God, it runs in families.* "Come, my friend," Fernandez said as he came to fetch him. "It is far to ride."

Colonel Joaquín del Real Alencaster was tall, blunt-talking, and splendidly scarlet and blue in full-dress uniform. As acting governor of Nuevo Mexico he sat behind a bare oaken table in the *palacio,* like a gaudy tropical bird consigned to the drabness of an old wicker cage. The room was poorly lighted, the windows small and glazed not with glass but with slabs of mica from the mountains. The floor was earthen, stomped hard by the tread of the colonel's boots and the sandaled feet of his many servants. The adobe walls bore no tapestries, no niched icons, no gilt-framed paintings. They were gray-white and filmed over by the dusty webs of spiders long dead. A burning candelabra, hanging above the colonel's head, cast its own shadow down upon his desk but did little to lighten his stern face.

"*Buenos dias, Señor Teniente,*" he said to Wilkinson, thus indicating that he considered the lieutenant to be the leader of the party. And from then on, to the relief of all, he spoke no more Spanish. Wilkinson glanced at Freeman to see if he wanted to assert a civilian presence, but he made no sign. So Wilkinson responded.

"I am James Wilkinson, Second Infantry, and my father is General Wilkinson, the commanding general."

He's doing it again. Rafe thought it might even help, this time.

"Is it your father who sends you into Spanish dominions? Is this father of yours the one who sent Teniente Pike across the Rio del Norte to raise his flag over Spanish soil?"

Freeman coughed quietly and stepped forward. "Sir. My friend the lieutenant is not responsible for our party. That is my privilege. I carry a letter of instructions from President Jefferson which, as you will see" (he fumbled in his pocket for the tattered paper), "directs us to the western edges of the Louisiana Purchase for purposes of scientific study."

"Ah, the Purchase!" the governor exclaimed. "Let us talk of that infamous transaction." He opened a carved wooden box, the only object on his table, and Rafe supposed he would offer cigars. Instead, the box contained thin, brown cigarettes which Rafe declined. By this time a silent male servant, in shapeless white-linen pantaloons and homespun shirt, had crept into the room and placed three chairs for the Americans.

Alencaster lit his *cigarrillo* and addressed Rafe: "You are the doctor from Birheenia. Splendid tobacco grows in Birheenia, not like this miserable weed. I thank your countrymen for what little of it I have had." He leaned back and clasped one hand behind his head, the cigarette sending a rill of blue smoke into the air toward the candelabra. "I will take your president's letter and have it translated, sending copies to Chihuahua, Madrid, and to our boundary commissioner in New Orleans. Also our *encargado de negocios* in Philadelphia. I can tell you now what they think. What my government thinks. Or, to put the supreme touch on it, what His Most Catholic Majesty thinks."

"About the boundaries, you mean," Freeman said.

"We shall come to the boundaries. First, about the Purchase itself. We do not recognize the validity of that transaction. France had no right to sell that vast area to the United States. I believe she had specifically agreed with my government not to do so. In our eyes there was no sale, so talk of boundaries is dubious. Still, let us speak of them. I ask this question: What is your president's view of the western boundary of this illegal purchase?"

"The Stony Mountains, without a doubt," Freeman replied.

"What kind of boundary is that! Do you mean the Sangre de Cristos? Or the range beyond that? Or the one even farther west? Do you imagine the Stony Mountains to be a single *sierra*, like a fish's backbone, that makes a sharp dividing line?"

"We came to find that out," Freeman said. "Now I ask you a question, señor. What is the southwestern boundary of the Purchase?"

The governor inspected his fingernails while considering his answer. "The Arkansa River. No question."

"We say it is the Red. No question."

"*A dios!* Again you have a misconception. Do you think the

Red River comes nicely up to the mountains and makes a neat corner like a box? In truth, the Red has its beginning far to the east of here, rising in many little streams so that we scarcely could say where it starts."

If that were true, Rafe thought, then Freeman's trip up the Red last year would have led to nothing. He wondered if Alencaster knew that Freeman had conducted such an expedition.

Freeman moved to another subject quickly. "Let's talk about the northern boundary, Señor Governor. Where do you say that one is?"

Alencaster shook his head. "The guessing game is over because neither of us knows enough. Even if we had a map that we could spread here on the table, we could not comprehend the boundaries because no man has been there. How many square leagues? We are all a little bit ignorant. I have a dispatch from General Salcedo, the commander general, stating that the territory of New Spain includes all the land south of the Missouri River from where it joins the Platte. But you and I know that the Missouri runs *north* in that region. Or do we?"

"We do," Rafe cut in. "Captain Lewis has been there to confirm it."

Alencaster looked at him in surprise. "Now I am debating two Americans! But this Captain Lewis, his name is familiar. We sent an emissary to stop him not once but three times. Then my militiamen went out to look for Teniente Pike for six whole weeks, in vain, and later another search party found him. We intercepted your Red River expedition before it had gone very far. Isn't that correct, *amigo?*" He winked at Freeman.

So he knows, Rafe realized. But Freeman, giving nothing away, only said "possibly."

"Here is my government's position. If we do not concede that the Purchase is legal, and if we do not know the boundaries, and if we feel the Americans are greedily eager to take everything, anyway — then we have no recourse but to resist. And those are my orders. Some of my compatriots are despairing already. They say: '*No es posible poner puertas al campo.*' You cannot put gates in an open field. But I will put the gates here and here and here, wherever the Americans try to enter, as long as I am ordered to do it."

The governor's position was disarmingly reasonable from his

point of view. He seemed to Rafe an honest public official who had been decent to them under exasperating circumstances. It was news that he had tried to head off Lewis and Clark. Did Jefferson know it?

Alencaster broke into the moment of quiet with a laugh. "We drink now! Then I take you to your quarters."

The *presidio* where the Spanish troops were garrisoned lay behind the governor's palace, the entire complex forming a hollow square. His military status drew a private room for Wilkinson but not for his waiter, who was consigned to barracks. Rafe and Freeman had an adjoining room. They were not under guard and were free to move about the compound and into the village. Alencaster seemed perplexed and unsure of how to handle the problem they had presented him. He undoubtedly was awaiting instructions from Chihuahua.

Wilkinson spoke often of Smith and the men left behind in the cove. Freeman predicted trouble getting home under winter conditions, if they were released. Rafe spent hours with his journals and specimens until the villagers began to realize that a new doctor had come to town. There was no civilian *médico*. The military detachment had its own physician who kept to himself, in the little hospital near the barracks, and seemed not to recognize Rafe as a professional peer.

One morning a man with wife and child were waiting outside the door of Rafe's quarters. Snow had fallen and they were shivering, although the woman's *reboso* seemed an ample wrap and the man's coat was coarse and heavy.

"*Tengo el dolor aquí,*" the woman said, pointing to her breast. "*Tengo fiebre,*" the man said, indicating his flushed and feverish cheeks. While Wilkinson and Freeman went out for an extended breakfast, Rafe treated them both and checked the infant, who seemed well. After that episode it was arranged for Rafe to hold a morning sick call in a back room of the *cantina* facing the town plaza. Fernandez translated for the male patients first, then his sweetheart — a lithe and dark-haired girl name Elena — came in and translated for the women and children. Elena said she had learned English at the church school.

"You are fine *médico*," she told Rafe after the first day's patients had gone. "I like all *inglés.*"

"I thought you called us *gringos*," Rafe teased.

"Only some. The traders who do not bathe." There were at least two so-called Americans in town, both French traders who had become citizens with the Purchase. Freeman and Wilkinson spoke with them often.

Fernandez was always about, as any devoted *novio* should be, and there were good times among them. Elena brought memories of Callie, whose face was now growing dimmer in Rafe's fantasies. Sometimes he substituted Elena's face. One day he gave her Burgoo's flute, a gift she truly admired. There was a padre, she said, who could teach her to play it.

About two weeks after his arrival — Rafe thought it must be early November but had lost count of the days — Alencaster sent for him with orders to come alone to his quarters. The governor's rooms were even darker than before, as if the late autumn sun had tired of trying to penetrate the stubborn panes of mica. But a corner fireplace now glowed bright with chunks of aromatic mesquite. Rafe was offered a cup of chocolate, darker and sweeter than the pallid drink of his childhood.

"You do not take *cigarrillos*. I remember that," Alencaster said. "How is your Spanish by now?"

"Worse, I think. My accent is good enough to deceive people into thinking I am fluent. So when I say three or four words, they respond with a hundred."

"I speak with Mr. Freeman and the teniente every day or so, and always ask them to be patient. I hope they tell you that."

We aren't patient, damn it. Rafe nodded in acknowledgment.

"I have a delicate problem which I do not wish to take to the garrison doctor. It would oblige me if you would consider the matter. It is necessary for you to be very —" He groped for the word.

"*Discreto?*"

"*Sí. Muy discreto.* The district commander of my military has been — to make a little play on words here — rather *indiscreto* in his social life. His recreational life. Do you understand? He is very uncomfortable and fearful, and does not wish to consult that old fool of a garrison doctor for obvious reasons."

That night Rafe made this entry in his journal: "A patient with a primary syphilitic ulcer, ungranulated, callous edges slightly elevated on body of penis. Phymosis & profuse discharge. Mercurial ointment to be rubbed daily, 3 or 4 drams; as much calomel to be taken as can be tolerated. Bread & milk poultice for the ulcer."

Rafe was becoming well known in the plaza now. It was a rectangle of bare soil, without a tree or shrub or any bench to soften the view. The New Mexicans only came here to mingle. In their private moments they turned away from the plaza, living in their hollow-square homes with a courtyard or patio opening into the street. Flat-roofed structures of adobe, the inside walls plastered with mud and whitewash. The national garb of the men seemed to be shapeless trousers, loose jackets, and low-crowned hats. The women wore skirts and their colorful *reboso* shawls. The Indians from the country pueblos kept to themselves, dressing more and more like their Spanish *conquistadores* and festooning themselves with jewelry.

As he strolled across the plaza, Rafe felt the December sun lay a touch of warmth as well as light upon his shoulders. Near the center of the square, three young men were playing guitars and singing, their *sombreros* hanging on their backs. Indians stood about in silence, offering silver ornaments and fried bread for sale. Children played in the dust and mothers ran to gather them up for fear of their catching cold. *"Un resfriado terrible!"* one distraught young mother predicted, as she bent to rescue a startled child from the evils of the season. She looked at Rafe for a nod of approval at her prudence. Some of the children ran to him for a pat on the head, and men greeted him with cries of *"Hola!"*

He knew he had only to step into the *cantina* for free drinks in any quantity, but he had decided to explore. He crossed to the south side of the plaza, turned east toward the newly renovated Church of Saint Francis, then swung south until he reached the creek that came down from the eastern mountains. The birds were old friends, as if all the species he had found in the north had come to Santa Fe for the cold weather. The black-billed magpie, mountain chickadee, robin, yellow-eyed blackbird, finches, juncoes — he knew them all. The song of a mourning dove might have been coming from the trees outside his bedroom window at Fox Run in the early hours of day.

Santa Fe Creek was a botanical surprise, and Rafe longed to collect an armload of specimens. The governor had showed some reluctance to encourage his collecting, as if the matter had never arisen before but was not worth writing to Chihuahua about. Along the warm sides of the little ravine, where green plants had not yet been struck down by frost, Rafe could not resist cramming a few specimens into his pocket. He found a *Geranium,* a *Senecio,* and a strange *Dodecatheon.* A sort of needle grass, standing in tufts, seemed new to him — and so did a low barberry with fruit the size of currants.

He had found a warm place to sit and make some notes, when Fernandez came riding out to look for him.

"You are wanted," he called as he pulled his horse to a halt.

"Someone sick?"

"No, but the governor wants to see you and the other Americans. A woman in the plaza said you had come this way."

Rafe climbed up behind Fernandez for a ride back to the *palacio.* Freeman and Wilkinson were already there, seated before Alencaster's table.

"Welcome, welcome," Alencaster said, sounding rather more amiable than usual. "I feel somewhat guilty, señores," he began. "Please remember that when you arrived I was suspicious of you and a little angry that I had spent so many *reales* sending my men to find you. So I must apologize for having withheld this letter from you." His hand lay across a sheet of paper. With a flourish he picked it up and thrust it at Lieutenant Wilkinson, who gasped in surprise.

"My father's handwriting!"

"Read it and pass it on," the governor said.

His Excellency Governor Alencaster: *New Orleans. 1 Aug. 1807.*

Had I perceived the events which were to be put in train by my dispatching Captain Pike in your general direction, I should have ordered him to be more circumspect. By recent mail he has advised me of his arrival in the United States, to which place he was courteously escorted by a detail of His Majesty's troops. Other letters of mine and no doubt of the President will deal further with the Pike episode.

I apprehend another problem which I hasten to lay before you. My son

James, lieutenant of infantry, left this place in the spring en route to the upper reaches of the Arkansa pursuant to instructions from Mr. Jefferson. Your government cannot have been ignorant of his tour. As he was particularly attached to Captain Pike and would be anxious to have news of him, it is possible that he may have led his party near your boundary and been taken up. Should this be the case, I beg Your Excellency to believe that my son's expedition was strictly of a literary nature, meant by the President to advance the general knowledge. You would bestow a personal favor upon me if you would release Lieutenant Wilkinson and the two civilian observers who accompany him, should they have entered your sphere of influence.

Should Dr. Raphael Bailey be with the detachment, kindly advise him that his army appointment with the rank of surgeon's mate has been forwarded to St. Louis, where he will present himself to the commanding officer of Cantonment Bellefontaine at the earliest opportunity.

I beg to remain, Sir,

Yr. Most Huml. Servt.
Ja. Wilkinson
Commanding, U.S. Army

Alencaster smoked complacently until all three had read the letter. "The commandant general in Chihuahua has complied with General Wilkinson's request, although reluctantly. You are free to go. I am instructed to say that this generosity reflects our esteem for General Wilkinson, who has been most cooperative with us in other matters. We shall be making it plain in letters to President Jefferson, however, that Spain is determined to resist these incursions."

Freeman came down at once to specifics. "Will I be allowed to take my maps and geographical notes?"

"*Ciertamente.* We have made copies for ourselves, of course."

Wilkinson said nothing. He reached for a *cigarrillo,* and a servant who had stood quietly by the fireplace brought a lighted taper. Then he paced about the room, silently smoking while Freeman discussed arrangements with the governor.

The party must return to the cove and rejoin Smith, then start down the Arkansa with great dispatch if the storms of January and February were to be avoided. A small escort would accompany them to the cove, taking a shipment of supplies to ease the expedition's return.

"There is one thing more," Alencaster said. "I congratulate Dr. Bailey on his new appointment and acknowledge that he is ordered to St. Louis at once. But 'at once' is a relative term, is it not? I don't think his new commanding officer would object if he stayed on for a while."

It's that awful syphilitic major.

"Why must I stay? I want to go with the others," Rafe said.

"Not what you might think," Alencaster said with the lift of an eyebrow. "I am sure you know about the new vaccine for smallpox. Slowly, too slowly, my government has come to believe in it. During the winter of 1782 this village lost nearly a hundred and fifty soldiers and townspeople to the pox. Now the commandant general has a new program. When we send our annual caravan to Chihuahua at the end of the year, we send several children to be vaccinated. Then they are brought back home with the cowpox pustules on their bodies, and we get from them the vaccine for the rest of the population. But the program is going poorly. Last year we did not succeed in getting the vaccine to 'take' in enough cases."

"Any midwife can do the vaccinating," Rafe insisted.

"I tried midwives and, of course, that good-for-nothing military doctor. And now I want Dr. Bailey. I am going to insist that you stay on and help us. We still have some vaccine — which we hope is alive — for you to start with. In the spring we shall have live vaccine coming back with the children of the caravan."

Freeman objected. "Surgeon's Mate Bailey might have a hard time on a trip alone to St. Louis. This is his first expedition."

Wilkinson had thumped his cigarette into the fireplace and now seemed very angry. "Rafe can have my waiter. He's an old hand. What do I need with a waiter? Holy Jesus! I'm just a kid with toy soldiers, playing under the watchful eye of his father. Growing up under a general's wing. If I come close to trouble, he steps in and stops the game. Take my waiter, Rafe, and welcome to him."

He left the room abruptly, and it seemed probable to Rafe that he was heading for the *cantina.*

The morning clinics continued. Wilkinson stayed in seclusion from the time of Alencaster's interview to the day of his departure, and Freeman had to make all the arrangements. Then Wilkinson, Freeman, and their escort left for the north with little notice. They carried a bundle of letters that Rafe had written to his father, the president, and "the officer commanding at Bellefontaine," promising to report for duty as soon as possible.

Freeman would see that the natural-history collections still at the cove were carried down to New Orleans, then shipped to St. Louis by the first keelboat in the spring.

"Please don't address them to Governor Lewis. Send them to Clark." *I'm getting paranoid.* Rafe had dreamed one night that Lewis had got hold of his specimens and weeded out those which duplicated his own. It shamed him to dream such a thing. He had no reason to think that Lewis was dishonest — merely troubled.

Rafe's only confidant now was Fernandez. They took their meals together, and Fernandez urged new foods upon him. The taste of ground chilies was in everything, Rafe decided, but he was beginning not to have heartburn after a large meal of *tamales, enchiladas,* or *chili con carne.* One of his woman patients, a fine cook, had made up a packet of chili powder for him to take home, containing *comino* and other mysterious herbs that now seemed pleasant on his tongue.

The vaccine saved from last year had lost its potency. Rafe tried in vain to induce cowpox in several adults and a couple of children. It was now obvious that no viable vaccine would be available until spring.

"You must go away soon," Fernandez said one day. "The governor's vaccination program can get along without you, no matter what he says. Sometimes I think he keeps you on to treat that fool major with the venereal disease. You cannot cure that one, so why stay?"

"He has a rash now," Rafe said. "I had hoped to see it improve. But you are right about the vaccine. The people of this place must learn to use it by themselves."

"Then you will go. I will help you."

The next day, Fernandez brought him a small but detailed map drawn on goatskin, showing a route leading northeast from Santa Fe and pointing diagonally toward the confluence of the Missouri and the Mississippi where St. Louis lay. It not only showed the rivers and streams he would cross — the Cimmaron, especially — but it located small springs or *ojos* where water and forage might be found. Apparently the route crossed the Arkansa somewhere above the Great Bend.

With a recklessness that Rafe feared might be costly later, Fernandez began to stockpile food and equipment in the house of Geronimo Lopez on the *cañón* road. Jonas Gardner, the waiter, helped when he could, one day slipping away to the Lopez house with Rafe's specimens and some medical supplies. Later he deposited a sack of *masa,* the corn flour that Rafe had come to like so well.

A few days after Christmas, Rafe slipped out of his quarters and walked to the Lopez house. Gardner had the horses ready: his black gelding bought from an Indian hostler, Rafe's little Mancha, and old Blue.

"That mule will be lucky to make it," Fernandez said. "He must be twenty years old."

"He's a Virginia mule. They just go on and on."

"No, my friend. Mules die like you and me. Please be very careful. *Vaya con Dios.*"

10

Winter Crossing to St. Louis

~~~~~~

IF THEY made it across the prairie, Rafe decided, it would be in
spite of their equipment. He and Gardner were encapsulated in
their own gear and the extras given them by their Spanish friends.
Rafe rode Mancha like the skipper of an overladen barge, a sack
of food across the saddle pommel, leather bags sagging at the
pony's withers, and a cluster of skin-wrapped miscellany bobbing
at the rump. Behind walked Blue, carrying the collections and
medical supplies with no hint in his gait that he knew he was
going home.

Equally burdened, Gardner's rangy mount bore his load with
a resigned looseness of tread and dullness of eye. The breath of
the men and horses, in the chill of a frosty morning, merged into
a veil of gray vapor that rose and hovered above them like a
swarm of summer gnats.

Their goal for the first day was to camp near, but not at, the
mission church and pueblo near the Pecos River east of Santa Fe.
By nighttime they were building a fire within sight of the old
relic, a vast adobe structure with twin towers, an adjoining *con-
vento,* and a three-story Indian dwelling that was falling into rubble like the church. Eddies of smoke, and an occasional figure
hurrying along beside the vine-draped walls of the complex, were
signs that the church of Nuestra Señora de Los Angeles de Por-
ciuncula was not yet a deserted ruin.

At the campfire, Gardner was talkative. "I understand you've
been ordained —" The statement ended abruptly, as if he had
meant to say "sir" and had deleted it.

"Are you speaking of my appointment to the army?"

"I notice you didn't call it a commission."

"Should I have?"

"Not exactly. You'll be a warrant officer."

"And not a real officer?"

"Not according to most commissioned officers I've served with." Gardner had rinsed their camp kettle in a stream and filled it with water for coffee. "Don't worry, most commissioned officers aren't worth a bean fart."

"Any exceptions?"

"Well, Lieutenant Smith, maybe. He was always decent to me and I wouldn't mind serving under him. But that Wilkinson is a sniveling toad. In civilian life you wouldn't notice it — might even get to liking him — but in the army he's a gone case."

By the next night, with the weather still holding, they camped near the village of San Miguel — a scattering of huts dominated by a new church surrounded by fallow fields. They bought corn for the horses, blue tortillas for themselves, and filled their kettle with steaming pork and chilies at the hearth of a farm family. From this point their route would lead them northwest and away from the Sangre de Cristos.

The landmarks, as the days passed, appeared much as they were noted on Rafe's map. The pocket compass he had always carried, but never used, now reassured him. The curious formation that Fernandez had called *El Montecillo* was sighted, duly noted, and passed by the travelers. Days later, they reached a double-peaked aggregation of rocks that the map called *El Conejo*, the rabbit, perhaps because its promontories suggested two long ears.

The streams were making ice at the margins but none was frozen over, and clumps of buffalo grass were ample forage for the animals. Thus far the weather had been perfect. "It can't last," Gardner predicted. "Probably not," Rafe agreed. The mountains had long since sunk below the horizon.

One morning the sun rose but dimly and the sky was milky from one horizon to another. The horses noted the change first, nickering and snorting, breaking now and then into an unaccustomed trot.

"That change you mentioned," Rafe said, pointing to the pallid, orange sun. "I can smell it now."

They were looking for a place called *Ojo Frio*. Fernandez had promised not only water, but also grass for the mounts and sheltering rocks for a campsite, at the Cold Spring.

In midafternoon the first flakes came down, tentative and sparse, just a hint of snow which stopped after a few minutes. The northwest wind heightened and turned colder. Long before the snow had thickened to a steady, slanting screen that blurred their vision, Rafe and Gardner had sighted the spring. Seen through the whiteness, it was a grassy hollow broken by piles of soft sandstone, and at the base of one sheer stone face lay a stream bed that had widened into a small pond. A few scrubby willows would provide branches for shelter, and gaunt greasewood snags would burn for warmth. By the time darkness had fallen, Rafe had tethered the animals among the rocks and Gardner had built a hearty, sputtering fire.

"Everything a boy could want," Rafe said as he scorched a length of dried beef on a stick.

"Not this boy," Gardner said, snorting. His feet had been cold all day and now he sat with his boot soles pushed almost into the fire.

Not waiter material. Rafe decided that Gardner was not even soldier material. "How'd you wind up in uniform?"

"Just by bungling my life all the way along. My father is a silversmith in New York and I was learning that trade when I decided to enroll in the College of New Jersey. That didn't work out — I was a terrible scholar — so I tried for an army commission. My father thought he had the secretary of war in his pocket, and maybe he did, but the commission never got past the floor of the Senate. Advise and consent. They forgot to consent. It made me so damned mad that I enlisted one day. Ended up in New Orleans, and when Wilkinson heard I had gone to his school he got me posted to him as a waiter. And that's how I learned to hate officers. I'm a lackey, a spy, a bootlick, asslick, and scullery maid. My tour of duty is over when I get back to New Orleans, thank God."

They sat by the fire without speaking, until a shift in the wind brought a gust around the corner of their rocky shelter and scattered the live coals. Rafe scraped them back into a pile with a greasewood stick.

"I suspect you could teach me a lot about army life."

"Stay away from it. Decline your appointment and get the hell back into civilized society. You aren't like them."

"Don't know who you mean by *them*. They're a diverse lot. I don't think there's a *them* that you could put your finger on."

"You haven't had to wash their dirty underdrawers."

"Do you actually do that?"

"Hell, doctor, who else? There aren't any washerwomen out here."

They found four inches of snow on the ground the next morning. The wind had died, however, and the sun felt faintly warm on their faces. Before breaking camp, Rafe scratched a message on a flat, chalky surface of the rock that had sheltered them. He tried to manage *Paso por aquí*, but had to abbreviate it to *P.p.a. R. Bailey & J. Gardner 1808*. Then, with one backward glance at his artistry, he led out on foot and Gardner followed. It took several tugs on the reins to get the animals started.

Studying his map, Rafe decided they had two choices. They could continue traveling northwest and finally strike the Arksana, but that was a long trek and the map showed no water. Also, there was the risk of bearing too far east and missing his cache of specimens at Pike's Rock. If they went due north they would strike the river much earlier and have some wood and water, even if it meant traveling more miles. Gardner agreed. So Rafe drew a line from the Cold Spring to the Arkansa, straight north, and started off with a quick glance at his compass.

"Good-bye, hypotenuse," Gardner said. "Old Euclid would call us crazy. What's the good of inventing a hypotenuse if nobody uses it?" He was still enjoying the opportunity to castigate the officer class. "Wait till the first time some ignorant captain orders a sick man back to duty after you've taken him off the roster. Wait till a drunken officer tries to commandeer your last bottle of medicinal brandy, and even dips into the raisins and ginger, or whatever you've laid up for the sick bastards."

"You're forgetting I'll have a sword. I can defend the brandy."

"Ever seen a surgeon's mate's sword? About as long as your prick. You couldn't even lance a boil with it."

By the end of the following day, Rafe was thoroughly tired of

Gardner's caviling banter. The cold was severe and there had been less forage than expected. Gardner had shot an old buffalo and they had packed up the tongue and some hump meat for future use. Mainly, however, they were eating sparsely from the diminishing *masa* and salt pork.

Rafe glanced back at Blue, limping slightly and hanging back more and more against the lead rope. "I'd waggle my ears at you if I could, old chap." They say you lose track of time on a trip like this, he told himself. *So what day is it?* January, he was certain of, but not the day.

The glimmering snow eased to the ground with a fluttery grace, and blobs of it clung like rabbit tails to the tips of the greasewood branches. Rafe gasped as the wind stole his breath and the biting air attacked him everywhere. It got into his sleeves and past the turned-up collar of his coat. It pulled at his ankles, even through his heavy socks and boots.

Gardner had been walking less and less; his horse felt the strain. While waiting for them to catch up for the third time in an hour, Rafe thought of frostbite. How do you treat it? *Don't think about that.* Then Gardner came up with him, riding his mount like a teetering bag of potatoes. "I think I will just lie down and very seriously die," he said. And he laughed.

When at last they approached the Arkansa, sand hills appeared and the land became more broken by ravines and patches of dark, windswept vegetation. They moved sometimes along the crest of a sand butte, sometimes along the side, avoiding deep snow and trying to nurse the animals along. It had been a good crossing from the Cold Spring, Rafe thought, considering their lack of experience. A Virginia doctor and a New York silversmith. He nodded at Gardner, who waved with more than his usual animation when the valley of the Arkansa came into view. Scaphoid, Rafe thought, the old medical term for a boat-shaped configuration coming suddenly to him from one of Dr. Wistar's lectures. A boat-shaped valley with a frozen twist of river in it, and a fringe of sticklike willows on either side.

That night along the river, when they had chopped a hole in the ice for the animals and bedded themselves on a sandbar with a willow windbreak, the doctor and silversmith sat on a cushion of boughs and watched the fire. Half asleep and cozily warm,

Rafe fantasized an appearance he would someday make before the monthly meeting of the American Philosophical Society.

So you see, gentlemen, altitude or elevation — with its variation not only in annual rainfall but in nighttime temperatures and total sunlight — has an effect on plant life as strong, perhaps, as variations in latitude and longitude. The overlapping that you see between the specimens I have laid out on this table, and those reported to have been brought back by Lewis and Clark, is striking evidence. My own findings will be reported in detail in the work now in press. Captain Lewis will publish his own studies later for the future enlightenment of the scientific world.

"Now I feel as if I'm going home," Gardner declared. "Couldn't quite sense it out there in the barrens."

"The river seems like an old friend. Behind us to the west is the mouth of the Purgatory where we fought the Comanches. Up ahead is Pike's Rock and the Great Bend." Rafe was glad for a chance to see the same vegetation in winter condition that he had seen in summer bloom.

They stayed on the south bank until they found that the north side was flatter, easier. The weather was kind. A small buffalo herd provided a generously fat cow.

By the time they had sighted Pike's Rock it was apparent that Gardner was not well. He seemed weak — did not like to walk and lead his horse — and his finger joints had begun to swell. It was not until he showed Rafe his ulcerated gums and a couple of loosened teeth that his ailment became identifiable: he was suffering from scurvy.

They rode directly to the great monolith and found a crevice at the southeastern base which would give them the most shelter they had enjoyed since Cold Spring. Gardner brought in willow branches and dry grass, to transform the crevice into a comfortable shelter, and dragged deadwood from a gully to stockpile beside the campfire. Rafe rode over to the site of his cache, a pile of rocks with a drift of dirty snow along the north edge. Dismounting, he rolled a few of the rocks aside and poked at the soil underneath with his hunting knife. He was not surprised to find it frozen solid.

He would get no help from Gardner in digging up his specimens until the scurvy was better. Too bad his little keg of lime juice, like that which Captain Cook had used to doctor his sailors, had never reached Louisville. He counted off in his mind the foodstuffs that he and Gardner carried: cornmeal, cured pork, coffee, tea, salt, and whisky. Nothing in that assortment even suggested the essence of freshness, of fruity acidity, that scurvy seemed to call for. He thought of the cellars of home, crammed with red apples and great, round cabbages.

Foraging down along the river, he found a patch of wild roses whose bare and bristly stems were topped by bright red berries, or hips. When he chewed one he found it astringent and seedy. But the berries were a fresh fruit, of sorts, and he decided to try them on Gardner.

"Chew them and swallow them," he ordered when he had returned to the rock. Gardner put one in his mouth and spat it out quickly.

"God, doc, that's a bad one. Give me a sweet one."

"They're all bad ones. Just chew some more." He made an infusion of the hips for the evening meal and drank a cupful, as did Gardner. "You're right. They're pretty bad."

They compared beards. Rafe's was darker than his hair but still definitely blond, while Gardner's was thin and black and grew not at all on his pale, thin throat.

Next day, he left Gardner in camp while he returned to his cache. He supposed that together they could hack away the frozen earth, but he decided that a fire would help to thaw it faster. He spent the morning dragging willow snags from the riverside and stacking them on the area from which he had rolled the stones. Using dry grass for tinder, and his flint-and-steel fire starter to produce sparks, he made a blaze about four feet across and fed it until a base of coals had started to accumulate. Then he returned to their shelter.

"The Indians will think you're calling a council," Gardner complained. "Every snot-nosed, shitty Indian in the world will come drifting in here to get warm and then scalp us."

"I don't think so. With no more buffalo than we've seen, and as cold as it is, we can hope there won't be any Indians. I must have those buried specimens. Everything I collected from the Three

Forks to this place last summer is tied up in deerskin under that fire. But just in case, we can take turns climbing the rock about once an hour to see if we're alone."

While the afternoon sun still warmed the air, Gardner spent an hour laying out their firearms and checking their ammunition. His own rifle, army issue, was in good condition. Rafe's little birding musket did not really count, but Fernandez had made him bring along an old *escopeta,* a Spanish musket with a British lock and a crude stock probably carved in Santa Fe.

"I know a man once shot a buffalo bull with three balls," Gardner said, and waited for Rafe to acknowledge his play on words. "A bull with three balls," he repeated.

"I understand drollery," Rafe said, as he rode off to feed his fire. He thought Gardner's health was improving.

A day later they scraped away a portion of the ashes and coals to test the ground. It had softened to a depth of six inches.

"Not ready yet," Gardner said.

"No, but we can dig away what's thawed and put a new fire in the resulting pit."

"I'm a waiter. We don't get assigned to fatigue duty."

"Neither do surgeon's mates. Start scraping."

With an axe, a pan, and a couple of knives, they worked all afternoon to remove the traces of the old fire and dig away the thawed soil. The new fire was better than the first, being submerged below ground level and sheltered from the wind.

The depression became a hole two days later. Gardner, feeling much stronger, showed Rafe his pink and healthy mouth and set about to help with the final digging. Two large packets came out of the cache, seemingly intact but with rotted leather fastenings. Rafe was inclined to retie the bundles as they were, but Gardner suggested he sort through the material to see if any decay had set in.

"Men of science are never practical," he said. The plant specimens, pressed between sheets of absorbent paper, were in good condition but could be improved by a day of drying in the thin prairie air. Some of the preserved bird and animal specimens were in poorer shape.

"This one smells a bit blinky," Gardner said.

"Blinky?"

"Sort of gamey. Like a grouse that's hung too long."

Most of the collection was intact, however, and Rafe was able to rewrap the specimens in the same deerskin that had protected them for six months.

"Lucky for Blue they aren't very heavy," Gardner said. "That old coon gets more swaybacked every day."

They left the security of the great rock and moved eastward the next morning, following the river that was now taking them northeastward toward the Great Bend. Gardner's recovery was so remarkable that Rafe had made several pages of notes in his journal about the case. Gardner had learned to like the mouth-puckering rose hips, but he had fallen silent again, hours on end.

"We must be halfway to St. Louis," Rafe said as they rode side by side.

Gardner said nothing.

"Bull with three balls," Rafe said.

The soldier managed half a grin. "I feel like I have four from all this riding, and all of them sore."

In camp at the Great Bend, where they were to leave the river and set out toward St. Louis, they found the expedition's old campfires. Five circles of ash, now plastered into the sand by the rains and snows. They sat by their own fire, knowing that tomorrow there would be no trail to follow when they veered from the river.

"Wish you were still Wilkinson's waiter?" Rafe asked.

"I don't miss the young crupper in the least."

Before they let the fire go, Gardner asked for a sheet of paper. Rafe had nothing to offer but a blank page torn from his journal. He watched Gardner scribbling at what might have been a letter home, to be posted in St. Louis.

"It'll be pretty stale by the time you mail it."

Just before bedtime, Rafe broke out his bottle of whisky and shared it. He thought it tasted of Virginia husking bees, or Saturday afternoons in the Chestnut Street taverns of Philadelphia. He plunked a palmful of snow into the cup and swirled it.

They had learned to sleep near each other for warmth, with a buffalo robe beneath them and another on top, their feet toward the fire. Rafe looked at his watch as he crawled in beside Gardner. If it was right, the time was about 8:00 P.M. — too early for grown folk to be in bed. He wore his fur cap and all his clothing except the boots, and through the narrow slit between cap brim and the robe's edge he looked high into the starry night. The horses and his mule were picketed close at hand, huddled close to the rocky wall. The howling of a wolf was multiplied into a chorus that seemed to be everywhere, then subsided utterly. His beard itched.

Cantonment Bellefontaine was said to lie along the very lower reaches of the Missouri, just before it joined the Mississippi. About ten miles above St. Louis, he figured. He supposed the commander would be expecting him about now. How long, he wondered, before he could go down to St. Louis and see about his specimens? And talk at last with Meriwether Lewis and William Clark?

Toward morning he began to dream his old, recurrent dream, that Lewis had somehow laid claim to his collections and added them to his own. His beautiful Louisiana cuckoo and those bright little birds of the mountains, and the plants he had so carefully pressed to crispness between papers. He was a stranger in St. Louis, walking the streets and looking for Governor Lewis, asking for him, lost so thoroughly that he could not even find the cobblestone wharf that edged the town. Worse still, the towns-folk in tonight's dream were laughing at his uniform. The coat was too small. The chapeau bras was crushed and tattered, without a plume. The sword was a tiny dagger.

He awoke at dawn and felt cold. Immediately he sensed that Gardner was not beside him. He felt for him to be sure, then sat up quickly, the robe dropping to his lap and letting body heat escape from his chest and shoulders.

Gardner was gone and so was his horse. The fire was burning briskly — Gardner had nudged it to life and fed it — and before the bed of flaming coals a stick had been propped upright between two stones. At the top of the stick, a folded piece of paper reflected the flicker of the thriving fire. Rafe reached out for it and retreated to the shelter of the robe to read Gardner's message:

Doctor —

> *To save argument I am starting down the river before you are awake. Don't call it desertion. I am only rejoining my unit at New Orleans. I am leaving you most of the food, as I will be among the Osages at Three*

Forks long before you reach St. Louis. If there are still some around.
Please be wary of that Spanish musket and remember that the rammer
slides out of its bracket if you are not careful.

Gardner

Too dispirited to walk, Rafe left the camp astride Mancha, leading the faltering Blue and looking frequently at his map to verify that the trail now shifted more eastward. As Mancha's hooves stabbed through the crust of snow, and the little horse shook himself to settle the newly shifted burden into something he could carry hour upon hour, Rafe glanced often toward the receding Arkansa. It would soon be out of his view, dipping down to warmer country, the cypress standing in the fetid bayous, the moss hanging to the water's edge.

Gardner must have forgotten that the Osage village at the Three Forks was just a hunting camp. *Serves the bastard right if he misses them.*

He stopped early in the afternoon because Mancha had sighted a patch of brittle grass and made for it at once. The two animals tore at the tangled blades while he stomped about in the snow to warm his feet and chewed on a slice of dried buffalo hump. Don't ever think your horses can eat snow, he told some imagined tenderfoot in a St. Louis tavern. If they don't find real water they'll go without.

After one more dry camp there was a stream every day. At times he camped by these watercourses, breaking the ice, because they provided not only drink but a scant gift of spindly firewood. Sometimes his shelter was only a ravine made by a creek, and occasionally there was no shelter at all. *One big blizzard will finish us off.* He waited fearfully for it, pressing on eastward, hunched against the bitter wind.

When a wolf approached the fire one night, he shot it and tried to eat some of the flesh next morning. He gulped down one mouthful of the flank meat, scorched over the fire, but could take no more. He munched on the rose hips and tore at a strip of dried buffalo meat with aching teeth. A long-legged hare, killed at close range with his small musket, was more succulent fare that lasted him a whole day. He skinned it hastily, glad that he did not feel obliged to preserve the hide intact as a specimen; he had another one.

One day at dusk, during a nearly opaque snowstorm which lasted but a short time, he became aware of dark forms on the move, ahead and to the rear. He was making his way through a herd of silent buffalo. Too cold to get the rifle out of Blue's pack, and too anxious about finding a haven soon, he let the hulking beasts go on their way.

His thoughts flicked back to Fox Run Farm in winter. His father and the hands would be skimming ice off the stream and pounding it into a solid chunk in the icehouse. Pork shoulders and hams curing in the smokehouse. He could almost smell the kitchen where his favorite foods were ready: corn dodger, beaten biscuits, grape conserve, tomato relish, red-eyed gravy, grits and butter, spoon bread, greens, yams. Summer foods now: watermelons were fine when cooled in a tub in the springhouse, but they were not bad just pulled off the vine and carried over to a fence and busted on the top rail. Warm watermelon juice ran down his chin and neck like pink wine, and dried to stiffness on his shirt.

Back to the pantry and kitchen again and again: catfish chowder, chestnut soup, gumbo thick with oysters and okra. Oh, God, send some steak and ham pie. Toss down a wild duck with mushroom catsup. Kindly pass a bit more of that jugged hare. Or, if nothing else, just some apples, please. A couple of yellow New Town pippins. Good keepers. You're out of those? Give me a rambo, then, or a Rhode Island greening. You say it's too late — they're all made up into pies? — don't apologize, God. Just one more slice and then I really must stop.

He first believed he would make the crossing successfully when the land became more rolling, better vegetated, and when he stumbled into a small grove of trees after dark that provided a welcome windbreak. On awakening in the morning, he saw that the trees were elms. He broke off a sliver of bark and checked for alternating layers of cream- and chocolate-colored fibres that identified the species. American elm. An eastern tree. Sometime during his head-down shuffling across the plains he had crossed the invisible meridian that separated East from West.

Mancha and Blue were hungry and ailing. Rafe discarded some of the heavier items from his gear and, finally, after Mancha had fallen once, he sacrificed his case of medical instruments. He relieved Blue of some mineral samples ("Away with these damned rocks, my good old companion") and a ten-pound bag of salt which somehow had ridden all the way without being opened.

Willows along the streams were taller, stronger, and had been joined by cottonwoods and a varied underbrush. The air seemed heavier and damper. In the second substantial grove of elms, doubly welcome because they grew on the south side of a sandy ridge that broke the wind, he made camp one night and dined on a hare and a couple of quail. The wet firewood sizzled. When a draft of air swirled down from the crest of the ridge and whistled in the treetops, he thought he sensed a hint of warmth in the breeze. He sniffed it. Nothing there, really, to speak of spring, and yet — just maybe.

In the morning, Mancha lay dead.

Rafe and Blue shared the security of the grove all the next day. The weather was kind, with little wind, and a stream below the trees provided water for them both. The problem was Mancha's carcass, which Rafe looked at as seldom as possible. He moved his campsite a few yards so he could at least pretend during meals that it was not there. He made a special effort to collect small game, because the dark and awesome thought had come to him that he might have to sustain himself on Mancha's flesh. He killed two rabbits and set the meat to dry. He was lucky to find a large raccoon which had ventured out to forage along the shallow creek. On a southern slope, warmed by the sun, he was able to dig deep enough to bring up the bulbous roots of a few ground apples, *Solanum* species, which he found not too bitter except just under the peel.

That night he dreamed he was fending off an enormous grizzly. All the horror of his encounter on the mountain was gathered into a few tense moments of nightmare, and he awoke to find that wolves were gathering near him — drawn by the presence of Mancha's remains. He kicked the fire to brilliance, sent a rifle shot into the darkness, and lay awake for the rest of the night while whining, yipping wolves crept closer to the grove. He would have to push on in the morning.

Soon after sunrise, he and Blue were on the trail. When they had gone a few hundred yards, Rafe left the mule and hurried back to cut a souvenir lock of Mancha's mane — telling himself it was for Jefferson. When he resumed his march, Blue's progress was even slower because of the added weight that Mancha had carried before.

He saw the Missouri River first from a point of timbered land in the curve of a sweeping bend, which the river made as it swung from northwest to east. On the opposite shore, the usual fringe of willows and cottonwoods began at the water's edge and reached back across the bottomland. Beyond, on higher ground, was the familiar skyline made by leafless oaks, hickories, and hackberries. At home in Virginia, confronted by such a scene, he would have seen a dozen columns of blue smoke rising from the chimneys of settlers in the hollows. There was no smoke here to soften the horizon line.

The Missouri was not a river that others could be compared to: he often had thought that parts of the lower Arkansa resembled the Ohio — and parts of the Ohio reminded him of the Potomac — but this was a new breed. Awesome power beneath a lid of gray ice. He saw the jumbled tree trunks along the banks and could imagine the roil and crunch of flood time that had tossed them there. For an instant he envied Lewis and Clark, who had toiled to the ultimate wellsprings of this surly monster.

Realizing that Blue had been on the move for hours and would chill soon, Rafe sought shelter by descending to lower land along the river. He found a ravine — a dry creek bed — and led the mule through it until they encountered a clay wall that cut the wind. The fire he built soon burned hot and steady, untouched by the breeze; he pulled off Blue's packs and made camp for the night.

Lately, Blue had been lying down to sleep instead of standing in his usual way, and the change worried Rafe. It was good, though, to feel the moist warmth of the great body when man and animal stretched out together on a pile of dry leaves. *Goodnight, sweet and hairy prince.*

In the morning he found that by felling a tree across the ravine he could produce a kind of canopy. When he had trimmed away the unwanted branches with his axe, and laid a thatchwork of brush across the top, he had made a tolerably secure haven. He hoped that the campfire just outside the shelter, if urged on with frequent feedings of dry wood, might send a bit of heat into it.

His purpose in staying by the river was to rest his bones, and Blue's, and to think. Blue had taken to sleeping late, not scrambling to his feet until long after Rafe had stoked the fire and made tea in his canteen cup. When led out of the shelter to a patch of wiry foxtail, he showed little desire to eat.

Rafe guessed that they were still two hundred miles from St. Louis and knew that Blue was the key to the completion of the journey. A healthy mule could sustain himself on the dormant weeds, but Blue needed cracked corn and sweet, green pasture grass. To coax him into eating, Rafe spent hours cracking acorns, digging roots, and scraping off the inner bark of cottonwood branches. Blue liked the cottonwood.

"There's plenty of it, but you've got to learn to strip it off for yourself," he said as he brought in another armload.

As for his own food, there was plenty. He ate the acorns spurned by Blue and shot a red squirrel or cottontail rabbit every day. His tea was reduced to crumbs in the bag, and he hated that.

Because he had seen no Indians since leaving Sante Fe, he took no precautions, supposing that he would be out of luck in any case if he encountered an unfriendly band. The appearance, then, of the two Indians was a stark surprise.

They stood just beyond the campfire, the morning sun at their backs, their muskets trained upon him. He sat beside the fire, holding a cup of tea and feeling completely off guard. His own musket was leaning against Blue's packs at the back of the shelter. The men were not Osages, he knew. Their horses tethered on the bank of the ravine looked fresh and well kept. Pawnee horses. The men were young — perhaps his own age — and because he was seated they did not bother to take a menacing stance.

Rafe did the right thing. He extended his steaming cup toward one of the men, who declined with a shake of the head but lowered his musket. The other lowered his. Rafe got cautiously to his feet, forcing a smile, and extended his hand.

"Friend," he said. "American friend."

Neither man spoke until they had warmed themselves and sat down. Rafe marveled at their sparse winter dress, for they were bare from the waist up except for buffalo robes thrown loosely over their shoulders. They offered him a lighted pipe, and no one spoke until it had been sucked at noisily by all three.

"Where come from?" the older of the two asked.

"Santa Fe."

The Indians exchanged blank glances. They doubted him.

"Spanish would not let that."

He would try some names on them. "Alencaster. Governor Alencaster. Sotelo, a soldier. Fernandez, also a soldier. All my friends."

One of the Pawnees found a sturdy twig and scraped a patch of leaves down to the bare earth. He handed the twig to Rafe and motioned for him to draw with it.

Rafe jabbed a hole. "Santa Fe." He scraped a line. "Mountains, very high." Then a long, sinuous line. "Arkansa River." Finally he drew a diagonal line that represented what he supposed had been his route. Pointing to the Spanish musket behind him, he said, *"Escopeta.* From my friend Fernandez."

The men spoke briefly to each other, then the younger one addressed Rafe for the first time. "Plenty damn far," he said. It seemed to be a compliment.

After spending the winter in St. Louis, and with the weather now abating, the Indians were returning to their village on the Republican River — a branch of the Arkansa. The older one wore a Jefferson medal; that probably meant that he was a person of some distinction in his village. They questioned Rafe probingly about the two large packs, supposing they were beaver skins. Fearing they might be thinking of robbing him, he untied one of the bundles to show the pressed plant specimens and aromatic birdskins. But when he told them he was taking the packs to St. Louis, they shook their heads.

"Mule too old," they said.

One of the Pawnees climbed out of the ravine to where Blue stood with his back to the wind. He looked at the mule's teeth and ran his hand along the rib cage. Then he came back and sat down.

"Shoot mule."

Rafe shook his head.

"Shoot mule, take raft. When ice go, take raft."

"I won't shoot my mule and I don't have a raft."

They led him up to a spot where they could look out to the river. On a sandbar, half covered by trash and partially upended by the last flood tide of the previous year, was a platform of cottonwood logs.

"Raft," the older man said. He repeated the words as if unsure that Rafe knew what he meant. "Good float raft. Hold packs, keep plenty dry."

And as they all scrambled down to take a closer look at the thing, the Indian repeated his advice. "Shoot mule, take raft."

11

The Governor and the General

IT HAD BEEN an incredible evening, for he had not been cold or hungry, exhausted or alone. He had drunk a glass of fine Madeira — trying not to gulp it — and replaced the glass on a silver tray held by a white-coated mulatto servant. He had drawn his fingers across the glossy tops of walnut and mahogany tables. He had stood within four walls beneath a chandelier of flickering candles without feeling the sense of entrapment he had known during the first few days after his river trip.

All other delights were trivial compared to the dancing. In a blue and red uniform, with a stiffly ruffled white shirt and the squeakiest of black jackboots, he had danced the minuet and gavotte with a yellow-haired French girl. Now they were promenading — he and Marie-Louise Gratiot — on the gallery that encircled the stone mansion of Auguste Chouteau, the wealthiest merchant in St. Louis.

On this cool May night the air was heavy with the scents of a ripening springtime. From inside the house came the sweet voices of violins, banjoes, and a clarionet. Marie-Louise seemed fascinated by her dancing partner.

"Shall I tell you what *ma cher papa* told me only this evening? *Non?*"

"Tell me." He could not keep his eyes off the ringlets that edged her brow, and the loosely rolled curls upon her bare shoulders. His mother must have looked like that once.

"He say that you are but one of many *voyageurs* to visit Santa Fe, but one of the few to come away safely. *N'est-ce pas?*"

"It was easy. With some connivance by a Spanish friend, I just rode off one morning and didn't look back."

"It was much more difficult! A marvelous feat. And for one so young!"

"I like having you think so." He thought he heard from infinities away the derisive snickers of his schoolmates. *Listen to that, will you,* they jibed.

"And my father is *tres jaloux,*" Marie-Louise said. "As are all his business friends. The Chouteaus, the Papins, the Carrs, and those dark, bearded fur traders who live along the waterfront and sing such terrible songs in the taverns. All jealous of you."

Then she added: "Even Governor Lewis, perhaps. *Est-ce possible?*"

"Not for any reason that I can think of."

"Well, when he was dancing with me earlier, I thought he seemed envious of you."

"He certainly should envy me right now, walking arm and arm with so beautiful a lady." (*And listen to him now,* his classmates cried from back there; old Rafe is learning charm.)

Mlle Gratiot swung her golden curls, squeezed his arm, and led him back to the ballroom where the musicians were playing a French waltz. It was their last dance of the evening, for every man at the ball was anxious to speak with Rafe. Pierre Chouteau, Auguste's half-brother, wanted to inquire about the Osages he had seen at Three Forks. Did they seem hostile? How was Chief Clermont, and did he inquire after his old friend Pierre? Lawyer Edward Hempstead asked if Rafe had seen anything of Captain McClallen, and when Rafe told of finding the remains of that unfortunate party the news ran through the assembly within minutes. "McClallen told me he was going trading up the Platte," Hempstead said. "He must have been trying to deceive any competition."

Dr. Antoine Saugrain, physician and devotee of scientific studies, wanted to talk new plants — especially cacti — and instruments. "Some of my neighbors are saying that I made a thermometer for Governor Lewis by scraping the mercury off the back of Mme Saugrain's mirror. That's nonsense. She would have killed me. And the governor had perfectly good thermometers from Philadelphia."

On two or three occasions Rafe felt that Meriwether Lewis wanted a word with him, but someone always intervened. Once it was Joseph Charless, who was starting a newspaper in town and wanted Rafe to write a piece about the species of plants and animals he had found. "We'll be off the press with our first issue of my *Missouri Gazette* in July, if I can ever get my machinery off the boat." Auguste, founder of the Chouteau dynasty, had a particular interest in Rafe's route from Santa Fe, insisting on seeing it sketched on foolscap. He was concerned about distances between watering places. "Only an intrepid man would try that journey in winter. You are very lucky."

Colonel Thomas Hunt stood always near, listening dourly. The ageing Revolutionary soldier now commanded the First Infantry with headquarters at the cantonment; he and Rafe had ridden to town together, overland, instead of coming down by boat. The colonel was tired and bitter, with a large family and a modest salary. Lately he had filled a succession of dull billets up and down the frontier. "At Fort Wayne it was the damned Miamis and Shawnees. Up at Mackinac — one hell of a place in winter — it was the Ottawas and Menominees. Now I've got the cantankerous Sauks and Foxes, the beggarly Ioways, and the tricky Osages."

The most welcome intervention of the evening came from William Clark, whose young new wife Julia was the honored guest at the ball. Clark cupped his palm around Rafe's elbow and steered him into a drawing room, motioning to a servant for brandy.

Rafe felt at ease with him. "Lewis and Clark. That was the name of our boat."

"I'm honored. But the world now has to start thinking of the governor and me as two separate human beings. Not just Lewis-and-Clark."

He looks almost like Jefferson. The hair not so red as his, but rather the color of a newly dug sweet potato. Better dressed than Jefferson, as if the years in the wilderness had whetted an appetite for the shining buckles on the slippers, the extra starch in the shirt, the superb cut of the black coat and pantaloons.

"I expected to see you in uniform as General Clark."

"That's the beauty of being just a militia general. We don't get into our regalia until there is an uprising somewhere." Clark held the brandy glass near his nose to catch the aroma, but did not taste it.

"Tell me about that bodacious grizzly," he demanded. When Rafe had related the tale of the fight on the mountain, Clark's face was aglow with excitement. "Wondrous animals. Scared the calibogus out of me a couple times. Chased one of our men clear up a tree."

He finally took a sip of the brandy and added: "I don't want to hear about that raft trip down the Missouri. It would remind me of some labors of our own on that same river. What I want to hear is a tale about that great mountain you climbed. We didn't have that pleasure." It was apparent that Clark knew a lot about the Arkansa expedition. Rafe described the ascent of Mount Bailey, or Bailey's Peak (he had not really settled on a name).

"You know," Clark confided, "I'm not surprised at how few Indians you saw. There isn't one behind every rock or tree, as most folks think. We had to go looking for ours a lot of the time. But I sure do regret that little dust-up you had with the Comanches. I blame McClallen for that. He should have stayed out of that country. We've got to come to terms with the Comanches sooner or later around a peaceful council fire."

He had kicked off his slippers and now sat with his elbows on a table, eager to keep talking.

"See if you agree with me on this. You're out on the river, say, and you've left the boats and walked off over some damned hill or other, and you know there's not a solitary human that has ever set foot on the spot where you're standing. That's the first thrill. The second comes when you look down at your feet and there's a beautiful flower. And, by God, it's a new one. No other person has ever set eyes on one like it. You bend down and dig it up, and walk away from that place feeling like a possum in the hen house. Am I right?"

Rafe nodded. *I like this man.*

Clark went on. "I'd go back out there in a minute. Already I'm tired of this bickering and all the political maneuvering in this town. I'd go to the Mandans — there's a crowd for you! Best damn bunch of folks in the world."

"I guess my best experience was with the Quapaws," Rafe said, recognizing the exaggeration but not caring. One beautiful Indian girl doesn't make a tribe.

"How are your journals coming? Have you started to put them into shape?" Clark asked.

"I've done a little and can't wait to do more. My assignment to Bellefontaine is going to allow me some time to work on them."

"Good. What you must do is come down here and stay with Julia and me every time the colonel will let you. We can compare notes. I've got some books you'll need, and you could use the Chouteaus' books and also Dr. Saugrain's. We have a quiet place for you to work and sleep." Then Clark fell silent for a moment while he inspected the ash on his cigar. The brandy and the heat generated by the dancing had given his face a ruddy glow which Rafe compared to that of a globe radish straight from the garden. Hair the color of sweet potatoes, face like a radish. He was turning Clark into a kind of human vegetable patch, but the earthy similes seemed apt.

"I'll confess something," Clark said. "I can't write a decent sentence. Can't even spell. It's always been a joke in my family. So any journal writing from the pens of Lewis and Clark will have to be done by the governor. Here's the sad part of that" — Clark glanced at the door to make sure they were alone — "I don't think he's getting on with it. He stews a lot and gets caught up in territorial politics, or goes wild-eyed about investing in farmland, and the whole world is waiting for those journals. I'd do anything in my power to help him, but he's got to get hold of himself and hunker down."

Rafe made no comment. The rest of their conversation was trivial. After his time with Clark, the evening seemed to lose its structure. The wine and liquor had raised the volume of the voices, and Rafe felt that he had reached for one too many cordials. He met more men and women whose names he simply must remember and feared he would not. A chatty old trader, Nicholas Boilvin, who spoke a rapid amalgam of French and poor English, had an urgent message for the secretary of war and said he couldn't get Colonel Hunt to forward it. He hoped that Rafe would convey it; but Rafe already knew about going through channels and conveniently forgot the message.

What the evening still lacked was a meeting with Lewis. The

governor had always been surrounded by men in urgent conversation, while his eyes seemed to seek those of women in far corners of the room. Rafe thought he seemed ill at ease: the hand-rubbing, the slight grin that stayed with him as he listened to endless talk, as if not wanting to be caught off guard if a quip were made. He seemed capable of withdrawing into himself, the half-grin posted on his face like a sentinel. The eyes were deep green and they looked past you, toward some high horizon. The queue that used to dangle over his collar was now securely pinned up and tied with a black velvet bow.

At last the governor approached Rafe with two glasses, handed him one, and invited him into the room where Clark had taken him.

"We're all glad you're safely home. Saw you talking in here with my good friend Will Clark."

"Thanks, Excellency." *Is that the right title?*

"Come on, now. We fellow explorers must use first names. My friends call me Mere — pronounced like a female horse. You'll get used to it. My mother finally did."

"I'll try to work around to Mere," Rafe said. "I might have to try Mr. Lewis a few times to break myself in."

Lewis's laugh was not the hearty burst of open-throated appreciation that Clark produced. It was three little coughs strung together as if by hyphens. Eh-eh-eh, coming from somewhere behind that half-grin. Except to rub his palms together, he never let go of his brandy glass. He twirled it, groped it, drummed his fingers against it, and soon summoned a refill from a servant who came to the doorway.

"Now then," he said. "I want to know how your journals are coming."

"They're started. My collections that Lieutenant Smith had charge of are coming up from New Orleans, then I'll have everything together. General Clark — Will Clark — says I am free to come into town when I have spare time and work at his place. Of course I can do a lot at the cantonment, where my quarters are pretty good. My medical chores won't take up all of my time."

Rafe noticed that Lewis had scarcely listened. He had drained another glass and spent some time staring at the candelabrum on the table. In the smoky yellow light, his face called up another memory of that moment in Philadelphia when, through a half-opened door, Rafe had seen him in Mahlon Dickerson's quarters. "Well, that's good," Lewis said. "Now I'll fill you in on what I'm doing with our own material. I'm pretty far into the initial stage of organizing our notebooks — Will's and mine — and I've sent a great bunch of stuff off to Dr. Barton. He's going to help with the scientific end. I've set aside a little time each day, when the cares of running this chaotic territory will permit, and I really feel that I've got something in hand that will catch the interest of the country. I guess you know that I've made all the arrangements with a publisher in Philadelphia. But have you seen the little brochure he has put out?"

Lewis pried a folded pamphlet from his waistcoat pocket. "You can keep that copy." Rafe scanned the first page.

PROSPECTUS
OF
LEWIS AND CLARK'S TOUR
TO THE
PACIFIC OCEAN
THROUGH
THE INTERIOR OF THE CONTINENT OF NORTH AMERICA

Performed by order of the Government of the United States, during the Years 1804, 1805, & 1806.

This work will be prepared by Captain Meriwether Lewis, and will be divided into two parts, the whole comprized in three volumes octavo, containing from four to five hundred pages each, printed on good paper, and a fair Pica type. The several volumes in succession will be put to press at as early periods as the avocations of the author will permit him to prepare them for publication.

I'll never top this. He saw that the pamphlet promised "a narrative of the voyage, with a description of some of the most remarkable places in those hitherto unknown wilds of America." *I can match that part.* "Accompanied by a Map of good size, and embellished with a view of the great cataract of the Missouri." *We'll embellish ours with Mount Bailey.* "Whatever properly appertains to geography, embracing a description of the rivers, mountains, climate, soil and face of the country; a view of the Indian nations distributed over that vast region, shewing their traditions, habits, manners, customs." *I'll beat that with a description of Santa Fe.* "It will contain a full dissertation on such subjects as have fallen within the notice of the author" — *he doesn't include Clark, I see* — "under the heads of Botany, Mineralogy, and Zoology." *I've got him there. I can botanize circles around him. I'll zoologize him into a corner.*

When his talk with Lewis broke off, Rafe went out to the gallery again where a few celebrants still were standing in small groups, enjoying a quickening southern breeze. Except for the lights from bobbing lanthorns, and the glow from a dozen windows, St. Louis was invisible. As he had seen it earlier in the day, it was a village set against a rolling prairie, with forest to the north and west. Built on a narrow savannah between the river and the hills, it consisted of three streets paralleling the river — the Grand Rue, the Rue de l'Eglise, and the Rue des Granges. The cross streets were narrow lanes, tending to divide the town into blocks, and the homes of tamped earth and vertical wooden beams were scattered and irregularly placed. The great house of Auguste Chouteau rose like a castle among the modest, whitewashed buildings.

The wharf was crowded with keelboats and flatboats, bearing planking from the upper Ohio and cotton from Kentucky; peltries and lead from up the Mississippi; corn on the ear and cider in the barrel; ladings of pork, flour, whisky, hemp, tobacco, and bale rope. This could be the Philadelphia waterfront, Rafe thought, except for the lack of tall-masted ships.

As the party waned, Clark came around with Julia, a girl in her teens whom he had met and courted in Fincastle, Virginia. He had brought her from home only lately, and her hazel eyes and auburn hair reminded Rafe of Ethelinda Pettefish from Brown's Cove. Why had so many moments of this evening brought Ethelinda to mind? While dancing with Mlle Gratiot, the sense that her body was so close — under all those yards of rustling, wilting fabric — had called up a recollection of Ethelinda. He had never loved the girl but had lusted often for her. Now he remembered one golden afternoon.

٭

He is sixteen and home from college, strolling along Fox Run and watching for minnows in the sparkling water. He had waded in to pick up a smooth stone of variegated green and brown for his rock collection. He stands by the brook, inspecting the stone, and when it begins to dry he spits on it noisily to bring back the shine. That is when he sees Ethelinda across the brook, laughing at him. They say she is twenty and was married to a boy who died. Now she has drawn him to a green plot in the shade — he remembers that much — and she pulls him down upon the cool grass. She runs a finger around the V where his shirt lies open. Then she grabs him *down there* and squeezes. Oh, double damn! He has never seen a girl's body, not even his sister Franny's. Legs so long, breasts so — oh, Jesus! A million times he has called back those incredible moments of his first intimacy with a girl. There have been others (including two or three nameless women in the cribs along the Philadelphia waterfront). None like Ethelinda with the flashing brown legs.

Will Clark stood with his arm around Julia's waist. "I hope you enjoyed the rollicking."

"It wasn't all partifying," Rafe said. "I had that good talk with you, for instance."

"True. But of course I was referring to Miss Gratiot."

"I felt pretty clumsy, dancing with her."

"She seemed to enjoy your company," Clark said. "But I advise you not to think of escorting her home."

"It crossed my mind. Why shouldn't I?"

"Because she came with the governor. He's been seeing her for quite a while now."

So that was what she meant when she said that Lewis seemed envious. She meant *jaloux*. An innocent maneuver on her part, for she could not know of the tension that already existed between them. *Now you've done it, Rafe.*

Bellefontaine was still called a cantonment although it was now a fully established and permanent fort. Only three years old, it was nearly obsolete. It sat on the banks of the Missouri, just above the confluence with the Mississippi, its purpose to provide soldiers to guard the factory where the Indians came to trade.

Colonel Hunt ran the post, usually billeting one or two companies of his strung-out regiment, with disdain for the kind of soldier he was getting these days. His orderly book was rife with sarcasm: "Corporals that place sentinels must be very particular that they inform them the course they are to walk and the distance. The colonel has observed lately that the sentinels placed to take charge of the contractor's store and the hospital have rather guarded a large tree in front of the store."

The reasons for the obsolescence of the cantonment were varied. Tribes upriver on the Mississippi, mainly the Sauks and Foxes, did not like to come down through the settled areas to trade. As for the Osages, the distance to their villages far to the west was too great to make trading practical. There was talk now of building two more factories, with accompanying military posts, one in the Osage country and one up the Mississippi, perhaps about where the Des Moines River came in from the west.

To a dry old ramrod like Colonel Hunt, trying to man the only real army garrison west of the Mississippi (he did not count that measly little Arkansa Post somewhere down south), the actions of younger men who wanted to get things done fast was provoking. Doing things took men and supplies. The eager territory-builders tried to nibble away at his regiment and the hoard of powder kegs in the magazines to carry out their damn-fool operations.

When Rafe and the colonel returned to Bellefontaine the day after the ball, it looked to Rafe like a fine place. He had been there since his memorable float down the ice-laden Missouri, and still liked it. The buildings were so new that, in protected niches, the peeled logs had not completely weathered to gray. His hospital quarters were more than adequate, though located so that the wind brought in barnyard odors from the cattle pen behind the post. A few cattle were kept so that the contractor could supply fresh meat to the men, and the aromas that came from their log enclosure were pleasant to Rafe and redolent of farm memories. His patients from the urban areas of the East were quick, however, to hold their noses and complain.

Two young officers had quickly made friends with Rafe. Lieutenant Alpha Kingsley, second-in-command below the colonel, was a thin, sandy-haired man from Vermont who had once been to Philadelphia with his father. Second Lieutenant Nathaniel Pryor ("call me Nate") was a blunt-talking Kentuckian who had been a sergeant on the Lewis and Clark expedition. More recently, after being commissioned, he had led a party of soldiers up the Missouri in an attempt to return a Mandan chief to his village. The attempt had failed, there had been an exchange of gunfire from hostile Arikara warriors, and Nate Pryor had fallen back to Bellefontaine. No one blamed him for the debacle.

"Did you meet my old commanders, General Clark and Governor Lewis?" he asked Rafe, pronouncing their new titles with a proud emphasis.

"Had good talks with both of them."

"I hear you danced a lot with the governor's intended," Pryor said.

Intended? Nobody said intended. Rafe marveled at how the word had spread in a single day.

"Not a serious encounter but very pleasant."

"How did Governor Lewis seem?" Pryor asked cautiously, as if it were not his business to be asking.

"Friendly, but I think I enjoyed talking with Clark a lot more. Still, the governor seemed amiable."

Not really. Rafe had been thinking since meeting Lewis that he had not been asked anything at all about his own expedition. The governor seemed obsessed with the prospect of publishing his own journals. On the other hand, Clark had talked more about Rafe than of his own exploits.

"I'd go to hell for either of them," Pryor said. "And let me tell you something. Captain Lewis has changed a lot since we got back. I don't know what it is. Just something different about him."

"Tell me how he used to be."

"He was looser. You know that tight little laugh he's got now? I never heard that in the mountains. He'd open his mouth and really laugh. I've seen tears coming down his cheeks when we were all bent over with amusement from something somebody said in camp. And then the other side of him: when we lost Sergeant Floyd from the colic, up in Yankton Sioux country, Lewis personally laid him out for burial. Wouldn't let any of us touch him. Read the service, too, and then took a long hike along the bluffs and we could see his outline, right up till sundown, standing on the highest rise he could find. We talked about him among ourselves sometimes. How he'd tried so hard to find a woman to marry. I once heard him say, 'All the women I fall in love with are bad for me.' It can't pleasure him much to see General Clark so happy with that little bride of his. Do you know they both named rivers after women? Clark's was Judith's River (his wife's real first name), but we never knew who Captain Lewis had in mind when he named Maria's River. Clark probably knows.

"Tell you what kind of person Lewis is. Or was. When he picked a second commander for the detachment — that was Clark — the second man was supposed to get a captain's rank. Well, the goddamned War Department or somebody wouldn't approve that rank, so Clark ended up as a lieutenant. Lewis was so angry — and us men never found out until after we got home — that he insisted on Clark calling himself a captain all through the trip. We all thought he and Lewis had the same rank. They were a perfect team because what Lewis couldn't do, Clark could."

Pryor paused as if wondering how to finish his monologue. "I wish to God we were all out there in the mountains again."

That evening, with only one patient to look in on, Rafe had spread out some of his plant specimens and was rechecking the labels, refreshing his memory as to the nature of the localities in which he had gathered them. Evening parade was over and there was still a good bit of time before lights-out. Lieutenant Al Kingsley dropped by the hospital with a bottle of wine.

"It's from the Chouteau vineyard. Too sweet for me and probably for you. But tolerable, eh?"

Kingsley was not a dashing officer. His military destiny would within a year or so consign him to the role of district paymaster. "Brought you a message from town," he said. "A rider came in with it just before supper and couldn't find you."

Rafe supposed it would be from Lewis or Clark, but it was from neither. He read it twice:

Dr. Bailey,   *St. Louis. Tuesday.*

I must tell you with regret that it will not be possible for the Missouri Gazette *to run your essay on the natural history of the Arkansa and the*

Santa Fe region. We have a large backlog of material for our early issues, as you might expect, and I must make some hard decisions about what to print. With pleasant memories of our meeting last evening, I remain, Sir, your most obedient servant,

Jos. Charless

A disappointment. Rafe had planned to describe some of his finds, supposing that if he chose his words properly, with a Latin description for each, he might qualify as the first to present those species to the scientific world. Curious that Charless would change his mind so soon after his invitation to write the article.

"Nothing important," he said. "A matter between me and that newspaper fellow in St. Louis."

"I understand that Lewis is one of his big backers," Kingsley said. "Helped to raise the money to bring him here. Nice thing for the town, don't you think?"

Next morning after sick call, Rafe walked along the banks of the Missouri, so powerful that downstream its brown water pushed into the greener, more placid flow of the Mississippi almost as a solid mass, as if determined not to surrender its identity. Next month would come the dreaded June rise, when snows melting in the mountains would swell the stream and bring floating trees and occasionally the bloated carcass of a buffalo down from the high plains.

Along the banks near the cantonment, hornwort and carrion flowers were showing green, together with scouring rushes and arrowleaf. Up a ravine that ran along the west side of the garrison the blackberry tangles were flowering and the frost grape was in leaf.

When Rafe returned to the fort and started across the parade to his quarters, he was hailed by Lieutenant Pryor. Wearing a sword to signify that he was officer of the day, Pryor hurried to Rafe with an urgent look.

"The colonel's been calling for you. Like to busted my ass because I couldn't locate you."

Colonel Hunt welcomed Rafe into his cramped living room, where there was evidence that it was home to several children. Neither Mrs. Hunt nor the children were present. The colonel sat behind a handsome desk of polished oak, which Rafe supposed had been shipped from post to post during the thirty-odd years the Hunts had been an army family.

"Been out collecting?"

"A little, sir. It's about a month too early for good plant specimens."

"How'd you like to collect where nobody else has ever done it
before?" the colonel asked.

Something's up. "I thought I'd been doing that for the last year,
colonel."

"So you have. Let me get to the point. You may have heard
rumors that the factory here is not really doing its job. Hell, we
haven't had twenty customers from the Mississippi tribes in the
last week. Now, what you don't know, and what I didn't know
until this morning, is that the factory is to be closed. Bellefontaine will continue as an army post, but the trading activity is to
be split into two new factories. One will be up the Missouri. I
think the spot that Clark has in mind is about where you spent
some time before you came down the river last month. As to the
other location, we've got a little problem — somewhere near the
mouth of the Des Moines, but whether above or below is the
question. Lewis is sending a couple of traders to parley with the
Indians and get them to sign over some land. Soon as we've picked
a good spot, I'm leading a company up there to get started with
the building. I want to get something under a roof before snow
flies, at least, and then complete the thing by next summer. When
she's looking good I'll come back down and leave the company
there along with a new factor — fellow named Johnson — who's
on the way out here from Baltimore right now."

Here it comes.

"Kingsley will be going and so will Pryor. And so will you. We
need a medical man up there and you're the best. Those stinking
Sauks and Foxes will give you plenty to do."

"Well, sir, I'm not exactly a seasoned surgeon. All the action
I've seen is that one skirmish with the Comanches."

"Good enough. One murderous savage is no different from another. One tomahawk wound's same as any other."

Now there could be no trips to St. Louis to work at the Clarks'
and use their library. No more access to paper and ink powder,
blank journals, and blotting sand. A hut full of wounded soldiers
to tend round the clock, no doubt, not to mention whatever kinds
of disease might take hold in that country. Living in a compound

that might even be too dangerous to leave on collecting trips. It sure as hell was going to set his schedule back.

The colonel added: "Governor Lewis suggested specifically that you go along. Made quite a point of it to me, in fact. You should feel proud of that."

Tricked and trapped. He would give it a try, see how things went; he would do his doctoring, wallow in homesickness, polish his buttons, and maybe try to figure out Meriwether Lewis. Was Lewis sending him away to hinder work on his journals, or to get him away from Marie-Louise Gratiot? Either way, it was rotten.

12

A Fort by the Rapids

THE SAUK and Fox Indians were loosely confederated tribes living in scattered villages on the upper Mississippi, between the Des Moines and Rock rivers. A troubled people, they were torn between allegiance to the Americans down in St. Louis, who offered them trade and protection, and to the British in the north, who whispered to them of rebellion and war.

In the fall of 1804, a delegation of five Sauk and Fox chiefs had been called to St. Louis to confer with William Henry Harrison, specially appointed by President Jefferson to buy Indian lands. The little delegation had been led by Quashquame, a minor Sauk chief and prominent drunkard. When the parley was finished the Indians had signed away their homeland: millions of acres, mostly in what would later become the state of Illinois, but also other lands west of the Mississippi. In return, they got the promise of a thousand dollars a year, the services of a blacksmith, a farmer to teach them agriculture, and a factory house where they could bring their furs — and chunks of lead from their crude mines far upriver — to exchange for goods. They were told they could stay on their land until settlers began to take it over, then they must move west of the river.

Later, Quashquame claimed that Harrison had got them drunk. (Officially the army prohibited all issuance of liquor to the tribes, but every post commander kept a barrel of common spirits for the chiefs and warriors who came to council or trade.) Besides, they had not known before going to see Harrison that they were expected to barter for land; their tribesmen at home had not authorized them to do so.

Back up the river went the five chiefs, holding their pirogues to the quieter currents near the shore and breasting a stream that was speckled with color from the cottonwood and sycamore leaves riding flat and limp on the water. Around Quashquame's neck hung a silver medal on a buckskin thong, bearing the likeness of the Great Father; on his back was a fine new coat; but his red and orange forests on the hills had passed into alien hands. The alcohol that had set him glowing was now burned from his veins. His throat must have ached for it, his skin thirsted, and he might gladly have let the river bear him swirling downstream like an empty cask, to be replenished in the smoky Creole taverns. Yet up the river he went, to tell his people that the graves of their fathers were now the property of the United States government.

In the heart of the Sauk-Fox country lay a twelve-mile system of rapids so deceptive that in high water not a ripple broke the surface above it. Even in August, when the flow of the Mississippi was sluggish and the water level down, there were only fretful swirls to mark the chains of limestone and blue clay that reached across the river shore-to-shore. Going upstream, a boat crew would reach the first chain about two miles above the mouth of the Des Moines. If the craft was not drawing too much, if the boatmen knew where to pass the first chain near the eastern shore, and if a crosscurrent did not send them against a tooth of rock, they would be clear to make for the next chain two miles farther on. By the time they had poled and rowed themselves to the head of the rapids, they had climbed a twenty-four-foot drop in the river.

At the head of the rapids, in Quashquame's village, the Sauks and Foxes watched their better world begin in the summer of 1808, as six large keelboats and several smaller craft toiled across the rapids. Colonel Hunt had planned to be there, but five days before the embarkation he grew suddenly ill and died, in a way that he might never have expected at Stony Point and Yorktown, when the British grapeshot was hissing past his boyish cheeks. He died in a four-poster under a patchwork quilt.

Lieutenant Kingsley draped the hilt of his sword and put on a black armband. He was now in charge of the flotilla.

Rafe could not decide whether to take his collections or leave them with Clark. The bird and animal skins would need frequent treatment, but he wondered how well he could protect them from decay in the damp bottomlands where the new fort would be erected. The plant specimens, many now in need of remounting, could not endure too many more transshipments. Will Clark had told him: "Don't ship anything home unattended. I sent a crate of prehistoric bones back to the president and they wound up strewn along the banks of the Ohio, the box torn open by vandals."

In the end, Rafe could not bear to leave a single root or stem behind. "Half a boatload of weeds and rabbit hides," Kingsley joked, but there was plenty of cargo space.

The line of boats that filed down the murky estuary of the Missouri and into the mile-wide Mississippi was the largest convoy ever seen in the upper country. The task of getting it to the rapids and above would take more than two weeks.

Ordinarily, Kingsley's company would have included a captain, a first and second lieutenant, an ensign, a surgeon's mate, four sergeants, four corporals, four musicians, and sixty-four privates. Now the only other line officer was Pryor, and the enlisted men fell far short of the normal complement. There were, in fact, barely enough men to move the boats.

To a man, these soldiers had heard of Rafe's success with Marie-Louise Gratiot at the "big doings," and to a man they believed he had been sent along because of it. The story gained him their respect and a few sly glances.

The convoy dragged itself to the mouth of the Des Moines in mid-September, when passenger pigeons were surging down from the north and flights of white pelicans passed in the western sky, alternately flapping and gliding across the scarlet flare of sunset. The woods were not yet touched with fall color. The riverside foliage, down to the waterline, showed the dust-dry green of late summer. On the east side the bluffs came to the edge of the water, but on the west there was bottomland with patches of sycamore, cottonwood, and black walnut.

"Damn," Kingsley said. "If we put a fort on the east bank, opposite the Des Moines, we'll be high and dry, and well below the rapids. But that's not the land we bargained for with the

Indians. My orders from the colonel are to build on the west bank. Someone wasn't thinking."

Pryor hated the decision. "If we build above the rapids we'll have a problem in low water. We'll get a boat stove in now and then, and lose a lot of time crossing those damned shoals."

But up the rapids they went, to a location negotiated by the government, and found it was no bargain. The place was about ten miles above the rapids, where the river made a long turn to the east, and the only logical place to build was one that never could be defended. Behind it ran a high bluff from which the Indians could fire down upon the garrison. And along the southwest, a hundred paces from where the stockade would be, was a ravine where war parties could infiltrate without being seen.

Pryor saw the risks, but Kingsley did not. He wrote home soon after the landing: "This situation is high, commands an extensive view of the river, has an excellent spring, and is advantageous to the Indian trade."

"We can't get into permanent quarters until spring," he told his two officers. "First thing is to put up some cabins to keep us warm in the winter. And Rafe, I'm going to see that you get one that will provide some privacy for your writing as well as a place for the sick men.

"Hand me an axe," Rafe said with a wry smile. *My surgical axe.*

When they had made a temporary stockade around the whole area, Kingsley named the place Fort Bellevue. He authorized factor John Johnson to open trade with the Indians in a hut outside the walls, near where a factory building would be built later. At roll call one morning, he announced that an express would be going to St. Louis with mail, and Rafe spent an hour writing to his father:

Fort Bellevue above the Des Moines

My Dear Father,   *15th Oct. 1808*

Since writing you last my life has taken a strange turn. Picture me sitting in a shack about two hundred miles up the Mississippi from the nearest settlement, helping to build a fort and caring for a company of infantrymen. The circumstances that brought me here are not to my liking. I shall outline them to you with the sure knowledge that nothing I say will ever fall upon the ears of my patron and mentor at Monticello.

Captains Lewis and Clark (of course I mean Governor Lewis and General Clark) are now established in St. Louis and I have met them both. I found Clark to be an estimable man and a ready friend. Knowing how urgently I wish to put my journals in train for printing, he let me know that I could come to his house and work on my materials whenever time allowed.

The Governor is another case entirely. I think the President made a terrible mistake in appointing him to run this unruly territory. He cannot cope with the political climate. He is caught up in the fever to speculate and has made some bad investments — or at least investments beyond his means.

The Governor showed me an elegant brochure describing a work that will contain the findings of his expedition. For reasons that I cannot explain, he seems to feel that he and I are in a race to publish. There is a certain element of truth there, for many of the new discoveries of mine are the same as his. I should naturally like to be first, but have never deceived myself into thinking I have a right to prior publication, considering that Lewis and Clark were first into the field and that their exploration was much more extensive and perhaps more important than mine.

Apparently to make sure that he publishes first, the Governor has used his influence to get me assigned to this place.

I perceive some habits of the Governor's which are distressing to his friends and must eventually contribute to his failure in public life, if not to his total dissolution. But this is none of my concern.

I think of you daily and of my departed Mother, and I long for the bright waters of Fox Run. Believe me, my dear Sir, that I want only to come home and will do so as soon as possible. Kiss my dear Sister. I remain your loving and respectful son,

Raphael

Winter struck hard that year. First came the nighttime rains of November, battering the coarsely riven shingles, thrumming in the ears of the men on watch, and pocking the river, while the wind jostled the boats nosed into the shore. The fresh earth tamped against the pickets of the stockade turned to cold ooze that came down the bank and muddied the water. Then the heaviest freeze in twenty years caught the valley unprepared. Boats were frozen in the channel as far down as the mouth of the Ohio. Inside Fort Bellevue the men wore their blue woolen pantaloons and their heaviest socks, relieved sentinels often, and went on with their work. In the night the snow swept across the parade ground, and where the pickets dulled the wind the drifts began to build.

As spring came on, the ice crumpled and rose into piles that fell over and disappeared. Canada geese spent the nights standing in the shoal waters along the shore. Ducks came in pairs or flocks, and by April the soldiers were bringing in mallards, baldpates, gadwalls, blackjacks, and butterballs.

Even before work had begun on the permanent fortification, Nate Pryor had come to Rafe with a tempting idea. He was resigning his commission and wanted Rafe to do the same.

"My friend, we've done our share of knocking around for someone else. Let's go into business for ourselves."

"Doctoring is my business," Rafe said. "I wouldn't mind doing it somewhere else, but that will have to wait."

"Not so, Rafe. Do like me and resign. I'm sending my letter down to the new colonel with the first express."

Pryor spoke of the riches he hoped to gather at the lead mines up north. For decades the Indian women had been mining and smelting the ore, dragging it in baskets or buckskin bags to pits scooped in the earth, where they melted the lead into seventy-pound "pigs" of very impure metal.

"They mix the ore and hot coals together and drain the liquid metal off into shallow holes to harden," Pryor explained. He hoped to find a partner who would help him build a sidehill log furnace, where the ore could be melted and drained into a stone basin.

"Look at the figures," he argued. "With a little help I can float about forty-five thousand pounds of those pigs down to St. Louis in a year, and get five cents a pound. I can haul a good ten thousand pounds in a big boat."

"Unless you get stove in. You'd plunge right to the bottom with all that concentrated weight. Too much empty space in the hull."

"I'm the best boatman on the river. Ask General Clark."

"And you want a doctor for a partner? What for — hernias? Strained backs? Lead burns?"

Rafe declined, and in fact gave the offer almost no serious thought, but Pryor had put a new plan into his head. What would happen if he turned in his resignation? Would Lewis see it and persuade the colonel to ignore it? The governor seemed aware of all military matters in the district. Still, it was worth a try.

When a civilian with a horse, the assistant to the factor, volunteered to go express in mid-March, Pryor's resignation went in the saddlebag along with this letter from Rafe:

Above D.M. Rapids
15th March 1809

My Dear Colonel,

 I hereby tender my resignation from the U.S. Army, in the role of Surgeon's Mate, an appointment I have held but a short time. I have in my possession many specimens of natural history, vital to an understanding of the western country, which I find I cannot get into shape for publication at this remote post. I remain, Sir, Yr. Most Obt. Servt.

Raphael Bailey

Lt. Col. Daniel Bissell
Regimental Commander, 1st Inf.

The possible resignation of two officers did not seem to bother Lieutenant Kingsley; his own request for a six-month furlough was in the same saddlebag. The three men watched the express rider ease his way along the riverbank, and when he rounded the first bend they turned to the task of building a permanent fort.

When the willow buds had begun to swell and the gray edges of the river were livening daily, there were stands of timber in the bottomlands which would not be the same for a century. The crippling axes of the fatigue parties were laying the forest open to the sun. The builders decided to concentrate first on the blockhouses and the stockade fence. Once the little wicket gate in the rear and the big front gate a few paces from shore could be slammed and barred, the garrison would be secure. Then the barracks and factory building could be worked on at a slower pace.

Kingsley had decided he needed four blockhouses instead of three — the last to be built atop a gentle rise behind the fort. One of the sergeants had called his attention to the chance that the Indians on that rise could rake the parade ground with musket fire. He would build a kind of alleyway, of smaller pickets, to connect the little blockhouse with the main fort.

"Sure don't resemble no fort ever I seen," said a private who had fought with General Wayne.

"Puts me in mind of a kite, with that tail onto it," said a corporal who carried a Shawnee musket ball in his shoulder.

Kingsley's instructions about the stockade were carefully spoken at evening muster: "I want peeled logs at least a foot thick. Oak and nothing but oak. Set the logs upright in a trench, and be sure they are butted square at the bottom and hewn to a point at the top. Later we can build a bench around the inside wall, a foot or two above the ground, for our people to stand on while firing through the loopholes."

"Sir," said the sergeant in charge of construction.

"Yes?"

"I want to adjust the bench and the loopholes in the wall so the shortest man in the company — that would be Glockner — can fire at the belly of an enemy twenty yards away."

"Sounds good," said Kingsley, who had never seen an enemy's belly at any distance.

The likeliest targets, the Sauks and Foxes, were still on their winter hunting grounds below the Des Moines. Soon they would be coming up past the fort, on the way to their summer homes near the mouth of the Rock. Even though the tribes kept winter homes, there was a good deal of horse and foot traffic past the fort all winter. Some of the old folk, the invalids, and women and children were still up on the Rock River. And straggling men, wandering through the forests with bags of beaver traps, were all over the valley. Many curious warriors had stopped at the post during the winter and inspected the rising fortification, waited around in vain for an offer of whisky, and gone away troubled and grumbling.

Rafe's crude hut was adequate as a clinic and working space; the sick men were housed in an adjoining hut. At first he kept his collections carefully wrapped and stacked in a corner, as if to protect them from prying eyes, but later he piled the mounted plant specimens around the room by genus and species and took pride in showing the soldiers some of the curious bird and animal skins. He worked daily with his journals but was constantly interrupted to attend men with smashed thumbs, sprained ankles, whipsaw cuts, and other injuries incident to carpentry. Every day he longed for the use of the books he remembered in Philadelphia. This was no place to work on a journal.

To the Indians who were waiting to bring in their winter's accumulation of pelts, the new fort obviously was going to be a bastion too strong for any weapons they had. They felt two ways.

They wanted to trade for American goods, but British traders from Canadian posts had fine goods, too — and the knack of making the Americans seem like sinister invaders. With relations between England and the United States crumbling rapidly, there seemed a special urgency in the race to win the allegiance of the tribes.

A young Sauk war chief named Black Hawk, and his elders such as the Blue Chief, Pashepaho, and Quashquame, thought the unfinished fort was still vulnerable. The temporary pickets were low and easily scaled, and the blockhouses were unfinished. If any mischief were to be done, now was the time.

Increased Indian movements around the post so alarmed Kingsley that he sent Pryor and six soldiers down to St. Louis in late March to report to Governor Lewis and General Clark. The stockade fence could be jumped over easily, there was not even a platform from which to fire the six-pounder, and the enclosure probably could not be defended by the short complement of men stationed there. Pryor improved upon the report by saying he had heard from "spies in different quarters" that the fort was to be attacked. Lewis, with confidence in Pryor's opinion, took immediate action. The next day he issued a call for two companies of volunteer riflemen, to be augmented by some regular troops from Bellefontaine. His order — printed in the *Gazette* — said the volunteers were to equip themselves with arms, furnish their own provisions, and receive seventy-five cents a day.

It did not work; nobody volunteered. A week later the governor sent out another general order, putting the regular militia into action in place of the reluctant volunteers. In the end, both militia and regulars were dispatched to Fort Bellevue, but all seemed quiet when they arrived. They went home.

Pryor brought the mail when he returned from his mission. His own resignation request had been forwarded to Washington, along with Kingsley's application for a furlough, each with a covering letter in which the colonel at Bellefontaine voiced no objection. But Rafe's request to resign was still on the colonel's desk, Pryor said. It was under consideration.

Pirogues by the dozens came up across the rapids in early April, crowded with Sauks and Foxes. The black-eyed children trailed their fingers in the water, laughed to feel the new spring sun on their backs, and called out to the band of furry dogs that pattered along the shore. Heaps of loosely rolled furs lay in the larger boats, destined for some rendezvous with a British trader. Another winter hunt was done and it was time to test the resolve of the Americans who were building the fort.

The Indians camped on the southeast side of the river, across from the garrison. If they stood in the right place and sighted between two willowed islands, they could see the peeled and gleaming logs of the new picket walls going up side by side. For more than a week the migrants lingered about the area, crossing over in small parties to cruise the shore for a closer look.

Then a party of braves came over, led by Black Hawk and Pashepaho. The events of that day became a passage in Rafe's *Remarks & Occurrences.*

11 April 1809. The Sauk named Pash-e-pa-ho asked to be admitted to the parade along with an interpreter, telling Kingsley that his people wanted to dance there. He said it was too rough & rocky outside the stockade to dance. Kingsley refused, saying they could dance outside the fence or not dance at all. The young men of the party got restless, somebody struck up a beat on a drum, & they all began to move to the front gate. The sentinel there came to the charge position with his bayonet. Kingsley had put the six-pounder inside the gate, & now a soldier with a lighted portfire stood beside it so that all the Indians could see the smoldering twine.

When I glanced toward the barracks, half-constructed across the back side of the parade, I could see bayonets glistening through the doors and windows.

A young chief named Black Hawk was now in front of about ten Indians who filled the gateway, all being pressed forward by others in the rear.

As the artillerist moved the portfire closer to the fuze hole on the cannon, Black Hawk raised his war club in the air, gave a mighty whoop, & waved his men into a withdrawal.

This morning an old chief named Quashquame came over with a white flag & said that Black Hawk was a headstrong young man, greatly influenced by the British. Kingsley had the six-pounder wheeled out to the riverbank & fired, and the old Indian looked truly frightened by the noise.

The affair spurred the builders to greater effort. Kingsley burned fires on all sides of the fort to conceal the movements of the men, and the great white logs slipped faster and faster into place to form the palisade fence. The blockhouses were at last roofed over with shingles. On the evening of April 14 the men tamped earth around the last log, hung the front gate and barred it, and felt at last secure. Kingsley had instructed a musician to beat a whisky call on the drum the moment the gate was locked.

Among the items of news that Lieutenant Pryor had brought back from St. Louis was the selection of James Madison to succeed Jefferson as president. At evening parade, Kingsley announced that the new post would no longer be called Fort Bellevue. Now it was Fort Madison.

After a walking tour of the prairie that lay beyond the bottomland, Rafe was scolded by Kingsley for going out unescorted. It had been a futile venture, for he found no new plants and knew that the birds and animals he saw had all been reported long ago. He noted but did not collect such plants as green amaranth, wild garlic, phlox, snakeroot, two clovers, tickseed, and several grasses.

"Now then, tell me what you found," Kingsley demanded, "that was worth the risk of getting your skull creased."

"You ready?" Rafe asked, reading from his notes. "Fern species on moist shaded slopes, along with *Woodsia obtusa* and *Cystoperis fragilis*. Doesn't that just make your skin tingle?"

"Weeds, aren't they?"

"To some, perhaps."

"Point made," Kingsley said.

He's a gone case. Rafe was to make no more collecting tours during his assignment to Fort Madison. He tried to write daily, worried about what was happening to his resignation, cared for his patients, and even showed a brief interest in the commerce that John Johnson was trying to carry on with the Indians. Once he found the factor unwrapping a bale of furs bought from the Sauks and was given a grumbling lecture on the care of animal skins:

"Piece of fur is a troublesome thing. The moths love it. It don't pack down well. If you don't get the ears and other fleshy parts skinned out, it will rot. And once you get it into storage you've got to bring it out and beat it every few weeks to flail away the larvae. These Indians don't give a damn about supplying a good product. Hell's bells, I just found in one pack alone a pair of shanks and four hooves."

One of Rafe's duties was to supervise the food supply for adequacy and quality. He fought with the contracting agent, an employee of a large supplier in Lexington who delivered food and liquor to most of the garrisons in the valley. For this service the government paid thirty cents per daily ration. Rafe fought for live cattle instead of salt pork; for better vinegar when the supply appeared to have been cut with water. He demanded flour without weevils and salt without sand.

Then he started a campaign to promote gardens. The country boys loved it and seemed not to mind when the city soldiers from Charleston and Savannah slacked off on the hoeing and spading.

"Beats killin' Injuns on a regular basis," was the consensus. The gardens soon were producing drumhead cabbage, salad greens, onions, peas, turnips, and bush beans. The food that everyone longed for was potatoes.

"Red Russetings," said one soldier with a hoe.

"Irish Whites," said another. "Fried with onions, of course."

"Your instincts are right," Rafe told them. "Potatoes seem to have some element that prevents scurvy. Damned if I know what it is. Maybe we can get some this fall from St. Louis."

The thought that he would still be there in the fall sent him into an afternoon of despair. He walked down to the boat landing and watched a flight of pelicans, their bodies forming a lacy network of shimmering lines in the sky. Callie. Did her vaccination take? What would she be doing today?

With the sound of carpenters' hammers in the air, suggesting that both he and Fort Madison were going to be there for a long time, he went to his desk and wrote another letter of resignation to the colonel in St. Louis.

13

The Practice of Physick

~~~~~~~~~~~~~~~~~~~~

OFFICERS of the army sent one another letters sealed with red wax, crumpled a little, rained on a time or two, and bearing the thumbprints of many a boatman and frontier postmaster. In St. Louis, editor Charless often fretted in his newspaper columns about the poor mail service. "We are compelled to complain of the wretched state of the post-office department in this quarter; by especial grace we sometimes receive one mail in two or three weeks."

Lieutenant Kingsley had applied for his furlough in mid-January. Eventually it cleared St. Louis and reached the desk of the adjutant general in Washington, who promptly approved the request. A letter so stating left Washington on the first of April, sent not to Kingsley but, as the chain of command required, to Colonel Bissell at Bellefontaine. Orders also went down to Fort Adams, instructing Kingsley's replacement to proceed to his new post. By that day in June when Kingsley learned that his furlough had been granted, the officer who would take command at Fort Madison was already on the river. And since men traveled no faster than mail, many more weeks would pass before the arrival of Captain Horatio Stark, his wife Hannah, and his tiny pink mite of a daughter, Mary, who was only five weeks old at the start of her voyage.

The hazards of river travel were well known to the Starks, for they had plied the waters of America as army man and army wife from Detroit, Niagara, Mackinac, and New Orleans; from Hannah's farm home in Connecticut to Horatio's plantation in Virginia. The difference this time was the baby. They had not been able to weigh her on the day of her birth in April, but three days later she weighed in at five and a half pounds.

Stark was in his thirties and no fledgling, having entered the service in 1799 as an ensign. Now that he was going to command his first post, he should have been filled with pride, confidence, and swagger, but probably was not. At the end of a long period of arrest and a court-martial, he had just received an official reprimand for the cruel beating of a soldier. Stark seemed unashamed of the beating but chagrined by the verdict of his fellow officers and irked by the months of stagnation during which he had waited out his reprimand from the pen of General Wilkinson himself.

The distinction between a beating and a *cruel* beating was not very clear in the army, but in Stark's case the brutality had been readily apparent. He had taken Private Joel Dempsey outside the garrison at Cantonment Columbian Springs, on the lower Mississippi, "and having four pins of wood driven in the Earth, to which he was tied, then having him flogged in so Savage a manner as to disable him so that at this time it is with Difficulty he can move out of his Bunk in consequence of which he is now on the Sick Report." So read the charges and specifications preceding the trial.

Wilkinson's rebuke had come in the form of a general order circulated to all commands: "The General cannot forbear expressing his disapprobation of the conduct of Capt. Stark in the lawless and inhumane mode he adopted to gratify his personal resentment on Dempsey when the law provides a regular remidy for every Trespass."

At Fort Madison, the first sergeant was laboriously copying the text of this reprimand into the orderly book, late in July. Tiny gnats were swarming in off the glassy water of the river and circled in a nervous little cloud above his head, and the sweat from his writing hand oozed down the pen holder and diluted the ink before it struck paper. Regulations required that the reprimand go into every orderly book in the army.

It seemed to the sergeant that the name of Stark was familiar. He checked the incoming mail containing the documents ordering Stark's transfer to Fort Madison. Then he swore — and hurried to Kingsley's quarters with the papers. And Kingsley swore.

✶

"I was terrified for the child," Hannah said. She had brought the infant to Rafe for an examination soon after her arrival. Baby Mary had a tight purchase on Rafe's thumb and they were cooing at one another like passenger pigeons.

"The boat was so beautiful when we left the landing. The men had painted it white and it was really inviting. We had our own little cabin with panes of real glass in the windows. Not the blurry, wavy kind of glass, but clear glass. I couldn't have dreamed how horrible the trip was going to be."

Hannah Stark was a sturdy, large-boned woman with a pleasant face and a braid of jet-black hair. Her full gingham dress and smock gave her a lumpy look and the sun had turned her face and neck to leather. But Rafe surmised that she would have cut a fine figure at any officers' ball. She had been too long on the frontier to have the bloom that a wife in her early thirties might have had back East; but she had traces of brunette beauty left over, serenity in the eyes, and grace in the hands. To live within a prison of logs two hundred miles from the nearest town; to comfort frightened children when musket balls and arrows came whining in from the dark woods; to remain decent in the midst of brutality and coarseness — these were the challenges to Hannah's youth and beauty.

There was a kind of tenacity about her. At home in Connecticut, some steady tradesman might have found and wooed her. Instead, she had gone out to visit her sister in Mackinac and had met her young lieutenant at that northern post. Now she had a daughter Caroline living back home, tiny Mary in her arms, and she wanted more babies from the rough and earnest officer who had brought her here.

"For one thing," she said as she continued the story of her trip, "the spring rise was on and the current was fast. We had only nine men in the command (the captain had lost his company but that's another story), and those poor dears just puffed and grunted all day long to keep us moving. That first night we had a plague of mosquitoes. They stayed until we got above the mouth of the Arkansa."

"I've tasted those Arkansa mosquitoes," Rafe said. "I used to get one in every mouthful of food."

"I stayed under the mosquito bar for ten days, almost never

venturing on deck, and still this poor little tyke was almost eaten up. I had to put on my thickest clothing, despite the heat, and keep a towel in hand to defend myself all the time. Finally the men began to get sick. We put in at Chickasaw Bluffs because four of them couldn't stand up.

"I felt so bad when we passed St. Louis, thinking of all the shops and homes we might have visited. But now that I'm above those terrible rapids I may never want to cross them again."

The Starks had reached the Des Moines rapids ten days after leaving St. Louis. Even if they had been well briefed, and the men old hands instead of untried ones, they could scarcely have coped with the rapids. The oarsmen had spent a day feeling their way into the lower chain of rocks, guessing from the swirls and ripples what kind of bottom lay below. By nightfall, Stark and his men had muddled themselves into a trap. Even if they threw over an anchor and waited out the darkness, there was danger of being stove against the rocks as the boat swung on her cable.

"It was one of those sweltering August days," Hannah continued. Big thunderheads piling up in the west. Mary and I just lay in our bunk and listened to the hull scraping against the rocks. About midnight, I guess it was, we went aground right in the middle of the river."

Next morning a Sauk hunter had come up to the fort with word of the stranded boat, and help had been sent. Stark and his crew had got the craft afloat again, but they were still in a maze, not knowing whether to go on upstream or try to fall back below the rapids. Rafe had written in his journal: "With our smaller boat, & a couple of privates who knew the channel, we got Captain Stark & family off safe & they arrived at this place on 26th August. Everyone apprehensive about the Captain's past record."

He felt good about having this reliant and comely woman at the post. "The most beautiful baby I've ever seen," he declared, patting the bare buttocks of the child. *And the first I ever examined.* It occurred to him, probably for the first time in his life, that he might be a father one day. The idea pleased him.

During Stark's first weeks as commander, he made a policy decision regarding Indians that was patently wrong. A party of Ioways from the Des Moines had come up to trade, and Stark learned that the tribe had been harboring a fugitive. He refused to let Johnson trade with them. In a council with Chief Hard Heart, he lost his temper and so did the chief. Hard Heart threatened to return his Jefferson medal.

"Go ahead, you ugly savage. Turn in your medal and declare war on us." That is what Stark reportedly had said; Rafe was not at the council.

"The man's a bufflehead," Pryor decided.

After that incident, Stark stretched his authority by "demoting" Hard Heart, telling him he was no longer principal chief of the Ioways. "If I can break a man from corporal to private I can break a goddamned Indian from chief to thieving warrior," Stark insisted.

Morale at the fort declined rapidly. The garrison court-martials increased, the men being put on trial for the pettiest of offenses. Still smarting from his reprimand, Stark was reluctant to use outright physical punishment. He ordered the guardhouse doubled in size (Kingsley had never counted on more than two prisoners at a time); he canceled the whisky drum several times a week; he invented needless chores for the fatigue parties, such as ordering them to drag logs in from the forest by hand, although a team of oxen was available.

One morning in October the orderly sergeant brought Private Michael Keough to sick call, complaining of a sprained back. Keough had spent the previous day at the charcoal pit, tending the smoldering logs, keeping them covered with earth, and sacking up the chunks of finished coal. On bending down to pick up an especially large bag ("I can show you the bag that done me in, sir"), he had felt a twinge and could barely straighten up.

Rafe said, "I'm going to take you off the duty roster for a day or so and give you a bottle of liniment." He had been keeping a supply of camphor, olive oil, and laudanum mixed for the men who did the heaviest lifting. "Get plenty of rest."

Before the soldier could leave, the orderly sergeant returned with a worried look.

"Sir, this man has got to report back to duty."

"Who says?"

"The captain."

"Jesus," said the injured man, groaning. He looked at Rafe expectantly, hopefully.

"Did the captain say why?" *I shouldn't have asked that.*

"I don't question any officer's orders, sir."

"Of course not. Dismissed."

Private Keough leaned against the log wall and waited as if it were not his problem. He uncorked the liniment and sniffed it, held it up to the sunlight coming through the doorway.

"I'm going to have to send you back to the coal pit," Rafe said, laying a hand on Keough's shoulder. "Maybe the corporal in charge of the detail can find something easy for you to do."

The boy left, shaking his head as if silently insisting there was no easy work in the making of charcoal.

For a long moment Rafe seriously considered an untenable plan. When night fell he would load a pirogue, slip the mooring and float downriver until out of rifle range, then row like hell to the middle of the river. The current would take him to St. Louis. It made him feel better to think of so brazen an act, but the idea was ridiculous. *I guess I won't do that.*

Who had warned him that a line officer might overrule his medical judgment and take a man off sick report?

The doorway darkened as a figure appeared. It was Hannah, without her baby, carrying two cups of steaming tea. Her dress was fresh, her hair neatly coiled and skewered, or whatever women did with long hair, and there was a kitchen fragrance about her.

"I'd have brought you a biscuit but the captain ate the last one," she said, coming in to put the tea on the examining table. "May I set these here?"

"Cleanest place in the room."

"The room looks fine. That's camphor I smell, isn't it? Such a comforting aroma."

"I was just thinking the same about the aroma of fried bacon and fresh bread that you brought in with you."

"Oh, dear. I must smell like a scullery maid."

"No. Like my mother or my sister, Frances. Someone from home."

"That's nice. And the tea will add to the illusion. I make splendid tea. I hope you like hyson."

"I like it better than sumac bark, which I tried on my trip from Santa Fe."

"The Freeman and Bailey expedition," Hannah said.

"That sounds good. You're the first person who's ever used that term in my presence. Except me, of course."

"It was in the *Intelligencer*. A long, exciting story." She looked at the mounted plant specimens piled in a corner of the room. "Those wonderful new things. And you aren't working on them much, are you?"

"As much as I can. But I need books, articles, things like that."

"Mr. Pryor told me about your dilemma. It upsets me." She was cupping the tea in her hands, and the knuckles were grainy and dark as if they had been soaked in the brew itself.

Rafe rubbed his chin. "I've been in the army just over a year and have run into two men who have outmaneuvered me. One won't let me get on with my research and the other won't let me practice medicine as I think I should." He drained the tea and hesitated, not sure if he ought to continue. "I have to talk to someone and I hope you won't mind if it's you, especially as it concerns your husband."

She smiled wanly. "It wouldn't be the first time a friend has come to me about my husband. What is it this time?"

"He took Private Keough off sick report without my consent and put him back at what I consider hard labor. The boy has a badly sprained back."

"I don't interfere," Hannah said, running her forefinger around the rim of her cup. "I tried to once, in Detroit, and it nearly ruined our marriage. I've seen him do terrible things. Perhaps you wonder why I stay with him."

"I've thought about it. Especially since you seem so independent."

"Independent! Try being an independent woman two hundred miles from the nearest settlement, Indians camped across the river, a babe in the crib, salt pork going bad in the kitchen. Independence lasts about a year in the army."

"You could leave him and go back home."

"You're forgetting something. I love the man. Do you still think I'm independent?"

He was trying for a word and could not come up with anything that would get them off the subject. He settled for the obvious. "I don't know," he said.

Another shape darkened the doorway as the orderly sergeant

returned, obviously distressed. He had been working at the coal
pit and his shirt was smudged. His hands were black and he was
trying not to wipe them on his pantaloons. He clenched his fists.

"Sir, I'm worried about our sick man. He's having a real bad
time. That back of his is going to go out on him."

"Is he using the liniment?"

"No, sir."

Rafe stood up. "I told him to rub it on his back whenever he
needed it. It won't cure him but it will help the pain."

The sergeant unclenched his hands and stared at his soiled
palms. He seemed hesitant to speak further in Hannah's presence. She looked away into the fireplace, as if to remove herself.

"He ain't got the liniment. The captain came and took it," the
sergeant said.

Rafe got up to go, waiting until the sergeant had turned and
left the doorway. Hannah touched his hand as tears came to her
eyes.

"Incredible," Rafe said.

"I know."

Although Stark's office was smaller and more primitive, it reminded Rafe of Governor Alencaster's headquarters in New
Mexico. The clean table with all the papers neatly stacked. The
fireplace, not used since spring but still smokily rancid like the
rubble of a burned barn. A few oak leaves had blown in and
Private Lytle — Stark's waiter — was crouching to pick them up,
one by one, and stuff them into his pocket.

When Rafe stormed in, the captain waved Lytle outside. He
showed no surprise, as if he had timed Rafe's arrival to the minute.

"Mr. Bailey," he said.

"Dr. Bailey."

"Not here, my friend. Warrant officers are just misters. You
want to be a doctor, go back to the Piedmont in Virginia and
hang up your shingle. Charlottesville, I believe."

"I'd like that," Rafe said. "But while I'm doctoring on this
post I would thank you to leave my medical decisions alone."

Stark ignored the remark. "How was tea? Did you cry on Mrs.
Stark's shoulder?" He reached into his stack of papers and pulled

out a couple; but instead of turning to their contents he shoved them to one side.

"I don't like doctors," he began. "I've had gout, bilious colic, pleurisy, catarrhal fever, chronic headache, and so many rashes it's a wonder I've got any skin at all. No doctor ever cured me of a blessed thing. You know why I haven't still got all those ailments? They're self-limiting! That's a term I learned from another doctor. My wife's father. Did she tell you her father was a doctor? That old quack rubbed me and drenched me with everything on his shelf."

"Someone has treated you for a venereal, I see," Rafe said.

"How do you know that?"

"The dark patches on your arm where you rubbed mercuric ointment into it. You should have put it where it wouldn't show."

"Piss-ant!" Stark cried. "Don't get insolent with me, sonny. You aren't out of here yet."

Out of here yet? He's got some news.

Stark picked up a letter, the broken red seal showing brightly on the back. He started to hand it over and then did not. He only glanced at it.

"Colonel Bissell says your resignation has been to Washington and is accepted. You must stay until a replacement gets here from Georgetown. I hope to God he comes tomorrow, but I'm afraid we won't see him until next spring. You will probably drink a lot of tea between now and then."

"I trust we'll all survive the wait, captain."

"I survive everything. Your own survival is up to you." He groped for another letter and read the address deliberately before handing it to Rafe. It was still sealed and marked "personal."

"You get some pretty fancy mail, mister," Stark said, and stood up to watch Rafe leave the room with the unopened letter in his hand.

He was halfway across the parade before he looked at the envelope. The return address astonished him. "Meriwether Lewis, Gov., Dist. of La. Per express." The postmark was two months old. *Stark must have been holding it back.*

Rafe always took his mail to the boat landing in good weather and sat on an empty keg or crate to read his letters. The contractor's boat had just left, leaving the month's supplies, and someone had broken open a box of wine-red apples. He crunched into one as he scanned the letter. It seemed to be in Lewis's handwriting — he had seen that hand often enough — but it was erratically scrawled. Several words had been crossed out. Rafe picked his way through it.

Dear Rafe,

As I am on the point of leaving for Montichello, Washington, &c. &c., to put some affairs awrite with the Govt. and see to the forwardness of my ~~journals~~ publication, I take this oppty. to advise that I believe you are badly placed at Ft. Maddison. I had advised my ~~frend freind~~ colleague Col. Bissall that you shd. be spending Full Time on the materials of yr. late ~~tour~~ expedition, & can scarcely do same in yr. present situation.

The Col. advises me he will see to this. I confess I forget the ~~occas~~ circumstances that put you in that wretched place.

As the British are at some lengths to get aholt of my papers, I am not going by ~~water~~ way of N. Orleans but reather taking the old trace across the country per horse. I shall be going to Philada. & shall take pleasure in carrying a Greeting from you to all our mutual ~~freinds~~ friends including Mr. Dickerson.

These are new times, Mr. Jefferson not being in power. Do not be entrapped by his old enemies. These are times ~~that try~~ that try —

Did I ever. tell you that I know yr. Father? I used to ride past your place on my rambles when you were very young. Autumn leaves will soon be bright on the Blue Ridge.

Yr. Most Obt. Servt.
Meriwether Lewis

"Read this and tell me what you think," Rafe said when he had found Pryor.

Pryor studied the letter, puzzled over it, shook his head over it. "Poor devil has forgotten that he sent you up here. That's what I get out of it. This bothers the hell out of me. I'd sure like to talk to General Clark right about now."

"It's a worrisome piece of paper, all right. Takes all the fun out of my resignation."

Rafe put the letter in the bottom of a portmanteau trunk. He did not ever want to read it again, but he thought of it on many a long night when autumn rains tore at the shingles and the wind on the river was shrill and wild.

When the contractor's boat came in November with the mail

and newspapers, word spread throughout the garrison — as it already had spread across the nation — that Meriwether Lewis had reached Tennessee in a state of derangement and intoxication. Later, at a country tavern where he was spending the night, he had fired two pistol shots into his body and gone off to explore one last range of shining mountains.

14

A Spark in the Willows

~~~~~~~~~~~~~~~~~~~~~~~~~~~

IT WAS the dullest winter of his life. Rafe wore away the season hour by hour, sometimes discovering that his teeth were clenched as he lay in his bunk at night or even in midafternoon as he strolled about the compound.

The day after he had learned of Lewis's death, he had written a letter of condolence — not to Lewis's family in Charlottesville but to William Clark in St. Louis. The reply had been gracious, and for the first time, Rafe had seen Clark's wondrous spelling: "I most sincearly Thank You for Yr. Sentamunts of greef, and I jine with Mrs. Clark in the fervan hope that you will soon be spending som time with us to werk on yr. jls., now that Dr. Simpson is proseeding to relieve you."

With the heavy construction at the fort completed, including the two-story factory building outside the stockade, there were few injuries. Rafe's practice consisted of treating a few colds. *No malarial fevers in winter, thank God.* He might have had a regular patient in Captain Stark, but the captain refused to consult him.

"My husband is filled with aches," Hannah said. "And he's worried about keeping the company up to strength. He has thirty men whose enlistments are expiring in the summer and another thirty due before the end of the year. He's actually written the colonel that he might be able to find some usable men if he were allowed a bit more latitude in recruiting habitual drunks!"

With the prospect of war with England growing stronger, the

secretary of war had eased up on floggings and other harsh punishments in the hope of attracting enlistees. But Stark's reputation as a martinet was now widely recognized in the valley. The colonel sent him two hundred dollars for enlistment bounties, telling him to use his own judgment in signing up drunks. Still, nobody signed.

During Rafe's daily spasms of homesickness, he once spent a few moments of regret for offenses against his sister, Franny. He regretted chasing her out of the barn with a pitchfork when she was nine, because she would not tell him where in the haymow the cat was having kittens. He agonized mildly over his unsuccessful attempts to watch her bathe, before the kitchen fireplace, when she thought he had gone to bed (someone always happened by to spoil the game). He sorrowed briefly upon recalling the time when, in the courthouse square, he had struck her full in the abdomen for not buying him a penny candy. He must have been six years old then. *Her belly at about eye level.*

Contacts with the Indians were few and unremarkable. A few came to the factory out of curiosity, but it was not the season to deliver furs and their lead ingots could not be brought down the river until the spring thaw. Even the members of the British band seemed less menacing.

It bothered Rafe to know that although another surgeon's mate had been assigned to replace him, he would probably not arrive until the ice went out. *He's not straining to get here, I'll bet.* Dr. Robert Simpson was twenty-three, a lad from Port Tobacco, Maryland, who had studied medicine under a preceptor in Georgetown and attended one session in Philadelphia. Upon receiving his orders he had gone by stage to Pittsburgh and joined a detachment bound down the Ohio at a time when the ice was running so hard they had lost their boat. Now he was stalled in St. Louis, awaiting passage on the first spring trip of the contractor's keelboat.

"The day that sawbones gets here, I go over and kick the captain in the scrotum," Rafe told Nate Pryor. Pryor was still awaiting his own replacement. "Then I'll hand him a jar of Turlington's balsam for his swollen joints and start running right down the riverbank toward Home, Home, Home."

Although the roster of soldiers remained about the same, the population of the fort and its environs steadily grew. George Hunt (son of the late colonel) had established a sutler's shop inside the stockade and was selling the soldiers coffee and tea, refined loaf sugar, imported molasses, butter, raisins, and more exotic alcoholic beverages than their army ration provided. He stocked cherry bounce, applejack, peach brandy, and a sweet, flaccid wine.

Then John P. Gates appeared, having ridden a horse from the lower settlements, and began to serve Johnson as an interpreter to the Indians. He was a veteran, having once enlisted during a festive evening at Shape's Tavern in St. Louis, signing up with an eager captain who was drunker than he was.

The first boat of the year, sighted quickly by idling soldiers and bringing Rafe to the landing with high hopes, did not carry Dr. Simpson. It was a special craft assigned to bring five new residents: Lieutenant Thomas Hamilton and his wife, Catherine; a young son; and a black servant girl named Jessette; and Lieutenant Robert Page, who was Nate Pryor's relief.

Page adapted quickly to garrison life, spending his first day helping Pryor pack his gear for the trip to his dreamed-of smelter at the lead mines. But the Hamiltons found they had come to a hostile place; something had happened in recent years between the Starks and Hamiltons. "It was a little misunderstanding," Hannah explained to Rafe. "I've managed to forget it but Horatio hasn't."

The new couple was from New York City and seemed entirely urbanized. The lieutenant was slightly built, thin-haired and fair-skinned, with eyes that seemed too blue — like a robin's eggs — to withstand the glare from the river. His wife, despite her recent residence at Fort Dearborn on Lake Michigan, had not yet adjusted to living on the ground floor. "Our rooms at home were always upstairs, away from the street smells, you know."

Sensing tension between Stark and Hamilton, the men soon uncovered the secret. While the Hamiltons had been stationed at Dearborn, the Starks had come through on the way down from Mackinac. A corporal who had been at Dearborn told what had happened. Stark had taken the girl Jessette into the powder magazine and was discovered in mid-dalliance by Hamilton. He had challenged Stark to a duel, not necessarily for his affront to Jessette but for his presumptuous use of Hamilton's chattel. The matter was settled without violence when Stark expressed his regret in public to Hamilton.

Rafe considered the story outrageous and probably true. *No regrets necessary for Jessette, apparently.*

With little else to do, Stark kept the orderly sergeant busy posting new standing orders for the troops: an inspection every Sunday, weather permitting. Squad drills every day except weekends. Chopping wood on Sunday prohibited. Card playing never allowed on any occasion. No fish or game to be brought into the company rooms or cook houses until it had been cleaned.

By the first of May 1810, the Sauks and Foxes were on the move, not only going about their seasonal chores but also planning special mischief for Fort Madison. They were to be joined by small bands of Winnebagoes, from farther north, who were coming more and more under the influence of British traders.

Daily, said an item in the *Missouri Gazette*, Lieutenant Page took a few picked men and made a circuit of ten to twelve miles around the fort. He was said to be teaching the Indians to respect the establishment. It was not true. There was little to gain from reconnoitering a ten-mile circle when parties of Indians could escape detection in the ravines and thickets a hundred yards from the palisade wall. No sensible commander with only fifty-odd men fit for duty would have sent his only subaltern and a party of scouts to be ambushed in the marshy willowlands and woody slopes about the fort.

Stark had declared it a singular instance of bad judgment that Kingsley had located the fort fifty paces from a shallow ravine that ran to the river, carrying spring water down from the foot of the bluffs behind the garrison.

"Every cutthroat redskin in the valley has got his eye on that ravine as a perfect place to fire from," he declared. "I'm going to name it Kingsley's Run, and then by God we're going to do something about it."

In a conference with the officers, the factor, the sutler, and Rafe, Stark announced that he would build a small stronghold, barely more than a hut, on the point of land where the ravine joined the river. He could then rake the ravine with rifle fire for sixty yards and render it useless to the Indians.

The structure went up in a couple of days. It was about eight feet square, just large enough for four men to load and fire with ease, and was hastily chinked with plaster as high as a man's head. A guard of one corporal and three privates was posted there. On the afternoon of their posting, a sign went up above the door: "Kingsley's Run Tavern." Stark let it stay.

"I wish Pryor hadn't gone north so fast," Rafe said to Page one night at dinner. They messed together in their quarters except on Sundays, when Hannah Stark usually invited them to a midday dinner.

Page agreed. "In my bones I feel we are going to have a little uprising this spring." He spoke from scant experience, having been a tinsmith's apprentice in Delaware just four months earlier. But he was right.

It was the morning of May 10, when the grays of dawn were still on the river and a fragrant fog hung in the valley, that a party of a hundred Sauks, Foxes, and Winnebagoes filed into Kingsley's Run and squatted there to wait for daylight. The surly Black Hawk was there, and Cut Nose and Quashquame, grunting orders to a line of tense warriors who, being so close to the Americans, could scarcely hold themselves in check. All were young men, angry, painted for war, and armed with spears, bows, and muskets.

The fog roiled across the water, combing through the willows on the bars and islands. At sunrise the tops of bluffs appeared, shaggy with cedars and newly leafed oaks. In the mists of the shoreline a flock of hoarse crows began to sing out. Then the broad watercourse turned graygreen and picked up the glints of morning as the fog began to leave.

Rafe awakened early, and by the time the drummer had done reveille and the guard had fired the morning gun, he had dressed, shaved, and stepped out onto the parade. He went to the second floor of a blockhouse for a clear look at the river. From an open port on the south side he could see the ravine and the tiny cabin where four sleepy sentinels had been on duty since midnight. One of the men was inside, two were walking near the door, and the fourth was sitting in the open doorway with his musket propped against the jamb. *Not exactly an alert gang.*

While he was peering through the port at the growing brilliance of the day, and at the exact minute when he glanced into the ravine, he saw an Indian with a musket creep over the edge of the bank and race toward the sentinels' cabin. His stocky body, bare but for a breechclout, was shiny with grease and streaked with vermilion. On his head was a bright plume of roached deer hair that bobbed and waved as he ran.

"Indians!" Rafe shouted. "Watch out, there!"

The men outside the cabin scrambled for the door. The man in the doorway got up quickly, but already the Indian had shoved his musket barrel through a loophole in the rear wall and shot him in the back. He fell, and the others dragged him inside. As they barred the door, a second Indian sprang upon it and tried to force it open with his feet. He was shot from inside, through a loophole in the door.

Inside the fort, where Rafe's shout and the firing had been heard, and the drummer was beating the call to arms, a gun crew raced toward the blockhouse. Within a minute a six-pounder was throwing shells into the ravine, the crew working frantically while Rafe stood awed in a corner and waved the blue smoke away from his face.

By this time several Indians were thrusting spears through the high, uncaulked cracks between the logs of the cabin, where the plaster had not yet been applied — but the angle was wrong and they did no harm. One frenzied Sauk had gained the roof and was firing through a hole he had pounded through the shingles with his musket butt.

The bursting shells cleared the ravine quickly, and musket fire drove the attackers from the cabin, but not until they had pulled away a part of the stone underpinning and dragged out one of the sentinels. When the firing stopped, all four of the soldiers appeared to be dead. Up and down the river the crows were flapping huffishly and scolding as they circled the area.

As Rafe left the blockhouse, Stark and his junior officers had positioned the whole command around the stockade walls, each beside a loophole. Members of the old watch, just coming off a long night's guard duty, had hurried to the kitchen to wolf a breakfast of johnnycakes. The women and children peered anxiously through the front windows of the officers' quarters. Stark was striding about the parade with a pistol in hand.

"Check your flints and keep a close watch. The bastards are still out there."

The first sergeant had opened the door of the powder magazine and was rolling out a cask of musket powder. No attempt was made to recover the bodies from the cabin; four men were enough to lose.

"What can I do, captain?" Rafe asked.

"Write a prescription or something. What the hell do I care?" Stark said, and hurried off to make sure the water barrels were filled for fire protection.

Rafe looked to the bluffs behind the fort, where the limestone outcroppings were white in the sun, and saw a dozen Indians moving along the ridge. They were too far away to worry about. Nearer at hand, the rest of the war party had taken cover. A few had bellied along the shore and were lying out of sight behind a rotten log. Others had crept into the stable behind the fort, where a pair of oxen were tied, and were preparing to fire from the windows.

The signal to attack was a tremendous yell from one of the war chiefs. At once the firing began on all sides of the fort. A few of the Indians had good British rifles, but most of their weapons (including some bought from Johnson's factory) were typical trading-post items with shoddy flints and with balls cast too small for the off-size caliber of the barrels.

Along the stockade walls, the soldiers fired only often enough to keep the attackers pinned down — holding fire until a tawny, bare arm could be seen wielding a ramrod or until an Indian changing position showed too much of his plumed head above a tangle of hazelbrush.

"Dr. Bailey, check that man for injuries," Stark called, and only then was Rafe aware that he had been standing with his mouth slightly open, motionless. It was the Comanche raid all over again, but here inside four walls he felt more fear than he had known at the mouth of the Purgatory. He went to the firing line and walked behind the men. There was blood on the sleeve of a tense, sweating soldier, and the red stain showed brightly as he rammed down a charge in his musket.

"Let me see that arm," Rafe said.

"Can't stop for that, sir," the man said as he thrust his weapon through a loophole and fired. He wore a crude bandage on his wrist, dirty and loose, obviously several days old.

"What's wrong with your wrist?"

"Carbuncle, sir."

"What are you treating it with."

"Cattail fuzz. Works just fine as a poultice. An old Indian remedy." *Cattail fuzz?*

When he had circled the quadrangle without finding anyone else injured, Rafe stood distractedly and watched the men load and fire. The sergeant had brought out a few spare guns and leaned them against the wall of the powder magazine, together with a stack of cartouche boxes filled with paper cartridges. Rafe took a musket and found the best vantage point he knew of — the port in the blockhouse from which he had watched the attack on the outpost.

The air in the blockhouse was blue and warm, faintly touched by the aroma of burnt powder. No crew was tending the gun now, but a soldier was firing a musket from an open port when Rafe knelt beside him.

"I'll load and you fire," Rafe said.

"Yes, sir, if you can do it fast."

One of the sentinels was lying outside the cabin, shoulders hunched, arms bent wrong, face pressed into the earth. Rafe thought he saw movement. He looked again and was sure the man was alive.

Bounding down the blockhouse steps, he ran to the stockade gate and slipped out, then raced along the log wall toward the man on the ground. Later he would remember thinking there must be a military way to do this, but he would have to do it his way. He heaved the soldier across his back and set out, stooped and unsteady, for the gate.

"Open that damned thing," he yelled, and the gate swung back for him. He was safe inside and had not seen a single Indian. *Got me a patient, by God.*

When the Indians began to use flaming arrows in an attempt to burn the fort, the soldiers made "squirts," or syringes, from old musket barrels. With these they kept the roofs of the blockhouses damp but could not protect the other buildings. A bucket brigade was formed. Led by Hannah Stark, the women (including the slave Jessette) filled pails from the fire barrels that were kept filled for the purpose, and volunteer soldiers climbed ladders to slosh the water onto the shingles.

"I can't load rifles," Hannah later explained. "Horatio never let me learn. But I can sure dip water out of a barrel."

By noon the stable was burning, and Stark feared that the factory might be set afire at a time when the wind could blow sparks toward the fort. He sent Hamilton and a soldier with a smoldering stick of artillerists' portfire to set the factory ablaze during a time when the breeze had calmed. The building burned with a great roar, heaving sparks into the willow fringe along the river and filling the air with the stench of scorching fur as the bales of pelts were consumed. The loss was not total, for much of Johnson's merchandise was stored on the lower floor of Blockhouse No. 3. But the factory itself fell to coals and smoking debris.

Late in the afternoon the attack began to wane. A tall Winnebago ran close to the stockade and fired a quiverful of arrows, arching them high over the wall. They struck the hard earth beside the flagpole and clattered harmlessly, end over end, across the parade. The dozen shots aimed at the archer went wild, and when he disappeared into the thicket the firing died away on both sides.

With the factory gone, the principal reason for maintaining the fort was gone, also. Johnson was already packing his goods, intent on getting to St. Louis as soon as possible. With all the cattle dead, there was no way to haul furs to the dock. The haystacks were burned, so there would have been no forage for the oxen, anyway.

When word of the attack reached St. Louis, Colonel Bissell sent a meager relief party of twenty men, carrying orders to Stark to maintain the integrity of the post, despite the loss of the factory, in case of general hostilities. "War clouds are gathering," he had said, repeating a popular phrase in the newspapers. "If our country goes to war with the British, our local war will be with the Indians under British influence. Our outposts, such as yours and the ones at Fort Osage and downriver between here and New Orleans, will be essential to our defense." The relief party, traveling in two boats, would not reach Fort Madison for another ten days.

Rafe carefully nursed his patient, whose arms had been broken by tomahawk blows. A gash at the hairline showed how nearly he had missed being scalped before the Indians were driven away. Keeping an eye on the river, Rafe once felt so sure that Dr. Simpson must be approaching that he spent an afternoon airing his plant collections and bundling them up for transport. He unwrapped all his skin specimens and gave some a new application of white arsenic.

Hannah brought beef tea to the wounded man and hyson tea to Rafe. Once she brought — with guilt in her eyes — a small cake she had baked despite the low sugar supply.

"It isn't as sweet as it might be," she said.

"It's just right."

For some time Rafe had suspected that Hannah was pregnant, but he was waiting for her to mention it. She never did. It was comforting to know there would be a doctor on hand, after he was gone.

"I dreamed last night that I was at a beautiful lawn party," she said, musing. "I was wearing a sheer, full skirt trimmed in white satin. A bodice of silk, in some nice color. And wonderful morocco pumps and silk stockings. And, oh yes, a great scoop bonnet with violets."

Her life could have been worse, Rafe supposed, since the typical frontier woman did not have the dubious protection of the army. To be a settler's wife in a solitary cabin, far from the shelter of stockade walls, would be far more grim. Still, he wished that Hannah could be back in Connecticut, secure from the weathering of body and soul that eroded western women. Five more years in this valley, he guessed, would beat her down. Where now she was spare she would be gaunt. Where now she was brown she would become winter-burned, sun-dried. She had touched something in him — some acutely tuned sensor — a nerve ending unresponsive to the mother-and-sister ministrations of his youth at home. She did not inflict the lightning damage so often done to his composure by the look and feel of women his own age. *A solacing woman.* And somehow she loved the posturing boor who was her husband.

He wondered if she longed for the miscellany of home. He thought of his mother's cupboard with its goblets, salvers, cruet frames, fish knives, toast racks, japanned coffee jugs, and sugar and cream ewers coated inside with rich gold.

"A fiddleback chair," he said to Hannah.

"A what?"

"Wouldn't you rather have a fiddleback chair than a crude, homemade bench by the fireplace?"

"I never thought much about fiddlebacks. But now that you mention it —"

"What else do you miss?"

She thought about it. "I miss muffs and tippets of ermine. And maybe a saucy beaver hat with a feather and a band."

"Suppose you could have something special right now. What would it be?"

"That's easy. A jar of Conner's balsamic lip salve of roses, to give me a coral mouth like the women at home."

"You should have brought some with you. It's not expensive."

"Captain Stark disapproves of it."

Rafe wanted to ask: "Is that the Captain Stark who took Jessette behind the powder kegs at Fort Dearborn?" But instead: "I'd love to see you wearing the Conner's, not to mention the beaver hat."

"Thank you, dear Rafe. I expect to miss you very, very much."

He supposed he loved her. But as protective as he felt, and as sure as he was that he might willingly die to protect her, he was sadly aware that he would not spend another day on the frontier to be near her. It was their last teatime.

The boats dispatched by the colonel reached the rapids at midmorning on Sunday, and the news of their approach — brought by a passing trader — made a shambles of Sunday inspection. With the river high from the spring runoff, the boats would clear the rapids easily and arrive at the landing by late afternoon. Stark ordered Hamilton to parade the company under arms, then set the men to preparing quarters for the new soldiers from Bellefontaine.

There was a doctor aboard the second boat, the trader had said. How he learned of this was a mystery, for he had communicated with the commander of the detachment only briefly by shouting across a quarter-mile of river.

"It was told to me as God's simple truth," the trader insisted. The news sent Rafe to his quarters to see to the brushing of his uniform, the blackening of his boots, and the fluffing of the white plume on his cap. Private Arthur Cox, all but healed from his injuries, begged to be discharged. Rafe inspected his fast-mending wounds and wrote him off the sick report, making it easier to straighten up the hospital room and put a freshly aired blanket on Cox's bunk.

The first boat tied up just as the stockade logs were throwing a jagged line of shadow across the parade. Stark had drawn the company into formation near the flagpole. As the new men marched through the gate, their commanding officer drew them into a similar formation facing Stark's company. The officers exchanged salutes, the men were dismissed, and Rafe's attention turned to the second boat drawing up to the riverbank.

French watermen tied it fast and immediately turned to the unloading of its cargo, including a six-pounder and several kegs of salt pork lashed together and made secure to the mast. When the gangplank slammed down, and the fore and aft lines were tossed ashore, the first person to step off was Dr. Simpson. Rafe hurried toward him. *Bless that silly white plume.*

"I've just discharged your only patient," Rafe said, extending his hand.

"Never mind. I'll find others, won't I?"

Rafe had not expected a short man. Simpson was about five feet five and on the pudgy side. When he removed his cap to dry his brow, his prematurely balding head glistened pink and damp.

Now Rafe was staring beyond Simpson with a look of total surprise. A slim, dark girl was coming ashore, a deerskin bundle under her arm. She came carefully, in moccasins, stepping smartly across a puddle in the sand. She stopped, shifted the bundle to her other arm, and scanned the faces of the men on shore.

"I guess you have seen my traveling companion," Dr. Simpson said. "She's been waiting all winter in St. Louis for passage up here. Like me."

The name he had called so many times in his dreams came haltingly to Rafe's tongue. In his heart it was a shout of exaltation but it half-died on his lips in the excitement of seeing her.

"Callie?"

She did not run toward him, but walked — in grace and serenity, her long wait and toilsome journey ended, her dark eyes confident that she had done the right thing.

"I told you I would learn English. Now I have learned it."

15

Under Their Vine and Fig Tree

In St. Louis, Editor Charless had been putting more and more
social notes into his newspaper. An example:

SEPT. *1, 1811 — Dr. and Mrs. Raphael Bailey left this place today for the
Doctor's plantation at Fox Run, in Albemarle County, Va. After his notable expedition to the mountains, and his heroic crossing of the plains in
winter, Dr. Bailey served for a time as Surgeon's Mate at Fort Madison.
He has spent the past few months in the home of Gen. Clark, working
on an edition of his Travels.*

Rafe and Callie were on the road, conveyed in an old calash
drawn by one horse and designed to carry three passengers. Its
folding canvas top was cracked and patched, and its leathers had
not been oiled in years until Rafe had doused them with neat's-
foot; but the body of the carriage was bright with new paint and
fresh brass nail heads. One strong bay mare drew the vehicle, and
two roan packhorses followed behind as the Baileys headed across
the Illinois prairies. They would take the old trail from Kaskaskia
across to Shawneetown, then ferry across the Ohio and continue
toward Louisville.

Rafe scanned the newspaper as they jolted along. He could
think of a few things left out of the story about their departure.
"The lovely Mrs. Bailey is the daughter of an itinerant beaver
trapper and a Quapaw Indian mother. Until recently she lived on
the banks of the Arkansa in a hut made of reeds, and her recipe

for stewed raccoon is second to none. She has more class and heart than all the high-born ladies of Philadelphia."

Another bit of news, Rafe thought, might have been added to complete the article: "Dr. Bailey's father knows his son is bringing home a wife, but knows nothing of her ancestry. That is to be a surprise."

Women's traveling garb ran to browns and blacks, and Rafe would have preferred to see Callie in her almost-white buckskins and her bright beadwork, as she had been that first day on the expedition when she had demanded to be vaccinated. Still, he had grown accustomed to her European dress and so, apparently, had she. Feet born to moccasins now were encased in patent leather. Hair worn so many years in braids now was teased into soft ringlets.

She waited for him to put the newspaper away. "When is my reading lesson?"

"When we stop at noon. We'll sit under a sycamore and you can read Joe Charless's latest tirade against the British."

"The print is too small. It hurts my eyes."

"Nonsense. I've seen you thread a needle by candlelight."

"The words are too hard." She screwed up her face and stuck out her tongue, a gesture that Rafe had decided was universal.

"Do you want to be just another squaw?" The term he once had shunned he now used to tease her.

She hammered on his shoulder with both fists, not very hard. "I will read the goddamned paper."

"Don't use that word anymore." He leaned over and kissed her.

"Which word?"

"Fifth word. *Cinquième.*" She fell silent as if wondering which was the fifth, but he knew she had purposely provoked him. "Learning what words are bad is the worst part," she had complained more than once.

Crossing the lower tip of Illinois Territory was an uncomfortable trip, with flies, midges, the hot sun of late summer, and a lame packhorse. Stumps in the road could destroy a wheel on the light vehicle. At one tavern where they lodged, the food was so bad that they had dug into their own supply of nutmeats and dried fruits which Julia Clark had packed for them. But the innkeeper's wife had given them a jar of watermelon pickles so delicious that Callie copied the recipe from the woman's tattered household book, scrawling it out with Rafe's help. "Let you Mellon rinds lay in salt water till they get yallow, then boil in spring water till they cook up plump," and so on. Of all the new foods she had encountered, Callie loved pickles best.

After they had crossed the Ohio at Jim Lusk's ferry, they would be on a well-traveled road that would carry them on a seemingly circuitous route, first southwest and then northeast to Louisville. From there they would follow the road that had brought Rafe west in 1807. He glanced at the *Gazette* again, taking pleasure in "his notable expedition" and "his heroic crossing of the plains." He wondered if the Richmond *Enquirer* or the Philadelphia papers would pick up the item. Fame was addictive, he decided. He recalled the time he was toasted in St. Louis. It was Independence Day, and after the big dinner at Christy's a great many toasts had been drunk and many a patriotic song played by the band. Then, Governor Ben Howard, who was Lewis's successor, had risen with glass in hand, looked squarely at Rafe, and proposed: "Wealth, honor, and happiness to the naturalist who makes us acquainted with the hidden treasures of our country." The band then played "Jefferson and Liberty." A fine occasion.

The months just passed had served a welcome purpose. They had cut him off from the hardest memories of his expedition and his unhappy stay at Fort Madison, given him a wife, and allowed him time to think hard about his journals — even if most of the actual rewriting was still to come. He thought less and less about Bid Wilkinson (down near Mobile Bay, he heard), and Tom Smith (already a colonel or something). He knew that Freeman was surveying in Mississippi Territory and had not yet sent in his report of the expedition.

Two letters from Hannah Stark had come down from the fort: she had borne a baby named Rosanna, and she sent Rafe her love — taking care to include Callie.

Once he dredged up a fading image of Santa Fe and wondered if Major What's-His-Name had recovered from syphilis. That had led him to felicitous thoughts of Fernandez, the dear young Spaniard who had befriended him and helped him to leave New Mexico. He supposed that later he would remember every moment of that hard year, but now he wanted to think only of Callie, of home and friends, and the journals.

The miracle that had brought Callie to him came often to mind. Aboard the boat going down from Fort Madison, he had asked her, "How did you find me?"

"Jonas told me."

"And who is that?"

"The soldier Jonas. Came to the Arkansa Post where I was learning to speak English. Very ill, very cold."

Jonas Gardner? Of Course! The son of a bitch. "Tell me about Jonas," he had asked, somewhat anxiously.

"He came to the fort. Mr. Treat was teaching me, and my grandfather was paying him with furs. While Jonas was getting better he asked if he could help. Told me stories about you. How well you treated him before he ran off from you — sad about that. How you fought the grizzly. How you climbed a great mountain. How you fed him nasty berries to cure his teeth and mouth."

"Did he — did he try to —"

"Make love with me? Not when he found out that I belonged to you. He just told me to go to St. Louis and you would be near there. He called me Downstream Girl. He was kind to me."

Days had passed before Rafe had asked one more question about that episode. "You told Jonas that you belonged to me?"

"*Certainement,*" she had said, and while Rafe held her close on the feather bed in William Clark's spare bedroom, and stroked her hair, she corrected herself without his prompting. "Certainly," she said, and ran her tongue playfully around the rim of his ear.

"My Downstream Girl," he had whispered, and tears had washed into his eyes — tears that did not sting but soothed.

At Louisville they spent a night at the Indian Queen. Callie thought the painted carving of an Indian girl above the door was ugly and crude. "Never mind," Rafe said. "I brought my own Indian queen and she is beautiful."

At the bookstore in a corner of the newspaper office he bought a copy of Zebulon Pike's *Expeditions,* the first he had seen, and read from it while Callie drove the horse between Louisville and

Lexington. "Terribly short on natural history," he muttered. But it was a pleasure to read of the places he knew: the Great Bend, the Big Cottonwoods, the Purgatory. He understood the excitement of Pike's men upon first sighting the Stony Mountains. Rafe learned for the first time that Pike and a few of his soldiers had made a futile effort to climb Mount Bailey. They had approached it in November, in summer uniform, and had left the creek too soon and got involved with the foothills before turning back in deep snow.

Pike wrote: "The summit of the Grand Peak, which was entirely bare of vegetation and covered with snow, now appeared at the distance of 15 or 16 miles from us, and as high again as what we had ascended, and would have taken a whole day's march to have arrived at its base, when I believe no human being could have ascended to its pinical."

"It didn't seem that hard a climb," Rafe told Callie. "We had good weather on our side. At least he didn't have to fight a bear."

"You are better than him," Callie ventured.

The days had stretched out, October had begun, and the horses were flagging when the Baileys reached the stage road that ran from the Holston River northeast to Rockfish Gap, and on into Albemarle County. A broken axletree had delayed them at Wytheville, and they had spent an extra night in Fincastle to bring the Hancocks news of their daughter, Julia Clark. Now they had reached Charlottesville and were in the final two hours of their journey. "Forty-five days on the road," Rafe said.

"My new home," Callie said.

Instead of taking the old Three Chopt Road, a much-traveled thoroughfare, they chose the smaller trail that led out past the site of the Hessian barracks where, during the Revolution, a captured army of mercenaries had been lodged. There was no sign of the camp now; even the fieldstones that the soldiers had used to support the walls of their huts had been hauled to the fence rows and piled up, by farmers. Scrubby young pines were crowding in from the woods. Looming ever closer in the west was Rafe's personal part of the Blue Ridge, bright with autumn colors. His eyes swept from left to right as he identified the gaps. Wood's Gap, Turk's Gap, Brown's Gap. He had traversed them all, including Old Rag itself, lying so far north that he could barely make it out.

At White Hall settlement, where the trail turned north into the valley of Doyle's River, and the dogwoods had turned to red and orange, Callie entertained him with her own botanical lore.

"What is that plant called?" she asked, pointing to a patch of meadow rue.

"*Thalictrum*," Rafe said. "That's the Latin name."

"It is a love medicine. Married couples take it when they have been quarreling. I will remember where it grows." She pointed out the purple rocket and said she had made a rouge from the boiled root with which to paint her face. The *Eupatorium*, she claimed, was another love medicine. "Men hold it in their mouths and nibble on it while speaking to girls who might want to make love."

They topped the last rise in the trail just as the sun was hanging red above the Blue Ridge and shadows of the pines were long upon the grasses. There in the valley lay Fox Run Farm and all his fond memories of boyhood.

The river ran straight beside the trail, coming down from the high places in Brown's Cove and other hollows to the north. On the south side of the river was the farm, laid out into small fields enclosed by rail or hedge fences. Halfway up Pigeon Roost Mountain, behind the fields, were the woods in which the Bailey hogs ran free and fed upon acorn mast until brought in for butchering.

Facing the river, on a little rise near where Fox Run coursed down to join the larger stream, sat the old farmhouse. It was colonial in style, one end built two full stories of brick in the Georgian manner, and the other end, a story and a half, made of wood with three dormers. A chimney at each end and the white-painted wooden wing made the house a fine example of two architectural styles combined.

The dependencies were typical farm buildings, built of sawed boards and roofed over with cedar shakes. The barn was large enough to have a threshing floor where, in winter, a team of oxen circled endlessly to tread the wheat kernels out of the chaff. There was an icehouse, a small tobacco-drying shed, two granaries, and four small cabins that housed the hired help. Despite Anthony's opposition to slavery, he kept two families who had been freed but simply declined to leave. The other cabins housed part-time labor, usually farm boys from about the county who were glad to learn agriculture from a man who once had farmed for Washington.

A glance at the fields told Rafe the state of the harvest. Shocks of Indian corn dotted one field. Another was newly sown, probably to wheat. The second cutting of native hay had recently been taken from lands along the river. Behind the barn, rows of flax had been spread out for retting.

"Under our vine and fig tree," Rafe said, half aloud.

"What is a fig tree?"

"A fruit. But the phrase is from the Bible and I've heard my father use it many times. It means contentment on one's own land. It fits my father."

Rafe looked toward Bluebird Meadow, on the mountainside, and realized with a pang that he would never again be welcomed by Old Blue. In earlier times, when Rafe was returning from school, he would send a piercing whistle up the mountainside. The black head would raise up, the ears swivel forward, and the stiff-legged mule would walk as briskly as he could to the gate nearest the barn to wait for his friend.

Rest in peace, Blue, and thank you for dying in your sleep like Mancha. I don't think I could have put you away.

Four and a half years after leaving home, Rafe pulled up to the front of the house and tied the horse to the hitching rail. The place was quieter than he would have expected (one strange foxhound on the porch raised its head but did not bother to get up), and the flower beds needed attention. The asters and marigolds near the veranda had escaped the early frosts, but weeds had almost hidden them.

He used the call he had learned as a boy to summon hogs to the feeding trough.

"Whoo-ee! Whoo-ee!"

Anthony Bailey appeared in the doorway. He had been reading, and the thick-lensed spectacles kept him from recognizing his son at once. He raised the glasses and peered out from under them. (*My God, he's aged.*) Then he rushed to the porch steps, paused as if reminding himself not to stumble, and hurried down to embrace Rafe. They stood clasped in each other's arms, swaying silently, for nearly a minute.

"Prayed for this day, Rafe," the old man said.

"Thank you for that."

Anthony released him and looked at Callie, who was still in the carriage. She seemed so alone, so overwhelmed by a world newly hers, that Rafe almost wished he had stayed with her on the frontier.

Anthony went to her and reached for her hand.

"Callie?"

She nodded. "Under my fig," she said, and took his hand.

As autumn deepened, and the first gentle snow came briefly to the highest ridges, Rafe adjusted to a home forever changed. He had never before slept for a night in the house without the comforting sense that his mother was near. Now there was only his father and Black Sally (Peter had fallen and died in the garden six months ago, and Franny had remarried and moved to Norfolk).

Rafe spent most of his time in his father's study, where his specimens were spread out in disarray and his papers lay in deep stacks on the library table. Three letters had come for him. From Philadelphia, the publishing firms of John Conrad and of Bradford & Inskeep had each offered to publish an account of his expedition. A letter from a businessman on the Eastern Shore — who had known his mother's people — inquired about his setting up a medical practice at Onandock. As he ordered his priorities, he thought he would first produce his book and then accept the offer of a medical practice while he decided how to spend the rest of his life.

Callie surprised him with the ease of her adjustment. She studied English daily, took long walks along Fox Run, and wandered into the mountains ("If you half close your eyes it looks like where I lived before"). Sally had accepted Callie graciously and announced one day that she wanted to be called Auntie so that Callie would not be puzzled by the sound of the two names.

He had written to Jefferson and mailed the note in Charlottesville, announcing his return. On his list of "things to do" he always wrote "Monticello," but had not yet gone to visit there. He was embarrassed by his negligence, when in the early days of November the former president came to him.

When they sat down in the study, Jefferson declined a glass of

Madeira and said he would prefer an iced drink; his icehouse had been empty since September and he craved the taste of something cold. He looked hale to Rafe; he was less stooped than before, his face was brighter, but he walked with some difficulty and seemed anxious to explain why he had come in his gig instead of on horseback. Rheumatism.

"I am a happy farmer, though, despite my infirmities."

He was filled with small talk that had to be disposed of before he brought up the subject of his call. His daughter Martha Randolph and her family had moved back to Monticello to care for him. The harsh weather of last spring had cost him the Morello and Duke cherry saplings sent him by George Mason, and some Spitzenburg apples as well. He had four hundred and fifty acres in wheat this year and had increased his tobacco to sixty. With those two cash crops he hoped, as he said, "to clear myself of all the financial difficulties I brought on myself in Washington."

When Jefferson asked to meet Callie she could not be found. Unready to meet her former Great Father, she had fled to the banks of Fox Run.

"She's really doing well," Rafe insisted. "I wrote you that she is half Quapaw. My father doesn't know that yet, but thinks she's all French. I am ashamed that we haven't told him."

"It's a splendid union. The red and white races must eventually merge," Jefferson said. "I wish I could say the same for the blacks and whites. That, I fear, can never be. Black men must be free, of course, and I blush for my country (and myself as well) that they are not so now. But they are a race apart. Have you read my *Notes on the State of Virginia?*"

Rafe said he had.

"Then these troubled views of mine are well known to you. Let us get on to the state of the world. What do they say in St. Louis about the problems with England?"

"I suppose the same as here, sir — that a war seems inevitable. But out there they don't expect to see British redcoats so much as hostile tribes aroused by British beguilement."

"Oh, we'll see troops here all right. And we must seize the day. Canada has ever been a dear dream of mine — it belongs in our union — and we must take it if war comes. Cuba must come into our family of nations, also. With Canada and Cuba in our camp we could be a bastion of liberty that all the wretched kings of Europe could not breach."

He fell silent for a moment, rattling the ice in his glass gently. "Now that I am refreshed, I believe I shall accept your kind offer of the Madeira."

Rafe poured two ample glasses. *He came here for something.*

"I suppose you are hard at work on your journals," Jefferson said. "I heard from General Clark that you drive yourself sternly in that regard."

"Every moment I can spend. I am considering John Conrad as publisher and may go up to Philadelphia soon to discuss the matter."

"Then you must give my best to everyone you see — Rush, Wistar, Barton, and half the city. Tell them I miss them, but not nearly enough to make the journey. I apprehend I shall never see those dear faces again."

"Happily, they are my friends, too. I shall be glad to carry your message."

Jefferson had brought with him a small trunk, the kind a gentleman kept near him to hold his books, papers, and small items of comfort when traveling. Now he brought it to his lap and opened the lid.

"I have some things of interest here and I hardly know where to start." He closed the trunk but held it. "Eventually we must go through the pain of speaking about Governor Lewis. My friends in the West tell me you suffered somewhat at his hands, and I wish to be clear in my mind that you realize he was a tormented man."

"I came to know that. It took a while."

Jefferson opened the trunk again and removed a letter. He unfolded it and scanned it, as if deciding whether to divulge its contents. Rafe thought he saw his eyes grow moist as he read the document to himself.

"I have a communication from someone I have never met but to whom I am deeply indebted. He is Captain Gilbert Russell, who was in command at Chickasaw Bluffs, in Tennessee, when Lewis stopped there on his last journey. The governor was not himself. The word 'deranged' has been used and perhaps that is too harsh. He was not able to get himself under control alone.

The captain took him in — almost forcibly detained him, as I understand — for a few days. But a mere captain cannot keep a governor under house arrest, of course. So Mr. Lewis rode on to the fate we all lament so sorely. Later the captain wrote me the letter I now quote from: 'The fact is, which you may yet be ignorant of, that his untimely death may be attributed solely to the free use of liquor which he acknowledged very candidly to me after his recovery, and expressed a firm determination never to drink any more spirits.' "

Jefferson put the letter away and shook his head ruefully. "In such cases a firm determination can be fleeting. I tell you all this to make it undeniably plain that Meriwether Lewis was much changed in those last years. He was not the boy I watched grow up in these mountains, or the young man who became my private secretary and served me like a son. Especially, he was not the bold explorer who went forth — and Heaven knows you are aware of all it takes, doctor — to those wild places and performed such a service that his country will never forget him."

Jefferson turned his head to hide his face as he continued. "I should have known something was wrong inside him. After he left here for St. Louis, to be governor, he wrote me only three letters — all on affairs of state. Three cold, detached letters."

He was crying.

Rafe stepped to the window and looked out anxiously, hoping to see his father down by the granaries or, better yet, on his way to the house. Anthony would know how to handle this moment, but he was not in sight. There was an awkward pause while Jefferson regained his desire to talk. He waved away Rafe's offer of more wine.

"Dr. Bailey."

"Sir, I would be flattered if you would call me Rafe."

"Rafe. Yes. I have to impose upon you a request that may cause you some resentment. I feel the time has come to set it before you."

"Your last request took me three years to fulfill. Am I in for another three years?"

"Possibly. I do hope not. I want you to take over the Lewis and Clark papers and put them into readable form for publication. You would be 'editing' them. The French would call it *rédaction*. Will you do it?"

"Before I do my own, you mean?"

"Before that, yes. Starting as soon as possible."

Double damn. What's happening here?

Jefferson said: "It's worse than my last request, isn't it? Back then I offered you fame and adventure. This time I propose tedious work and my gratitude. Only you can do this work. You have the knowledge and personal experience. You are the voice of authority."

"I thought General Clark already had arranged for someone to do a book."

"A book, yes. But not the book that the world needs. Mr. Nicholas Biddle in Philadelphia has kindly agreed to write a narrative based on the Lewis and Clark materials. Indeed, he has already redrafted some of it and returned the notebooks to me." He patted the trunk on his lap. "But even if that book sees the light of day, it will not be the definitive, instructively scientific report that the exploration deserves. There will be a single map, not very detailed. There will be no drawings of plants; no Latin descriptions of new species; none of Lewis's elaborate descriptions of animals or General Clark's marvelous discourses on Indian life. All these things you could prepare wonderfully well. I ask it of you with great seriousness."

"Must I agree today? May I think about it?"

"Naturally. Let me fuel your determination — if, indeed, there is a spark to be fed. We have had two great explorations into the West — yours and the other one — which represent real dilemmas to the planners of this nation's development. Much as it might pain you to realize it, there is some reason not to place too much emphasis upon the fine work that you and Mr. Freeman have done. Not with the Spanish in so truculent a mood. We have narrowly escaped armed encounters with them, and their interception of Mr. Pike on the wrong side of the Rio del Norte was most unfortunate. It would be best if we did not add to Mr. Pike's recent edition still another treatise on those disputed regions in the Southwest. We must wait until diplomatic means have brought an end to these boundary disputes with Spain.

"On the other hand, Lewis's tour — I should say his and Clark's tour, for I sometimes make that ungracious mistake — their expedition must come to the attention of our people soon, with all its implications for western expansion. The British would like to get their hands on the mouth of the Columbia. They would not lose the sale of a pack of furs for the freedom of the whole world. But Lewis and Clark have strengthened our claim to that country. Now we have Mr. Jacob Astor, who has sent two vessels round the Cape and a party overland to establish a post on the Columbia.

"I view that post as the germ of a great, free, and independent empire on that side of the continent. One from which the idea of liberty and self-government will spread in this direction, just as our own concepts must go westward with our people.

"But the people must know. We are a land-hungry lot, and as soon as our citizens know what lies out there, they will support the government in ultimate control of those regions. They will read about them — in the work you must prepare!"

Jefferson rose and put the trunk on the table. "I think I am straining too hard. Let me leave these with you and you can let me know what you think in a few days." He laid out half a dozen red-morocco notebooks and a couple of others bound in marbled boards. "This is a start. There will be more as soon as I can get Dr. Barton to send down some of the scientific materials he has been reading. Wonderful, fascinating." He opened a journal and Rafe recognized Lewis's handwriting.

"My father will be sorry to have missed you," he said.

The Baileys loved a big breakfast. Anthony had eaten johnny-cakes every morning of his adult life, always suggesting mildly that the next stack be just a shade browner. Usually there was a plate of thinly sliced ham, cut from a mold-crusted, salt-ridden chunk of meat that had to be soaked forever to make it edible. Only Anthony was addicted to johnnycakes, so Auntie (née Sally) usually rose early to get some kind of hot bread into the oven. She fried eggs and potatoes and made sure there was plenty of applesauce, dark with cinnamon and ground cloves. The breakfast drink was strong tea. Something new was present now: a cut-glass side dish of assorted pickles for Callie. She was partial to the bread-and-butter kind but also liked pickled beetroot, peach chutney, tiny pickled onions, and corn relish.

"Auntie, you could do wonders with a buffalo tongue," Rafe suggested.

"Glad you ditten bring me any. Ah wouldn't tech it." Auntie hovered, mumbled, and served.

On this morning after Jefferson's visit the conversation focused wholly on that event. It was the great misfortune of Anthony's entire year, he complained, not to have been at home.

"Have you decided what to do, Rafe?" he asked after saying grace.

"Not yet. Sometime after midnight I gave up on it and went to sleep. I seem to be casting about for a reason. I don't want to do those journals just because my former commander-in-chief has asked me to, when I've got my own project before me. Maybe that's selfish, but it's how I feel."

"Then do it for Lewis and Clark," Anthony said. "Fellow explorers. Band of brothers. Kindred spirits."

"Not quite right, either. If I do it for Lewis I may always think he has reached out from the grave and put his hand on me, holding me back, as he once did. I might always think I was editing his journals under duress. I don't want to remember Lewis that way, now that I sense what made him act as he did toward me. I want a better memory of him than that."

"Then what about Clark?"

"A great friend who can't write a decent sentence and can't spell worth a damn. If I say I'm doing it for him then I'm just a secretary, a corrector of infelicities. There are dozens of good writers who can do that. Some printers even correct an author's English while they're setting type."

Callie had something to say, waiting as usual to make sure the men had finished speaking. Her eyes glistened.

"Two books to be written. Yours and theirs?"

"Right, my dear. I would be doing theirs first."

"What about this? Do their book first — for your country. You went out to the mountains for your country. You were a soldier and doctor for your country. Now do this. What is the difference?"

She's closing a trap. "And after that?"

"Do the other book for Callie. I waited for you, and now I wait for this book. There is plenty of time for me to have you, your book, babies, and my fig tree."

Anthony clapped his hands as if applauding a ringing political speech in the courthouse square. "Spoken with all the sagacity of an Indian princess!" he cried.

Rafe looked inquiringly at Callie and knew he had been left out of something.

She smiled. "I told your father yesterday that my mother was a Quapaw and my grandfather a chief. I wanted to surprise him but he seemed to know. Anyway, he hugged me and kissed me on the forehead, and made me feel glad."

Anthony was busy with johnnycakes. "New World blood in the family is a fine thing. And royal blood at that."

After breakfast, Rafe gathered up half a dozen of the Lewis and Clark notebooks and went to the barn. All his life he had struck out for the barn when there was a serious matter to be worked on, faced up to, or simply pondered. When he was five he had retired there after his father had told him that human children were generated in precisely the same manner as calves, little pigs, and kittens. In adolescence he had spent an evening there after a distressing argument with his father, who wanted him to enroll at Washington Academy instead of William and Mary. When Franny's husband died and Rafe, well along toward becoming a doctor, realized that medicine could never have saved him, off he went to the barn. If the weather was hot the barn was cool. In winter it was warmed by the bodies of cud-chewing cows and kind-eyed horses. Every piece of wood in the building seemed to have been smoothed and polished by long contact with animals.

He turned over a wooden pail and sat down, behind the stalls where his three new horses from St. Louis were tied. They had no names yet, and that must be attended to. Callie would have some suggestions. He was beginning to rely upon her, he realized. "The sagacity of an Indian princess," he said aloud, and settled back to browse in the journals that had been carried to the Pacific and back.

Soon he was deeply involved in the record of that great trek, so different from his own. Lewis and Clark had handled a nearly disastrous confrontation with the Teton Sioux admirably, considering how little they knew of what the Sioux were thinking. Their winter near the Mandan villages was a fine example of two races co-existing. Lewis's description of their encounters with grizzlies made him nod and reach unconsciously for the scar on his neck. The misery of their crossing the Bitterroot Mountains was misery he had known. Their excitement at finding new species he understood well, and their sighting of the Pacific ("Ocian in view! O! the joy!") reminded him of the day his own group had first discerned the Stony Mountains lying deep in the west under a blue haze.

He came across a musing of Lewis's that touched him:

> *This day I completed my thirty-first year, and conceived that I had in all human probability now existed about half the period which I am to remain in this Sublunary world. I reflected that I had as yet done but little, very little indeed, to further the hapiness of the human race, or to advance the information of the succeeding generation. I viewed with regret the many hours I have spent in indolence, and now soarly feel the want of that information which those hours would have given me had they been judiciously expended. But since they are past and cannot be recalled, I dash from me the gloomy thought, and resolve in future, to redouble my exertions and at least indeavour to promote those two primary objects of human existence, by giving them the aid of that portion of talents which nature and fortune have bestowed on me; or in future, to live for mankind, as I have heretofore lived for myself.*

Brave and elegant words, hardly those of a man who four years later would stop at a country tavern, his mind befogged and his world asunder, and end his life. *I wish I had known the old Lewis. The good one.*

Rafe turned to the first notebook, which Clark had been keeping the day the expedition had shoved off from the starting point at the mouth of the Missouri: "I set out at 4 oClock P.M. in the presence of many of the neighbouring inhabitents and proceeded on under a jentle brease . . ."

Jentle brease? Clark misspelled his words with charm and confidence. Could these passages be made into a book the world was waiting for? Well, at least Lewis's notebooks would be easier going. Rafe lifted the open book to his face and thought he caught the odor of pine bark, high country streams, and early snow in the passes. He went to the barn door (the upper half had swung open) and looked out toward the Blue Ridge. Callie was right; if you nearly closed your eyes, those dark mountains could lie far to the west.

So he would edit the Lewis and Clark journals — for his country, as Callie had said. Then he would do his own journals, turning them into a tale of wondrous travels and a treatise of scientific value — and this he would do for Callie. After that he would load up the old calash, taking his wife and the children he hoped for, and set out again for the Stony Mountains.

That was a thing he would do for himself.

A gust of air came up from Doyle's River and touched his face. My gentle breeze, he thought, telling me to get busy. He walked toward the house, reading as he went.

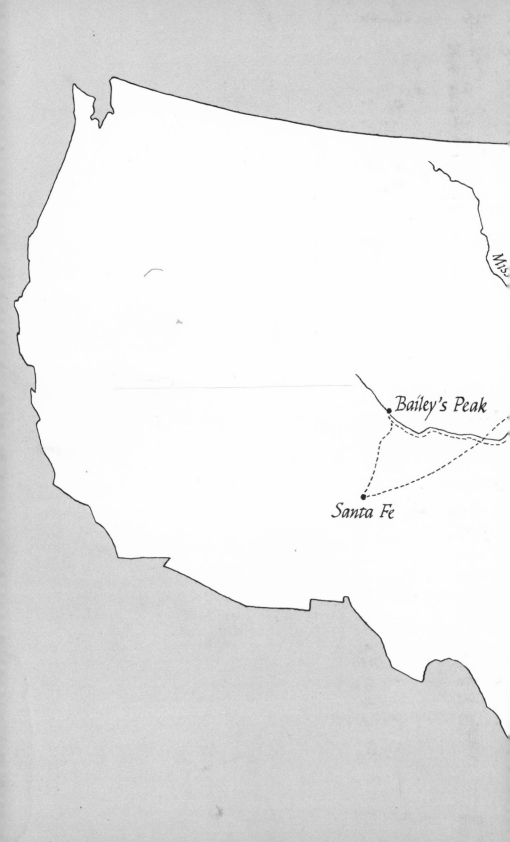

Bailey's Peak

Santa Fe

Miss